TOXIC METAL SYNDROME

D0096303

Finally, hope for millions of people
with early signs of alzheimer's
and their troubled families.
An authoritative book by
a visionary physician on
preventing and treating
this mind-destroying killer.

Jane Heimlich

Author of
What Your Doctor Won't Tell You

TOXIC METAL SYNDROME

Dr. H. Richard Casdorph
Dr. Morton Walker

A DR. MORTON WALKER HEALTH BOOK

Avery Publishing Group
Garden City Park, New York

The medical information and procedures contained in this book are based upon the research and personal and professional experiences of the authors. They are not intended as a substitute for consulting with your physician or other health care provider. An attempt to diagnose and treat an illness should be done under the direction of a health care professional.

The publisher does not advocate the use of any particular health care protocol, but believes that the information in this book should be available to the public. The publisher and author are not responsible for any adverse effects or consequences resulting from the use of any of the suggestions, preparations, or procedures discussed in this book. Should the reader have any questions concerning the appropriateness of any procedure or preparation mentioned, the authors and the publisher strongly suggest consulting a professional health care advisor. It is a sign of wisdom, not cowardice, to seek a second or third opinion.

Cover design: William Gonzalez
In-house editor: Karen Hay
Typesetter: Bonnie Freid

Cataloging in Publication Data

Casdorph, H. Richard (Herman Richard), 1928–
      Toxic metal syndrome : how metal poisonings can affect your brain
   / by H. Richard Casdorph and Morton Walker.
      p. cm.
      Includes bibliographical references and index.
      ISBN 0-89529-649-7

      1. Alzheimer's disease–Treatment. 2. Metals–Toxicology.
   3. Chelation therapy. 4. Alzheimer's disease–Pathogenesis.
   I. Walker, Morton. II. Title.
      [DNLM: 1. Alzheimer's Disease–pathology. 2. Brain–drug effects.
   3. Metals–poisoning. WM 220 C336t 1994]
   RC523.C38 1994
   616.8'31–dc2
   DNLM/DLC
   for Library of Congress   94-28053
                                                              CIP

Copyright © 1995 by H. Richard Casdorph and Morton Walker

Printed in the United States of America

10 9 8 7 6 5 4

Contents

Part III: The Heavy Metal Connection

Part IV: The Chelation Connection

Part V: The Dietary Connection

Dedication from H. Richard Casdorph, M.D., Ph.D.
*To my parents, Herman Russell and Dorothy Meadows Casdorph
who made all of this possible*

Dedication from Morton Walker, D.P.M.
*To Leonard and Anita Elkies,
my friends for forty-five years
and
my mother-in-law, Martha Bloom*

Acknowledgments

We acknowledge the invaluable work of Miss Heidi Encz for her administrative assistance as well as the typing of segments of this book.

Heather Browning Casdorph has been of invaluable assistance in the collection of and contributions to the recipes included in the book. Heather's devotion to animals and her dedication to vegetarianism has taught us a lesson.

We wish to acknowledge the invaluable assistance of Mrs. Lois O. Clark, MLS head librarian of the Johnson Medical Library at Long Beach Community Hospital, for retrieving medical literature and performing MedLine searches.

Foreword

If you are concerned about Alzheimer's disease, you picked the right book to learn from. Drs. Casdorph and Walker have written not another book about senile dementia, but rather a book about the *successful treatment* of senile dementia. And further, they have written not only about the theories behind promising leads that will one day provide a major breakthrough in this heart-wrenching deterioration of the minds of so many productive citizens, but rather about therapies that are being done today by dozens of dedicated physicians aware of Dr. Casdorph's protocol and about exciting successes that have already been achieved with consistent regularity.

If this statement is received with skepticism, I should not be surprised. For we all *know* that Alzheimer's is a relentless disease for which nothing can be done. And we *certainly know* that doctors are not having success at the present time. But, as Drs. Casdorph and Walker will show you, both statements are false.

I practice, as does Dr. Casdorph, a different type of medicine, which I like to call Complementary Medicine. The name derives from the principle that all healing arts can and should be made to complement one another. One of the major premises of Complementary Medicine is that the consensus of medical experts is too often wrong and too often rejects medical techniques that work better than the ones they accept.

Thus, I am never surprised to learn of medical practitioners who can accomplish successful patient outcomes in conditions in which the official pronouncements of consensus panels of leading professors indicate that cure is impossible. And, in the case of dementia of the Alzheimer's type, I can tell you why Dr. Casdorph is able to provide case histories of successful treatments, when all the while the professors are telling you nothing can be done.

The explanation for this discrepancy between the authors' success and the party-liners' gloom-and-doom prognosis centers around a well-used but controversial treatment called chelation therapy.

A brief explanation is in order.

There is overwhelming evidence, as Drs. Casdorph and Walker will show, that much of the Alzheimer-type dementia is caused by the accumulation in the brain of toxic metals that simply do not belong in the human body. Metals like aluminum, mercury, and lead.

Well, a treatment effective for removing these toxic metals has been around in clinical medicine, and all doctors are taught about it; it's called chelation therapy. One of the first therapies a doctor might think of as a technique for combating Alzheimer's would certainly be chelation therapy. But the removal of toxic metals by chelating agents simply was not a "quick fix," so it took Dr. Casdorph, with his patience and perseverance, to teach his colleagues that chelation worked all right, but that it simply had to be done frequently enough to get those impressive results.

But why hasn't your doctor heard of this application of a therapy proven safe and effective over two generations of usage? The simple, unadorned truth is that the consensus-makers in organized medicine, the ones that set the "accepted standards of medical practice," have an irrational contemptuous abhorrence to the very idea of chelation therapy. Just a few years ago, for example, the FDA issued a bulletin citing chelation therapy as one of the ten greatest health frauds in our society. They had to retract their statement when they learned that another department in the FDA had issued an Investigative New Drug (IND) application for the treatment.

The net result of this rancor is that mainstream doctors are afraid to investigate or confirm the exciting results obtained with chelation overseas. They accept what they are told—that chelation is ineffective and dangerous. But the scientific observers of chelation therapy have proven and reproven that it is neither.

This is how it came about. In 1951, Dr. Norman Clarke, in Detroit, noted that his lead-poisoned patients with heart disease were getting better with their cardiac angina while the lead was being removed via chelation. Over the next decade following Dr. Clarke's paper, the idea of using chelation to help heart patients became an exciting development in many teaching hospitals, and by 1960, two major nationwide conferences on chelation therapy were held. All studies showed positive results. Chelation therapy's popularity was growing.

But, in 1963, a strange event occurred. The two researchers with seven of the most exciting clinical papers of all published another paper in which they described that the benefits of chelation ceased and the illness returned when the treatment stopped. This was a logical enough observation: insulin stops benefiting the diabetic when insulin dosage stops. But what was not logical was their conclusion: That chelation has no role in the management of coronary heart disease. The other mind-boggling development was that the entire American medical community stopped research on chelation at that time, as if by prearranged agreement. Most medical historians explain these facts with the assumption that chelation, an inexpensive office procedure, threatened to remove the lion's share of income for heart disease treatment from the hospitals, whence all the consensus panelists came.

But by that time, "the cat was out of the bag," and a group of courageous practitioners continued and perfected the system of administering chelation therapy, along with other appropriate nutrients, to the point where virtually all toxic responses were eliminated. These doctors formed a group which grew and took on the name of American College for Advancement in Medicine (ACAM). One of the most recent past presidents of ACAM, which is now the preeminent group of complementary practitioners in the United States, was Dr. H. Richard Casdorph.

ACAM physicians have administered chelation therapy to over 700,000 patients. The treatment's safety record is nearly unblemished. But it takes money away from hospitals, mainly because it allows heart patients to get better without bypass surgery or angioplasties. For example, a recently published Danish study showed that fifty eight of sixty five heart patients who received chelation therapy while they were on the waiting list for bypass surgery *did not need the bypass* after several months of chelation. the mainstream response—continue the vilification of chelation, don't let the doctors know it works—"stonewall" it.

So now that Dr. Casdorph has developed a protocol centering around the perseverant use of chelation treatment, you have window of opportunity to restore your loved one with senile dementia to more normal functioning. Ask your doctor, and for all the reasons I have given you, that window will most likely be closed.

Read *The Toxic Metal Syndrome* and it will be opened.

Robert C. Atkins, M.D.

Preface

The book you are about to read has no competition, that is, no similarity with any other writings relating to mental dysfunction or brain dementia. Consumer books on the causes and treatments of Alzheimer's disease, to be presented here, as yet do not exist. Furthermore, no other persons with our combination of medical knowledge and writing skill are privy to this proposed book's information about the dramatically successful therapy to antidote Alzheimer's disease and allied forms of dementia. Almost everyone has a turning point in his life, and dissemination of knowledge set down in this published book is anticipated to be ours.

We are writing about a narrow group of diseases which affect the brain and begin in middle to late-adult life. About 30 percent of all people who live in industrialized western countries will develop Alzheimer's disease or another form of dementia if they live long enough. It is likely that someone you know already has been diagnosed as having some form of dementia. It might be a loved one. The dementia could be either Alzheimer's disease, vascular dementia, or one of the other brain syndromes. Whatever the name of the disease, a person close to you may have lost some of his or her ability to think and remember.

The few disorders that cause symptoms of forgetfulness, personality change, depression, moodiness, withdrawal, and other mind phenomena have been chronic and irreversible. Until now! What we offer in *Toxic Metal Syndrome* are revelations of causes and procedures that if acted upon, will reverse or sharply reduce the signs and symptoms of Alzheimer's disease.

The audience for our proposed book is the patient and his or her family, friends, neighbors, health care professionals, and myriad others in thousands of communities around the world. The audience, in fact, numbers in the multi-millions. Alzheimer's disease touches everyone. It is becoming an illness of increasingly larger proportions as our elderly population expands.

A few other books have skirted the subject with various guides to caring for persons with dementing illnesses and memory loss in later life. Some books have offered programs for life extension and physiological health. Unlike what we are presenting for your use here, none of those books have responded to the problem of people whose lives are destroyed by loss of brain function even though they are otherwise healthy and have many years ahead of them. If acted upon, the information we are providing can bring back people's minds to clear thinking.

Our information is completely authentic and backed by the reputations of highly placed physicians and totally competent clinicians. The treatment program offered actually has been in place since about 1952, but organized allopathic medicine in the United States has failed to focus on it because of political and financial reasons unrelated to the scientific method. Patentable drugs that bring profits are seldom involved in our mental health presentations.

As the proportion of the U.S. population over age 65 increases, an ever greater number of people become susceptible to a brain syndrome designated "dementia." The syndrome is marked by memory disorders, changes in personality, deterioration in personal care, impaired reasoning ability, and disorientation. It is a chronic or persistent abnormality of the mental processes due to organic brain disease.

The prevalence of dementing illness increases geometrically with life extension. Investigators have ascertained that cognitive impairment sufficient to justify the diagnosis of Alzheimer's disease affects up to 10 percent of persons over sixty-five, 25 percent of those over eighty, and nearly 50 percent over eighty-five. About five million Americans suffer from some form of dementia, two-thirds of them diagnosed as suffering from Alzheimer's disease. It is the fourth leading cause of death in the United States with an upward trend producing approximately 350 thousand newly diagnosed cases of Alzheimer's disease annually.

At the Institute for Basic Research in Developmental Disabilities, Staten Island, New York, a specific protein antigen has been identified in large quantities in the spinal fluid of Alzheimer's patients. This antigenic factor, known as the "tau antigen," is associated with peculiar tangles of paired spiral filaments and plaques displayed by the degenerating brain tissue of Alzheimer's victims. It is not found in almost any other form of dementia. Connected with the tau antigen is a neurotoxicity condition of the body and brain from the exposure to or the ingestion of toxic metals. The toxic metal most frequently involved is aluminum, but also present are mercury, manganese, and some other minerals (i.e. calcium) from the environment.

This book tells about a readily accessible treatment program which has been useful in removing toxic metals from the human body and brain. The therapy we describe mitigates the individual's mental deterioration from Alzheimer's disease.

The *Toxic Metal Syndrome* describes actual treatment being administered today in the offices of about 500 clinicians who are physician/members of the American College of Advancement in Medicine (ACAM). ACAM's stated purpose is "to promote and advance any innovative and emerging research, therapies, and areas of preventive medicine that offer to aid health and prevent illness.

Under a new drug application, the treatment protocol for metal detoxification and enhancement of blood flow being discussed here and endorsed by ACAM is currently under investigation at two U.S. Army hospitals, the Walter Reed Army Hospital in Washington, D.C. and the Lederman Army Hospital in San Francisco. After completion of these placebo-controlled, double-blind studies, approval for broad patient administration of the treatment is expected to be given by the United States Food and Drug Administration (FDA). Although the double-blind study codes remain unbroken, the progress of the patients seems to point to metallic detoxification and increased blood circulation treatment being 200 times (20,000 percent) more efficient and productive than any other procedure as yet developed.

Chelation therapy not only enhances body function but also improves mental processes so that dementia of the Alzheimer's-type tends to fade away.

—H. Richard Casdorph, M.D., Ph.D.
Long Beach, California
and
—Morton Walker, D.P.M.
Stamford, Connecticut

Part I
The Brain Connection

The Disease That Produces Alzheimer's Disease
With Some of Its Related Illnesses

It is now well-recognized by the medical community that Alzheimer's disease is totally different from the ordinary memory lapses that plague almost everyone as he or she grows older; it is a specific organic condition that develops in some human brains, but not all. Still, ask any family and it is likely that you will hear a sad story of relationships, close or distant, to one or more of the four million Americans who have been diagnosed with Alzheimer's disease.

CHAPTER 1

Restoring Healthy, Well-Functioning Brains

Nothing seems as full of hope and promise as watching the growth and development of a new baby, watching as the child stretches and reaches each day on its way to attaining its own unique humanness. Conversely, nothing is so hopeless and devastating as watching someone you love slip into the abyss of Alzheimer's disease. This degenerative killer of the mind and body begins with loss of memory, and progresses to personality changes, language irregularities, illogical thinking, and physical malfunctioning. It ends in death.

Just ask Jim S., and he'll tell you about his wife of forty-three years, Dolores, a patient with early Alzheimer's disease. While he tries to put a smile on his face and crack a joke or two, tears role down his cheeks as he speaks of her deterioration. When he describes himself as having "the soul of Fred Astaire with the feet of a duck," you sense that Jim is calling on all the resources he can muster, including a strong sense of the ridiculous, to help him through.

A loving, dedicated family man, at seventy-six years old, Jim has chosen to take care of his wife for as long as he is capable. The couple spends as much time together as possible, even if Dolores is not often "her old self." She is seventy-two. Both of them know that their time together is coming to a close.

Jim first began to notice signs of Dolores' mental deterioration when he retired in September 1987. He told us about when he first began to notice her condition:

> Maybe because I was spending more time with her I noticed that things just weren't right. It was nothing big, just that she was letting jobs around the house go undone. Right now, things still aren't too bad if you don't get upset about small things, like

Dolores' stocking the pantry with enough tea bags for five years
and sufficient soap to wash an army. She puts the dishes in the
refrigerator and the cold storage food in the cabinets, unless I
keep close watch.

Jim knows that it is coming to a time when he is going to have to separate
from Dolores. He will be left to live alone, and she will need to live in a
nursing home so she can receive the care that he cannot manage. Of course,
he is aware that many others are required to cope with the same problem
as his wife's.

The National Institute of Aging (NIA) has stated that 4 million Americans are currently suffering from Alzheimer's disease. According to NIA
estimates, 14 million people will suffer from the condition by the year 2050.

Dr. Donald R. McLaughlan, a professor of medicine at the University of
Toronto, has shown that, when left untreated indefinitely, Alzheimer's
disease patients reduce by one I.Q. point per month. Under grants for
physiological studies provided by the Canadian Government, Dr.
McLaughlan, a world authority on dementia, has proven this fact by using
recognized psychometric studies. Once the disease starts, Alzheimer's
disease patients become demented, lose their mental faculties, lose memory retention, and cannot keep control of their mental functions.

Formerly used as the general word for insanity, the term *dementia* is now
used by doctors only for the loss or impairment of mentality resulting from
organic causes. It is a disorder in which mental functions deteriorate and
break down. Dementia grows worse with time. Symptoms and signs of
dementia are marked by personality change, confusion, lethargy, inability
to remember, loss of pride in personal appearance, impaired reasoning,
and disorientation as to time and place. Judgment, reasoning, and thinking
go awry. There are several types of dementia, which is caused by brain-cell
damage. Their identifying names are *Alzheimer's disease, dementia para-
lytica, Pick's disease, senile dementia, secondary dementia,* and *toxic dementia.* Alzheimer's disease is the type that most commonly affects middle-
aged and elderly people in Western industrial societies. Alzheimer's disease is sometimes referred to as *presenile dementia.*

H. Richard Casdorph, M.D., Ph.D., treats Alzheimer's disease patients
at The Casdorph Clinic in Long Beach California. When an Alzheimer's
disease patient is brought to Dr. Casdorph for treatment, he is often able
to stop the progressive dementia and, not infrequently, actually reverse it.
The Alzheimer's disease victim may then be returned to loved ones as a
whole person. Although, nearly all patients he treats show improved

intelligence quotients and memory scores, the doctor offers no promise of improvement to the patient or family members.

Frequently, Dr. Casdorph is able to stop the progression of deterioration with chelation therapy. (Chelation therapy is the administration of chemicals which bind to toxic metals in the body, and help to flush them out.) Victor, the subject of the following interview, was just such a deteriorating Alzheimer's disease patient.

Victor F. was brought to the Casdorph Clinic by his wife, Minerva, for the treatment of Alzheimer's disease. Minerva related the events leading up to his treatment and his reaction to treatment to Dr. Morton Walker in an interview one afternoon while her husband was in therapy. Minerva readily disclosed her experiences about Victor's receiving intravenous treatment, nutritional supplementation, and dietary improvements for reversal of the sixty-four-year-old man's Alzheimer's disease.

> Dr. Casdorph has been giving my husband chelation treatments for three years. This is after Vic was diagnosed as suffering from Alzheimer's disease. For eight years previously I was aware that something was terribly wrong with Vic's thinking. As an engineer, my husband had been a very logical person, but back then he began to do things illogically. For instance, Vic had possessed a marvelous sense of direction, but when we were driving on vacation in Hawaii seven years ago he was unable to find his way. Repeatedly he took wrong turns. This happened often in other places, too, especially if they were of unfamiliar surroundings.
>
> About three-and-a-half years ago Vic's memory loss and other symptoms had progressed to the point where an evaluation needed to be done. So I agreed that he should go through the mind assessment center at St. Jude's Hospital in Long Beach, where his diagnosis was given. Calling together the whole family, the consulting neurologist at St. Jude's told us what was wrong. As treatment, the doctor said: "Enjoy life and travel if you want to," then he got up and walked out of the room. That was it! The brain specialist offered no other corrective or maintenance program, and we were left stunned.
>
> Later, I read a book written by Dr. Morton Walker [*The Chelation Way*]. It suggested chelation therapy as a possible way of reducing senile dementia. When I asked our family doctor about chelation treatment he did not object to Vic taking it.

Rather, he said, 'If we can buy time for Vic by using chelation therapy, let's do it.' So my husband started on the treatment, administered by Dr. Casdorph, in the fall of 1987. He has received well over 200 treatments, and I saw major improvements develop in him. He did become much more alert—was with it again! In fact, he has been doing much better all the way around, and these benefits have continued for a couple of years.

Later, though, he was hit by his third pulmonary embolism and became very ill. The embolic attack kept him in the hospital for three weeks, which was a giant step backwards. Vic had had his first embolism at age twenty-seven; the second one struck eleven years ago. Then he overcame a third embolism three years ago within six months and resumed showing remarkable improvement over Alzheimer's disease. He functioned like his old self again until a hernia struck him, just two years ago. Following his hernia operation, an infection of the wound occurred and this set him back again.

But chelation therapy pulled Vic out of the physical and mental problems brought on by the hernia complications, too. His mind is competent once more. Vic's logical thinking has returned. He participates in intelligent discussions with friends and family, even about philosophical subjects and current events.

His memory is so much better. He has been receiving chelation therapy twice a month. When once he hadn't been able to take care of his physical needs, such as going to the bathroom by himself, for the past year he has had almost no problems in that area. I've been able to reduce my caretaker role considerably and make arrangements so that I can leave him for short periods of time. When I'm out of the house he takes care of himself, totally. I go to work daily as a real-estate broker for a half-day and remain at home the rest of the time.

There is a definite correlation between the chelation therapy and Vic's mental state. It's not long term, but for two days following his chelation treatment, Vic just functions a whole lot better all the way around. His competency lasts for about a week and a half; something good happens in his brain. But then he seems to lapse back into wrong-thinking. This lapse occurs in particular if we miss a biweekly appointment with Dr. Casdorph. I'm so grateful that chelation therapy is available for my husband. It is keeping him a whole man.

Victor's medical history included multiple medical problems, including three pulmonary emboli, deep thrombosis (a blood clot) in the right calf, an irregular heart beat, hypertension that had been present for three years, and type-II diabetes that had been present for nine years. Since beginning chelation therapy, Victor has fared well, with no interruption in his normal life. His intellectual capabilities have stabilized, instead of gradually declining. His normal ability to communicate with family and friends was maintained throughout the treatment period. Family members, in fact, have recognized the treatment's benefits and remain quite responsive to bringing Victor to Dr. Casdorph's office for the administration of intravenous infusions with ethylene diamine tetraacetic acid (EDTA), a synthetic amino acid and the primary component of chelation therapy.

Unfortunately, it takes more than one case to prove the effectiveness of any new treatment, and, even more unfortunately, there are many more victims of these degenerative diseases out there to help us do this. The following cases of Rita and Robert cite the use of chelation therapy to inhibit, and even to reverse, the progression of Alzheimer's disease.

Fifty-eight-year-old Rita B., the petite, beautiful wife of a wealthy, prominent Chicago industrialist, began to develop symptoms of memory disorder. At first it was only that she appeared quite forgetful, but then her family, friends, and servants noticed other disturbing characteristics about her. She developed what seemed to be neutralized emotions: smiles were wiped away, tears dried up, verbal communication with others tended to be nonexistent, and she drifted in her own sort of dream world. Her formerly expressive, lovely blue eyes became hard, and devoid of expression.

The symptoms had come on gradually, but Charles, her husband of thirty-four years, noticed some obvious changes in his wife's mentality. Because his business often kept him away from home, the change in Rita was first pointed out to Charles by the people around her. While he was away on business some shocking disclosures were related to him over the telephone. Once he recognized that a problem existed, the determined tycoon resolved that nothing would be an obstacle to getting Rita well again.

In the spring of 1988, Charles took Rita to Los Angeles for examinations by neurologists and other medical specialists at the University of Southern California School of Medicine. At the medical center associated with this institution, he and his wife were treated as "VIPs." The tycoon was a major contributor to USC and a member of its board of trustees. There, his wife obtained the best medical care available with an extensive study in the departments of internal medicine and neurology, including a brain scan involving computerized axial tomography (CAT scan). The extensive medical workup, utilizing the latest technology available to this university medical school, resulted in a final diagnosis that Rita, was indeed, the victim of Alzheimer's disease.

As treatment, the most learned specialists employed in the hospital could offer nothing for Rita. Combined drug therapy was vaguely mentioned once as a means of stimulating neurological pathways in her brain, but none of the doctors followed through with it. Instead, the patient was sent home to Chicago with a poor prognosis. What was unsettling to Charles was that he could do nothing for her steadily deteriorating condition.

He sent employees of his own international company's department of industrial medicine to search out alternatives to the existing inadequate conventional medical approach for Alzheimer's disease. He couldn't let his wife, who was now being taken care of by servants, just linger and die.

It was three weeks later that the efficacy of EDTA chelation therapy for brain disorders, detailed in a paper written by H. Richard Casdorph, M.D., Ph.D. (published in the Fall/Winter 1981 issue of the *Journal of Holistic Medicine*), was brought to Charles' attention. Additional published information on the subject about this form of treatment strongly suggested that chelation therapy might help victims of Alzheimer's disease. He telephoned Dr. Casdorph for discussions, asked many questions, made an appointment, and, in short order, Charles and Rita flew back to southern California.

After undergoing Dr. Casdorph's initial history-taking, laboratory examinations, and physical examination, Rita was started on intravenous (IV) infusions with EDTA chelation therapy. It turns out that besides her mental impairment, two serious physical problems uncovered by her laboratory and clinical tests would also be aided by the treatment.

Following the very first series of IVs, it was as if a switch had been turned on for Rita. Her mind began to function again. She seemed brighter and more alert. With subsequent intravenous injections, her eyes took on their former expression. They had brought an attendant with them, and by the sixteenth IV Charles reported that the attendant no longer had to feed his wife. She could feed herself.

Rita and Charles remained in Long Beach until she had completed the prescribed series of thirty treatments. She continued her improvement in mental and physical performance and now recognized the different neighborhoods as they strolled around the southern California city. Sometimes she was able to lead Charles back to their hotel.

Because of lack of coordination, diminished reflexes, and the general mental confusion that had been coming over her, Rita had stopped driving her car two years before. By the time she received her twenty-ninth chelation infusion, Charles had Rita practicing driving a rental car in a nearby empty parking lot. She was thrilled with getting back into the driver's seat once more. It was symbolic that once again Rita was taking control of her life.

At the completion of her series of infusions, they flew back to Chicago to resume more normal activities and to pick up the treatment with another specialist in chelation therapy. That was when Rita resumed driving a car by herself, something she had been unable to do for those depressive preceding years. She accomplished her own food shopping, too, and drove girlfriends to the clothing stores along Michigan Avenue. Indeed, she did a lot of driving. The women made known their amazement at their friend's restored vivaciousness and presence of mind.

A little less than ten weeks passed before Charles once again recognized his wife's need for further treatment. The initial brain enhancement was not holding, and more chelation therapy was obviously mandatory. This became quite apparent when she drove her car onto the sidewalk on a busy Chicago thoroughfare. She hit a fire hydrant but was not hurt seriously.

"Rita . . . took chelation therapy in my office beginning February 13, 1989," said Cal Streeter, D.O., in his written interview. Dr. Streeter is in family practice at the Highland Medical Plaza in Highland, Indiana, where he conducts a pain clinic and administers preventative medicine, including IV nutritional therapy. Like Dr. Casdorph, he has diplomate status with the American Board of Chelation Therapy. Charles had been referred to Dr. Streeter by the Casdorph Clinic, as a physician who was qualified to continue with Rita's treatment program.

> I was told that she had been diagnosed as having Parkinson's syndrome, epilepsy, and Alzheimer's disease. It seems that she had experienced a cerebral-type seizure one year ago and progressively deteriorated until she was treated with chelation therapy by Dr. Casdorph, the last of those treatments being given in early November 1988. When she came to my office it was about two months since she had been treated and once again had begun to deteriorate mentally. I agreed to give her at least ten chelation treatments on an every-other-day basis to see if improvement again could be obtained and normal mental function realized.

Rita did tolerate the procedures well, wrote Dr. Streeter, but he fell short of seeing any dramatic reversal of the patient's mental incapacitation.

> I did not see significant return of her normal mental functions as I had anticipated and had observed in other Alzheimer victims that I had treated with chelation therapy. Physically she did fine, but mentally it was frustrating for her, her husband, and me during the time of her treatments. I did do laboratory and clinical studies and an echocardiogram on her, all of which proved to be normal. She did take a total of thirteen treatments from me between April 4, 1989, and August 2, 1989.

Dr. Streeter reports that he did not have contact with the couple thereafter, but is convinced that if he were to treat her again, his preference would be to administer chelation therapy on a one-time-per-week basis over an extended period of time. "I believe that such a slower and more prolonged treatment program would give her much better results than either she or her husband realized on the initial series."

All cases of "senility" are not due to cerebrovascular disease as once was believed by medical scientists. Recent innovative research in the United States and in Canada by Professor Donald R. McLaughlan, M.D., has shown increased concentrations of aluminum in the brains of patients with Alzheimer's disease. This form of brain disease responds to chelation therapy, inasmuch as EDTA binds most toxic metals such as aluminum, mercury, lead, cadmium, and other elements and carries them away from the brain and then out of the body.

Such metallic binding causing reversal of Alzheimer's disease is illustrated by the case of Robert L., a chemical engineer who is fifty-seven years old. His mother, Agatha, learned of Dr. Casdorph's success with treating Alzheimer's disease, and telephoned the internist to discuss the wisdom of bringing her son for chelation therapy.

Robert was experiencing a memory disorder that had become progressively more severe during the past five years. His mental capacity had been thoroughly tested in medical centers, including the Department of Neurology at Johns Hopkins University School of Medicine, and he had been diagnosed with Alzheimer's disease.

Robert had previously proven to be very intelligent. He had worked for a large chemical company for thirty years until he had to take disability retirement because of his apparent mental disability. He still recognized his wife and three children, but his formerly bright intellect no longer sparkled.

Robert had been brought to a nearby neurologist by his wife, Cynthia. The doctor, who performed brain-flow studies on Robert, advised the couple that there was no treatment available for his condition. The diagnosis, he affirmed, was Alzheimer's disease.

Conflict arose between Robert's wife and his mother. Cynthia had accepted the diagnosis and was satisfied that nothing at all could be done for her husband. She was assured by the experts at Johns Hopkins University Medical School that Alzheimer's disease responded to no known treatment. Her conviction was reinforced, as well, by their daughter who had recently graduated as a registered nurse and was instilled with beliefs acquired during her conventional medical instruction.

Still, Agatha volunteered to pay for the entire cost of her son's treatment at the Casdorph Clinic, so Cynthia finally gave in and dropped her objections to Robert receiving chelation therapy. Agatha and her son flew to Long Beach.

There, Robert underwent a complete physical examination and some sophisticated laboratory investigations. At Dr. Casdorph's request, he was subjected to psychometric studies performed by a nearby and independently practicing Ph.D. in psychology who gave Robert a reference-memory score and I.Q. score. Such baseline studies proved to be significantly reduced from Robert's normal brain function and consistent with the diagnosis of Alzheimer's disease.

Robert then received his first in a series of chelation treatments from Dr. Casdorph. Within three months there was noticeable improvement in Robert's memory and in his ability to function and perform everyday tasks, which he was having great difficulty with before he arrived at the Casdorph Clinic. After the first thirty IVs it became apparent to Agatha that her son's intellectual functioning, as well as his physical ability, was returning to the way it had been ten years before. He was able to go bicycling and cross-country hiking. But more than that, his mind was returning to mental astuteness.

Of special interest is that Robert has an identical twin, Wilfred, who, also being an engineer, works for an aircraft company, and resides in southern California. At separate times, both brothers consulted Dr. Casdorph for medical care and received physical evaluations from him. Wilfred was found not to have the dementia being experienced by his brother Robert.

Of special importance, the hair-mineral analysis performed by the internist on Robert revealed that he showed a marked accumulation of toxic minerals in his tissues, including lead and cadmium. Lead accumulation in the body certainly affects the brain's function, including memory. Robert apparently had been exposed to increased metallic concentrations during the course of his job at the chemical company. It was determined that heavy-metal toxicity was the main source of the memory problems he was experiencing. Also, the patient suffered from hypertension, and accumulation of cadmium in the body is a known cause of high blood pressure.

After six months, Robert's mental and physical conditions were considerably changed for the better. Because chelation therapy assuredly corrects hypertension, his recorded blood pressure was now remaining steady at a normal reading.

Following his sixty-third intravenous infusion of EDTA chelation therapy, Robert repeated the series of psychometric studies that had been done before he started the chelation treatment. The psychologist who had been retained to record the first set of tests, Kathryn Holden, Ph.D., was astonished to discover that Robert's I.Q. had improved by 13 percent and his memory score had increased by 12 percent. Any psychologist or psychiatrist can tell you that this amount of I.Q. elevation is a spectacular improvement. The increase was proven by objective testing performed by this independent health professional who is not in any way affiliated with Dr. Casdorph's clinic.

Agatha was so impressed with the results of chelation therapy on her son, that she elected to undergo physical evaluation and start the treatment for herself.

The immediate and dramatic responses of Robert, Victor, and Rita are typical of many cases reported, not only by the Casdorph Clinic, but by other healthcare facilities around the country that participate in following the chelation-treatment protocol.

In addition to becoming aware that treatment for Alzheimer's disease does exist, the fact that patients just like Robert improve so well gives us new insight into the role of metals such as aluminum, cadmium, calcium, lead, mercury, and others in the cause of the condition. With five million cases of Alzheimer's disease in the United States, one out of every six people suffering similar dementia in Australia, something approaching two million struck by it in Great Britain, and every third family struck by it in countries in Europe, it seems as if the longer one lives the greater will be the chance of falling victim to this so-called incurable ailment.

We wonder why the governments of these affected countries, and, specifically, their publicly-financed Alzheimer's disease societies, have not taken more interest in the accumulating international research that incriminates aluminum and other toxic metals. Toxic metals tend to collect in the brain as the major etiologic factor in this disease. Chelation therapy is the only treatment that passes through the blood-brain barrier (BBB) and removes toxic metals from body tissues, including the brain cells.

Agatha, Wilfred, and Robert have each voiced their wonderment that chelation therapists don't try to win the Food and Drug Administration's (FDA's) approval for this marvelous treatment. "Why don't you bring chelation therapy to the masses by conforming to the FDA's requirements of performing those various placebo-controlled, double-blind studies on its safety and efficacy?" they ask. In fact, such controlled studies are being performed now for proving the treatment advantageous for peripheral vascular and cardiovascular diseases. Yet, other more practical studies, clinical investigations, some 1800 of them, have already been carried out but remain unrecognized or ignored by government authorities and orthodox medical practitioners. The masses of medical consumers needing care are martyrs to such obtuseness.

In Part IV of this book we will discuss at length the "chelation connection" for Alzheimer's disease and other mind dysfunctions. Then we will fully disclose everything one must know about the treatment, including the medical politics involved. For the balance of Part I and for all of Part II and Part III, however, we will focus strictly on the signs, diagnosis, pathology, causes, and avoidance of Alzheimer's disease.

The message of this book is that a real breakthrough exists for stopping the deterioration of brain cells. Fast or slow progress of the dementia need not continue inasmuch as, since 1952, the medical profession has had the means to reduce or reverse the signs and symptoms of Alzheimer's disease.

CHAPTER 2

Signs and Symptoms of Alzheimer's Disease

Eighty-year-old Edna T., a long-time resident of a nursing home in Montgomery, Alabama, had been confined to bed for four years. She was partially blind, and could see only to one side of her head. Because of some erratic behavior she occasionally exhibited, and a detached, "out-of-this-world" attitude, the home's regularly consulting medical doctor had branded Edna as "witlessly demented" and "woefully mentally deficient."

This unkind double-label remained with her until an elderly, but progressive, wholistic physician, H. Ray Evers, M.D., of Cottonwood, Alabama, was asked by Edna's granddaughter to examine the patient. Dr. Evers visited the nursing home and evaluated Edna. He determined that she simply had no new visual environment—just looking at the bare walls all day long—which, compounded with the brain loss she had suffered from a stroke, made her seem and act demented.

In medical terms, Edna actually had only a vision defect called *homonymous hemianopia,* an uncommon condition that results in the loss of sight in the corresponding right or left lateral halves of the eyes. A stroke had also caused Edna's right eye to be mostly sightless, what she could see was blurry. Edna had spent nearly four years bedridden in an alcove of the nursing home in such a position that the functional part of her vision was turned to a blank wall and the blind part was turned to the outside world.

Upon Dr. Evers uncovering Edna's problem, and providing the simple remedy of turning her bed around so that she could see the outside world, the patient underwent a remarkable mental improvement. Her withdrawn behavior had been brought on by a lack of meaningful visual stimuli, which compounded the effects of her stroke.

With the passage of time, and with mental stimulation, Edna became bright, cheerful, friendly, responsive, well-groomed, and thriving. Her family was thrilled that their grandma was back to normal.

Edna's case is an example of the needs of a normally operating human brain. She did not suffer from Alzheimer's disease, as implied by the home's unobservant consultant doctor.

In contrast, there was another woman whom no one could help. For several years Margaret F., of Seattle, Washington, had known that her memory was slipping away. Names that went with faces of friends suddenly became unrecallable, telephone numbers she had always used were now forgotten, and thoughts she had one moment and lost the next stood out as undeniable signs that senility was quickly approaching. "Senility? How can that be?" Margaret asked herself. "I am only fifty-six years old."

Her husband, Ted, noticed the mental deterioration but did not admonish her. He did, however, mention the situation to their daughter, Rose Ann. Ted said in sadness, "I think Mother is losing her foothold on life." Rose Ann had noticed Margaret's memory lapses, as well. The father and daughter commiserated and then discussed possible eventualities if the condition worsened. They were realistic with each other about what needed to be done.

Meanwhile, Margaret tried to compensate for memory lapses by writing down ideas, tasks, required information, and more—even her own street address. One day while shopping, the piece of paper on which she had noted her house number was missing from her purse. In Margaret's neighborhood, unfortunately, most of the row housing looked alike. Although she was standing on the correct street, Margaret could not locate her own attached bungalow. A neighbor found her wandering around and brought her home.

Ted was finally forced to turn to three physicians—an internist, a neurologist, and a psychiatrist. After carefully considering her case, all three doctors agreed on Margaret's diagnosis—Alzheimer's disease.

Gradually, Margaret lost the ability to make sense out of what her eyes and ears told her. Noises and confusion caused her to feel panic, which became overwhelming, and forced her into hiding under the bed clothes or in a dark closet for hours at a time. Repeatedly she misplaced her possessions. Nothing in her surroundings seemed familiar. Often a terror washed over her, clutching at her heart. At other times, anger would spring from deep inside, and she would take it out on Ted, her daughter, her three young grandchildren, or anybody else who was around.

The time finally arrived when the physical and emotional burdens of caring for Margaret became too much for Ted, and he and Rose Ann brought her to live in a nursing home. Margaret's family came to visit. They put their arms around her frail body, held her hand, and sat silently, or sang old songs. Sometimes she remembered who they were, but more often she did not.

She liked it best when these strangers, who appeared to mean no harm, just held her and loved her. Six years later, Margaret died.

The producers of the film, "There Were Times, Dear," put it best:

> Of all the dread-filled diseases, Alzheimer's is a singularly awful way to go. All that makes us human—memory, the ability to love, intelligence—is stripped from the Alzheimer's patient. The caregiver is left with a familiar stranger incapable of response. We want a cause and cure to be found now, while there is still time for us.[1]

ALZHEIMER'S DEMENTIA

The most common symptom related to Alzheimer's disease is memory loss. No evidence of stroke exists, and at autopsy there is no atherosclerosis (hardening of the arteries of the brain). As recently as 1979, it was wrongly believed by the medical community that Alzheimer's disease was a disorder involving degeneration or hardening of the blood vessels of the brain, with brain shrinkage (atrophy) and thickening of the brain covering. It was, in fact, erroneously referred to as *presenile sclerosis*. This is no longer used as a pathological description for Alzheimer's.

Alzheimer's disease progresses through three major stages: from forgetfulness, to confusion, to total dementia or loss of mental function. In the final stage of deterioration, victims tend to regress to infantile dependency and become completely incapacitated. The life expectancies of Alzheimer's disease victims are reduced, and a variety of complicating mental and emotional symptoms arise for them: acute anxiety, paranoia, restlessness, irritability, insomnia, aggressiveness, depression, and more.

Alzheimer's disease—also referred to in medicine as presenile dementia, primary senile dementia, *dementia presenilis,* and primary neuronal degeneration—is progressive mental deterioration marked by memory loss, confusion, and disorientation beginning in late-middle life and resulting in death in five to ten years. Pathologically, as seen during autopsy, the brain is shrunken or wasted (atrophic), especially in the frontal, occipital, and temporal regions.

The official histological description of Alzheimer's disease brain tissue, as seen under the microscope, is that it is characterized by thickened, gelatinous, and distorted intracellular neurofibrils (designated as neurofibrillary tangles) and by senile plaques composed of granular or filamentous argentophilic (having an affinity for the mineral silver) masses with an amyloid core, found predominantly in the cerebral cortex, amygdala, and hippocampus parts of the brain. The amyloid core is an abnormal protein deposited in tissues, formed from the infiltration of an unknown substance, probably a carbohydrate.

The cerebral cortex has only a few shrunken brain cells (neurons) that may contain spaces (cytoplasmic vacuoles) and granules that attract silver (argentophilic granules) displacing the nucleus to the outside of the cell. These neurons, therefore, are cells that are filled with molecules that attract silver in place of the nucleus. Granulovacuolar degeneration of this kind is seen mainly in the sections of the brain that affect memory (the anterior hippocampus) in Alzheimer's patients.[2]

The disease was first discovered in 1906 and described in a clinical journal article in 1907 by Alois Alzheimer, M.D. a German neurologist. He had first recognized the peculiar symptoms in one of his patients, a fifty-five-year-old woman. Dr. Alzheimer then referred to this disease in a published article as *presenile dementia.* Neurologists now agree that the dementia that occurs in the elderly is the same as or similar to the presenile condition. It is usually referred to today as senile dementia of the Alzheimer's type (SDAT—more commonly leaving off the word "senile," medical specialists designate it just as DAT or Alzheimer's disease).

Of the patients with Alzheimer's disease, 20 percent have complicating factors, such as depression, that make their symptoms worse. Another potential complication is that Alzheimer's disease patients may develop nutritional deficiencies, such as a lack of vitamin B1 (thiamine) from routine, excessive, drinking of alcohol.

Besides the memory loss that is typical of Alzheimer's disease, other signs and symptoms prevail. The more frequently seen symptoms include confusion, depression, temper tantrums, irritability, change in overall mood, negative attitude, hallucinations, poor coordination with clumsiness, shuffling gait, plus other physical, mental, and emotional difficulties. There are potential complications accompanying Alzheimer's disease, as well. The physical and immunological debilitation of Alzheimer's patients leaves them at risk for many illnesses that ordinarily would be shrugged off by other people. Even a chest cold can easily lead to pneumonia, which is a common killer of elderly Alzheimer's victims.

The second most common type of dementia that arises used to be labeled senility from arteriosclerosis (hardening of the arteries) but now is designated as "multi-infarct" (a series of strokes) or "vascular dementia." Also there is a third type labelled as "mixed dementia," which is a combination of atherosclerosis and Alzheimer's disease.

Alzheimer's disease can affect any race or social class. It can affect anyone in middle-age and beyond. There is no one common demographic denominator that can pinpoint a victim from birth.

THE FREQUENCY OF ALZHEIMER'S DISEASE

It is estimated by the *Medical Advertising News,* that the elderly—people age sixty-five years and older—will account for more than 21 percent of the population by the year 2030. Today, the elderly account for about 15 percent of the population. Alzheimer's disease poses the greatest risk for this older group, because it takes approximately five decades to develop.

The Alzheimer's Association, an advocacy group based in Chicago, says that Alzheimer's disease is the nation's fourth leading cause of death for people living in western industrialized countries, such as the United States, Great Britain, and Canada.[3] After heart disease, cancer, and stroke, Alzheimer's disease accounts for the deaths of a minimum of 150,000 Americans per year.

Within the next five years, in fact, one of three American families will be affected by Alzheimer's disease. Most of the victims are older than sixty, but the disease can strike persons as young as forty years of age and Down's syndrome patients as young as thirty. At a minimum, about 50 percent of patients with such non-reversible dementia are properly diagnosed as suffering from Alzheimer's disease.

DRUG PROFITS FROM ALZHEIMER'S DISEASE

In July, 1991, it was estimated that four million Americans were already Alzheimer's victims. Each year the number of Alzheimer's victims grows in proportion to the entire United States population. The result is that many pharmaceutical companies are engaged in crash programs of drug-product development, in order to cash in on the huge profits to be made from sales of brain-conditioning drugs to the millions of Alzheimer's-disease sufferers.

Sandoz Pharmaceutical Corporation manufactures the only FDA approved drug for the treatment of Alzheimer's disease, *Hydergine* Liquid Capsules. The product helps a few patients, usually in the early stages of the disease. Hydergine is off-patent (in the public domain), but it carries an exclusive indication in it's package insert for symptoms of declining mental capacity. Still, it is used for a variety of other purposes, such as alertness, longevity, memory retention, and much more.

Because Hydergine's patent has run out and left the product as public domain, other companies can now compete with Sandoz for the sales of the drug. Therefore, Sandoz will not make as big a push for Hydergine, but it will concentrate on other drugs for which they hold exclusive patents.

Thus, because the population of the U.S. is currently skewing toward old age, the market for drugs to treat problems associated with aging is steadily increasing in importance. A recent poll of physicians sponsored by the Bristol-Myers Squib Company predicted problems associated with aging will be the most important field of healthcare by the turn of the century. The major pharmaceutical manufacturers are gearing up for the market shifts.

The Warner-Lambert Company, believed to be the leader in the search for an Alzheimer's drug, is working on at least four agents for the disease, among them are Tacrine (recently FDA approved) and the memory activator Pramiracetam. Bristol-Myers is in clinical trials with BuSpar, already approved by the FDA for anxiety. The Ayerst Laboratories division of American Home Products Corporation has a new drug application (NDA) filed for Ceractin; G.D. Searle & Company is researching Sulocton; and Hoechst-Roussel Pharmaceuticals, Inc. is looking into the Alzheimer's indication for Trental, already FDA-approved for intermittent claudication (a circulatory condition). The Lederle Laboratories division of American Cyanamid Company, the Roche Laboratories division of Hoffmann-La Roche, Inc., the Ciba-Geigy Corporation, and Du Pont Pharmaceuticals are also working on Alzheimer's drugs. It will probably be years before several of these drugs that effectively treat Alzheimer's disease reach the market.

One of the most promising markets is for memory activators which could be used for relief of Alzheimer's-like symptoms. Analysts foresee a $1 billion-per-year worldwide market for memory-enhancing drugs. Parke-Davis (a division of the Warner-Lambert Company), Syntex Laboratories, Inc., and The Upjohn Company each have memory activators in their research and development pipelines.[4]

Drug therapies for the elderly, especially those connected with Alzheimer's disease treatment, turn out to be big business in the short and long run.

SUSPICIOUS INDICATIONS OF ALZHEIMER'S DISEASE

To friends, neighbors, and loved ones, the beginning indications that an individual may be developing Alzheimer's disease may be mild, undramatic, and may seem harmless. The early Alzheimer's disease patient may only exhibit minor difficulties, like forgetting familiar places, such as the city in which one lives; losing frequently-used objects, like house keys; or show the inability to form meaningful sentences when describing common activities. Then again, the afflicted person's behavior could become bizarre or tragic.

The following quote was taken from an old issue of *Modern Maturity:*

> I look at him and wonder who exactly is asleep in the chair opposite me. It certainly isn't the man I married. I've become quite ambivalent about my dear mate because Alzheimer's disease is slowly but treacherously consuming him.

This comment, from the wife of an Alzheimer's disease victim, illustrates that Alzheimer's disease is far from being merely a natural loss of memory that is inevitable with advancing age, as so many once believed. The sad truth about the nearly epidemic ailment is that it is a slow, mind-destroying killer that can turn a beloved spouse or parent into a difficult, even troublesome stranger.

Or consider the following description of another typically impaired person as reported in an excellent book on Alzheimer's disease titled, *The 36-Hour Day:*[5]

> Mom is so paranoid. She hides her purse. She hides her money, she hides her jewelry. Then she accuses my wife of stealing it. Now she is accusing us of stealing the silverware. The hard part is that she doesn't seem sick. It's hard to believe she isn't doing this deliberately.

Then there is a second heartbreaking statement cited in the same book from the caregiver of an equally ill Alzheimer's disease patient:

> The worst thing about Dad is his temper. He used to be easygoing. Now he is always hollering over the least little thing. Last night he told our ten-year-old that Alaska is not a state. He was hollering and yelling and stalked out of the room. Then when I asked him to take a bath we had a real fight. He insisted he had already taken a bath.

Yet, there are numerous examples of people who have aged and not lost their mental faculties or talents. Examples of public figures who remained vigorous into old age, even until the time of their deaths, include the actress Mae West who died at age eighty-eight, Margaret Mead gone at seventy-seven, the cellist Pablo Casals at ninety-seven, the painter Pablo Picasso living to ninety-one, the conductor Arturo Toscanini who died at eighty-nine, the jazz musician Duke Ellington who died at seventy-five, the novelist Rebecca West living to ninety-one, the ragtime pianist Eubie Blake dying at ninety-one, and the German statesman Konrad Adenauer who died at ninety-one. Congressman Claude Pepper was Chairman of the Congressional Committee on Aging, and causing havoc in the natural foods industry with his "Pepper Bills" when he died at age eighty-eight. The painter Georgia O'Keeffe lived and worked into her nineties. The writer Malcolm Cowley was eighty-seven when he wrote a stirring article for publication on the Op-Ed page of *The New York Times* called "Being Old Old."

One of the most outstanding examples of elderly vigor and ingeniousness was Linus Pauling, Ph.D., the two-time Nobel Laureate who worked into his nineties, conducting research at his Menlo Park, California Institute. Obviously, the high-dosage vitamin C that Dr. Pauling ingested daily offered him long life and a fertile brain.

As demonstrated by their personal creativity, job-related production, and active lives, none of these people had dementia.

SERIOUS SIGNS AND SYMPTOMS OF ALZHEIMER'S DISEASE

Symptoms and signs in a patient with Alzheimer's disease are numerous and variable. All of the symptoms and signs listed in the three subsections to follow are not likely to be present in the same patient. Symptoms are experienced internally, within the mind or body of the affected individual, or they are noticed by the patient as subjective responses to the condition of his or her health. Signs are those indications obvious to an observer. For instance, the examiner might note a type of behavior, a fever, a rash, or something else witnessed objectively.

With increased awareness of Alzheimer's disease, there is a tendency on the part of even clear-thinking people to confuse "benign forgetfulness" with pathological senile dementia. The *Diagnostic and Statistical Manual of Mental Disorders (DSM-III)* of the American Psychiatric Association officially recognizes dementia as "the deterioration of mental faculties that is of sufficient severity to interfere with a person's ability to function normally for an extended period of time." This qualification marks the dividing line between senile dementia and the minor memory lapses of normal aging. For example, if an older person forgets the name of one of the guests at a grandson's bar mitzvah, that is the normal, benign forgetfulness of aging; if the bar mitzvah itself is forgotten, that is symptomatic of dementia.

The word *dementia* does not mean crazy. It was chosen about two decades ago, by neurologists and psychiatrists, as an inoffensive designation of a series of symptoms. Quite simply, *dementia* is a combination of Latin words that mean *away* and *mind*—the mind has gone away for an Alzheimer's patient. The symptoms of dementia are disorientation, intellectual impairment, memory loss, mental confusion, and others.

In people with Alzheimer's disease, the impairment of memory and other cognitive functions is progressive and continuous. These victims find it increasingly more difficult to carry out the routine activities that they have performed efficiently for years, such as balancing a checkbook, driving a car, and food shopping. This applies to technical skills that are used regularly, as well. The radiologist who finds it harder and harder to read x-ray films, for instance, may be exhibiting early signs of Alzheimer's disease.[6]

We have broken down the signs and symptoms into three categories: mental, emotional, and behavioral. The following subsections give outlines and definitions of the different things that may be felt or witnessed.

MENTAL CHANGES SYMPTOMATIC OF ALZHEIMER'S DISEASE

Almost all of the processes involved in awareness and knowledge—including memory, orientation, comprehension, attention and concentration, general information, abstract thinking, judgment and problem-solving, and formation of delusions—deteriorate in people affected by Alzheimer's disease. Each change or loss of a mind process is another symptom adding to the impaired individual's diagnostic confirmation of Alzheimer's disease.[7]

- *Memory Loss.* No matter how sharp a person's memory is from early life onward, as one gets older, usually there is a gradual onset of forgetfulness. There may be trouble placing names with faces, finding descriptive words to complete sentences, and remembering the times or locations of events in the past. Often we manage to compensate for what medical science refers to as mild, moderate, or *benign forgetfulness.*

It is only when *severe forgetfulness* takes hold of one's daily life that noticeable mental impairment, typical of Alzheimer's disease, becomes apparent. The symptom of memory loss is considered severe when the individual's forgetfulness interferes with normal functions, such as his or her being unable to prepare a simple meal. Memory loss can come on in stages, and certain types of memory are lost more quickly than others. In the following chapter we will discuss the different kinds of forgetfulness that strike during Alzheimer's disease. Meanwhile, know that there is immediate memory, recent memory, and remote or distant memory. Generally, recent memory, such as the news of the day as seen on television, is lost first. The loss of remote memory occurs as Alzheimer's disease deepens, one may even forget where and when one was born.

Memory loss is the most insidious of symptoms, for it affects all other mental processes. When one loses his or her memory the self is gone, as well as the ability to think.

- *Disorientation.* One of the tests used by psychiatrists to determine Alzheimer's disease or other mental impairment is to ask questions about present time, day, year, place, and familiar people. The more severe a person's involvement with Alzheimer's, the fewer questions are answered quickly and correctly.

The sense of time goes first: early or late, day or night. Disoriented people may be unaware of their own disorientation to time and muddle through the day performing routine tasks in familiar settings. For instance, they may eat when served but not know if they are eating lunch or dinner. In contrast, different surroundings disorient them entirely and often lead to fright, anxiety, or withdrawal.

The recognition of other people may go next. Confusion strikes when the ill person cannot connect a name with his or her caregiver. Distress is felt when the Alzheimer's disease victim realizes that he or she is coming up blank when trying to recall, or even speak to, loved ones or friends. While medical personnel often record *confusion* as a diagnosis, it is not. Rather, confusion from disorientation is one of the symptoms of dementia.

- *Loss of Comprehension.* As the disease worsens, an Alzheimer's sufferer may have difficulty understanding what he or she is told or what he or she has read. Comprehension of new information eventually disappears and is replaced by complete confusion. When it becomes apparent to the victim that there is difficulty with processing new information, such a person may either become agitated with anxiety or passively withdrawn.

- *Loss of Concentration.* Short attention span accompanies memory and comprehension problems. Easy distraction results in a lack of concentration. This may be manifested by the patient repeating over and over of only a few ideas. Lack of concentration sometimes prevents absorption and integration of activities and information around the patient. Energy might be at an ebb too.

- *Loss of General Information.* The Alzheimer's disease patient sometimes loses everyday information, such as the city in which he or she resides, the current president of the United States, and significant dates such as Christmas. Recognizing that such general information is elusive, the Alzheimer's patient will likely declare in alarm, "I am losing my mind."

- *Loss of Abstract Thinking.* Insight and logic, especially involving topics of philosophical precepts, lose interconnection. One concept cannot be tied to the logical next and problems remain unconsidered and unresolved.

- *Loss of Judgment.* Loss of judgment can be extremely harmful to a person with Alzheimer's disease. The most elementary of tasks, such as taking a bath, could become a dangerous activity if one does not exercise proper judgment. It would not be too unusual, in such a circumstance, for the impaired person to drop his or her body into scalding-hot bath water.

- *Delusions.* An inability to distinguish between real events and imagined ones combined with a loss of insight could cause delusions to arise. The delusions could be anything. They may be related to people that are not there, sounds, such as disembodied voices, or objects disappearing into outer space.

THE EMOTIONS EXPERIENCED BY ALZHEIMER'S PATIENTS

Alzheimer's disease patients must confront the alarming mental losses occurring in their own minds, so it is not unreasonable for the individual to respond with bouts of fear, anxiety, anger, frustration, sadness, hostility, depression, and other emotions. Ingrained personality traits become more apparent to the point of exaggeration. For instance, an individual suffering from Alzheimer's disease who was always slightly suspicious of the potential for people to be hurtful, is likely to become more paranoid than ever. The emotional reactions of Alzheimer's disease patients will differ from person to person, and it is important to understand where they originate.[8]

- *Loss of Emotional Control.* People who have inappropriate fits of crying or laughing, are referred to by psychologists as *emotionally labile* (unstable). Control over mood is gone, which causes wild swings to occur ranging from uncontrollable rage to being completely docile. This overreaction one way or the other is a predominant sign of emotions affected by Alzheimer's.

- *Lack of Emotion.* A person who is apathetic and unable to respond with usual animation is labeled by psychologists as displaying *flatness of affect*. The person appears withdrawn, incapable of feeling happy, and unable to express sadness, anger, or much of any emotion. There is a dullness of mood that resembles depression but actually is not.

- *Anxiety.* Anxiety, the manifestation of uncertainty and fear, is a symptom of distress felt by the patient. Anxiety tends to heighten other symptoms and signs such as irritability, nervousness, and agitation. Usual daily functions may be suppressed by states of anxiety.

- *Irritability.* An irritable reaction occurs when feelings of anger are expressed out of proportion to a provoking situation. In truth, this irritability is an inner cry for help, but it can alienate those who are able to help, simply because the irritable person seems so hostile.

- *Hostility.* Open anger projected at caretakers and others may take the form of verbal attacks or even physical aggression. Such hostility is not meant to hurt or offend, it merely shows a reaction to situations that the patient cannot understand.

- *Stubbornness.* In attempting to maintain a sense of control over life's frustrations, the Alzheimer's patient becomes stubborn to the extreme. An insistence on "being right" is a form of obstinate behavior that probably seems unreasonable to the observer. In reality, it is a panicked reaction to the idea of "losing your mind." Having a temper tantrum is another sign of this stubbornness.

- *Lack of Sense of Humor.* Healthy people use humor to quell anxiety, but humor is often difficult for the Alzheimer's disease patient. Many undergo total personality changes and lose their habitual patterns of humor. For some, quips, poking fun, and joking may be lost forever.

- *Suspicion.* Misplacing items without remembering that they were moved causes the person with Alzheimer's to be suspicious without reason. Because there is no memory of hiding objects, there is a tendency to blame others for stealing or losing them.

- *Jealousy.* Jealous rage and accusation that the caregiver is favoring someone else in the family is not uncommon. This response occurring on a continuous basis indicates that loss of judgment or insight has taken over the brain.

- *Paranoia.* Paranoia differs from suspicion in that the paranoid patient definitely blames others for his or her situation. Distortion of perception has set in.

BEHAVIORAL ALTERATIONS FOR THE ALZHEIMER'S PATIENT

Mental and emotional changes bring on behavioral alterations. It is a cause-and-effect relationship between brain failure and personality fluctuations. Behavioral characteristics—signs to the observer that something is very much wrong for the Alzheimer's patient—follow the affecting mental and emotional symptoms and signs.[9]

- *Lack of Initiative.* A previously independent person displaying an inability to initiate acts or tasks is a nearly sure sign of Alzheimer's impairment. The basis for such behavior is an organically blocked mental process.

- *Inability to Follow Through.* The inability to finish what is started, so that no meaningful action takes place, is tied to memory loss.

- *Apathy.* Being unresponsive or showing no interest toward daily activities is a sign of mental deterioration.

- *Personal Neglect.* Among the first clues that dementia is taking over the brain of a loved one or friend is poor grooming and lack of routine housekeeping. Dirt, stains, odor from not bathing, and other forms of poor hygiene are the signs.

- *Restlessness.* Hyperactivity is an opposite effect of brain deterioration. We already mentioned withdrawal and apathy as obvious symptoms and signs, but restless rummaging through drawers, moving furniture, shuffling papers, and ongoing sorting and organizing can be an indication of Alzheimer's disease being present.

- *Lies and Confabulations.* A once "with it" person may begin to tell stories that are completely irrelevant or mixed with fantasy. Psychologists call these lies *confabulations* and recognize that they are the person's attempt to compensate for blank areas in the memory.

Repetition by telling of the same tales over and over—known among psychologists as *perseveration*—is a form of rambling caused by interrupted thought processes. *Irrelevant conversation* is still another sign of brain deterioration. It comes from the patient wanting to participate in social conversation but not having the ability to understand the nature of the conversation. It can also be caused by the problem of words and thoughts not coming together to respond coherently.

- *Loss of Inhibitions.* Performing shocking sexual acts, using vulgar language, engaging in abusive actions, and making tactless statements is caused by failed function in the part of the brain that usually controls learned social behavior.

- *Impulsiveness.* Buying items that are actually unaffordable or giving extravagant gifts may be done on impulse because of dysfunctional intellect, a form of mental derangement.

- *Hoarding and Hiding.* The need to accumulate and protect possessions, even those with no apparent value, is characteristic of Alzheimer's disease patients. Newspapers and magazines may be collected until they rise to the ceiling and form a household hazard. Rancid and moldy food might be stored in the refrigerator. Other people's discarded garbage might be taken into the home and hidden in closets.

- *Misperceptions.* What is seen, heard, felt, or sensed by the individual with Alzheimer's disease may be incorrectly organized and left unintegrated in the brain. Consequently, his or her response to stimuli may be inappropriate, bizarre, or erratic. For example, during winter months the patient may have felt cold. Later, on a hot August day, the memory of coolness may cause the person to turn up the furnace in his or her home.

All of these possible signs and symptoms of mental, emotional, and behavioral entanglements for the individual suffering with Alzheimer's disease will probably lead loved ones to seek an authentic medical diagnosis. Particular diagnostic procedures have been recognized by gerontologists so that Alzheimer's disease is confirmable. Chapter 3 goes into the make-up of those procedures.

CHAPTER 3

The Stages of Alzheimer's Disease

John H., a top executive in the San Francisco offices of an international corporation, gradually lost interest in his work, his friends, and previously pleasurable activities. His memory failed. Easily confused, John frequently wandered away and became lost. Reluctantly, but for the good of their division, his colleagues asked him to resign.

A certified public accountant, Nora P., who, together with her husband, had built a successful and highly respected actuarial firm in Dallas, Texas, could no longer subtract seven from ten. She is kept away from the firm's office suite permanently.

At the very peak of his career, Charles D., an attorney in one of the nation's most renowned Wall Street law firms began to make surprising errors in fact and judgment. The mental changes precipitate more serious deterioration including alterations in the attorney's personality, behavior, and intellect.

While the symptoms differ somewhat, each of these individuals is diagnosed as suffering from the same disease, Alzheimer's disease. Their dementia shows up as severe enough to preclude independent living. They must receive constant attention from supervising adults who are either their close relatives, paid live-in companions, or nursing home personnel.[1]

Alzheimer's disease has been called the "disease of the century" by Lewis Thomas M.D., the former Chairman of the Medical Board of the Sloan-Kettering Cancer Institute, due to the growing number of elderly Americans being diagnosed with the disease.

When dementia strikes, individuals who were once resourceful and capable gradually become totally dependent. The process is so insidious that colleagues, friends, and relatives unconsciously begin to assume responsibilities that were once routine for the afflicted individual. For instance, a secretary or a coworker provides extra support to get the ailing person through the work day. Even friends and close acquaintances may dismiss bizarre behavior changes—even as they begin to unconsciously avoid socializing with the ill person. Often, years go by before the peculiarities of behavior and the declining intellect are viewed as the symptoms and signs of dementia.

The diagnosis of Alzheimer's disease, indeed, is never made lightly or in any offhanded manner. Labeling an individual with such a diagnosis means that he or she is branded as having an incurable affliction.[2]

The diagnosis is given only after the patient advances through a series of stages. Barry Reisberg, M.D., clinical director of the Geriatric Study and Treatment Program at New York University Medical Center, affirms that the distinguishing characteristic of Alzheimer's disease "is that it is an illness of stages, a slow progression through which the patient walks down a highly predictable path." He and his colleagues see seven distinct stages, beginning with moderate confusion and ending in total physical and mental helplessness.[3]

THE SEVEN STAGES OF ALZHEIMER'S DISEASE

The seven stages of Alzheimer's disease were collectively developed by four attending psychiatrists at New York University's Geriatric Study and Treatment Program. They are Dr. Reisberg, Steven H. Ferris, M.D., Mony J. de Leon, M.D., and Thomas Cook, M.D. Their Alzheimer's disease measurement scale was described in an article published in the 1982 issue of *The Journal of Psychiatry*.[4]

Stage One

Simply normal behavior with no clinical signs or symptoms.

Stage Two

The New York University psychiatrists refer to this stage as the forgetfulness of "normal aging," characterized by minor memory lapses. Forgetting names of people—even those known for years—is not clinical evidence of memory deficit. It is common for people over the age of forty-five to occasionally forget or fail to identify certain dates, names, places, events, or objects. "Most aging individuals believe their memory is not as good as it used to be, that they can't remember names or where they put things as well as they once did," Dr. Reisberg said. "In fact, one-third of the people who come to our program are troubled enough by these symptoms that they are terrified they have Alzheimer's disease." Fortunately, most turn out not to.

Stage Three

This early "confusional" stage is characterized by a mild cognitive decline during which people demonstrate decreased ability to remember a name after pointedly being introduced to someone new. Or, items of value seem to misplace themselves, concentration noticeably diminishes, and doing complex tasks becomes difficult. Testing of the potential Alzheimer's disease patient at this time may show evidence of memory deficiency.

Dr. Reisberg kept track of thirty-two people with these symptoms, and after three-and-a-half years, one of the patients had died, one was in a nursing home, and three had deteriorated dramatically. The remaining twenty-seven, however, experienced no progression of symptoms and were perfectly fine. The so-called third stage of Alzheimer's disease, therefore, cannot serve as a diagnostic platform. "This seems to be a borderline condition," notes Dr. Reisberg, "which does not presage marked decline in most cases, at least for the next three years."

Stage Four

Designated as "late confusion" or "mild Alzheimer's disease," this stage shows increased cognitive decline. During testing by means of a psychiatric interview, the doctor will likely find definite mental abnormalities in the patient. There will be an inability to continue serial subtractions or to travel distances or to handle finances. One has marked decrease in the knowledge of current and recent events. Faces and friends may be recognized, however, and traveling along familiar pathways is accomplished. Still, complex tasks that once were performed with no trouble cannot be done anymore. The patient may deny his or her failings, but repeated mistakes or errors of judgment eventually become obvious.

In continuing his research, Dr. Reisberg followed twenty-two people in stage four Alzheimer's disease. After three-and-a-half years, six of them had died, six had entered nursing homes, and the rest remained at home under care of loved ones. None of the patients in stage four improved, but six of them had not grown noticeably worse.

Stage Five

Considered "early dementia" or "moderate Alzheimer's disease," stage five witnesses a more severe decline with the patient unable to survive without assistance. He or she probably won't be able to recall his or her own home address, telephone number, birthdate, and the names of some family members. "An educated person will probably have lost the ability to count back from 40 by fours or from 20 by twos," explained Dr. Reisberg. "If you ask direct questions, persistently, you can see the deficit. They may know who the president of the United States is now, but won't know in a half hour. If you ask them the year, they may know it, but they'll be way off on the month or the season." The individual may look healthy, and in a social situation, no one is likely to notice anything wrong. Attending to personal needs, like going to the toilet, is still a viable possibility, but there may be difficulty choosing correct clothing for the prevailing weather conditions.

Stage Six

In "middle dementia" or "moderately severe Alzheimer's disease," symptoms may accelerate rapidly, often to the point where home care is no longer possible. Severe cognitive decline is quite apparent. Patients can't dress themselves: buttons remain open, shoes get put on the wrong feet, jackets are put on backwards, and outer clothing is often worn over pajamas or nightgowns. Taking a bath becomes a terrifying experience. With hot and cold water taps not being adjusted, skin burns occur. Memories of recent events are barely remembered; memories of past events are forgotten, as well. Spouses' names blur or disappear altogether. Assistance for daily activities is mandatory.

Physical, mental, and behavioral derangements set in. Incontinence may occur. There is confusion between night and day. There are delusions, such as talking to spirits or to reflections in the mirror. Accusations may be levied that the spouse is somebody else. A person may scrub the kitchen sink for hours or repeat some other simple activity over and over again. Some Alzheimer's disease patients become violent in this stage and punch visitors or even attack their loving caretakers.

Stage Seven

In the "final" stage or "late dementia" the patient exhibits very severe cognitive decline. There can be a total loss of speech with only grunts or humming remaining. There can also be incontinence and loss of basic psychomotor skills, such as the inability to feed or walk. The brain seems to function on its own, without any attention to the body. The personality is gone. "Alzheimer's disease seems to progress in the reverse order of normal development," said Dr. Reisberg. "It is the smile that goes last."[5]

PEOPLE WHO ILLUSTRATE STAGES
OF ALZHEIMER'S DISEASE

The confusional phase of stage-three Alzheimer's disease is typified by the expert carpenter who has trouble constructing a simple wooden box. A teacher may forget his or her students' names. The assembly-line worker notices deterioration in job performance by two criteria: he or she is unable to keep up with the ordinary speed of products being assembled on the moving line, and actual mistakes are made in the assembling process.

The late-confusion phase of stage-four "mild" Alzheimer's disease is another story. Here, people lose the ability to handle such routine activities as food shopping or managing personal finances. The most common lament is, "I can't balance a checkbook anymore."

Hortence W., a homemaker in Monterey, California, whose husband has been diagnosed with Alzheimer's disease, said, "His checkbook looked like a Chinese puzzle. Our lawyer told me to keep the finances out of his hands." This is the stage at which Grandma, who once baked batches of cookies every Christmas and Easter, can't even whip up a batter. In another instance, Uncle Herman comes to your home on Thanksgiving, and the next day can't remember having been there.

The early-dementia phase of stage-five "moderate" Alzheimer's disease has people forgetting the names of their grandchildren or the college from which they graduated. They may wander from home and not be able to find their way back. As victims, these stage-five patients are stripped of their physical skills, their sanity, and their self-esteem. It is the mind that goes while the body functions well enough.

In the middle-dementia phase of stage-six Alzheimer's disease, symptoms speed up in occurrence and reach the point where living alone becomes impossible. The patient forgets simple actions, like how to step into a tub, resulting in great physical damage to the body. Sometimes the names of one's mother and father are remembered, sometimes not. The name of a spouse may be forgotten, or the spouse could even be looked upon as a complete stranger.

Fifty-six-year-old Norman T., a former police officer in Milwaukee, Wisconsin, plagued by sixth-stage Alzheimer's disease, will sit in the living room with his coat on all night, banging on the locked door every half-hour or so demanding to go out. The situation became so intolerable that his wife and children sought an institution in which to lodge Norman.

The final phase of stage seven, "late dementia" Alzheimer's disease, represents the eventual loss of nearly all basic abilities, including toilet training and self-feeding. Social inhibitions are also lost in this stage. Efficiency even with life-saving personal functions, such as coughing and swallowing may be lost. Abusive habits are adapted in an automatic way.

CASE STUDY OF A POTENTIAL STAGE-THREE ALZHEIMER'S DISEASE PATIENT

At the beginning of 1992, sixty-year-old Mickey V., an attractive, divorced woman residing in Patterson, New Jersey, had complained to her physician that the executive-secretary position she held was being adversely affected by lapses in her memory. Weekly, to prevent any recurrence of breast cancer, Mickey traveled to Suffern, New York, to receive immune system reinforcement from orthomolecular psychiatrist Michael B. Schachter, M.D. There was no problem with the patient's anticancer treatment; in fact, her immune system had been responding magnificently, and, as a result of her metabolic enhancement program, she was probably healthier than most so-called "normal" persons.

Mickey's problem was that she was having trouble retaining short-term memories. She was also having difficulty concentrating. For example, the chief operating officer of the corporation, for whom she worked directly, might give the executive secretary a small task to accomplish in the near future and then give her another vital job to be done immediately. If Mickey did not jot down the latter task, invariably she would forget it. Various details during the work day were recalled only with difficulty.

In many instances, Mickey told Dr. Schachter, she would dash for the notepad, bump into a door post or a piece of furniture (because of poor body orientation), and by the time she reached her desk, the matter she needed to mark down had already been forgotten. This forced her to ask again about those details. It was becoming increasingly embarrassing for the secretary and annoying to her superior.

Mickey slept too long and deeply, as well, and sometimes would nod off inadvertently when watching television, attending a lecture, or sitting through a sermon. She hardly ever felt wholly awake. Her eidetic imagery (power to visualize objects previously seen) was faulty, too, in that she found herself losing the ability to look at a painting, leave the museum, and remember what the painting looked like.

Unlike when she first began her executive-secretary position, thirty years before, Mickey found herself doing almost no creative work. It was all she could manage to get through the day performing merely those tasks being asked of her. It was obvious that the patient needed help with many aspects of her memory.

TYPES OF MEMORY

Mickey was exhibiting flaws in several types of human memory. Memory is more than the ability to recall past events and act on the thoughts. Instead, memory can be divided into different forms in accordance with the brain's immediate needs. The following are aspects of memory classified by psychologists:

Episodic memory is past event or episode recall, such as remembering your graduation day, the circumstances of meeting your spouse, or the moment you paid off your mortgage.

Factual memory is the remembering of facts, such as the number of people populating your city, who discovered America, or the address of your office building.

Semantic memory is knowing the meaning of words, such as butterfly," "data processing," or "Cadillac."

Sensory memory is using "the mind's eye" to remember a person's face, the sound of a piece of music, or the smell of some delicious food.

Skill memory is the ability to perform a function with accuracy such as swinging a tennis racket, driving an automobile, or getting dressed.

Instinctive memory is a calling on instructions stored in the genes for performing individual physical and mental functions such as inhaling fresh air, sucking at mother's breast, or escaping from imminent danger.

Collective memory is application of archetypal feelings and symbols resulting from collective race or cultural memories. An example of this would be a black person's suspicions of whites, a Chinese antagonism for Japanese, or a Jewish person's wariness of Germans.

Past-life memory is the ability to relive events such as regression under hypnosis to one's earliest age or the assumption of a character out of some bygone time, from even long before birth.

Imagery memory is the sensory-type experience in the mind without an actual corresponding situation to provide the immediate sense stimulus such as seeing oneself floating on a sailboat, climbing a majestic peak, or engaging in sexual interplay with a celebrity movie star.

DIAGNOSING MICKEY'S MEMORY PROBLEM

Dr. Schachter checked Mickey for dementia after using laboratory and clinical tests to rule out the yeast syndrome, food allergies, environmental sensitivities, and a variety of other physical ailments that could be affecting her brain.

There are more than 50 identified causes of the intellectual deficits of dementia involving the loss of recent memory. The dementias are classified as primary, vascular, and secondary, and subclassified according to specific pathogenetic or systemic features (see Table 3.1 below). Dr. Schachter set out to determine whether Mickey was experiencing benign forgetfulness or stage three senile dementia, and if so, from which cause. Once he did so, he was able to reverse her brain syndrome in several months by utilizing a chelation-therapy protocol similar to the protocol illustrated by the case studies cited in Chapter 1.

The first step to confirm the presence of dementia was relatively simple, based on the patient's history and response to a mental-status examination. Being a trained psychiatrist, Dr. Schachter had enough information, including Mickey's history of memory loss, various cognitive failures, and her mental-status test ratings.

The second step was to identify the dementia and its underlying disease. Dr. Schachter carried out additional, thorough, clinical evaluations, based on the versatile use of office and laboratory procedures, and the clinical correlation of these findings. The office workup consisted of a detailed medical history and systems review, a family history to rule out genetic disease, a social history stressing the patient's food, alcohol, and drug habits, and physical and neurologic examinations.

Laboratory examinations included a computerized axial tomography (CAT) scan, an electroencephalogram (EEG), a complete blood cell count (CBC), a metabolic screen (including thyroid, serum vitamin B_{12}, other vitamin levels, blood glucose, electrolytes, liver and kidney-function tests), and a hair-mineral analysis. These tests pointed to the most likely causes.

OTHER CLINICAL AND LABORATORY TESTS
FOR ALZHEIMER'S DISEASE

The primary characteristic symptom of Alzheimer's disease, memory loss, can be most precisely estimated by clinical examination and psychological tests. The individual types of memory tests—spacial, verbal, and written—

Table 3.1 Classification of Causes of Dementia

Classification	Subclassification
Primary Degenerative Dementia	Alzheimer's disease (50% to 60% of all cases) Pick's disease (rare in the United States) Huntington's chorea Progressive supranuclear palsy
Vascular Dementia	Multiple-infarct dementia Lacunar state dementia Binswanger's disease
Secondary Dementia	Hydrocephalus Korsakoff's psychosis (alcoholic) Traumatic (punchdrunk syndrome) Intracranial masses (tumor, subdurals) Metabolic (thyroid, B12 deficiency, liver, kidney) Infections (Creutzfeld-Jakob syndrome, neurosyphilis, encephalitis, and fungal meningitis) Other neurological diseases (multiple sclerosis and Parkinson's disease)

are well established. The following multiple-choice questions are typical of the examination that a patient would receive:

- Do you notice that you have difficulty taking care of personal grooming needs?
    1. Grooming is no problem.
    2. It's a struggle, but grooming gets done daily.
    3. Daily grooming seldom gets done anymore.

- Have you observed yourself as having a nervous problem such as an inability to sit still or the presence of a facial tic?
    1. Nervous problems are not present.
    2. Sometimes people remark on my uncontrollable nerves.
    3. Unintended movement or restlessness is usual for me.

- Have you noted a change in your alertness?
    1. My alertness is present as much as ever.
    2. Occasional listlessness or dullness is noticeable.
    3. My unawareness is apparent to me much of the time.

- Please speak the following phrase: "No ifs, ands, or buts." Was there difficulty with saying the words?
  1. I had no trouble with remembering or speaking the phrase.
  2. There was some difficulty, but I managed to say the phrase.
  3. I had much trouble saying or even remembering the phrase.

Besides furnishing numerous check-off questions about someone's speech and language, general appearance, and mental inventory, the doctor provides test questions that ask about motor functions, intellectual abilities, long-term memory, short-term memory, and more. According to the response numbers scored, the testee's points added together may be compared with a range that shows a healthy, well-functioning brain or one that is in a dysfunctional condition.

The EEG (eletroencephalogram), or brain-wave test, produces a recording of voltage patterns from the brain that are measured through electrodes at varying positions on each side of the head.

A diagnostic test has been developed by scientists at the Institute for Basic Research (IBR) in Developmental Disabilities, an arm of the New York State Office of Mental Retardation and Developmental Disabilities, and Immuno-Product Industries who created the test format under contract with Senetek PLC of St. Louis, Missouri. The clinical data obtained from the diagnostic testing of spinal fluid from Alzheimer's disease patients rules out other forms of dementia as a source of symptoms. Until now, this test has not been revealed to medical consumers through the media. Although it is safe, the spinal fluid test has not yet been tested on a large enough number of people to be made public.

Research at IBR is also completed on an Alzheimer's-disease diagnostic test using the patient's blood serum. However, stringent regulations from the United States Food and Drug Administration (FDA) are holding up the extensive tests necessary to make this test available to the public.

Conventional X-ray examinations are of limited value in Alzheimer's disease because they cannot produce an image of the brain itself. They are used instead as a crude screen to catch other pathological processes.

The CAT scan and magnetic resonance imaging (MRI) outline the brain, including its surface and ventricles, allowing an actual view of small injuries such as strokes or tumors, that can produce other forms of dementia. Although CAT scanning and MRI do not provide any definite diagnosis of Alzheimer's disease, still they must be performed on most patients (especially MRI) to rule out other brain pathology. Sometimes they just show brain atrophy.

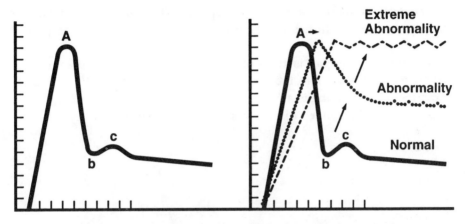

BRAIN FLOW STUDIES WITH TECHNETIUM 99M.

Figure 3.1. This artist's rendition indicates the computer printout pattern of brain-flow studies performed on patients utilizing the injection of the isotope Technetium 99m. The rise of the heavy solid line to point A, as shown on the left, indicates blood flowing into the brain. As the line descends to point b, the the blood carrying the isotope is leaving the brain. Point C indicates a recirculation wave of blood and then the radioactivity in the brain levels off as well as the blood level. In contrast, the dotted and dashed lines separately show abnormal and extremely abnormal blood flow to the brain that invariably manifests in patients with Alzheimer's disease.

Central nervous system abnormalities associated with delayed blood flow into and out of the brain would be indicated by point A being shifted to the right. Delayed outflow of blood from the brain is manifested by a rise of point b as indicated on the right side of the illustration.

The diagnosis of vascular dementia may be assisted by blood flow studies using Technetium 99m. Technetium is an artificial radioactive element that emits gamma radiation and is used as a tracer for the examination of the brain and the thyroid gland in the technique of scintigraphy. (Scintigraphy is a diagnostic procedure that allows the examiner to determine the competency of brain cells through observing the activity of a radionuclide injected into the patient.) It is useful in determining the paterns of brain-blood flow as depicted on page 39 in Figure 3.1.

Alzheimer's disease can be diagnosed with brain biopsy, but the procedure is painful, and causes discomfort into the recovery period. A major drawback to using this method is that if it is done too early in the course of the disease, the damage may not have spread throughout the brain, and the changes in brain tissue may not appear in the small sample taken for biopsy. Because of this, brain biopsies usually are done only as part of research procedures.

At present, autopsy is the only way that a conclusive diagnosis of Alzheimer's disease is established. Even so, by means of the complete examination, including testing with MRI, it is possible to make the clinical diagnosis of Alzheimer's disease with a high degree of accuracy.

CHAPTER 4

The Pathological Brain Changes in an Alzheimer's Disease Patient

In July of 1989, President George Bush officially declared the 1990s our "Decade of the Brain." The Decade of the Brain signifies a pledge by the federal government to focus vital resources on brain research. This pledge stems specifically from the needs of almost 55 million Americans with disorders and disabilities of the brain, about 5 million of whom, in the current decade, suffer from dementia of the Alzheimer's type (DAT), commonly referred to as Alzheimer's disease (AD). (The terms Alzheimer's disease and dementia of the Alzheimer's type are used in medicine interchangeably.) With the rates of Alzheimer's disease doubling every 5.1 years,[1] it is projected by the United States Census Bureau that close-in to the next century a minimum of 10.3 million persons with Alzheimer's disease will be burdening our sociological and financial systems.[2]

The remarkable advances that have occurred in brain research in the past decade, coupled with the former President's announced timely support from the federal government, promise opportunities for research on Alzheimer's in the 1990s. Medical investigators do have some information on the pathological brain changes in patients with Alzheimer's disease, but not enough. We need to uncover the true brain pathology involved and root out its cause. To do this, we must first examine all of the evidence available on Alzheimer's disease.

During the fifty-seven years following the discoveries made by the Bavarian neuropsychiatrist, Alois Alzheimer, M.D., in 1906, virtually no research was done on dementia. Then, in the 1960s, three English scientists, Dr. Bernard E. Tomlinson, Dr. Garry Blessed, and Sir Martin Roth, followed fifty demented, over-sixty-five-year-old patients through to the ends of their lives. After the deaths of these selected people, autopsies were performed. The researchers made comparisons with the brain matter of twenty-eight nondemented, age-matched adults who died during the same period.

More than half of the demented adults were found to have pathological changes in their brains indicative of Alzheimer's disease. The British scientists concluded that, in most cases, senile dementia and presenile dementia were the same disease. Both should be labelled dementia of the Alzheimer's type (DAT) or Alzheimer's disease (AD).

Another form of brain pathology in addition to AD includes multi-infarct dementia (MID), probably the best-known of the additional dementias, since it results from a series of small strokes (see Chapter 5 for a description of MID). Still, most researchers estimate that 75 percent of all dementia patients suffer outright from Alzheimer's disease.[3] Symptoms of Alzheimer's disease account for about half of all cases of dementia at any age.

THE DAMAGE OF ALZHEIMER'S DISEASE

What Dr. Alzheimer saw in his microscopic slides he described as malfunctioning brain tissue. There are neurofibrillary tangles and senile plaques occurring among neurons (nerve cells) that involve memory in areas of the brain designated in neurology as the hippocampus, cerebral cortex, the amygdala, and other tissues essential for cognitive function. A valid diagnosis of Alzheimer's disease requires the same microscopic testing that was done by Dr. Alzheimer.

Since it is illogical to remove a portion of the brain for such examination from a living person, technically no one can be absolutely certain of the diagnosis unless this examination is performed during autopsy. However, as part of the next chapter we shall describe how the neurologist, the psychiatrist, and their colleagues practicing in the biobehavioral sciences, go about recognizing dementia and making the diagnosis of Alzheimer's disease in a living person. More relevant to this current chapter is our task of discussing exactly what has happened to tissues in the brain of an Alzheimer's disease patient.

The neurons that are being destroyed are the working components of the brain. From these neurons come the commands that set muscles into motion, retain memories, receive the sights and sounds of surroundings, cause hormones to be secreted, and produce emotions. Nerve tissue affected by tangles or plaques looks as if it is nonfunctioning and dead. It probably is nonfunctional, but brain scientists have not yet proven the absence of life among the neuronic tangles.

Alzheimer's disease is unique to the human species. The loss of memory, judgment, and emotional stability that it inflicts on dementia victims occurs gradually and inexorably, usually leading to death in a severely debilitated, immobile state. The cost to American society for diagnosing and managing Alzheimer's disease, primarily for custodial care, is currently estimated at more than $120 billion annually, perhaps one sixth of the gross national cost of health care in the United States.

The earlier the onset of AD, the more severe the illness, and the shorter its course. Down's syndrome victims who live beyond the age of 40, invariably develop Alzheimer's disease. From ages 55 to 70, the average remaining period of life for an Alzheimer's disease patient is between four and twelve years, averaging around 7.5 years once the symptoms begin and become noticeable. But with the chelation-treatment program we describe in Part III, most of the signs and symptoms of dementia can be reversed or reduced if a good portion of neurons remain viable, and the individual eliminates the primary causes.

HOW ALZHEIMER'S WAS DISCOVERED

Dr. Alois Alzheimer was not the first medical scientist to describe the disease that now bears his name. Sixty-eight years earlier, in 1838, Jean Esquirol, M.D., a prominent French physician, told his colleagues about *demence senile* (senile dementia). Dr. Esquirol described his discovery as an illness that comes over the elderly gradually. Often it is accompanied by emotional disturbances, he said, that result in a victim's loss of short-term memory, ambition, energy, and willpower. The limiting factor, he offered, is that only those over the age of sixty-five are struck by *demence senile*.

For Dr. Alzheimer there was no limiting factor, for he identified a much younger victim. (The historical age record for Alzheimer's first recorded AD patient seems to be cited variably among the annals of medicine ranging from age fifty-one to age fifty-six. The most frequent age cited of the autopsied woman that we have found in the literature appears to be fifty-five.) It turns out that both Esquirol's and Alzheimer's discoveries are exactly the same condition. Dr. Esquirol referred to it as "old age" dementia and Dr. Alzheimer named it "presenile" dementia. In a well-accepted 1907 clinical journal article, Dr. Alzheimer described what he observed about the affected brain tissue when visualized under the microscope.

Other brain researchers were able to duplicate his observations in autopsies and so credited Dr. Alzheimer with uncovering a unique form of brain pathology. His findings were incorporated in the classic psychiatry text of the day, Kraeplein's *Textbook of Psychiatry*, and classified as a presenile dementia that strikes people under the age of sixty-five. The age classification no doubt set the study of this disease back by many years, for during the next five decades there was no agreement in the field as to whether people over sixty-five with dementia, whose autopsied brains exhibited the structures Dr. Alzheimer described, could be considered to have had AD. Further confusion was created by the mistaken belief among American psychiatrists that most cases of senile dementia were due to hardening of the arteries in the brain.

What Dr. Alzheimer did find were abnormal fibers and degenerated nerve endings. The nerve cells in the outer layer of the brain—the cerebral cortex—were riddled with jumbled-up fibers at the ends of those nerves. These fibers resembled tangled strands of wool or telephone cables that have been cut through with a dull axe. Dr. Alzheimer gave these jumbled fibers a name—"neurofibrillary tangles," literally meaning nerve-fiber tangles.

With the aid of a tissue strain, Dr. Alzheimer also noted that on the outside of the nerve cells there were deteriorating pieces of nerve cells grouped around a fibrous core. Later investigators, seeing the same grouping, named them "neuritic plaques." They look like mothholes eaten in cloth and are known to interrupt the passage of nerve signals, as if the brain is short-circuiting, cutting off memory messages and destroying the free flow of thought.[5]

At the center of each plaque is a substance that has been labeled amyloid—an abnormal protein not usually present. These amyloid plaques often are present with highly reactive types of molecular fragments that combine readily with other pollutant molecules, such as those of heavy metals. They bring about chemical reactions that lead to blood-vessel and cellular damage. When analyzed under the microscope, as the United States Department of Health and Human Services acknowledges, the amyloid core at the center of each neuritic plaque is always surrounded by pieces of deteriorating brain cells.

The intertwined wool-like neurofibrillary tangles look like coils on an innerspring mattress. They are also found in the brains of autopsied patients who suffered with Parkinson's disease. Thus, Parkinson's disease and Alzheimer's disease have similar pathological appearances, as do adults with Down's syndrome, and punch-drunk boxers. It is likely that the former heavy-weight boxing champion and principled role-model, Muhammed Ali, who unluckily had been struck with Parkinson's disease by age forty-five, has them too.

Dr. Alzheimer remarked in his journal article that the brain of the fifty-five-year-old corpse he had autopsied could have been taken from a woman who was ninety years old. Her brain appeared severely withered as if it had dried up and shrunk. While everyone loses brain cells during his/her lifetime, the inner spaces of this middle-aged woman's brain—the ventricles—were larger than usual and their outer layer of cells were thinner than they should have been. It looked like this woman had subjected her brain to much wear and tear.

Long after Dr. Alzheimer announced his findings, some pathologists and other scientists reported on "granulovacuolar changes" being present in the brains taken from victims of AD. They wrote that cells in the memory-storing hippocampus region became filled with fluid and grain-like material. They also said that amyloid in the core of plaques was discovered to be penetrating blood-vessel walls, which may signify an immune system abnormality. Additionally there are Hirano bodies that encase vital granules known to be responsible for bringing together proteins. Trapped within these Hirano bodies, certain tiny chemical factories (organelles) known as ribosomes, cannot perform their work and so memories fail to form.

THE TRUE NATURE OF AMYLOID MATERIAL IN THE BRAIN

In 1853, the great German pathologist Rudolf Virchow, M.D., made one of his rare mistakes in medicine by erroneously identifying a particular beta-protein in the cerebral cortex as "amyloid." His error is easy to understand. He made it because, in some brains of persons dying during that period, there were variable numbers of spherical plaques consisting of altered axons and dendrites (the long, tapering ends of neurons) present. The plaques surrounded an extracellular mass of thin filaments that resembled extracellular deposits that accumulated in other organs in a variety of unrelated diseases. The consistency of some other extracellular deposits could be a starch-like substance known as amyloid, but not the filamentous mass in the cerebral cortex.

The principal constituents of the brain's "amyloid" filaments are actually proteins, and such so-called amyloid proteins often are observed in other health problems. The identification of these proteins differs among the various diseases marked by the deposition of amyloid. A commonness among these disparate diseases showing amyloidosis is that they are characterized by innumerable extracellular deposits of normal or mutated-protein fragments. Such protein subunits are always folded in a three-dimensional pattern referred to by histopathologists as a beta-pleated sheet.[6] (Histopathologists are doctors who identify types of pathology affecting different cells.)

There are glial cells in the brain known as neuroglia. These are the special connective tissues of the central nervous system. Mature plaques contain two types of altered neuroglial cells. First there are microglial cells that scavenge and remove the inflamed or destroyed tissue of brain pathology. Then there are reactive astrocytes, which are the large, star-shaped glial cells that are assigned the function of providing nutrients for neurons that take part in information storage. These two kinds of neuroglial cells bind nerve-cell tissue together.[7]

According to Dennis J. Selkoe, M.D., professor of neurology and neuroscience at Harvard Medical School, the senile plaques and neurofibrillary tangles characteristic of AD actually are not made of the amyloid beta-protein once considered the accepted structure for the brain disease. Instead, Dr. Selkoe says, they are a modified form of a normally occurring neuronal protein called "tau." The neurofibrillary tangles and amyloid plaques occur in over a dozen chronic diseases of the human brain, all of which are made up of tau. What distinguishes AD pathology, however, is that there are a vast number of such tangles and plaques, much more than usually seen in the autopsied brains of elderly people who had behaved socially normal while living.

"For the most part, the distinction between normal brain aging and Alzheimer's disease is quantitative rather than qualitative," wrote Dr. Selkoe. "Usually patients with progressive DAT have moderately or markedly more mature neuritic plaques and neurofibrillary tangles than age-matched nondemented people do."[6]

Thus, amyloid-bearing neuritic plaques in the brain are an invariant feature of AD. All elderly people accumulate at least a few of them during their lifetimes, but an overwhelming number of such plaque formations will probably be the main brain pathology that identifies a patient with Alzheimer's disease.

Amyloid beta-protein is comprised of forty or so amino acids. It is part of the coding sequence of deoxyribonucleic acid (DNA), the exceedingly important 695-amino acid protein molecule that carries genetic cell information. Amyloid beta-protein occupies places 597 through 636 on the DNA chain. It is encoded by a gene located on chromosome 21. At least one form of familial Alzheimer's disease (FAD) comes about because of a genetic defect located on chromosome 21. The FAD we shall mention at the end of this chapter and discuss in the next is Cretuzfeldt-Jakob disease (CJD).

Also, people with Down's syndrome (who are born with an extra copy of chromosome 21) routinely develop beta-amyloid deposits at an early age.

AMYLOID BETA-PROTEIN AND TOXIC METALS

Beta-amyloid abnormalities can initiate some forms of Alzheimer's disease. This happens when environmental factors are present, such as heavy-metal toxicity. (For further information on heavy-metal toxicity, see Part II.) Then ". . . there will be a direct influence on Alzheimer's disease occurrence," affirms Dr. Selkoe. "One piece of evidence supporting this opinion is the observation that identical twins may manifest Alzheimer symptoms at considerably different ages."

The case history of identical twins Robert and Wilfred, which is described in Chapter 1, is a prime example of Dr. Selkoe's statement. The second twin, Wilfred, who did not come in touch with toxic metals at his job as a chemical engineer in San Diego, did not develop Alzheimer's disease. The first twin, Robert, whose case history we discussed at length, became very much involved in dealing with toxic metals while performing his job as a chemical engineer with the chemical company in Delaware. Robert developed and suffered from the symptoms of Alzheimer's disease until he underwent chelation therapy. (For more information on chelation therapy see Chapter 17.)

The theory, that we will discuss at length in Part II, is that the metallic molecules combine with beta-amyloid in the brain to produce pathology. This pathology so interrupts nerve impulses and thought processes that symptoms manifest themselves as Alzheimer's disease. "Debate swirls around the unsettled role of aluminum as a contributing factor," Dr. Selkoe concluded. And while aluminum and calcium are the two most likely abusive minerals for the many forms of dementia (see Chapter 5 for descriptions of other dementias), the many other poisonous minerals such as arsenic, beryllium, cadmium, copper, iron, lead, manganese, mercury, nickel, and titanium are culprits, too.[8,9,10,11,12,13]

Dr. Harold H. Sandstead, professor and chairman in the Department of Preventive Medicine and Community Health at the University of Texas Medical Branch, Galveston, Texas, wrote in *The American Journal of Clinical Nutrition*:

> Lead, mercury, iodine, cobalt, iron, copper, manganese, and zinc have important influences on brain development and function. Identity of thresholds at which effects occur is needed for determination of safe and/or essential levels of these elements in diet. Such knowledge will help define human needs for essential elements, and the hazards of toxic elements.[14]

As we've mentioned, therefore, Alzheimer's disease is thought to be some form of amyloidosis of the brain tissues. Remember that amyloidosis is a disease in which a waxy, starchlike, protein builds up in the tissues of any part of the body. The brain is no exception. In the brain, in regions of the hippocampus, which controls memory, and in the cerebral cortex, which controls higher order thinking and reasoning, you can find the same plaques and tangles identified by Dr. Alzheimer back in 1907 intermixed with high concentrations of beta-amyloid, the protein described as being present in many of the plaques.

In an excellent article published in *The New York Times,* Robin Marantz Henig discussed the "amyloid hypothesis" in which the first step in a sequence of destructive events in the brain involves beta-amyloid. In November 1993, medical writer Henig tells us, gerontologists and other scientists led by neurobiologist Allen D. Roses, Ph.D., at Duke University, linked a gene to an increased susceptibility to Alzheimer's disease that strikes after the age of sixty-five—the most common type of Alzheimer's. Dr. Roses and his colleagues declared that the first step in the brain cell degeneration involves a protein called apolipoprotein E (ApoE).

Henig wrote:

> The Duke scientists found that 64 percent of Alzheimer's patients had at least one gene coding for the type of ApoE protein known as E4. Among a control group, only 31 percent did. And they charted a clear relationship between the ApoE types and the age of the onset of the disease. For those Alzheimer's patients with two E4 genes, one from each parent, the average age of onset was 68. For those with a single E4, paired with another type, like E3, the average age was 75. For those with no E4, the average age of onset was 84.
>
> It became clear, then, that having ApoE4 is a risk for Alzheimer's disease, just as high cholesterol is a risk factor for heart disease. "If you have E4, you're more more likely to get Alzheimer's disease; if you don't have E4, you're less likely" Roses says. Research on how E4 works, he says, holds promise for a preventive therapy within the next ten years, perhaps as simple as a pill to supply a missing brain chemical.
>
> Just as diet and exercise can lessen the risk of heart disease for someone with high cholesterol, something in the environment might affect whether a person with E4 actually develops Alzheimer's.[14a]

We maintain that the environmental "something" definitely exists in the form of toxic metals—lead, aluminum, mercury, cadmium, iron, and manganese. These and other environmental toxins produce a syndrome of highly destructive interconnected etiologies, pathologies, symptoms, signs, and prognoses.

Once again our idea must be stated that amyloid beta-protein deposition can be the primary event initiating Alzheimer's disease when toxic metals that are present in the environment move from the blood stream, past the blood-brain barrier, and lock onto brain amyloid. The blood-brain barrier (BBB) is a specialized system within blood vessels of the brain designed to keep undesirable chemicals out of the brain. With the build-up of excessive amyloid, the BBB gets penetrated.

The three Harvard Medical School brain researchers, Drs. Catharine L. Joachim, Hiroshi Mori, and Dennis J. Selkoe, have decided that beta-amyloid deposition is not restricted to the brain alone. Dr. Selkoe stated clearly:

> The predilection of these extracerebral deposits [found in most other parts of the body undergoing degeneration] to occur near blood vessels also strengthens the parallels between Alzheimer's disease and certain systemic amyloidoses that we know have a circulatory origin. Most important, the deposition of small amounts of amyloid beta-protein in peripheral blood vessels in the absence of any preceding neuronal injury—indeed in the absence of local neurons and glial cells—supports the hypothesis that the release and accumulation of amyloid beta-protein precede rather than follow neuronal degeneration in the brain.[6]

THE CHOLINERGIC HYPOTHESIS

Even with evidence strongly favoring the amyloid concept of dementia, neuropsychiatrists have not pinpointed the exact cause of AD. To speak of a single cause may be misleading, in fact, because dementia probably is the result of a complicated sequence of events involving many contributing factors. There are other hypotheses about pathological brain occurrences that may cause dementia. One of the hypotheses considered most valid, relates to the enzyme that makes acetylcholine (ACH), a chemical messenger used by the body to transmit information between nerve cells. This catalytic enzyme, choline acetyltransferase (ChAT), is decidedly lacking in the cortex of brains belonging to autopsied Alzheimer patients.

The absence of choline acetyltransferase indicates that there is a deficiency of ACH, especially in the cortex, the part of the brain responsible for higher mental functions—such as memory, speech, and reasoning. Without ChAT there is not likely to be any ACH, the lack of which would bring on severe dysfunction of the memory.

Acetylcholine is one of the most vital neurotransmitters. Neurotransmitters function by being released from neurons, jumping across synapses (spaces between nerve fibers), and attaching to the next nerve cell at a specialized region called a receptor. Different nerve cell receptors accept only those neurotransmitters to which they have a specific affinity.[15]

According to Richard Mayeux, M.D., professor in the neurosciences at the Columbia University College of Physicians and Surgeons, "The pathogenesis of the core manifestation of AD, memory loss, is attributed to loss of neurons containing ACH." The 'cholinergic hypothesis' is based on compelling evidence that includes the following facts:

First, scopolamine [a sedative drug] blocks the post-synaptic muscarinic cholinergic receptors [receptors at the synapse], induces loss of memory, brings about a decline in cognitive skills in young people, and is reversible by an inhibitor or cholinesterase called physostigmine. [Cholinesterase is another enzyme known to break down ACH.]

Second, choline acetyltransferase, this rate-limiting enzyme initialed ChAT that's needed by the brain for ACH production, has activity significantly lower in the brains of AD patients compared to control patients.

Third, the severity of dementia is related to the degree of choline acetyltransferase reduction in AD.

Fourth, in immunohistochemical studies, both choline acetyltransferase and ACH have been found in neuritic plaques and neurofibrillary tangles, the pathognomonic lesions of AD.

Fifth, in AD there is also a reduction of cells in the basal forebrain cholinergic complex.

The drug Dr. Mayeux mentioned, scopolamine, was commonly used in the 1930s in conjunction with a pain medication during labor and delivery. Women so treated had pain relief but often failed to remember the events of the delivery. Scopolamine is known to prevent the normal action of ACH. It was administered to healthy young college students to induce memory disruption in a series of experiments in the 1970s. The effect was then reversed by administration of the other drug mentioned by Dr. Mayeux, physostig-mine, a compound that increases the availability of ACH.

NUTRITIONAL SUPPLEMENTATION
WITH CHOLINE DERIVATIVES

Trials with nutrients were undertaken to increase brain acetylcholine con-tent by feeding AD patients either choline (a B-vitamin) or lecithin (a phospholipid). Nutrients such as these, and other B-vitamins like inositol, are known as "neurotransmitter precursors." They nourish brain cells so that the chemicals that carry messages from neuron to neuron, the neuro-transmitters, may be created. This form of treatment with oral nutrients, known as precursor-replacement therapy, is based on the assumption that by administering a neurotransmitter precursor there will be a chemical reaction in the brain.

The conversion of swallowed choline into acetylcholine did produce mild improvement in AD patients. The trials have given some good clinical results. However, the double-blind, placebo-controlled studies (in which neither the patients nor the investigators are aware of who are on placebo and who are on active nutrient) count most in the medical community. In double-blind studies, oral choline has failed to demonstrate improvement. Why? It is thought that precursor-replacement therapy failed because there is an inadequate amount of the enzyme necessary to convert choline into ACH. Therefore, the diseased brain may not be capable of producing more ACH in sufficient amounts to pass psychomotor tests required in double-blind studies. But sufficient improvement occurred for observing loved ones. Perhaps their hopes and wishes overshadowed the requirements of the established scientific method.

As a further pursuit of the cholinergic hypothesis, the ACH inhibitor physostigmine was injected into AD patients. It prevents cholinesterase from breaking down acetylcholine. Four out of seven double-blind studies using physostigmine showed beneficial effects on memory and behavioral tasks for AD patients. Still, in no instance did an individual recover from dementia. Higher doses produce more positive responses, but there are side effects, including nausea, vomiting, altered blood pressure and pulse rate. (For Cholinergic Cognitive Enhancers, see Table 4.1 on page 52.)

GENETIC REASONS FOR AD

Other than a young-age dementia reference cited later in this chapter, the

Table 4.1 Cholinergic Cognitive Enhancers for Alzheimer's Disease

	Nutrients	Drugs	Choline Replacement Compounds
Acetylcholine precursors	choline lecithin		
Cholinesterase inhibitors		physostigmine tetrahydro- aminoacridine	
Agonists			arecoline RS 86 bethanechol
Miscellaneous drugs and nutrients		Zimelidine Nimodipine Vinpocetine chelating agents	

youngest recorded case of Alzheimer's disease was a Japanese woman who was diagnosed at age twenty-eight. She died from AD in 1981 when she was thirty-three-years-old.[3] Indeed, in Japanese society the prevalence of dementia is estimated to be 5.8 percent of the entire population. There is moderate to severe dementia in 2.2 percent and mild dementia in 3.6 percent of the Japanese aged population. Cerebrovascular dementia (CVD is any dementia caused by a blood-vessel disorder in the brain) and multi-infarct dementia (MID) were found in 2.8 percent, Alzheimer's disease in 2.4 percent, and dementia due to other causes in 0.6 percent. MID was diagnosed more frequently in Japanese men, and Alzheimer's disease in women.[4]

Of all the factors convincingly demonstrated to be responsible for Alzheimer's disease, an error in the genetic material passed down from generation to generation is at work. Genes basically respond to moment-to-moment changes in their environment.[16]

This being true, it is another verification of the rightness of our goal in drawing attention to metal toxicity as a reason for the onset of dementia. Since all people residing in industrialized western countries are exposed to excessive amounts of toxic metals, and about 20 percent of those over sixty-five are demented to some degree (as has been determined in statistical studies), anyone having twenty-five relatives aged over sixty-five, on average will see not less than five of them suffering from dementia. If toxic-metal exposure for these relatives has been much higher than average, it's probable that the number of demented elderly relatives could rise to eight or ten. Most of the genetic studies suggest that the close relatives of demented patients have a greater risk of developing AD.[17]

Alzheimer's disease occurs exponentially with age; it has an incidence of 5 percent at age sixty-five and increases to as much as 50 percent by the age of eighty-five. This gives the optimistic conclusion that therapeutic intervention (with diet, nutrients, drugs, or all three together) delays the onset or progression of the disease, and could possibly eliminate it from the current normal human life span.

Cees van Tiggelen, M.D., a Dutch psychogeriatrician who practices out of a clinic in Dandenong, Australia, agrees that genetic factors are, in a minority of people with AD, undoubtedly involved. "In its purest form, senile dementia of the Alzheimer's type is probably a genetically determined disease," said Dr. van Tiggelen. He added:

> Depending on your genes, everyone will get it by the age of one hundred and twenty. In some people, the genetic penetrance is very strong; they will get it at a young age. However, some people will develop early symptoms of Alzheimer's disease at a much younger age than determined by their genes because of their involvement with accelerating factors such as nutritional elements and toxic metals.

Dr. van Tiggelen names the additional brain-poisoning chemicals of alcohol, prescribed drugs (such as anti-epileptics and anti-rheumatics), and industrial products employed at home or work like solvents, herbicides, and pesticides as adding to one's genetic predisposition. "What I am saying is that in a significant proportion of patients currently diagnosed as Alzheimer sufferers, additional and accelerating factors do play an important role, aggravating the disorder beyond the genetic impact," Dr. van Tiggelen affirmed.

A problem that arises from blaming AD solely on genetic predisposition is the question: Why is the expression of a supposed dementia genotype delayed for half-a-century and more after birth? The answer could be that autosomal-dominant inheritance may operate in Alzheimer's disease. Autosomal inheritance is a pattern of inheritance in which traits depend on the presence or absence of certain genes on the non-sex determining chromosomes (the autosomes). The pattern may be dominant or recessive, and males and females are affected in equal numbers. Most hereditary disorders are the result of a defective gene on an autosome.

THE SLOW-VIRUS THEORY

The genetic explanation for AD has numerous supporters among psychogeriatricians and neurobiologists. Others add another source of difficulty to the concept, though, and assert that a slow-acting virus is a main or an adjunctive cause of symptomatic dementia. The popular guess is that viral infection brings about cellular death in the brain. Viral infection comes about by the invasion of one or more of about 200 viruses known to be dangerous to humans. Sometimes viruses are responsible for some of the most dangerous diseases known, such as the human immunodeficiency virus (HIV), what is thought to be the cause of autoimmune deficiency syndrome (AIDS).

Viral infection does occur in humans in two rare forms of dementia: Creutzfeldt-Jakob disease and kuru. Each produces plaques in the victims' brains that are quite like AD. Another disease called scrapie, found in sheep and goats, produces similar lesions in the brains of the affected animals.

The three mentioned diseases, Creutzfeldt-Jakob disease (CJD), kuru, and scrapie, are caused by slow-acting viruses that develop over an extended period. It can take years from the time the victim is infected until the symptoms of the disease appear.

In *The Lancet*, researchers at the Laboratory of Central Nervous System Studies, National Institute of Health, United States, and the Departments of Pathology and Neurology, University of Helsinki, Finland, reported on an association between the scrapie amyloid-precursor gene and CJD in fifteen affected members in four generations of a Finnish family.[18] Successive generations in this family have had a progressively earlier age of onset.[19] The most recently affected member in this family's fourth generation is the previously unheard of age of only twenty-six years. Brain tissue, extracted from one patient and used in laboratory research as the source of the slow-acting virus, transmitted the disease to a capuchin-laboratory monkey.[20] The average age at onset for the involved Finns is fifty, and the illness evolves as a progressive dementia with other associated signs including muscular rigidity, muscular spasm, muscle wasting, various uncontrolled movements, and above all, dementia. Deterioration is obvious week to week. It is bound to be fatal within one year.

Brain diseases associated with Alzheimer's disease are becoming more predominant in our Western industrialized society. The cost to us in terms of tragedy is immense. Because of such great cost, the public is demanding that something be done to reverse the trend of brain deterioration. In response to such alarm from medical consumers, finally the profit-oriented pharmaceutical industry is researching the subject. Also, medical investigators are beginning to uncover the true causes of brain pathology. Indeed, this book offers facts which have been known to the health professions but were disregarded. It is time to act on the knowledge at hand.

CHAPTER 5
Diagnosing Dementia

In surveying the medical professional literature for information about the reasons for mental impairment in mid-life and old age, we've uncovered a quirk in the field. It's a finding similar to one cited by Professor Florence Safford, D.S.W., Director of Graduate Certification in Gerontology for the School of Public Affairs and Services at the Florida International University.[1] Dr. Safford and the coauthors encountered repeated inconsistencies of terminology in Alzheimer's disease. Health professionals refer to this mind disability by no less than twenty-three different names. In alphabetical order, the terms they use to identify the singular condition, Alzheimer's disease, are the following:

Alzheimer's disease
atrophic senile psychosis
brain damage
brain dysfunction
brain failure
chronic brain syndrome
cognitive decrement
cognitive impairment
confusional state
degenerative dementia
delirium

dementia
mental disorder of the senium
mental impairment
mental infirmity
organic brain syndrome
organic mental syndrome
senile brain disease
senile dementia
senility
vascular dementia

In utilizing this variable terminology, health professionals do nothing more that confuse the affected public. The terms Alzheimer's disease and dementia of the Alzheimer's type, used interchangeably, are adequate terms that suitably describe the devastating effects of brain dysfunction of variable types, diagnoses, geography, and other characteristics.

THE GEOGRAPHY OF DEMENTIA

No longer regarded as a "presenile" malady or as arising from hardening of the arteries in the brain, Alzheimer's disease (AD), interchangeable with but perhaps more properly termed dementia of the Alzheimer's type (DAT), is steadily increasing among all industrialized populations around the world.

In Japan, for instance, the frequency of Alzheimer's disease is approaching 21 percent of cases reported for northern European countries such as Sweden and Denmark. The development of geropsychiatry (the study of mind diseases in the elderly) is increasing among Japanese health professionals. Japanese medical specialists have done an immense amount of work in the areas of brain biology, epidemiology, and nosology (science of disease classification). Additionally, clinico-pathological and psychological research involving normal as well as abnormal subjects have appeared in the Japanese medical literature.

A number of these investigative efforts have been translated and printed in English-language journals, especially the reports on biological and clinical studies of Alzheimer's disease. One characteristic of the dementias, particular to the Japanese, is that there is a higher rate of cerebrovascular disorders in the population before their people enter the major risk period for Alzheimer's disease. A marked difference exists between the prevalences of Alzheimer's disease and MID in northern Europe compared with Japan where multi-infarct dementia (MID) is the predominant type of dementia.[2,3,4]

There are, in fact, vast international differences in the relative prevalence of Alzheimer's disease and MID. As well as being more common in the Japanese, MID is also more frequently diagnosed in Russians. Studies of the populations of Finland and America, as well as other Western European countries, have shown an excess of Alzheimer's disease, rather than MID. There are differences in the ratios of MID and Alzheimer's disease found in Asia and Africa as well, but not enough is known about them yet to analyze possible contributing factors.

The obvious requirement for a consulting neuropsychiatrist or other attending doctor, then, is to differentiate between the various forms of dementia before concluding that the patient's brain problem is irreversible, such as simple forgetfulness or cerebrovascular impairment. MID and many of the other mental disorders, such as depression, have similar symptoms to Alzheimer's disease. As with a disability like pneumonia, dementia is not a specific disease but presents itself in a series of symptoms and signs—a syndrome—with many causes.[5]

When a doctor is faced with the decision as to whether or not his or her patient must be diagnosed with Alzheimer's disease, there is a major textural authority to consult. A "bible" for mental health professionals, *The Diagnostic and Statistical Manual of Mental Disorders*, third edition (DSM-III), offers definite criteria for internists, family practice specialists, neurologists, and psychiatrists to make such a judgment. It's one of the first places doctors look when attempting to diagnose dementia. The following syndrome traits are what doctors look for:[6]

- Loss of intellectual abilities that are severe enough to interfere with social or occupational functioning.

- Memory impairment of any degree.

- At least one of these characteristic difficulties: personality change, dysfunctional abstract thinking, impaired judgment, and other disturbances of higher cortical function.

- A clear state of consciousness (which distinguishes dementia from delirium and intoxication).

- Evidence, demonstrable or presumed, of an organic factor judged to be caused by related behavioral disturbance.

The clinical manifestations of dementia—at least for the beginning signs and symptoms—are not in themselves sufficient evidence that Alzheimer's disease is the patient's trouble. Alzheimer's disease is one of the most serious labels anyone can wear. Therefore, the person making the diagnosis must make a differentiation with other disturbances. An examiner has to go beyond the early signs of the patient's forgetfulness: repetition of the same phrases within a few minutes; word-finding problems and language difficulties; disorientation; difficulty with simple calculations; wandering or getting lost; nonrecognition of familiar places or faces; suspiciousness; and even frank paranoia. It is imperative that the doctor keep in mind that a diagnosis of Alzheimer's disease can be taken as a condemnation of "living death."

Even if the dementia progresses with the patient developing emotional instability, the inability to care for oneself or carry on the daily routine, incontinence, and hallucinations, physicians and family members should be reluctant to use the Alzheimer's label, when in fact, many people who display these symptoms may have a reversible or curable type of dementia.

THE TYPES OF DEMENTIA

There are three different types of dementia, which have all been broken down into the categories of primary degenerative dementia (Alzheimer's disease), multi-infarct dementia (MID), and extrapyramidal nerve dementia (END). Organic brain disease is the source of all of them. It is important that we understand the different types of dementia in order to know what to expect and how to treat the patient.

When a patient begins to show signs and symptoms that are gradually worsening, and all specific causes—such as toxic agents—have been ruled out, Alzheimer's disease is a prime suspicion. To determine if an organic or other physical cause is responsible for mental impairment, laboratory, radiologic, physical, and other clinical examinations of the patient are conducted. (See Table 5.1 on page 61 for the various kinds of physical tests which need to be carried out before rendering a firm diagnosis.)

The category of primary degenerative dementia corresponds roughly to Alzheimer's disease, and also includes some rare disorders, such as Pick's disease and Creutzfeld-Jakob disease, which will be discussed later in the chapter.

Multi-infarct dementia (MID) is diagnosed if the course of signs and symptoms is stepwise and more abrupt. The signs come in groups, suddenly, and the patient's mind deficits are patchy. The involved person's neurological difficulties may be present in a localized area, such as paralysis of an arm. MID may be caused by a series of smaller strokes rather than by one large one.

A dementia can also develop as part of various extrapyramidal nerve disorders. The extrapyramidal system involves nerve tracts and pathways connecting different parts of the brain and spine in complex circuits not included in the pyramidal system. The extrapyramidal system is mainly concerned with the regulation of stereotyped, reflex, muscular movements. The best example of extrapyramidal pathology is Parkinson's disease. A prominent movement disorder such as rhythmical contraction of the person's muscle in response to an applied and sustained stretch stimulus, such as reaching up to a high shelf, distinguishes these kinds of subcortical dementias[7] from a cortical dementia such as Alzheimer's disease. Alzheimer's victims do not usually show difficulty with motor abilities until the disease is well-established. MID is generally considered cortical (from the cerebral cortex), but it can include subcortical (tissues beneath the cerebral cortex) features as well, depending on the location of the cerebral infarction. The cerebral infarction is a localized area of decay in the cerebrum caused by an interruption in the brain's blood supply.

Table 5.1 Physical Examinations for Alzheimer's disease

Type of Test	Test
Laboratory	Calcium
	Phosphorus
	Vitamin B12
	Folate
	Complete Blood Count with Differential, ESR
	Thyroid function (including TSH)
	Kidney function, Liver function
	Urinalysis, VDRL
Radiologic	Chest film (if indicated)
	Computerized tomography of head without contrast
	Magnetic resonance imaging
Neuropsychologic	Formal Neuropsychologic Test
Other Tests	ECG
	EEG
	Lumbar puncture
	Drug-toxicology screen
	Heavy-metals screen

WHAT PHYSICIANS EXAMINE IN DEMENTIA CASES

As suggested, Alzheimer's disease is a diagnosis of exclusion, which entails ruling out all other conditions that could account for the patient's symptoms. There are many other disorders that display similar symptoms. Physicians must go through full medical histories, laboratory testings, and physical examinations of their patients suspected of dementia. They also must obtain extensive, thoroughly documented psychiatric, neurologic, general medical, and family histories of the patients under review.

Close relatives or caretakers are asked by the examining physician to participate in uncovering facts about the course of the dementia. This procedure is used because the patient may not be able to answer questions correctly, or their orientation to time may throw off the answers.

A patient and family members, both alone and together, are interviewed. The advantage to this procedure is that, together most questions are answered, and separately, both the family members and the patient are spared the embarrassment of filling in certain details—such as suicidal thoughts or catching the patient wandering the neighborhood aimlessly. Then, talking together in a group with everyone concerned informs the examiner about the level of stress, communication (or lack of it), and understanding in the family.

Through this question and answer process the doctor tries to establish when the patient's symptoms began. Did they appear suddenly or develop gradually? Have they worsened steadily or in sudden increments? The symptoms of Alzheimer's disease are usually gradual, as we have emphasized. It is rare that they come on abruptly, but it may seem to have come on suddenly in patients who have managed to muddle through each day following an old routine. Should illness or other circumstances disrupt the routine—for example, if the patient's spouse should go away on a trip—problems may "suddenly" surface although they were present all along.

A drug history is also taken, that includes any over-the-counter medications the individual uses. The examiner also asks about the individual's alcohol intake and the exposure to various types of toxins. If this information is difficult to obtain, a specialist, usually a geriatrician, is called in to interview the patient or review the information that was obtained. It is not uncommon to discover that a patient that was thought to have dementia, has been taking a drug that is known to effect the central nervous system. If the dosage can be decreased or another agent substituted, the symptoms of dementia may disappear altogether.

The examiner looks for physical difficulties. Perhaps the health history will reveal gait abnormalities or falls, incontinence, visual or hearing problems, head injury, seizures, stroke, heart attack or arrhythmia, high blood pressure, diabetes, elevated blood cholesterol, high blood fats, or thyroid disease. Any of these findings suggest that the dementia may have a potentially treatable biochemical or physical component.

The examination will also reveal any difficulties with daily living. Even after ruling out depression and other maladies, Alzheimer's disease may still be a suspect. This leaves the examiner to ask about the family's history of depression, mania, "nervous breakdown," dementia, stroke, or senility. A personal or family history of affective illness does help an examiner to distinguish between depression and dementia. This should point to possible associated conditions, such as Down's syndrome, leukemia, venereal disease, Parkinson's disease, and Wilson's disease. (Wilson's disease is an inherited condition in which the body is unable to metabolize copper properly and the free copper may deposit itself in the liver and brain, causing dementia.) These disorders, as well as advanced maternal age at birth of the patient, may be genetically linked to Alzheimer's disease, and help to pinpoint diagnosis.

The examiner also records the behavior of the patient during the exam. Confusion, gaps in memory, confabulation, apathy, anxiety, eagerness or reluctance to cooperate may all be early clues to forming the diagnosis.

There are also answers to be revealed in questions about who made the initial appointment, who brought the patient to the office, and how aware the patient is of the problems. In neuropsychiatry it's commonly accepted that people who seem relatively unaware of their problems, and who have been brought to the physician's office by others, are more likely to suffer from dementia than those who made the appointment themselves.

One rule that all examiners must follow is not revealing anything to the patient that he or she may not be able to handle. Aside from causing emotional trauma to the patient, it may also hinder any further examinations. Disclosing faults serves no purpose if that person has no control over correcting them.

HOW MENTAL EVALUATION IS DONE

Physical and neurological examinations are mandatory for the potential Alzheimer's disease patient. The evaluating specialist pays particular attention to signs of any neurologic trouble, cerebrovascular disorder, cardiovascular disease, and impaired vision or hearing. Then there will be testing for the patient's cognitive functioning and general psychiatric status.

In the cognitive examination, assessment is made for orientation, memory, language, attention and concentration, and visuospatial abilities.

In the psychiatric evaluation, the examiner looks into six recognized mental health areas. The patient is checked for:

- Behavior—agitation, general slowing of response from what is considered normal
- Mood—depression, anxiety, irritableness, anger
- Affect—emotions that are labile, restricted, inappropriate to the stated mood
- Thought process—logical, incoherent, rambling
- Thought content—delusional, suicidal, phobic
- Perception—hallucinations

A good test of measuring the severity of a person's mental illness is the Mini-Mental-State Exam (MMSE)[8]. Although this exam is not a diagnostic protocol or plan for carrying out the patient's treatment regimen, it is widely used. The test involves a series of questions, some spoken and some written, and ends in an evaluation of the patient's alertness. The MMSE is relatively accurate, complete, and comprehensive but short and easy to administer (see Table 5.2 on page 65).

In a study of a large population of elderly people living at home, 80 percent of those age sixty-five or older scored twenty-three points or higher on the MMSE.[9] The average score of a patient with dementia is twenty-five, but a score of twenty-two or less suggests that there is significant cognitive impairment. Occasionally, patients with dementia do score higher than expected, particularly if they were exceptionally intelligent before the onset of dementia, or if it is early on in the disease.

MMSE results are not infallible, of course; the examiner must interpret them in the context of the overall clinical picture.

PARTICULAR LABORATORY STUDIES CONDUCTED FOR DEMENTIA

The neuropsychiatrist uses a number of chemical, radiologic, and electro-physiologic procedures to identify potentially treatable causes of the patient's mental problems (see Table 5.1 on page 61).

Computerized axial tomography (CAT scan) of the brain will detect structural abnormalities, such as brain tumors or hydrocephalus. Although it may be common to find cerebral atrophy, it does not clearly indicate the presence of dementia.[10] An electroencephalogram (EEG) is a test that is run to determine brain-wave activity. It works by detecting the speed at which electronic messages are being passed through the brain. The read-out will show a line that will either be zig-zagging or flat. A flat line can be an indication of a nervous system disorder or that the brain is dead. The results of an EEG early in Alzheimer's disease may be normal, but it eventually shows slow-wave activity by the brain.

While some experts hold that all patients evaluated for dementia should have a spinal tap (lumbar puncture), others do not and prefer examining the cerebrospinal fluid (CSF) only when an infection such as syphilis or crypto-coccal meningitis is suspected. A spinal tap requires that a long, sterile needle be inserted into the spinal cord, which is only one centimeter wide. The cerebrospinal fluid that flows through and protects the brain and the spinal canal is allowed to escape or is withdrawn into a syringe. This fluid is then subjected to laboratory testing.

Although brain biopsy has been used to make a definitive diagnosis of

Table 5.2 Mini-Mental-State Exam[9]

Orientation (Maximum 10 points)
The examiner asks: "What is the (year, season, date, day, month)?"
"In which (state, county, town, hospital) are we?"

Registration (Maximum 3 points)
The examiner clearly names three objects and asks the patient to repeat the names of all three. If necessary, the patient is asked to repeat the exercise with the retrials counted.

Attention and Calculation (Maximum 5 points)
Known as "The Serial Sevens," the patient is asked to count down from 100 by 7. He or she should stop after five answers. Alternatively, the patient is asked to spell "world" backward.

Recall (Maximum 3 points)
The patient is asked to repeat the three words the examiner previously asked him to remember.

Language (Maximum 9 points)
The patient is shown a pencil and asked what it is.
The patient is shown a wristwatch and asked what it is.
The patient is asked to repeat the phrase "No ifs, ands, or buts."
A three-stage command is given, such as "Take this paper in your right hand, fold it in half, and put it on the floor."
The examiner prints "Close your eyes" on a piece of paper and asks the patient to read it and do what it says.
The patient is asked to write a sentence and then gets scored for the sentence's sense, but not for its grammar.
The examiner draws two intersecting pentagons and asks the patient to copy the design.

Level of Consciousness
The patient is assessed: alert, drowsy, stupor, coma.

Alzheimer's disease, it is not foolproof. The biopsy procedure is dangerous—removing a small piece of living brain tissue is a major surgical operation with all the accompanying hazards of surgery plus the potential of damage to the brain. Brains of normal elderly persons as well as those of patients with Alzheimer's disease show plaques and tangles. In addition, the area of the brain from which biopsy specimens are usually taken, the frontal cortex, may not show pathologic changes early in the disease. In the absence of an effective treatment for Alzheimer's disease until now, neurosurgeons have not been able to justify brain biopsy except under the most unusual circumstances.[11]

NEUROPSYCHOLOGIC TESTING

The coauthors recommend formal neuropsychologic testing to complete the initial patient evaluation of Alzheimer's disease. And it should be performed by a neuropsychologist to minimize the risk of either overdiagnosis or a wrong testing procedure.[12]

By themselves, no neuropsychologic test results are specific for Alzheimer's disease. Memory loss is the only cognitive deficit invariably associated with the disorder, although aphasia (lost speech) is common.[13] But test scores do provide the examiner with quite useful information about intellectual functioning. For example, they may reveal that someone has more trouble with spatial relationships than with language. In addition, the pattern of scores will point to unexpected strengths the patient possesses that can be applied in planning a program of rehabilitative activities. The pattern also provides a baseline for judging future performance in later tests.

As may be realized by now, Alzheimer's disease is progressive. Patients or their families could seek diagnosis, prognosis, treatment, or other medical intervention at any point. Several scales exist for clinical staging.[13,14,15] Staging for Alzheimer's disease is based on the emotional, behavioral, pathological, and physical status of a patient. In Chapter 3 we discussed the seven stages of Alzheimer's disease developed by four attending psychiatrists participating in the Geriatric Study and Treatment Program at New York University. We feel this scale is a helpful tool for determining exactly where the patient is is in terms of the development of the disease.

Another rating is the Clinical Dementia Rating Scale (CDRS) offered by a group of British neuropsychiatrists.[15] The CDRS provides numeric scores in six cognitive and behavioral categories: memory, orientation, judgment and problem solving, community affairs, home and hobbies, and personal care. Directions for scoring come with the scale.

THE DIFFERENTIAL DIAGNOSIS OF THE DEMENTIAS

When the patient's mental impairment is mild, it may be difficult for even the most knowledgeable neuropsychiatrist to differentiate between early Alzheimer's disease and certain other disorders (see Table 5.3 on page 67). Furthermore, Alzheimer's disease may actually coexist with depression, Parkinson's disease, drug effects, venereal disease, Wilson's disease, or even multi-infarct dementia.

Distinguishing between depression and dementia is especially difficult.

Table 5.3 Differential Diagnoses for Alzheimer's disease

Alzheimer's disease	Sedatives/hypnotics
Anoxic brain damage	Tranquilizers
Basal-ganglia calcification	Endocrine abnormalities
Benign senescent forgetfulness	Huntington's disease
Creutzfeldt-Jakob disease	Multi-infarct dementia
Depression	Normal-pressure hydrocephalus
Drugs	Parkinson's disease
Alcohol	Pick's disease
Anticonvulsants	Progressive supranuclear palsy
Antihistamines	Stroke syndromes
Antihypertensives	Syphilis
Anti-inflammatory agents	Vitamin deficiencies
Antispasmodic agents	Wilson's disease
Cancer chemotherapeutic agents	

Shared symptoms include apathy, slowing verbal and reflexive responses, altered sleeping and eating habits, poor concentration, decrease in activities, and impairment of thought processes. Although some physicians describe the cognitive impairment associated with depression as pseudodementia, it probably is a misleading term. It erroneously directs attention to the possibility of a treatable disorder. Thus, "pseudodementia" mistakenly implies that the depressed patient's cognitive impairment is not real when it may be considerably so.

The following clues point to depression rather than dementia in the patient:

- Recent and relatively abrupt onset of problems

- Personal or family history of depression

- Pronounced sense of distress

- Tendency to minimize cognitive abilities, especially memory

Anecdotal evidence from affected family members and family physicians indicates that, during cognitive testing, depressed elderly people often say "I can't" or "I don't know," whereas those with Alzheimer's disease are likely to confabulate answers. The dexamethasone suppression test, a research tool, may be useful as a means of differentiating depression from dementia.

Still, in many patients, depression and dementia cannot be distinguished with certainty. If the attending physician suspects depression as the cause of erratic behavior, emotions, and mentality, the reasonable approach for this doctor to take is antidepressant therapy prescribed in conjunction with the advice of a neurological consultant or geriatric psychiatrist. The patient is then watched for improvement in cognitive status as well as in mood.

BRAIN SCANS

There is a particularly valuable noninvasive brain test for Alzheimer's disease. Positron emission transaxial tomography (PETT) scans of the brain employ a labeled amino acid or glucose analogue to analyze the organ's metabolism. PETT is a computerized x-ray technique that uses radioactive substances to look at the brain. The patient either inhales or is injected with the radioactive tracer that is mostly harmless. The PETT device changes gamma rays into pictures that show the brain's interior. Certain regional alterations in the use of glucose (glucose and oxygen are nutrients for the brain) differentiate between Alzheimer's and the many other types of dementia.[16,17] They enable researchers to monitor how the brain reacts to drugs and what is happening when individuals are talking, thinking, and sleeping.

The PETT scan requires a cyclotron and must be performed by highly skilled professionals. The result is that they can see when disease begins to disrupt the brain's normal functions.

Single photon emission computerized tomography is a brain scan that shows better than any other diagnostic procedure just how well the impaired brain is functioning. It uses isotopes to measure cerebral blood flow, but not brain metabolism.

Magnetic resonance imaging (MRI), which uses the magnetic field of the brain to print out an image of its structures, cannot be used to diagnose Alzheimer's disease,[18] but it is useful for the radiologic evaluation of patients who have other forms of dementia. MRI gives better structural detail than CAT scan and can detect smaller infarctions.

Additional tests of physiologic function that have helped physicians differentiate between Alzheimer's disease and other disorders are highly technical. They include sleep studies,[19] neuroendocrine assays, immunologic markers,[20] philotherm response,[21] altered calcium metabolism,[22] and biochemical measurements. Investigations have turned up that there are biochemical changes in the cells and molecules of noneuronal tissues, suggesting that Alzheimer's disease may be a systemic disorder.[23] (A systemic disorder is one that involves the whole body system, not just one affected area.)

UNCOVERING WHAT THE DIAGNOSIS IS NOT

In no uncertain terms, the United States Department of Health and Human Services has advised the American medical profession that, since the diagnosis of Alzheimer's disease carries with it a dismal prognosis, all physicians must display extraordinary care before pronouncing it as the diagnosis. All the other illnesses that might cause the dementia must be discounted first (see Table 5.3). Once a doctor knows what the diagnosis is not, he or she may be left with the explanation that Alzheimer's disease is the most likely problem. The factors in a patient's life that may trigger dementia-like symptoms are:

- *Drugs.* Some 20 percent of people with disturbed behavior suffer from drug intoxication. This is hardly surprising when it's known that 65 percent of all prescribed drugs are for the elderly.

- *Dehydration.* Elderly people tend to drink insufficient liquids. In hot weather they can dehydrate within twenty-four hours. Also some drugs (diuretics) that help a person to pass water add to the problem.

- *Urine retention.* Fairly common in elderly people, failure to rid oneself of accumulated, toxic, liquid wastes can bring about disturbances in the mind.

- *Constipation.* Because of obstruction or for some other physical reason, constipation will cause an acute confused state.

- *Depression and environmental changes.* Following alterations in their environment, some people reach an acute state of confusion and depression. Moves from familiar surroundings can bring about a sense of loss and subsequent depression.

- *Pain.* By itself or if accompanied by infection, in particular, pain brings on severe confusion in the elderly.

- *Tumors.* Involvements of the lung, especially, are responsible for much mental upset. A fast-growing cancer extracts important nutrients from the system, which leads to disturbed behavior or a delirious condition in some people.

- *Multi-infarct dementia.* Damage to the brain from a cerebral vascular disorder affects speech, memory, and the ability to control movement. If the patient suddenly behaves strangely, it is usually a sign that a series of small strokes (transient ischemic attacks or TIA) have occurred. This is in contrast to Alzheimer's disease which creeps in slowly. Moreover,

MID usually appears between the ages of forty and sixty; Alzheimer's disease will often manifest itself beyond the age of sixty-five.

In most cases, those with MID have a history of high blood pressure, vascular disease, or previous strokes. The problem will strike one part of the brain only, so the symptoms and signs may be limited to just one faculty, such as loss of speech. MID offers localized symptoms whereas the overall effects of Alzheimer's disease are "global" in effect.

- *Multiple sclerosis.* MS is characterized by the progressive destruction of the insulating material covering the nerve fibers. One of the more well-known neurological diseases, it's progress is filled with symptomatic exacerbations and recovering remissions, but the patient seldom returns to the level of competence at which he or she had been functioning before the last increase in seriousness of the disease.

- *Parkinson's disease.* This is a disease that comes on slowly, usually striking people over sixty. The symptoms include tremors, weakness, bent posture, and in the end, dementia.

- *Huntington's disease.* Showing in early middle age, this problem includes a change in personality and mental decline. Twitching or "flickering" of the face, restlessness, and possibly severe uncontrollable flailing of limbs, head, and body may follow. Mental faculties disintegrate into dementia. Children with a parent suffering from Huntington's disease have a 50 percent chance of inheriting it.

- *Pick's disease.* Having similar signs and symptoms to those of Alzheimer's disease, the condition is really a different malady because pathological changes in the brain tissue are different.

- *Creutzfeldt-Jakob disease (CJD).* Caused by one of several infectious agents, but most especially a virus, the problem can lead to dementia. The CJD virus is suspected of lying dormant in the body for years; then it becomes activated to bring about rapidly progressing dementia accompanied by a peculiar gait and muscle spasms.

- *Delirium.* Delerium is a state of great excitement, confusion, speech disorder, anxiety, and hallucinations. It arises from an upset in brain functions that result from many physical disorders, such as hormonal, nutritional, and stress disorders, poisoning, or high fever. Not infrequently this condition is confused with dementia in older people because it has the victim behaving inappropriately.

- *Neurological symptoms.* Excessive amounts of fluid surrounding the brain and any type of growth (tumors, cysts, hematomas) inside the skull, may be the source of out-of-the-ordinary behavior. Nerve-related symptoms are the result, such as pain, parasthesias, drop foot, etc.

- *Senility.* Something amiss in the brain, an abnormal process while growing older, can include serious forgetfulness, confusion, certain personality changes, and odd behavior. The abnormality may stem from neuronal atrophy, infarction, or other degenerations. But these signs and symptoms are not necessarily the incurable effects of old age. Small lapses in memory do not signify senility, but perhaps only an overload of facts in the brain's storehouse of information. Many memory lapses are temporary and reversible. Tests have shown that the healthy, aged brain works as hard and efficiently as a healthy, young one. The majority of people retain, and in some cases raise, their intellectual competence as they age.

There are innumerable substances in the earth's environment that can affect sensitive brain tissues, so that it is a wonder more of us do not show signs of dementia at earlier ages than already occur. As we shall learn in Part II, toxic metallic components in the earth's crust that are turned into useful modern products become the sources of our brain dysfunctions—especially that of Alzheimer's disease. Our metal technology is poisoning the brain.

Part II
The Aluminum Connection

Human beings around the world are adversely affected by *metallic toxicity*, consisting especially of aluminum, in excess amounts. It is consistently found in the brains of Alzheimer's disease victims. Aluminum is abundant in nature, but it has no known biological function in the human body.

Moreover, toxins from heavy metals such as arsenic, cadmium, iron, lead, manganese, mercury, and nickel also induce in laboratory animals visible brain lesions that are similar to the neurofibrillary tangles and neuritic plaques seen in humans. Neurotoxicity from metallic poisoning is a primary cause of Alzheimer's disease. We discuss the different types of toxic metals here.

CHAPTER 6

Aluminum Products
All Around Us

From the time she was twenty-eight years old and returned from traveling for an extended period throughout Mexico, Diane V., of Milwaukee, Wisconsin, had suffered from sour stomach accompanied by heartburn and acid indigestion. Certain foods, enchiladas among them, she thought, triggered the chronic discomfort, but she also knew that other prime offenders, in her case, were smoking and stress, and the consumption of alcohol and caffeine. She habitually drank ten or more cups of coffee and smoked two packs of cigarettes every day. The job she had as an insurance broker was high-powered and tension-filled.

Diane's solution was not to avoid the offending outside factors but rather to take copious amounts of antacids. After each meal she swallowed a stiff double or triple dose of a popular antacid. She moved to progressively stronger versions of this brand of antacid, and eventually began mixing the weaker and stronger types together, and downing them with either coffee or water.

Today, millions of people use prescription and over-the-counter antacids of many kinds—liquids, gels, tablets, capsules, chewing gums, and powders—to relieve symptoms of upper gastrointestinal distress. An antacid neutralizes hydrochloric acid. When a person chews, smells, tastes, looks at, or swallows food—or sometimes even thinks about it—hydrochloric acid is produced. This is a potent gastric acid that is secreted by glands in the lining of the stomach to aid in the digestion of food. Why the same amount of acid secretion plagues some people but not others remains unclear. What is certain, at least by the sufferers of excess stomach acid, is that the smoldering distress felt in the upper abdomen, behind the chest, and as high up as the throat, must be relieved as quickly as possible. It is an absolute compulsion to neutralize the burn.

The antacids did provide Diane with immediate relief for heartburn and the sour burning she experienced with it. The only trouble was that for over twenty-five years, frequently three, four, and five times daily, the woman was ingesting voluminous quantities of the aluminum hydroxide that makes antacids effective, with varying amounts of aluminum content each time. The multiple antacid tablets she popped down contained from 95 to 208 milligrams of aluminum hydroxide per dose—a very large quantity. (See table 6.1, pages 77–80, for aluminum content of antacids.)

Moreover, Diane douched daily for several years, even well after menopause, with an ammonium aluminum sulfate compound comprising 16 percent of aluminum salts. Some aluminum was absorbed through the walls of her vaginal vault. She purchased and employed a brand containing boric acid plus ammonium alum. (See table 6.2 on page 81 for aluminum content of douches.)

Additionally, Diane worked ten-hour days at a high-stress job, and, more often than not, she would go home with an excruciating headache. These headaches lead her to take a lot of aspirin, that were buffered with aluminum hydroxide. The type that she favored contained 44 milligrams of aluminum in each tablet. After waiting three hours, it was usual for Diane to pop down more aspirin, raising her daily oral dose of aluminum from a minimum of 122 to 728 milligrams, depending on how severe and persistent the headache was. (See table 6.3 on page 82 for aluminum content of buffered aspirin.)

During a normal workday, Diane seldom ate a relaxed and healthy meal, but instead ate at fast food restaurants or merely consumed Danish pastries and coffee at her desk. This kind of eating brought on bouts of diarrhea that caused her to take popular antidiarrheal agents that have an aluminum content of 120 to 1450 milligrams per dose. For more effective bowel stoppage, she moved to more concentrated forms of this popular brand. (See table 6.4 on page 83 for aluminum content of antidiarrheal drugs.)

Eventually the stress of her job caused Diane to develop gastrointestinal ulcer symptoms, and she offset them where possible with anti-ulcerative remedies. In this case she took several different forms of aluminum sucrose sulfate prescribed by her physician. They had an aluminum content of 207 milligrams per dose. The products offered Diane the ingestion of a possible daily dosage amounting to 828 milligrams of the toxic metal.

ALZHEIMER'S DISEASE FROM ALUMINUM POISONING

Living in a large condominium apartment in a relatively affluent section of Milwaukee, Diane had few female friends but hundreds of business

Table 6.1 Over-the-Counter-Available Antacids That Contain Aluminum[3]

Brand/Manufacturer	Aluminum Salt/Concentration	Al/Dose
Albicon/Pfeiffer	aluminum hydroxide	
tablet	150 milligrams	44
suspension	60 milligrams/mililiters	87
AlternaGel/Stuart	aluminum hydroxide	
	120 milligrams/mililiters	174
Aludrox/Wyeth	aluminum hydroxide	
tablet	233 milligrams	68
suspension	61 milligrams/mililiters	88
Aluminum Hydroxide		
Gel/Philips	70 milligrams/mililiters	100
Alurex/Rexall	aluminum hydroxide	
tablet	not revealed	—
suspension	not revealed	—
Aluscop/O'Neal	dihydroxyaluminum	
capsule	325 milligrams	72
suspension	40 milligrams/mililiters	45
Amphojel/Wyeth	aluminum hydroxide	
tablet	300 & 600 milligrams	87 & 174
suspension	64 milligrams/mililiters	90
A.M.T./Wyeth	aluminum hydroxide	
tablet	164 milligrams	48
suspension	61 milligrams/mililiters	88
Antacid Powder/DeWitt	aluminum hydroxide	
	15%	—
Banacid/Buffington	aluminum hydroxide	
	not revealed	—
Basaljel/Wyeth	aluminum hydroxide	
	not revealed	—
Basaljel/Wyeth	aluminum hydroxide	
Extra Strength	200 milligrams/mililiters	—
Camalox/Rorer	aluminum hydroxide	
tablet	225 milligrams	65
suspension	45 milligrams/mililiters	65
Creamalin/Winthrop	aluminum hydroxide	
tablet	248 milligrams	72
Delcid/Merrell-National	aluminum hydroxide	
suspension	120 milligrams	174

Brand/Manufacturer	Aluminum Salt/Concentration	Al/Dose
Dialume/Armour	aluminum hydroxide	
tablet	500 milligrams	145
Di-Gel/Plough	aluminum hydroxide	
tablet	282 milligrams	82
liquid	56 milligrams/mililiters	82
Estomul-M/Riker	aluminum hydroxide	
tablet	500 milligrams	145
liquid	184 milligrams/mililiters	265
Flacid/Amfre-Grant	aluminum hydroxide	
tablet	not revealed	—
Gelumina/Amer. Pharm.	aluminum hydroxide	
tablet	250 milligrams	72
Gelusil/Warner-Chilcott	aluminum hydroxide	
tablet	200 milligrams	58
suspension	40 milligrams/mililiters	58
Gelusil II/Warner-Chilcott	aluminum hydroxide	
tablet	400 milligrams	116
suspension	80 milligrams/mililiters	116
Gelusil M/Warner-Chilcott	aluminum hydroxide	
tablet	300 milligrams	87
suspension	60 milligrams/mililiters	87
Glycogel/Central Pharm.	aluminum hydroxide	
tablet	175 milligrams	51
Kessadrox/McKesson	aluminum hydroxide	
suspension	67 milligrams/mililiters	97
Kolantyl/Merrell-National	aluminum hydroxide	
gel	10 milligrams/mililiters	14
tablet	300 milligrams	87
wafer	180 milligrams	52
Krem/Mallinckrodt	aluminum hydroxide	
tablet	not revealed	—
Kudrox/Kremers-Urban	aluminum hydroxide	
tablet	400 milligrams	116
suspension	113 milligrams/mililiters	164
Liquid Antacid/McKesson	aluminum hydroxide	
suspension	67 milligrams/mililiters	97
Maalox/Rorer	aluminum hydroxide	
#1 tablet	not revealed	—
#2 tablet	not revealed	—
suspension	not revealed	—

Brand/Manufacturer	Aluminum Salt/Concentration	Al/Dose
Maalox Plus/Rorer	aluminum hydroxide	
tablet	200 milligrams	58
suspension	45 milligrams/mililiters	65
Magna Gel/No. American	aluminum hydroxide	
gel	not revealed	—
Magnatril/Lannett	aluminum hydroxide	
tablet	260 milligrams	75
suspension	52 milligrams/mililiters	75
Maxamag/Vitarine	aluminum hydroxide	
gel	not revealed	—
Magnesia-Alumina Oral/		
Philips Roxane	aluminum oxide	
suspension	24 milligrams/mililiters	55
Mylanta/Stuart	aluminum hydroxide	
tablet	200 milligrams	58
suspension	40 milligrams/mililiters	58
Mylanta II/Stuart	aluminum hydroxide	
tablet	400 milligrams	116
suspension	80 milligrams/mililiters	116
Noralac/No. American	bismuth aluminate	
tablet	300 milligrams	55
Nutrajel/Cenci	aluminum hydroxide	
suspension	60 milligrams/mililiters	87
Pama/No. American	aluminum hydroxide	
tablet	260 milligrams	75
Riopan/Ayerst	magaldrate	
tablet	400 milligrams	51
suspension	80 milligrams/mililiters	51
Riopan Plus/Ayerst	magaldrate	
tablet	480 milligrams	61
suspension	80 milligrams/mililiters	51
Robalate/Robins	dihydroxyaluminum sodium carbonate	
tablet	500 milligrams	94
Rolaids/Warner-Lambert	dihydroxyaluminum sodium carbonate	
tablet	334 milligrams	63
Silain-Gel/Robins	aluminum hydroxide	
tablet	282 milligrams	83
suspension	56 milligrams/mililiters	83

Brand/Manufacturer	Aluminum Salt/Concentration	Al/Dose
Syntrogel/Block	aluminum hydroxide	
tablet	38%	—
Trimagel/Columbia		
Medical	aluminum hydroxide	
tablet	250 milligrams	72
Trisogel/Lilly	aluminum hydroxide	
capsule	100 milligrams	29
suspension	30 milligrams/mililiters	43
WinGel/Winthrop	aluminum hydroxide	
tablet	180 milligrams	52
suspension	36 milligrams/mililiters	52

acquaintances, both male and female. Her married sister, Janet, was the only person with whom she shared confidences. They saw each other about once a week when Diane visited the department store where her sister worked as a women's clothing buyer.

It was during these weekly visits that Janet noticed Diane's dressing habits had taken a curious turn. Sometimes she wore shoes that didn't match. Not uncommonly her color combinations were tasteless and occasionally even ludicrous. Diane would forget to button her blouse all the way down. She would walk into Janet's department on stormy days without a raincoat and resent being told about it. The sisters had a few rows relating to the rudeness and other discourtesies that Diane exhibited.

In business, she would grope for an easy word to express a simple idea or occasionally entirely lose track of what she was saying in the middle of a sentence. Her office manager received complaints from customers that Diane swore on numerous occasions and was uncharacteristically cranky. She lost a lot of sales that way.

For the manager, Janet, and the many acquaintances whom Diane offended, there really was no particular pattern to any of these deviations. Acquaintances began to avoid her, and her manager complained to his superior. When people let Diane know that her behavior was unacceptable, she professed unawareness of what they were talking about and became immediately offended. In fact, she made it seem as if the complainer was the strange one, "the sick one," she said, for bringing up such picayune matters.

It finally took the ultimatum of her firm's president and pleadings of her sister to get Diane to consult a medical specialist whom she disdainfully

Table 6.2 Douches That Contain Aluminum

Brand Name/Manufacturer	Aluminum Salt Content	Concentration
BoCarAl/Calgon	Potassium aluminum sulfate	not revealed
Massengil Douche Powder/ Beecham Products	Ammonium aluminum sulfate	not revealed
PMC Douche Powder/ Thomas & Thompson	Ammonium aluminum sulfate	16%
V.A./Norcliff-Thayer	Alum	not revealed
Summer's Eve/Personal Laboratories	Potassium aluminum sulfate	not revealed

labelled "a shrink." In advance of their visit, he was persuaded by Janet to check Diane for dementia.

The doctor happened to be an orthomolecular psychiatrist who prescribed nutrients instead of drugs as remedial agents, and did unconventional diagnostic testing. In this case the physician did a hair-mineral analysis, among many other diagnostic examinations, and discovered that Diane had an aluminum content in her tissues that was off the charts. He sent her for more laboratory examinations to test her sputum, urine, sweat, and blood. The reports came back indicating that the woman was suffering with metal toxicity.

After the thorough clinical and laboratory checkups, a complete neurological examination by a psychoneurologist, some hours of psychological testing, and a gathering together of the examination results, this attending psychiatrist called Janet and Diane to a meeting in his office. It seemed reasonably clear from the psychoneurologist's opinion and these tests, he said in sadness, that fifty-three-year-old Diane was the victim of a variety of dementia. In all probability, the doctor affirmed, it was Alzheimer's disease.

ALUMINUM IN OUR ENVIRONMENT

Aluminum (chemical symbol Al), constitutes between 8.4 to 14 percent of the earth's crust (depending upon the site of available measurements). As a result of this, aluminum is very common in most people's lives. Unfortunately this includes the daily human diet. Almost every individual will unavoidably ingest 30 to 50 milligrams daily of the metal, so it may seem surprising that aluminum has found no place or usefulness in any pathway

Table 6.3 Over-the-Counter Buffered Aspirin
That Contain Aluminum

Brand Name/Manufacturer	Aluminum Salt/Concentration	Al Dosage
Arthritis Pain Formula/ Whitehall	Aluminum hydroxide/ not revealed	not revealed
Arthritis Strength Bufferin/ Bristol-Myers	Aluminum glycinate/ 73 milligrams	15 mg/tablet
Ascriptin/Rorer	Aluminum hydroxide/ 75 milligrams	22 mg/tablet
Ascriptin A-D/Rorer	Aluminum hydroxide/ 150 milligrams	44 mg/tablet
B-A/O'Neal, Jones & Feldman	Aluminum hydroxide/ 100 milligrams	29 mg/tablet
Pabrin/Dorsey	Aluminum hydroxide/ 100 milligrams	29 mg/tablet
Bufferin/Bristol-Myers	Aluminum glycinate/ 49 milligrams	10 mg/tablet
Cama/Dorsey	Aluminum hydroxide/ 150 milligrams	44 mg/tablet
Cope/Glenbrook	Aluminum hydroxide/ 25 milligrams	7.2 mg/tablet
Vanquish Caplet/Glenbrook	Aluminum hydroxide/ 25 milligrams	7.2 mg/tablet

of animal metabolism. Nearly all of the other reactive and abundantly available metals—even toxic ones—have found such uses, but not aluminum. (*Aluminum* is the accepted and official spelling in the United States; abroad, the name is spelled *aluminium*.)

Check out the label of ingredients on such items as hair spray, cheese products, baking powder, pizza, deodorant, lipstick and other cosmetics, and toothpaste, just to name a few product types that contain aluminum additives. All are approved for human consumption by the U.S. Food and Drug Administration (FDA). Soda cans, beer cans, pots and pans, and foil wraps made of aluminum can be dangerous, because, besides what invades our surroundings from a natural leaching of the earth's crust, these processed items are a source of excessive aluminum ingestion.

Table 6.4 Over-the-Counter Antidiarrheal Drugs
That Contain Aluminum

Brand Name/Manufacturer	Aluminum Salt	Dosage/tab or suspension
Amogel/No. American	Kaolin	120 mg
Bisilad/Central	Kaolin	370 mg or ml
Diabismul/O'Neal, Jones & Feldman	Kaolin	170 mg or ml
Donnagel-PG/Robins	Kaolin	200 mg or ml
Donnagel/Robins	Kaolin	200 mg or ml
Kaolin Pectin Suspension/ Philips Roxane	Kaolin	190 mg or ml
Kaopectate/Upjohn	Kaolin	190 mg or ml
Kaopectate Concentrate/ Upjohn	Kaolin	290 mg or ml
Pabisol with Paregoric/Rexall	Aluminum magnesium silicate	8.83 mg or ml
Parepectolin/Rorer	Kaolin	180 mg or ml
Pargel/Parke-Davis	Kaolin	200 mg or ml
Pektamalt/Warren-Teed	Kaolin	217 mg or ml
Quintess/Lilly	Attapulgite	100 mg or ml
Rheaban/Pfizer	Attapulgite	600 mg/tablet 140 mg/ml suspension

To give you an idea of how much aluminum is in some of the other antacids millions of Americans use, relative to the brands that Diane ingested, look at the following over-the-counter pharmaceutical product dosages:

Gelusil	200 milligrams
Mylanta II	400 milligrams
Kudrox	400 milligrams
Mylanta	200 milligrams
Gaviscon 2	160 milligrams
Win Gel	180 milligrams

Alu-Cap	400 milligrams
Amphojel	320 milligrams
Alternagel	600 milligrams

There are forty more antacids besides these nine which contain aluminum additives that are listed in the broadly distributed reference work on prescription drugs, the *Physicians' Desk Reference*,[1] the brief but complete *Dr. Wigder's Guide to Over-the-Counter Drugs*,[2] and the pharmaceutical trade-produced, chart-filled *Handbook of Non-Prescription Drugs*.[3] (See Table 6.1 in this chapter for 49 popular, nonprescription antacids' aluminum contents, and notice how many of them duplicate each other by containing the same aluminum buffering ingredient.)

The United States, Canada, Australia, New Zealand, and Great Britain are not the exclusive users of vast amounts of these metallic-containing personal products. It's proven that aluminum contamination of populations is all-pervasive throughout societies of industrialized countries worldwide.

Aluminum is part of the food chain because mankind has put it there by means of his refining and manufacturing processes. Sodium aluminum phosphate is added to cake mixes, frozen dough, self-rising flour, and processed cheese. Sodium aluminum sulfate is in household baking powders. Aluminum sulfate is part of food-starch modifier. Aluminum ammonium sulfate and aluminum potassium sulfate are both used as pickling salts. Sodium aluminum silicate is an anticaking agent for nondairy creamers. Aluminum cans, foil, and other forms of packaging with the metal are depended on by all walks of society. (See Table 6.5 on page 85 for the aluminum salts content in some of the more common consumer food products.)

From 1906 to 1912 Harvey W. Wiley, M.D., directed the one-time government agency that became the United States Food and Drug Administration. In 1929 he wrote: "From the earliest day of food regulations the use of alum [aluminum sulphate] in foods has been condemned. It is universally acknowledged as a poison and a deleterious substance in all countries." Today, sixty-four years after Wiley published those words, alum is still used in water purification and for other sensitive consumer applications.

"Large numbers of people in our aluminum-using society are the victims of slow aluminum poisoning," wrote Stephen E. Levick, M.D., of the Yale University School of Medicine, in a letter published in the *New England Journal of Medicine* (July 17, 1980). Dr. Levick said there has been an increasing amount of literature implicating aluminum as the cause of a form of dementia, or mental deterioration. He declared that there also has been scientific literature discussing an association between aluminum and a form of Alzheimer's

Table 6.5 American/Canadian Food Products
That Contain Aluminum[4,5]

Common Household Product	Al Amount	Al Salt Content	Al Dosage
Cake mixes, frozen			5 mg/serving
Dough, self-rising flour	6.5%	Sodium aluminum	15 mg/serve
Processed cheese	3.5%	phosphate	50 mg/slice
Household baking powders	5.9%	Sodium aluminum sulfate	70 mg/tsp 5 mg/ser/tsp
Food starch modifier	1.3%	Aluminum sulfate	—
Pickling salts	6.0%	Aluminum ammonium sulfate	—
Pickling salts	5.7%	Aluminum potassium sulfate	—
Anticaking agents	16.0%	Sodium aluminum silicate	—

disease that brings on mental deterioration in people under 50 (Pick's disease).

This Yale Medical School professor went on to emphasize that aluminum chloride fed to rats ". . . was deposited in their brains and led to behavioral abnormalities. Furthermore, university researchers showed that a population of elderly people with high aluminum levels had a greater incidence of neuropsychiatric deficits, including poor memory and impaired visual motor coordination, than did elderly people with lower levels," Dr. Levick wrote.

THE COFFEE ALKALOID CONNECTION

You'll recall that the Alzheimer's victim we described, Diane, drank an immense amount of coffee every day. Diane wasn't alone in her addiction to coffee. Both socially and privately, coffee drinking is indisputably the beverage of choice among North Americans and many Europeans. Eight out of ten adults living in the United States drink it each day. We sip three times more of it than we do soft drinks, four times more than beer. We drink fifty times more coffee than hard liquor. We take it black or creamed, sweetened or bitter, hot or iced. So much of the beverage washes down the national gullet that the electric coffeemaker has displaced the trusty iron as the hottest-selling small appliance.

Coffee houses, coffee cake, and coffee break are all words which have been coined to accommodate the universal addiction to this brew. It has been used to substitute for other addictions. Alcoholics Anonymous members, for instance, have an average intake of twenty cups per day, although you needn't be an ex-alcoholic to consume that much daily. Many who are opposed to alcohol out of religious principles see no wrong in the drinking of a beverage that can be just as addicting and health-destroying as alcohol.

Caffeine, the white, crystalline alkaloid in coffee, acts as a temporary stimulant to the brain and artificially lessens fatigue. And it does other things which are less advantageous:

- After one or more cups of coffee, the stomach temperature rises 10 to 15 degrees.

- The secretion of hydrochloric acid increases 400 percent—a significant physiological change directly related to causing Alzheimer's disease.

- The salivary glands double their output.

- The heart beats faster.

- The lungs work harder.

- The blood vessels narrow in the brain (also significant) and widen in and around the heart.

- The metabolic rate increases.

- The kidneys manufacture and discharge up to 100 percent more urine.

- The cells respond by a greater tendency to mutate with the potential for cancer.

- Coffee being the major dietary source of cadmium, the body is burdened by an extra amount of this toxic metal.

Intensive tests on guinea pigs, who were given doses of coffee, indicated that the effect on their brain and nervous tissues caused more destruction than doses of morphine.

Regular coffee drinking produced dose-related changes in most standard electroencephalogram-electrooculogram sleep parameters of normal adult males monitored in a sleep laboratory. The changes were always in a direction that indicated sleep disturbance. Drinking four cups of regular coffee, without cream, milk, or sugar, produced equal effects.

Two cups of black coffee taken a half hour before bedtime had its greatest effect on parameters relating to the early part of the night—including delays in falling asleep that resulted in shorter total sleep time and lower sleep efficiency.

The four-cup equivalent of regular coffee affected all major measures of sleep. The result was insomnia in the experimental subjects. Their brain tissues were put into a state of temporary turmoil.[6]

When coffee is withdrawn from a habitual drinker for any period of time there is an enhanced brain response to a neurotransmitter, adenosine, the chemical messenger that circulates in brain blood. Adenosine in large amounts causes blood vessels to dilate and thus lowers blood pressure.

Conversely, coffee drinking constricts the brain's blood vessels and adenosine stops flowing. This is a main effect of caffeine, and probably part of the addictive process.

When a regular coffee drinker stops drinking coffee, adenosine comes rushing back into circulation and a headache results. These were the agonizing headaches that Diane experienced. She got rid of her headaches with buffered aspirin when actually the pain would have been relieved more quickly by drinking more coffee. Here is the explanation: Blood vessel dilation is a known cause of headache, and caffeine is often included in headache remedies because it helps to constrict painfully dilated blood vessels in the head.

In a 1982 report delivered to the annual meeting of the Federation of American Societies for Experimental Biology, Reid W. von Borstel, Ph.D., explained how caffeine can be both a cause and cure of headaches. Drinking more than one cup of coffee a day will block the inhibition of nerve message transmission by binding itself to the receptors normally occupied by adenosine. Adenosine normally does inhibit such transmission of messages from one nerve cell to another. Its action resembles that of a tranquilizer, in slowing down brain and other body functions.

Richard J. Wurtman, M.D., chief of the Laboratory of Neuroendocrine Regulation at the Massachusetts Institute of Technology, found that while coffee is being consumed, adenosine receptors are blocked and the body responds by producing more adenosine receptors so adenosine can exert its normal functions. When coffee drinking is stopped abruptly, a larger-than-normal number of receptors is available to bind adenosine. The result is a dilation of blood vessels with a subsequent drop in blood pressure; then a headache is likely to develop. Blood vessels within the cranium are most affected by the dilation, which results in an adenosine-induced headache.[7]

Worse, the caffeine alkaloid in coffee acts with the hydrochloric acid in one's stomach. It causes more than normal acidity to form in the stomach. The caffeine, being alkaline, causes the stomach to react by dumping more hydrochloric acid as a neutralizer. When the stomach fluids become excessively acidic, any aluminum present in the diet or from drugs will collect and be transported into the bloodstream. Such aluminum-tainted blood travels to the brain and nourishes the cells situated there with whatever is carried in the stream.

Medical anthropologist, epidemiologist, and nutritional enthnobotanist Michael A. Weiner, M.S., M.A., Ph.D., says in his far-sighted book, *Reducing the Risk of Alzheimer's*, "Medical science has known for more than a decade that even mildly elevated levels of aluminum can influence memory disturbances in adults as well as hyperactivity and learning disorders in children."

"Professor R.J. Boegman, Department of Pharmacology and Toxicology, Queens University, Kingston, Ontario, Canada, advises that when aluminum is deposited in the gray matter of the brain, it will inhibit nerve transport, increase the breakdown of various neurotransmitters, and stimulate the production of harmful proteins. The consequences of aluminum deposits can include seizures, a decreased ability to learn, impaired motor coordination, memory loss, and even psychotic reactions."[8]

A CONFIRMING ANECDOTAL LETTER
ABOUT ALZHEIMER'S AND COFFEE

Dr. Casdorph has been heard by thousands of health-oriented consumers on radio and television and from the lecture platform talking about aluminum as a potential cause of Alzheimer's disease. It is not unusual for him to receive telephone calls and letters from many who are captured by the significance of his advice. The following is a letter from one such listener, Meg Easling, of Ojai, California. Her letter reads:

Dear Dr. Casdorph:

A friend of mine, James Kennedy, gave me a tape from a conference you spoke at. I appreciate the research you're doing on Alzheimer's disease. I feel very strongly that aluminum is the villain.

My mother was a R.N. during her professional life. She spent several years as *nurse at the Alcoa Aluminum plant in South Texas* [underlined and starred by Meg Easling]. Today she turned 87—but isn't around to appreciate it—except physically. She was a bright, witty, and fun-loving person once. Aluminum can come into us from so many evasive sources that it is usually hard to track. She actually worked where it was refined. Also, no one else in her family has developed Alzheimer's.

I read somewhere once that the aluminum is not toxic or as toxic unless combined with an acid. My mother was also a very heavy coffee drinker.

I guess I'm writing this in case it would be of any use to you for research. I'd also appreciate any further info you have. I do feel that the toxicity she worked in is responsible. She lives in a nursing home and still gets along pretty well physically, *but she just doesn't know her own children and grandchildren.*

Sincerely,

Meg Easling

CHAPTER 7

Aluminum Dust and Other Metallic Air Pollutants

For decades, gold miners in the northern Ontario town of Timmins were deliberately made to inhale large amounts of aluminum dust every day. The belief was that aluminum would protect their lungs from silicosis, one of the health hazards of digging into hard rock. Silicosis is a chronic lung disease caused by the breathing of silica dust. Gold-bearing ore is loaded with silica, and the McIntyre Porcupine Mine set up a research institute, in the 1930s, devoted to the study of silicosis prevention.

"They came up with this bright idea that we should coat our lungs with this aluminum stuff. Then when we coughed it out, we would cough out the silica encountered at work," says Ed Vance, a former Timmins gold miner who still retains some mental competency.

Each day when the miners entered the headframe—a tall building where they reported to work, changed their clothes, and caught elevators underground—they were required to sit for ten minutes in the locker room while aluminum dust, called 'McIntyre Powder' (finely ground aluminum and aluminum oxide), was blown around them.

"My husband just hated it, I can tell you," remembers Mrs. Winifred Latendresse, a miner's widow from South Porcupine, near Timmins. "It used to burn his nose terrible. He used to spit up this awful black stuff. He said the taste was rotten. Some days, he'd just come home and he just couldn't eat his food. He'd say, 'I'll just wait,' because he still had the aluminum taste."

However disagreeable the inhalation exercise may have been for the diggers, it caught on at an unknown number of other gold mines—and, later, uranium mines—where silicosis is a concern. The practice of inhaling McIntyre Powder did not end until 1980, when officials decided there was no evidence that the aluminum dust was doing any good against silicosis.

Soon after the practice ended, Sandra L. Rifat, Ph.D., an epidemiologist at Clark Institute of Psychiatry in Toronto, heard about the miners and tracked down enough of them to make a sample for studying. Combining the records of chest clinics in the mining area known as the Porcupine District, Dr. Rifat came up with the names and addresses of 1,353 men who had been miners since the 1940s. Of those, she located 647 who were alive and willing to participate in her study.

She put the men through three cognitive tests. Two of her tests checked on memory, asking the miners, for instance, to spell simple words backward. The third test examined the miners' logical thought, asking them to complete patterns. Not only did twice as many miners from the aluminum-breathing group score in the "impaired" range, their amount of exposure worsened their difficulties. The longer they had inhaled aluminum dust, the worse were their present symptoms of Alzheimer's disease.

"I don't know if aluminum dust done something to me," says Ange Aime Camirand, a feeble Timmins ex-miner who suspects that he has silicosis. "But I know sometimes when I want to tell some people's names, I don't remember. And I worked with them for years! Do you think the aluminum could make me forget?"[1]

BREATHING ALUMINOSILICATES

You don't have to be one of those underground, hard-rock diggers of gold to inhale aluminum dust. In order to get Alzheimer's disease, all you have to do is breathe the air around you. That cruel, degenerative brain disorder, has already been proven to result from the types and amounts of dust inhaled over a lifetime.

A research physician at the City of Hope National Medical Center, neurobiochemist Eugene Roberts, Ph.D., affirms that complex ionic alumi-nosilicates—the same substances plaguing gold and uranium miners—actually do get into the brain through the nose and the olfactory system.

Dr. Roberts, who holds Distinguished Scientist status at the Beckman Research Institute of the City of Hope for his original findings in brain function, says: "It's known that changes occur in the nasal passages with aging. The sense of smell therefore deteriorates; the mucous membrane alters; small hairs in the nose designed to sweep airways of debris become less active or even cease to function. Aluminosilicates [dust particles of aluminum and silicon, combined], thus, can find their way close to the olfactory nerve."

Dr. Roberts pointed out that studies have shown how complex molecules of aluminum travel directly to the brain from the olfactory nerve into the first sensory/thinking station in the brain, the olfactory bulb. Much of the damage typical of Alzheimer's disease is found in olfactory regions of the brain.

Autopsies of the brains of Alzheimer's disease patients have invariably found concentrations of aluminosilicates in cores of neuritic plaques in various areas of the two brain hemispheres. Such findings are typical of Alzheimer's disease. As we mentioned, aluminosilicates from aluminum dust are ubiquitous, comprising in some places around the globe up to 14 percent of the earth's surface.

Aluminosilicates may be manmade, too, and then purposely incorporated into consumer goods. They are found, for example, in talcum powder, asbestos, cat-box litter, cement and asphalt, volcanic rock, tobacco ashes, and free-flowing table salt. Inhale cigarette smoke and you'll recieve a large share of disease- and death-provoking aluminosilicates. Since Alzheimer's disease does not strike all of the population, genetic makeup and the components of an individual's nasal passages seem to play a role.

"We are all governed by our genetic makeup, even to small areas like a spot inside the nose," Dr. Roberts said. "Aluminum inhalation first affects the nose—and then the brain."

Such aluminum poisoning is inescapable. Everyone around the globe is a potential victim. As a result of industrialization and processing of the metal, there is more aluminum dust than ordinarily present in nature.

ALUMINUM AND OTHER FINE METALLIC AIR PARTICULATES OF POLLUTION

Large portions of the entire atmosphere over sizable areas of the United States are dangerous to human health. Scientists have identified the chief culprits of this environmental assault as aluminum and other fine metallic particulates, which remain in the atmosphere for weeks and are transported hundreds of miles on the winds. Pariculates are aggregates of aluminum particles suspended in the atmosphere and in the air we inhale. They are distinct, minute dust constituents that pollute the lungs with toxic aluminum. These particulates are so small—one fiftieth the width of a human hair—that they cannot be seen, yet they are capable of inflicting the most extraordinary damage on human and other animal tissues. They are slipping right through elaborate air-pollution control devices installed at industrial sites around the nation. It's not that the heavier, visible metallic particles are harmless—they definitely are carcinogenic and poisonous—but scientists find that the finer ones are more menacing because their miniscule size lets them become part of the floating elements in blood, intercellular fluids, and other liquid elements of the body. They travel through cell walls and implant themselves in the cell nucleus so that they eventually affect the cell's DNA.

Because of the combination of their tiny size and durability, in fact, the fine metallic particulates penetrate the body's total physiological defense system. The Brookhaven National Laboratory, on Long Island, in New York, estimates that 21,000 more deaths from brain-, respiratory-, and heart-related diseases are occurring each year east of the Mississippi due to the presence in the atmosphere of just one class of these particulates. They are the diabolical toxic-metal, sulfate-complex-type emanating principally from aluminum smelters and coal- and oil-burning power plants that the Bush administration freed to pollute more of North America, especially the United States.

In an academic paper published in 1978, two Yale University researchers estimated that 140,000 deaths each year were related to all forms of metallic air pollution compounds, but principally sulfates.[2] The death toll caused by such metallic air pollution by now has almost doubled.

The pro-pollution ruling wrought by former President Bush, which still stands, allows for an increase in the fine metallic particulates. The total weight per cubic meter of air sampled by the Environmental Protection Agency (EPA) must not exceed 75 micrograms. But fine particulates are not measured by weight because they are too light.

Most fine particulates are emitted from industrial sources either as solid particles or as gases. The gases are converted into aerosols—tiny combinations of liquid and solids—by exposure to the sun's radiation, by condensation, or by attaching themselves onto other materials already in the atmosphere. Most toxic metallic particulates become even more dangerous once atmospheric reactions take place. The fine particulates consisting of toxic metals such as aluminum, titanium, beryllium, nickel, cadmium, arsenic, lead, mercury, iron, manganese, etc., plus converted sulfur oxides, nitrogen oxides, and hydrocarbons are antigens that cause cellular mutation. (An antigen is any substance that the body regards as foreign or potentially dangerous and against which it produces an antibody. Invasive metals certainly are considered dangerous by one's immune system.) The mixture of these air-borne pollutants is far more lethal than any of its individual parts.

IMMUNE DYSFUNCTION FROM TOXIC METALS

Heavy metals do an immense amount of damage to animals used in studies. Through such studies several things have been discovered about the fine metallic particulates in the air. These particulates can suppress all aspects of immune functioning, reduce cell-mediated and humoral immunity, depress phagocyte responses, increase susceptibility to infection, and stimulate fibrillary tangles in the animal brain.[3] The same dysfunction takes hold in human beings.

Michael Weiner, Ph.D., an epidemiologist and nutritionist, has written that heavy metal air particulates produce serious damage, especially to growing children, even at low levels not generally considered toxic.[4]

Elevated aluminum levels in the bloodstream, that have been inhaled, trapped within lung tissue, then released gradually, become precursors to Alzheimer's disease. Other toxic metals do damage, as well. For instance, cadmium levels impair host resistance, antibody response, B- and T-cell response, phagocyte response, and they depress bone marrow function. Excess lead in the body tissues is responsible for cancerous tumors of the brain and kidneys. Mercury excess inhibits host resistance and antibody response, too, and causes malignant changes in lymphoid tissue.[5]

In researching this book, we traveled to London for consultations with Stephen Davies, M.A., B.M., B.Ch., F.A.C.N. Dr. Davies is laboratory and clinical director of the Biolab Medical Unit on Weymouth Street, in London, England. On May 15, 1992 he was presented with the Carlos Lamar Research Award at the semi-annual meeting of the American College of Advancement in Medicine, in Dallas, Texas.

Over a seven-year period, Dr. Davies had accomplished the herculean task of measuring the amount of aluminum, lead, cadmium, arsenic, and mercury in the hair of 17,000 patients, the sweat of 15,000 patients, and the blood of 3,000 patients. Analysis of these in relation to age and sex reveals that males generally have higher levels of these toxic metals than females and that levels increase progressively with age in both sexes. During our interviews, Dr. Davies reaffirmed for us that such progressive increases in human heavy-metal toxicity come from ongoing inhalation of fine metallic particulates and other air pollutants. He condemned aluminum air particulates as the most noteworthy potential source of dementia pathology.

THE GOVERNMENT IN OUR AIR

On June 25, 1992, the Bush administration, led by Vice President Dan Quayle, issued a rule that gives manufacturers broad authority to substantially increase the amount of hazardous pollutants they pour into the atmosphere beginning in the mid-1990s. Extra particulate air concentrations should begin to be noticed by the people on the streets of all U.S. cities and towns at the start of 1995. The air will be more difficult to breathe, and the greenhouse effect will increase, so that there will be greater shifts in weather patterns. The EPA was coerced, even over the agency administrator's clear objection, to enforce the new rule, which was championed by President George Bush's Council on Competitiveness, a powerful Cabinet group at the time. The Council's new rule is central to a system of pollution permits being established over the next ten years under the Clean Air Act of 1990.

Chemical and drug manufacturers, concerned about the costs of meeting standards in the Clean Air Act, lobbied for the new rule, saying they needed it to avoid making changes in equipment or production practices that have them currently exceeding air pollution limits. At the expense of Americans' health and in furtherance of Alzheimer's disease, lung disorders, and cancers, U.S. manufacturers will now be able to save money and pollute the air even more than ever before.

If a manufacturing company merely states that it is forced to pollute more by a change in production methods, under the Bush/Quayle rule the company can increase the amount of pollution it emits into the atmosphere by up to 245 tons (490,000 pounds) a year without public notice or hearings. Any manufacturer is allowed to do this simply by applying for an increase. Shocking as it sounds, while the application is pending, the company may go ahead with its plans for greater air pollution. The Environmental Protection Agency has 45 days to reject the application and the Environmental Agency of each of the 50 states has 90 days to approve or disapprove it.[6]

THE COMPETITIVE COUNCIL VS. THE EPA

Under the 1990 Clean Air Act, the EPA is required to set minimum, uniform standards of air pollution, and to enforce them. But the Competitiveness Council's revised rule sets up the framework for states to alter those standards and issue operating permits to roughly 35,000 factories, power plants, refineries, chemical processors, pharmaceutical manufacturers, and other significant sources of air pollution.

A giant oil refinery typically emits millions of pounds of pollutants into the air in its normal operations over one year. A small manufacturing plant also generally discharges polluting materials, although smaller amounts. This reality did not sit well with William K. Reilly, the EPA Administrator. In April 1991, he first proposed the procedures governing pollution permits under the 1990 Clean Air Act. His proposal required that there be public notifications and public hearings before any company could exceed the level of air pollution on its operating permit.

The next month, Quayle's Council on Competitiveness reviewed Reilly's proposal and added the provision to allow manufacturers and chemical companies to increase pollution levels without public notification. It was a clear and distinct pro-business, anti-consumer move.

During the summer of 1991, EPA General Counsel Donald Elliott attempted to save medical consumers by issuing a memorandum declaring the Council's proposal to eliminate public review illegal. That important Clean Air Act signed by former President Bush in 1990 specifically directed the EPA to allow the public to intervene in proposals by polluting companies. Other legal experts in the Government concurred, including Charles Bowsher, the Comptroller General, and Richard B. Stewart, the Assistant Attorney General for Lands and Natural Resources. Unfortunately, nothing ever came of this.

Then in October 1991, William Reilly once again called for the public to have the right to be notified and intervene if a company asks to increase its pollution levels. Under Reilly's compromise, if such increases were under five tons, states may expedite the application. The Council on Competitiveness under instructions of Vice President Quayle rejected the EPA compromise.

By May 1992 former President Bush decided the issue in favor of Mr. Quayle's Council and directed Mr. Reilly to write a rule that eliminates public review. Mr. Reilly refused to issue the rule until the Department of Justice declared such a rule legal. Mr. Bush ordered Attorney General William P. Barr to issue a memorandum to that effect, which he did on May 27, 1992. Thus, the new Bush/Quayle rule increasing air pollution took effect June 25, 1992.

The disagreement on the pollution rule thus produced one of the angriest political struggles in the Bush administration between William K. Reilly and Dan Quayle. Quayle's position was strongly supported by the Chemical Manufacturers Association, the Pharmaceutical Manufacturers Association, refiners, individual drug and chemical companies, and other large industries. Of course, it was inevitable that Reilly had to lose, along with the American people.

THE ALZHEIMER'S ASSOCIATION AND THE ALUMINUM INDUSTRY

The Alzheimer's Disease and Related Disorders Association, Incorporated (usually referred to as the Alzheimer's Association) began its medical research grant program in 1982. It declared then that more and better research into the cause, treatment, management, prevention, and cure of Alzheimer's disease and related disorders was being encouraged through the issuing of financial grants. By the end of 1990, 365 grants and awards totaling more than $18 million had been funded by the Alzheimer's Association through its programs.

The Alzheimer's Association research grant programs are structured to complement the United States Public Health Service (PHS) funding programs and to stimulate investigation into Alzheimer's disease and related disorders. The major source of funds for Alzheimer's research is the PHS, which provided approximately $146 million in 1990. Congress appropriated $247 million for Alzheimer's research in fiscal year 1991, providing a 67 percent increase in budgetary funds over the previous year.[7]

Governmental representatives do recognize the growing seriousness of Alzheimer's disease. As we mentioned earlier, the 1990's have been declared the "Decade of the Brain," and as a result, much attention is being given to the environmental source of Alzheimer's disease. Because of this, the aluminum industry is beginning to cloak itself in a protective mantel of financial contributions and political moves. The aluminum manufacturers have taken a lesson from the successful holding actions of cigarette manufacturers, whose product was also linked to a deadly disease.

The aluminum industry is gathering together all research documents, marketing promotion documents, and trade association documents for that near-future time when individual populations worldwide will wake up to the dangers of its aluminum products. Court actions are inevitable. In the meantime aluminum company executives are attempting to win friends for themselves and the industry. For instance, Edward Truschke, the executive director of the Alzheimer's Association headquarters in Chicago, in response to our multiple inquiries, finally admitted that his organization has received unrestricted grant monies from the Aluminum Association of Canada (ALCAN) and from the Aluminum Company of America (ALCOA). He did not acknowledge, but we are aware anyway, that the international Alzheimer's disease medical meeting held in July 1992, in Italy, was sponsored in part by the Aluminum Association of Canada.

These associations are exhibiting two different ways in which they can cover their tracks. The Canadian organization takes the aggressive approach, so that in the eventuality that a lawsuit arises, they can say that they were actively searching for evidence against their own product—making themselves look very good. The other advantage to funding the research is that they can direct the outcome of their findings, and still come across as innocent. The American organization heads right in the other direction—denial. If they have nothing to do with the research, they can eventually say that the findings are not valid, or that they did not participate because they do not believe that their product could be implicated as the cause of such a destructive disease.

The tobacco industry has done the same thing. Smoking cigarettes has been shown to cause cancer, lung disease, various cardiovascular diseases, and other health problems. Although the industry continues to deny the connection, they know the consequences full well.

Aluminum products are not addictive in the same sense as tobacco, but because they are readily available and convenient, they pose a similar health risk. Moreover, the aluminum industry is keeping people ignorant about the hazards of using aluminum products.

We have some recommendations as to how aluminum usage should be controlled worldwide:

- Aluminum-control national legislation should be seen as an integral part of a comprehensive control policy.

- Scientific and medical organizations should be urged to help, support, and encourage groups that are free to lobby and take a more activist role against the spread of aluminum usage.

- There should be legitimacy of Alzheimer's disease victims and victims' families to obtain compensation from aluminum manufacturers through judicial processes.

- Governments should seek reimbursement from the international aluminum industry for all medical and other relevant costs which they must bear by taking care of the victims of Alzheimer's disease.

- Pro-health and other organizations should review the socio-economic and health costs of aluminum use to the individual and to the society.

- All countries should regularly increase taxation on aluminum products as a health policy measure.

- All appropriate bodies should consider higher insurance rates for persons taking internal aluminum compounds to reflect the true socio-economic and health costs of their use.

- Every country should recognize the complex nature of aluminum-products production methods and use and should implement appropriate and demonstrably effective cessation techniques.

- All forms of aluminum-containing product advertising, sponsorship, and any other direct and indirect forms of promotion in all media should be strictly limited or banned altogether in all countries. As a first step toward a total ban, governments should eliminate aluminum product advertising on television.

- Each country should set up a national coordinating body on aluminum control. There should be regional and global coordination of such bodies.

- As a minimum, no promotion of aluminum products should be allowed that is illegal in the country of origin. Aluminum should cease to be used as political leverage in trade matters.

- Non-government organizations in all countries should work to assure their own governments do not contribute to the promotion of aluminum product manufacture and use.

- Illness prevention should be the main objective of national and international aluminum-products control programs.

Aluminum and its particulates are poisoning the bodies—not only the lungs but also the brains—of all the world's inhabitants. The writers of the University of California at Berkeley Wellness Letter are giving their readers misinformation when the newsletter's writers deny this fact. There is heavy evidence that aluminum ingested from the usual sources is harmful, shortens lifespan, and brings about the early onset of Alzheimer's disease. Beware the aluminum health dysfunctions that are coming upon us.

CHAPTER 8

Aluminum Contamination in Drinking Water, Milk, Tea, and Cookware

It has been about twenty years since medical researchers first uncovered the connection between exposure to aluminum, the third most common of the Earth's elements, and Alzheimer's disease. The Alzheimer's and Related Diseases Association (ARDA) continues to draw no parallel between increasing amounts of aluminum toxicity and Alzheimer's disease. How can the ARDA Board of Directors remain so blind to the quite apparent linkage? Such a stand is equivalent to denying that cigarette smoking is a contributor to the incidence of cancer and heart disease.

As we mentioned earlier, in Chapter 7, a certain relationship exists between ARDA funding and the aluminum associations of Canada and the United States. We suggest that the ARDA be put under the spotlight about such funding. As a health-oriented reader of this book, you might contact the ARDA at 70 East Lake Street, Chicago, Illinois 60601, 1–800–621–0379. It is your right to ask how staff members use various charitable contributions, what proportion of monies goes into Alzheimer's research, and how much is spent on administrative costs, such as fancy offices and educational junkets. Find out just what is the cozy relationship between the ARDA and The Aluminum Association.

The aluminum industry argues against environmental factors being responsible for the prevalence of Alzheimer's disease. But as indicated in this chapter and others, the tie-ins are obvious. To offer the Aluminum Association your own piece of advice, you could contact its officials directly at 900 19th Street, N.W., Washington, D.C. 20006, 202–862–5100. The staff there would prefer not hearing from readers, but you and your loved ones are the recipients of its diverse aluminum pollutants that are poisoning our Earth's environment. Be aware, of course, that these staff members are going to denigrate the information we are offering here. It is in their financial interests to throw you off the track and disguise their polluting ways.

The thirty-eight footnoted references that we cite in this chapter show a definite link between aluminum and Alzheimer's disease. In the developed world, the incidence of Alzheimer's disease is constant. If you compare Canada, the United States, northern Scandinavia, southern Italy, Japan, and other Western industrialized countries, there is not a lot of difference in the incidence of the condition. Nearly all of these countries are exposed to similar amounts of aluminum contamination in their drinking water, milk, tea, and aluminum cookware.

DRINKING WATER

Six researchers in the United Kingdom conducted an evaluation of the geographical relationship between amounts of aluminum in drinking water and the rate of Alzheimer's among older people. Rates of Alzheimer's disease in people under the age of seventy were gathered from the records of the CAT scanning units that serve eighty-eight county districts in England and Wales. Aluminum concentrations in water over the past ten years were obtained from water companies.

These researchers found a 50-percent increase in the risk of Alzheimer's disease in counties of the United Kingdom with high concentrations of aluminum in the drinking water. This was particularly true in Wales. The researchers learned that the risk of Alzheimer's disease was 1.5 times higher in districts where the average aluminum concentration exceeded 0.11 milligrams per liter of drinking water than in districts where concentrations were less than 0.01 milligrams per liter.[1] There was no evidence of a relation between other forms of dementia, or epilepsy, and aluminum concentrations in drinking water.

Similar studies have been done in certain other counties in Australia, France, Norway, and the United States, and the results of the United Kingdom study were substantiated.[2,3,4]

The published articles describing these findings were criticized by the country's water authorities, understandably touchy about suggestions that they are driving the British prematurely "potty." The critics were quick to point out that of the 1 to 10 milligrams per liter of alum or other aluminum additives slipped into the United Kingdom's drinking water to reduce cloudiness, most gets filtered out again. Their claim is that the vast majority of Britain's water supplies contain less than the government's limit of 0.2 milligrams per liter.

Information Sources
on Drinking Water

Many consumers now test their kitchen tap water for the various contaminants specified in the Safe Drinking Water Act—even when they use public water supplies. They are most worried about synthetic organic compounds or inorganics such as toxic metals and minerals that could be naturally occurring. But what are the other, more subtle forms of contaminants? There are EPA "Recommended Maximum Contaminant Levels," but do you know what they are?

To receive information that answers these types of questions, contact reliable educational sources including the following:

National Sanitation Foundation
3475 Plymouth Road
P.O. Box 1468
Ann Arbor, MI 48106
(313) 769–8010

EPA Drinking Water Hotline
(800) 426–4791
(202) 382–5533 in Alaska
  and the District of Columbia

Water Quality Association
4151 Naperville Road
Lisle, IL 60532
(708) 505–0160

Request the telephone of your local Environmental Protection Agency Division of Water Quality and make your rightful taxpayer demands.

About half of the United Kingdom's water is treated with iron, as well, which we shall see in a later chapter could be almost as predisposing to dementia as aluminum.

These fault-finders of the researchers' water study also represented groups who have commercial interests in the aluminum industry. The aluminum industrialists argued that the evaluated data on aluminum involvement might be flawed among the counties in Wales, because the Welsh-speaking patients could be misdiagnosed as demented by English-speaking doctors who failed to understand their language or Welsh dialect.

How to Test the Tap Water in Your Home

Before an American invests in any technique of tap water home-purification, it is proper procedure to determine which major pollutants, if any, are in the home's water supply. By law, you are entitled to see the results of water tests conducted on your municipal system. To do so, contact the local water utility company directly and, by authority of your state's health department, demand information about contaminants in your drinking water, notices of any violations of federal or state regulations, and/or records of complaints made by consumers.

Most often, large cities, medium-size suburbs, and even rural communities have a municipal laboratory, a state hygienic laboratory, or a university laboratory which performs analysis tests for the public. Each state also funds EPA-certified labs that test public drinking water systems. Request lists of these laboratories from your closest EPA regional office. (There are eight EPA offices located around the United States.)

Home water testing outfits do offer mail-order water testing at fair prices. Complete tests cost $100 and up. When inquiring about the laboratory, learn what tests are performed, costs, and whether it is state certified and approved by the EPA, the Water Quality Association, or any other official organization.

The tests offered by different organizations may vary in exactly what they offer testing for. Often the company doing the testing will offer a pamphlet that describes what can be tested. They will test for things such as VOCS and gang VOCS, which are volatile organic compounds that come from living organisms, either alone or grouped together. They can test for nonurban items, which are simply organic items, or coliform, which is a bacteria found in the intestines of humans and other animals. Aside for looking for metal particulates in your water supply, the examiners can also check for pH level and chemicals that do not belong.

The following three mail-order laboratories offer a variety of home water testing options and prices:

Laboratory	Test	Price*
National Testing Laboratories	•Lead	$29
6151 Wilson Mills Rd.	•73 Nonurban items, 14 metals,	$89
Cleveland, OH 44143	Volatile Organic Compounds	
(216) 449–2525	(VOCs), coliform bacteria,	
(800) 458–3330	10 inorganics and physical factors	
	•Same as above plus 20 pesticides	$119

Laboratory	Test	Price*
Suburban Water Testing	•Lead	$19
Laboratories	•33 VOCs	$55
4600 Kutztown Rd.	•42 parameters—VOCs, radon,	$148
Temple, PA 19560	nitrate, bacteria	
(800) 433–6595	•Above with either 20 pesticides	$240
	or 14 metals	
	•With both pesticides and metals	$390
Water Test	•Economy Purity Test: pH, 8	$75
33 South Commercial St.	inorganics and coliform	
Manchester, NH 03101	•Without coliform	$65
(603) 623–7400	•VOCs and above (with coliform),	$115
(800) 426–8378	total of 59 parameters	
	•Or substitute either 12 pesticides	$115
	or 8 PCBs for VOCs in above tests	
	•Or gang VOCs, pesticides,	$305
	and PCBs	

*All prices are subject to change without notice.

Furthermore, criticism of Dr. C.N. Martyn, the study's chief researcher, and his five colleagues came from statisticians who condemned the completeness of the patients' clinical records, which may have varied from place to place. They took exception with the fact that some patients lived so far from CAT scanning devices that they may have been ineffectively used to arrive at the diagnosis. Similar to tobacco industrialists, the water sellers and aluminum manufacturers really were reaching for reasons to be critical of the study.

Nevertheless, a most interesting confirmation of the researchers' findings came from Bengt Lindegard, M.D. at the Department of Social Medicine and Clinical Epidemiology, University of Gothenburg, Vastra Frolunda, Sweden. Lindegard wrote:

> Your findings on aluminium and Alzheimer's disease remind us of similarities between this disease and amyotrophic lateral sclerosis (ALS) as a subset of the motoneuron diseases. In Guam and on Kii (Japan) where a 100-fold increased prevalence of ALS

was observed two decades ago, high levels of heavy and/or trace metals, such as manganese and aluminum and low content or lack of minerals such as calcium and magnesium, were detected in soil and water samples.

With this in mind, we compared, for those counties in England and Wales where Dr. Martyn and colleagues found the highest and lowest water concentrations of aluminium, standard mortality ratios for motoneuron disease.[5,6,7]

The data suggest that mortality from motoneuron disease, like the incidence of Alzheimer's disease, varies with the local water concentration of aluminium, especially among women.[8]

More Proof of Aluminum-Contaminated Water Causing Dementia

Additional evidence was brought to bear on the role aluminum plays in dementia, too. Further studies in the United Kingdom were conducted in 1988 by the same Medical Research Council's neuroendocrinology unit in Newcastle. At that time, the MRC team found neuritic plaques in the cerebral cortex of people exposed to low doses of aluminum over a very long period.

In their investigation, Dr. Martyn and colleagues, at the MRC environmental epidemiology unit in Southampton, uncovered that the incidence of Alzheimer's disease in the UK appears definitely to be related to levels of aluminum in the water supply. The researchers related the risk of having dementia to the concentration of aluminum in water.

Moreover, according to further estimates from the Ministry of Agriculture, Fisheries, and Food, the average adult aluminum intake in Britain is around 5 to 6 mg per day. A lot of it comes from drinking tea, both in the water and from the tea leaves themselves. When brewed, the tea leaf will provide half of the aluminum contamination.[9] (For a more complete discussion of aluminum contamination in tea, please see pages 108–109.) Still, tannin in tea tends to reduce the effect of the high aluminum content that comes with drinking hot or iced tea.[10] (Tannin from plants, such as tea leaves, ordinarily is thought to be used for tanning leather. Tannic acid, a mixture of tannins, is used in the treatment of burns.)

Professor James A. Edwardson, M.D., the MRC unit's director, told delegates at a Royal Society of Chemistry meeting in May 1988: "There is now a very strong case that must be taken seriously. Aluminum is an early, not a late, event in plaque formation and chronic low exposure from drinking water can lead to deposition inside neurons in the brain."

COW'S MILK

In 1986, *The Lancet* reported on the levels of aluminum in milk formulas for infants.[11] Thereafter other clinical research papers from around the world confirmed the findings. Compared with carefully collected human breast milk containing 5–20 micrograms (mcg) per liter of aluminum, aluminum concentrations are 10- to 20-fold greater in most cow's milk-based formulas and 100-fold greater in soy-based formulas.[12]

Aluminum concentration in infant formulas increases considerably during preparation as a result of the utensils used, the ambient air particulates, and the formula mixture itself. The permeability of the gastrointestinal tract is greatest in the first days after birth, enhancing the potential for absorption of substances from the diet that normally get excluded.[13] Consequently, the seeds of Alzheimer's disease may be planted during the first days of life.

This unfortunate finding is indicated all the more so from aluminum ordinarily being excreted through the kidney. When immature or reduced kidney function occurs in an infant, aluminum from a cow's milk-based formula is accumulated and stored thereafter for decades—perhaps from birth to death of the person. That is because the amount of aluminum stored in the kidneys as a result of their detoxifying functions (known as the urinary aluminum/creatinine quotient) at age three weeks is four times greater than at a mean age of five months for enterally-fed (fed through the intestinal tract) term infants. While urinary creatinine is lower in the newborn than in older infants, the difference is unlikely to account for the observed increase in ratio, possibly indicating increased absorption in the younger infants.[14]

In one infant with severe kidney failure reported on in a 1985 *Lancet* paper, the absorption and retention of aluminum from a cow's milk-based formula resulted in clinical toxicity. By one month of age the baby had a brain-aluminum concentration in the neurotoxic range. Aluminum poisoning of the neurons in this way may cause either mental retardation, learning disabilities, or set the scene for the early onset of Alzheimer's disease.[15] Premature infants are at increased risk of retaining absorbed aluminum until the kidneys have developed the full filtering capacity for full-term infants. For most infants that are born premature, this is attained by forty weeks after conception.

Zinc deficiency will cause a child to absorb more aluminum into his system in general, and into his brain in particular.[16] Aluminum will be absorbed by competing for binding sites on a zinc-binding ligand. A ligand is an organic molecule attached to a central metal ion such as zinc by many bonds.[17] This will be true especially if there is not enough zinc available in the diet. Infants at risk for zinc deficiency are those born to mothers who smoked tobacco or marijuana or consumed alcoholic beverages during pregnancy.[18,19]

Infants fed exclusively on soy-based milk risk a reduction of zinc availability due to the increased concentrations of phytate in such formulas, compared with cow's milk-based formulas.[20] The American Committee on Nutrition suggests that it would be prudent to avoid feeding soy-based formulas to low-birthweight infants and those with impaired kidney function, including premature infants.[21] The 1988 report of the Department of Health and Social Security committee advising on infant feeding said that soy-based milks "have been approved for prescription in the National Health Service as borderline substances for established forms of milk intolerance."[22]

Soy-based formulas have the highest aluminum and phytate contents of any available for newborn. They offer an avoidable hazard when gastrointestinal and kidney function are immature. These formulas should be available to the premature or low-birthweight infant only by prescription or on medical advice.

To offset the aluminum content problem with cow's milk, rather than drink this beverage yourself, or include it in infant formulas, or use it in cooking, people ought to consider the substitution of goat's milk which usually contains no aluminum.

TEA

Tea has been found to be a major source of aluminum in the daily diet, especially tea leaves that come from Assam, Darjeeling, Ceylon, and some supermarket blends. These contain a greater amount of aluminum in their physical makeup than do other teas.

It was reported by three researchers at the Water Research Centre, Environment Laboratory, MRC in Medmenham, England that 91 to 100 percent of the filtrable aluminum in tea infusions is bound to organic matter. Under simulated stomach conditions, laboratory experiments proved that large molecules of aluminum, even those with molecular weights of 20,000, shift towards mineral salt species of lower molecular weight, and hence they cross-link to form destructive free radicals in protein complexes that become quite bioavailable.[23]

British scientists concluded that concentrations of aluminum in brewed teas are commonly in the range of 2 to 6 milligrams per liter.[24] Water quality does have some effect on the release of aluminum during infusion; thus, for the same tea samples brewed using soft tap water there were consistently higher levels of the metal present. The average increase of aluminum in tea brewed in soft water was 1.6 milligrams per liter over tea brewed in hard water, although the highest observed value in soft water was 6.9 milligrams per liter.

Drinking tea with milk rather than lemon could be somewhat less hazardous for aluminum absorption. A 1986 experiment showed that the absorption of aluminum from the gut is greatly enhanced by citrate. Thus, lemon juice tends to increase the bioavailability of aluminum from tea.[25]

The total amount of aluminum found in an Alzheimer-diseased brain is just one milligram or less, hardly an overly large amount when one considers how much people consume with ordinary eating and drinking. Tea drinking or other dietary edibles, in fact, do offer sufficient microgram quantities of "neuro-available" aluminum complexes, when ingested over a lifetime. They would more than suffice to provide the required amount for the pathological process of Alzheimer's-type dementia.

COOKWARE

It is not uncommon for a restaurant to serve hot baked potatoes wrapped in aluminum foil. While wrapping food in foil is a convenient cooking method for the restaurant's chef, it is a hazardous practice for the patron who finally eats the potato. Organic foods cooked or stored in aluminum foil wrap or aluminum cookware invariably have some small quantity of the aluminum leached into them. For example, if you boil an acidic-type vegetable or fruit, such as rhubarb, for 30 minutes in an aluminum saucepan, you can measure between 300 and 400 milligrams per liter of aluminum escaping from that pan.

The same thing happens with tomatoes; a near-equal amount of aluminum becomes part of a pasta sauce when the sauce is prepared in an aluminum pot. In this case between 2 and 10 milligrams per liter of aluminum leaches from the cookware to form molecules of aluminum citrate.

If you mix a salad in an aluminum bowl and sprinkle in some vinegar and olive oil, you will be getting a goodly quantity of aluminum as a dressing additive. The vinegar's acetic acid joins in a chemical complex with metallic components in the mixing bowl and offers up to 10 milligrams per liter of aluminum acetate.

A little known chemical experiment can be conducted in your own kitchen to test your aluminum cookware's toxicity quotient. This method of leaching aluminum from aluminum cookware involves boiling acid water in the presence of copper (Cu) ions in such cookware. From prior electrochemical studies it is known that small amounts of dissolved copper can lead to the oxidation of much larger amounts of metallic aluminum. So, if you boil soft tapwater acidified with sulphuric acid to a pH4 and use cookware containing 2 milligrams of copper per liter of solution, the cookware will leach out 30 milligrams of aluminum per liter into the solution.[26]

In a study by two scientists from Sri Lanka, it was found that fluoride is responsible in many instances for aluminum leaching out of cookware. Most people get a daily dose of fluoride in their drinking water, because this element has been added to the public water supply to guard against cavities.

The experimenters, who are staff members of the Institute of Fundamental Studies, University of Ruhuna, said:

> We have found that the presence of only 1 ppm of fluoride (the permitted level of fluoridation[27]) in water adjusted with citric acid or sodium bicarbonate to pH 3 (a pH often realized in cooking conditions) and boiled in an aluminum vessel, liberates nearly 200 ppm of aluminum in 10 minutes, compared with less than 0.2 ppm in the absence of fluoride. Prolonged boiling produces a concentration of 600 ppm, which is reached more quickly the larger the surface-to-volume ratio of the water.[28]

These experimentors did a test with 50 grams of crushed tomatoes in 250 milliliters of water, cooked in the same aluminum vessel with 1 part-per-million (ppm) of fluoride. The tomato paste produced a concentration of 150 ppm of aluminum in 10 minutes.

Water consumed in some localities among certain western industrialized countries—such as the United States, Canada, and the United Kingdom—contains 10 ppm of fluoride. And cooking or prolonged storing of foods in aluminum cookware that contains large amounts of fluoride (500 ppm in tea or 100 to 700 ppm in fish) could easily release more than 100 ppm of aluminum.

One more word of caution: bottled beverages contain less aluminum than beverages that come in cans, an obvious finding, for the cans are manufactured from a combination of tin and aluminum. So if you have a choice, drink your beverages from bottles. The general rule to follow is reduce your use of kitchen aluminum altogether.

KIDNEY MALFUNCTION

Bone is the major storage organ (or dumping place) for excess aluminum that enters the bloodstream from drinking contaminated water, milk, coffee, tea, or from food. When the stored aluminum exceeds certain limits, it causes embrittlement of the bones, and then spontaneous fractures (osteoporosis). This physiological response is not surprising, since the toxic metal is a crosslinking agent for collagen. Particularly when phosphate groups are present, crosslinking occurs because phosphate salts are catalysts for crosslinkage. More damaging crosslinking comes from the North American and European public's extensive drinking of carbonated soda and the eating of meat, both of which contain an elevated amount of phosphate.

Crosslinkage occurs in human tissues when large, active, intracellular molecules produce bridges between themselves so that they join and form even larger, so-called macromolecules (very large-sized molecules). Crosslinking is pathological because it immobilizes proteins in a way that renders them irreversibly inert toward body enzymes. The enzymes are not able to break these proteins into smaller parts for use in metabolism. Thus, malnourishment of the cells occurs. Cross-linkages of deoxyribonucleic acid (DNA), the genetic factor in cells, may give rise to mutation and the subsequent formation of malignancies, aberrations, or some other abnormalities of cellular growth.

Another crosslinking pathology takes place in regard to low density lipoproteins (LDLs), the "bad" form of blood cholesterol. Crosslinkage is an important contributor to an individual's bodywide deterioration that accompanies hardening of the arteries and subsequent aging. Recent studies have shown that LDL cholesterol is changed through oxidation from a form that circulates freely in the blood to a form that can latch onto artery walls, narrowing their passageways and thus increasing the risk of heart attack or stroke, similar to the stroke that struck former President Richard M. Nixon on April 18, 1994. When LDL cholesterol clogs artery channels, it is from bridges forming between the macromolecular blood cholesterol and the cells lining arterial walls by means of crosslinking attachments.

Aluminum salts concentrated in the blood, which come from one's ingestion of antacids, absorption of antiperspirants, drinking acidic liquids (like citrus juice), from aluminum cans, especially are responsible for producing crosslinkages. The deleterious effect takes place in the elastin and collagen of our tissues, and thus seriously reduces the elasticity of blood vessels and neurofibrils, where aluminum lodges. Aluminum and other toxic metals disturb proper pH to produce an overacid serum state so as to lead to aberrant calcium accumulation in cells.

In any person who has a lessened capacity to excrete aluminum through the urine, the metal burden from even normal intake will markedly increase. Although the quantity of aluminum is small, in micrograms per day, over a lifetime this amount reflects in a major accumulation of heavy metal in the bone and brain. As with X-radiation in the body, aluminum toxicity is cumulative in the brain.

If an individual suffers from kidney malfunction, as in hemodialysis patients, the dialysate (the mixture that passes through a dialyzing membrane) is high in aluminum.[29,30] In Chicago between 1972 and 1976, 12.5 percent of the patients undergoing chronic hemodialysis treatment developed *dialysis dementia*. Water purification processes usually utilize iron and/or aluminum sulphates, a practice that we mentioned earlier about the United Kingdom. But Chicago water clarification plants switched, in 1972, from combining iron (Fe) and aluminum to the exclusive use of aluminum sulphate. Consequently, kidney specialists saw a significant rise in the number of dialysis dementia cases.[31]

One more 1982 investigation of a British population revealed that dialysis dementia was found in 18 out of 258 kidney patients undergoing hemodialysis in the home.[32] Analysis of the water supplies for these people showed that dementia was present only in dialysis patients living in those areas where the concentration of aluminum was in excess of 80 micrograms. The resulting recommendation from alarmed health professionals was that purification of water by the process of reverse osmosis should be used. They advised that there was no known safe level of aluminum for water used in hemodialysis treatment.

THE CROSSLINKAGE THEORY

A remarkable concept was developed by Johan Bjorksten, Ph.D., the present Laboratory Director of the Bjorksten Research Foundation of Madison, Wisconsin. Dr. Bjorksten revealed his theory in 1941,[33] and explained it in 1942 as follows:

> The aging of living organisms I believe is due to the occasional formation of tanning, of bridges between protein molecules, which cannot be broken by the cell enzymes. Such irreparable tanning

may be caused by tanning agents foreign to the organism or formed by unusual biological side reactions, or it may be due to the formation of a tanning bridge in some particular position in the protein molecule. In either event, the result is the cumulative tanning of body proteins which we know as old age.[34]

By now Dr. Bjorksten's theory is well accepted as fact by the scientific community. The process Dr. Bjorksten refers to as "tanning" is now called "crosslinkage." The aging process becomes hastened as a result of molecular crosslinkage. When molecular chains of polyvalent metals (which have more than one electrical charge in an atom), proteins, and nucleic acids (either DNA or RNA in the nucleus of living cells) combine together with other long protein molecules, an unnatural cross-link forms. This newly created giant cross-linked protein is no longer able to function normally and cannot be split or hydrolyzed, as usually is done by enzymes present in the blood circulatory system. Crosslinking produces free radicals that create pathology by preventing the usual splitting and hydrolization of proteins for use by the body.

The type of cross-linking we are speaking of is illustrated metaphorically by Garry Gordon, M.D., of Roseville, California. He describes the human cellular crosslinking processes as we have done before. Dr. Gordon states that crosslinkage occurs in the arteries similar to garden hoses that dry out and crack when they're old and no longer are soft and pliable, or by old rubber automobile windshield wipers that become hard and split. Cracked hoses and split windshield wipers, Dr. Gordon points out, have lost their elasticity as a result of cross-linking, which is recognized as one of the major contributors to "aging." They are dried and brittle from the inability of molecules in the rubber to slide over each other, which happens in the most solid of objects—even rocks.

The same sort of cross-linking-induced brittleness occurs in the protein chains of human beings, especially with metallic ions that permeate the cardiovascular system. Consequently, along with the increasing calcium content that occurs in all of our arteries as we grow older, we find a loss of elasticity, reduced ability of the arterial wall to expand and contract, a tendency to become brittle, and a loss of the artery's moisture content. These changes increase the *peripheral resistance* (opposing pressure of gravity) that a person's heart has to work against every time it tries to deliver another squirt of blood to the legs, arms, head, or any other part of the body—thus making the heart work harder just to maintain normal blood circulation.

Aluminum being a reactive metal, it readily enters into cross-linkage with the body's proteins. The uremic patients on dialysis that we mentioned earlier are typically exposed to about 180 liters of water two or three times a week. This exposure is directly through the arterial bed when the transfusion is received. Any substance dissolved in this water bypasses not only the gastrointestinal barrier, but also the kidneys, which normally remove much of the aluminum that gets through the gastrointestinal barrier.[35,36,37] It would appear that a person requiring periodic hemodialysis receives an abnormally large amount of aluminum directly into his or her bloodstream. The reverse osmosis technique used for purifying the hemodialysis fluids does not remove all of the alumimum and other metallic elements. Some get through and are not detoxified by the kidney. The contaminating metal cross-links with cellular proteins in the brain and elsewhere. If the dialysis patient lives long enough; therefore, he or she must suffer from aluminum toxicity, of which one of the resultant diseases is Alzheimer's disease. This makes Alzheimer's disease almost inevitable for dialysis patients.

Normally a person excretes about 15 mcg of aluminum daily in urine. This should, however, be viewed in the perspective that aluminum is present in almost all foods so that we ingest 30 to 50 mg daily. If we overburden ourselves with a greater amount of the toxic metal consumed in prescription and over-the-counter drugs, drinking water, milk, coffee, tea, and leachings from pots and pans used for food preparation, the accumulation will be immense over one's lifetime. A pathological quantity of dietary aluminum is destined to reach the hippocampic area of the brain, which may result in Alzheimer's disease.[38]

CHAPTER 9

How Aluminum Acts on the Brain

The connection to metal toxicity in the brain is proven by aluminum's presence in the neurons (brain cells) of autopsied patients who had suffered from Alzheimer's disease. Aluminum is the most commonly found toxic metal that permeates such affected brains.

In 1897, aluminum was analyzed for pathological reaction in animals and reported to be a selective neurotoxin (a nerve cell poison of specific affinity for the brain).[1] Shortly thereafter it was recognized as a human poison that caused loss of memory, jerking movements, and impaired coordination.[2] Experimentally, for instance, exposure of the central nervous systems of rabbits to aluminum salts produces a progressive encephalopathy (any of various diseases that affect the functioning of the brain).[3] The way this experiment is done is to inject aluminum powder such as the McIntyre Powder (finely ground aluminum and aluminum oxide) into the cerebral spinal fluid or the neural parenchyma of rabbits. You may recall from Chapter Seven that during the period of 1944 to 1979 Mcintyre Powder was forced upon miners in northern Ontario as an inhalant to act as a protective agent against silicotic lung disease. It was discovered much later that the majority of these silicon-mine workers developed Alzheimer's disease or some other form of encephalopathy.[4]

In 1980, Drs. D.P. Perl and P.F. Good, two neuropathologists at Mount Sinai Medical Center in New York City, discovered that not only did aluminum show up generally in the brains of Alzheimer's disease victims, but it was also present in precisely those tangled brain cells that characterized the disease. One of the research scientists, Daniel Perl, M.D., chief of research for the Mt. Sinai Medical Center's Department of Neuropathology, looked into identification of diseases associated with aluminum and found a baffling wave of degenerative brain disease in the Pacific island of Guam. About 10 percent of Guam's local population currently dies of one of two degenerative brain diseases, amyotrophic lateral sclerosis (ALS, or Lou Gehrig's disease) and parkinsonism with dementia (PD).

It has been known for nearly four decades that the Chamorro peoples of the Mariana islands in the western Pacific Ocean, particularly Guam and Rota, suffer from this inordinately high incidence of brain disease. Between 1957 and 1965 the ALS and PD syndromes accounted for 15 percent of adult deaths among Chamorro peoples. Medical scientists did not know why until aluminum came under suspicion as the source. There are high levels of aluminum in the drinking water and in nineteen common foods of Guam and Rota. Dr. Perl repeatedly has found the metal in the brains of deceased Mariana islanders who had been afflicted with ALS and PD.[5]

Low calcium and high aluminum concentrations in the soils, waters, and native foods are strongly suspected as the environmental factors contributing to the high incidence of the two dementias. The amounts of elemental aluminum and calcium were measured in foods of the native diet of the Chamorro people. Some of these foods consisted of taro, yam, arrowroot, cassava, radish, turmeric, pepper, banana, coconut, melon, pumpkin, papaya, mango, breadfruit, pandanus, guava, achote, betel nut, and cycad. Taro, a staple of the Chamorro native diet, contained the highest aluminum content and next were yam, arrowroot, radish, turmeric, peppers, and pandanu. They each had at least a concentration in excess of 100 micrograms aluminum per gram dry weight of the sample.

The amount of aluminum eluted (removed by dissolving) from topsoil by water was also measured. For comparison, food, water, and soil samples were collected from two islands that have not reported a high incidence of ALS and PD syndromes: Palau and Jamaica. Compared with the agricultural soils of these two islands, the agricultural soils of Guam averaged 42-fold higher yield of elutable aluminum. It has been proposed by researchers that the food-growing soils offering high dietary aluminum or low dietary calcium content, and the dusts of Guam are a major source of aluminum entering the body of the native people, particularly through the respiratory epithelium. The epithelium is tissue that covers the external body surface and lines hollow structures. Ingestion of fat-soluble organic ligands of aluminum more readily penetrate epithelial membranes of the nose, mouth, bronchioles, alveoli, and other tissues of the lungs.[6]

ALUMINUM INGESTION

In fact, ingestion of aluminum in any form—by inhalation, skin or scalp absorption, food, water or other liquid consumption, subcutaneous, intramuscular or intravenous injection, and/or additional means—is dangerous for the brain. Aluminum is known to be a potent cross-linking agent that acts to immobilize reactive molecules within brain cells. It also causes free-radical pathology inside the neurons. Free-radical damage of brain cells brings on molecular cross-linkage throughout the brain's tissues. (For a more complete discussion of the cross-linkage theory, see page 112.)

Crosslinkage abnormally develops at the very minimum two macromolecules (very large-sized molecules) that join together. Such linkage is pathological and brings on cellular damage. Once brain-macromolecular linkage takes place, molecular motion between the cross-linked molecules will cause further contacts with each other, thereby increasing the probability of additional crosslinkages being formed. Thus, additional macromolecules may join the aggregate. As this pathological process progresses, the cells become increasingly burdened with an accumulation of malfunctioning or inert large molecules that cannot be removed.

In addition to the cross-linkage pathology of macromolecules, irreplaceable nucleic-acid molecules that form part of the DNA (dioxyribonucleic acid) become damaged. Such damage leads to mutations or, more frequently, to cellular death in the brain. The cellular death is critical, because neurons do not divide and thus cannot be replaced. As brain cells die, or as the damage becomes progressivley worse, mental abilities of the affected person decrease.[7]

Free-radical pathology occurring from bombardment of the brain by additional aluminum ions, aluminum subatomic particles, or whole aluminum molecules penetrating the blood-brain barrier increases neuronal damage and advances dementia. The pathology is continuous if aluminum exposure continues and free radicals continue along the body's metabolic pathways.

Free radicals are atoms that become extremely reactive by virtue of having unpaired electrons. Nonradical compounds usually have their electron orbitals occupied by an even number of paired electrons, a state that is energetically most favorable and hence most stable. A free radical, on the other hand, usually has an odd number of electrons and a single unpaired electron in an outer orbital. It is this unpaired electron that is responsible for the instability and reactivity characteristic of all free radicals. Simply by losing or gaining an electron, any nonradical compound can be converted to a free-radical form and thereby undergo dramatic changes in its physical and chemical properties.[8,9,10] When a free radical strikes an atom with paired electrons, it is not unusual for one of the pair to be knocked loose so as to fall away from the electron pairing. Thus, a second free radical gets formed. Once the cycle of free-radical formation gets going, it is very difficult to stop it, except by the neutralizing or quenching effect of anti-oxidants, such as selenium and vitamin E.

Once initiated, free radicals tend to propagate, by taking part in chain reactions with other, usually less reactive atoms. These chain-reaction compounds generally have longer half-lives and therefore extended potential for cellular damage. Thus, the toxicity of a single radical compound may be amplified in subsequent reactions. The stages of *initation* and *propagation* are followed by the stage of *termination,* at which the free radicals are neutralized either by nutrient-derived antioxidants, by enzymatic mechanisms, or by recombination with each other. Enzymes and transport molecules tend to generate free radicals in living organisms (especially in humans) as a normal consequence of their catalytic function.[11]

One of the primary sources of free-radical activity in brain tissue is lipid peroxidation. Lipid peroxidation is pathology in tissues that takes place when lipids (fats) of the body actually turn rancid from oxidation. Such lipid peroxidation requires the presence of abnormally located metal ions, such as iron, aluminum, copper, lead, etc. All of these give rise to free-radical attack. The brain is especially vulnerable to this pathological peroxide process from the high concentration of biologically active lipids in the cellular membranes of neurons. The consumption of some of the dietary polyunsaturated fats, therefore, contributes to the damage caused by lipid peroxidation and its relationship to aluminum neurotoxicity. An individual's ongoing ingestion of the polyunsaturated fats increases lipid peroxidation to produce not only heart disease (which currently is a well-accepted concept among cardiologists), but also brain deterioration.

THE ALUMINUM/DEMENTIA CONNECTION

In a series of brilliant laboratory and clinical studies, Donald R. McLaughlan, M.D., Professor of Physiology and Medicine, at the University of Toronto, and his co-workers, caused a replication of the entire sequence of symptoms of Alzheimer's disease in cats. By a single injection of 100 nanomoles (one-billionth of a mole) of aluminum chloride into the hippocampic space, sometimes referred to as a brain ventricle, an area located in the hippocampus of the cat's brain, they caused the cats to develop a dementia similar to Alzheimer's.

Dr. McLaughlan and his coworkers watched the cats' reactions to the aluminum chloride injections. No change was observed during the first week following treatment, but at about the ninth day the cats began to fail to remember where they had seen food hidden. Approximately ten days after that the animals' short range memory was completely gone. Other signs and symptoms became apparent, additionally, and laboratory tests indicating distinct similarities to human Alzheimer's disease were striking.[12]

In this chapter we shall be referring frequently to the aluminum/Alzheimer's connection established by Dr. McLaughlan and his colleagues. To respond to the works we are citing, you may choose to address your queries to D.R. McLaughlan, M.D., F.R.C.P.(C), Professor of Physiology and Medicine, Director, Centre for Research in Neurodegenerative Diseases, University of Toronto.[12a]

An even more impressive study that Dr. McLaughlan performed, so as to counter any misapprehension that aluminum installation into the brain could be responsible for the animals' irregular behavior, involved his injecting aluminum chloride into a subcutaneous area of the cats' skin covering the abdomen. Again, for the ten days following the injections nothing special happened, but thereafter the felines developed a progressive dementia.

Dr. McLaughlan repeated this experiment innumerable times. In that way the researcher proved that similar abnormal responses take place in laboratory cats no matter where the aluminum is placed in their bodies.[13]

"Concentrations of aluminum that are toxic to many biochemical processes are found in at least ten human neurological conditions," stated Dr. McLaughlan. "However, four primary neurodegenerative conditions of late adult life are of particular interest: (a) senile and presenile dementia of the Alzheimer type, (b) Down's syndrome with Alzheimer disease, (c) Guam parkinsonism-dementia complex, and (d) Guam amyotrophic lateral sclerosis. Each of these brain diseases is linked by two important markers: (1) neurons exhibit neurofibrillary degeneration composed of aggregates of 10 nm paired helical filaments; (2) neurons with neurofibrillary degeneration contain elevated concentrations of aluminium."[14,15]

Dr. McLaughlan's conclusions were confirmed and broadened by other investigators around the world. They proved that what he uncovered is true: aluminum ingestion into an animal's physiology brings on symptoms of a kind of Alzheimer's disease. Upon autopsy of the cats in both types of studies—the brain injections and the abdominal injections of aluminum chloride—the impartial investigators performed histochemical (chemical studies of the brain cells) and microscopical studies. The aluminum was found to be preferentially absorbed by the chromatin in the pyramidal neurons in the hippocampic areas of the feline brains.[16]

The animal used most frequently for the study of aluminum neuroencephalopathy (abnormal functioning of brain cells), however, is the rabbit. These more docile laboratory animals furnish a faster readout than any other. Like the cats, rabbits injected in the brain ventricular system with aluminum salts or powder recover from the operation within an hour and develop clinical symptoms inside of two weeks after the injection. They show neurofibrillary degeneration with general motor inhibition and pronounced *ataxia* (shaky movements and unsteady gait). Their brains fail to regulate the body's posture and the strength and direction of limb movements.[17]

Ataxia is connected with dementia in humans, too, with clumsiness of willed movements, staggering when walking, and inability to pronounce words properly. The unsteady movements of sensory ataxia (blocked ability to coordinate movement with the senses) in a person are exaggerated when he or she closes the eyes (Romberg sign). Romberg sign is evidence of a sensory disorder affecting those nerves that transmit information to the brain about the position of the limbs and joints and the tension in the muscles. The patient is asked to stand upright. Romberg sign is positive if he or she maintains posture when eyes are open but sways and falls when eyes are closed.

From ataxia brain studies on animals and many other types of neurological brain studies that we shall describe in the next few sections, it has been established that aluminum is associated with the nuclei of neurons in neurofibrillary degeneration in senile human brains associated with Alzheimer's disease.

Additional immunologic tests on animals have confirmed the chemical similarity between abnormal, tubular, intracellular growths in Alzheimer neurons and similar tubules induced in laboratory animals—mostly rats but also rabbits—by the administration of aluminum in their daily diet and by injection into their skin.[18,19,20]

ALUMINUM IN THE HUMAN BODY AND BRAIN

When aluminum is inhaled or consumed by a person or absorbed through the skin and scalp, or ingested in some other way, it is metabolized in the body, transported through the blood stream, and either excreted in the feces and bile or absorbed into the brain cells.[21] There is an age-related increase in the level of aluminum absorption in several tissues.[22] Primarily, this additional age-absorption mechanism takes place from osmotic transfer through the gut wall as a result of the oral intake of aluminum that travels through the gastrointestinal tract. A good example of such source aluminum in food is the amount of the metal absorbed from aluminum foil when acidic fruit, such as pineapple, is stored in it.

In the laboratory, studies of elderly rats have shown that their uptake of aluminum increases over younger animals, and young rodents rather than older ones are used in investigations. When taken as part of the food supply, the toxic metal moves into the animal's general blood circulation, and eventually permeates the blood-brain barrier.

In the instance of aluminum absorption and toxicity, what's true of laboratory animals, in large measure, is true of human beings. In elderly people more than youngsters, such blood-brain barrier permeation takes place with certain amino acids, with peptides especially: the N-Tyr-delta-sleep-inducing peptide and the beta-endorphin.[23] These two peptides combine with aluminum molecules placed in the body from the use of aluminum foil and cookware. Thus, natural enzymes become body poisons by absorption of high-technology aluminum.

Other studies indicate that aluminum and the ions of the heavy metals cadmium and manganese join to inhibit the certain brain enzymes that are the source of cellular energy. The result is that enzyme inhibition in an animal or a person causes brain cell energy and reasoning ability to diminish, and memory to fade. When brain cell energy diminishes, the affected person feels utter fatigue. A perpetual tiredness becomes the overwhelming symptom for the individual.

Also, these toxic metals have other adverse properties. Aluminum, cadmium, and manganese are potent inhibitors of the uptake of choline and dopamine by membrane-bound sacs in the brain known as the synaptosomes.[24,25,26]Choline and dopamine are vital brain chemicals released by nerve endings to transmit impulses across synapses to other nerves, and across the minute gaps between the nerves and muscles or glands that they supply. The toxic metals obviously must bring about adverse effects for the brain's neurotransmission of thoughts, reasoning, and short-term memories, if these messages cannot be transmitted.

There is strong evidence that alterations in the enzymes involved with acetylcholine metabolism are caused by the ingestion of aluminum.[27,28] Acetylcholine is a substance in the body that allows messages to travel from one nerve to another. For example, a person who decides to pick up a pen can act on the thought only when the hand receives the message from the brain. This message is sent across the synapse between neurons by acetylcholine, which is then neutralized by cholinesterase, so that the message cannot be sent more than once. This process occurs in a fraction of a second in normal people. If aluminum is ingested in sufficient quantity over time, then there is an abnormal modification, either increases or decreases, of acetylcholinesterase (the enzyme that stops acetylcholine from being activated). An associated motor-lack takes place with reduced coordination, or non-transfer of the thought that the pen should be picked up. So, there will be a reduction or prevention of the movement of nerve signals and ataxia is the disease symptom that is likely to follow.

Increased levels of aluminum in the brain also affect the catecholamine neurotransmitters, noradrenaline and dopamine, in the frontal cortex, hippocampus, and cerebellum.[29] The neurotoxicity of aluminum depends on the dietary intake of other metal-nutrient ions (an atom or group of atoms with an electrical charge) such as copper, zinc, iron, and magnesium. For instance, both noradrenaline and dopamine levels in the cortex and cerebellum decrease when there is a copper deficiency in the diet.[30] High aluminum concentrations absorbed by individuals over a lifetime result in numerous other adverse physiological effects in the cells, such as increased amounts of proline, lysine, arginine, and other amino acids in brain cells. This accumulation of basic protein in the fluid surrounding the nucleus (the actual brain cell body called *perikarya*) leads to an alteration in neuronal excitability which turns out to be responsible for the erratic and convulsive effects seen in aluminum neurotoxicity.[31]

ALUMINUM NEUROENCEPHALOPATHY

In our beginning chapters we described Alzheimer's disease as being characterized by the presence of numerous senile plaques and neurofibrillary tangles within the neocortex and hippocampus. The neurofibrillary tangles comprise groups of pairs of twisted filaments 22 nanomoles in diameter with a constriction down to 10 nanomoles with every 80 nanomoles.[32,33] Investigations of enriched fractions of tables from patients with Alzheimer's disease show that these abnormal filaments have a substructure of six protofilaments.[34] The structure of each protofilament is beaded and joined by longitudinal and lateral crosslinks.[35] While the absolute causes of these protofilaments, twisted filaments, neurofibrillary tangles, and senile plaques remain unknown, toxic substances, and most especially aluminum, are strongly implicated.[36,37,38]

Investigations in mixed populations of patients with Alzheimer's disease and older people with brain diseases have shown a strong correlation between the amount of senile plaques and a decrease in the ability to perform mental functions, such as arithmetic.[39] There is a similar relationship between the numbers of brain cells containing neurofibrillary tangles and cognitive decline.[40] Thus, a well-established relationship exists between senile plaques and the loss of mental abilities.[41]

In autopsy examinations of the brains of deceased Alzheimer's disease patients, Dr. McLaughlan found concentrations of aluminum, which he had found to be cytotoxic in cats and rabbits during his earlier laboratory experiments.[42] (A cytotoxic substance is one that is detrimental or destructive to cells.) Similar amounts of the metal were not detected in the brains of neurologically normal patients.[43] The metal in the patients who show dementia was not distributed homogeneously within the brain. There was a significant elevation of aluminum in the brain with age.[44]

Carrying these findings further, studies of human autopsy material by using a combination of X-rays and electron microscopes have led to claims by research pathologists of a very precise localization of aluminum in the nuclei of neurons containing tangles.[45,46] The metal was found only in brain cells with neurofibrillary tangles in both Alzheimer's disease and non-demented elderly persons. Based on these findings, therefore, the investigators decided that strong circumstantial evidence prevails for the presence of increased levels of aluminum in the brains of Alzheimer's disease patients. Moreover, the investigations affirm that aluminum is localized only in those brain cells that have undergone neurofibrillary degeneration.

THE NEUROTOXIC EFFECTS OF ALUMINUM

Clear neuropathological changes caused by high concentrations of aluminum show themselves in the central nervous system. Behavioral, biochemical, electrophysiological (body repsonses tied to impulses generated within), and morphological changes have been recorded in live animals and in cultured cells. Evidence is clear that both acute[47] and chronic,[48,49,50] focal[51] and more generalized[52] changes in the central nervous system do develop from the living organism's ingestion of aluminum particles. The conclusion among researchers from animal experiments they performed using powdered aluminum is that the neurotoxic effect produced is dose-related. The more metallic material given, the greater the damage to brain cells over time.[53]

The major lesion seen in the brain cells of animals that develop Alzheimer's disease is the neurofibrillary tangle, the same as in humans. Many animal species develop these brain tangles through the course of life. However, for rabbits the brain-tissue tangles form within a matter of days of exposure to high concentrations of aluminum in neurons *in vivo* (within the live animal) and *in vitro* (within animal cells in the test tube). The protein components of the tangles formed in rabbits have been investigated, and they differ somewhat from brain tangles that form in larger animals such as cows. (Experiments were done on bovine 51K-dalton neurofilamentous proteins.)[54] Chemicals from the immune system counter-react to aluminum-induced tangle-protein which, in turn, reacts to serum prepared from 160K-dalton polypeptide of cow neurofilaments. There is also immunochemical cross-reaction between tangle-protein and blood antigens from both chicken brain and human sciatic nerves.[55]

As mentioned earlier, aluminum does influence the properties of enzymes in the synaptasomal membranes and also affects enzymes involved in neurotransmitter metabolism. Remember that aluminum ingestion has an effect on choline and dopamine uptake by synaptosome preparations. The effect of aluminum on the neurotransmitter enzymes choline acetyltransferase (ChAT) and acetylcholinesterase (AChE) is acknowledged among investigators. To illustrate, neurofibrillary degeneration occurs in regions of the brain showing pronounced deficits in the activities of ChAT and AChE. These findings highlight that the degeneration is a cause of the deficit in neurotransmitter activity. Conversely, as in a cycle, the inactivity could come from the degeneration.

The activities of both neurotransmitters, ChAT and AChE, were reduced in rabbits when they were dosed with McIntyre A1 powder to the point of neurointoxication.[56] Then there was a decrease in the activity of ChAT in the cholinergic neurons of the spinal cord.[52] An Alzheimer's disease investigator showed that when pregnant rats were exposed to an active chemical salt, aluminum chlorohydrate, found in cake mixes, there was a marked decrease in neurotransmission activity of AChE in the rat mothers' offspring.[57] An examination of the ChAT and AChE enzymes in the spinal cords of rabbits with aluminum neuroencephalopathy showed typical neurofibrillary degeneration but no significant alteration in the enzyme activities.[24] (The physiological activity of enzymes is another marker for how aluminum affects the brain.)

Aluminum lodged in the brain has an affinity for cancer causing agents.[56] Extensive studies of aluminum on DNA reveal certain changes in the binding of carcinogenic complexes because of interactions between DNA and aluminum.[58] In high concentrations, aluminum influences chromosomal structure in human lymphocytes and in glial cells (cells of the central nervous system) in the test tube. The investigator saw DNA-template damage, a precursor to brain cancer.[59] Aluminum also influences the physiological process of hormone-induced gene expression in insect cells.[60] Aluminum also binds corticosterone to receptor proteins in rabbits with aluminum neuroencephalopathy of the Alzheimer's type.[61]

All of these data show that DNA and aluminum do interact so as to alter cellular function. Histochemical and electron microscopical techniques indicate that the metal is localized in the nuclei of neurons with neurofibrillary tangles. The metal inhibits the coding reaction for genes that determine the formation of enzymes involved in the metabolism of neurofibrillary proteins.[62]

CONTROVERSY ABOUT THE ALUMINUM/ALZHEIMER'S CONNECTION

A prolonged period of controversy has been carried on among medical scientists about the presence of elevated aluminum concentrations in the brains of Alzheimer's disease patients. Now, finally, there is agreement about the source of discord. It turns out that the size of the population samples used in the different studies and the choice of control material had been the cause of this dispute. The controversy is dissipating at last.

Dr. McLaughlan showed that concentrations of aluminum were localized in several areas of the brain. Differences, he said, could be detected between aluminum accumulated merely in the brains of elderly people during their lifetimes and the metal content of Alzheimer's diseased brains. Another group of researchers led by William R. Markesberry, M.D., chairman of the medical and scientific advisory board of the Alzheimer's Association, said that the aluminum content of demented brains was not focalized at all but generally was diversified in the tissues. Then, Dr. Markesberry came up with the solution to their variable findings. He put forth that the reason for the differences between his group's observations and those made by McLaughlan's group resides in the use of aluminum compounds in water treatment plants. Dr. Markesberry pointed out that the patients sampled by Dr. McLaughlan came from the Toronto region of Canada where alums (colorless, white, astringent-tasting, evaporating aluminum compounds) are used by the majority of water treatment plants for producing a settling of sediment. Whereas the Markesberry population samples were taken from rural eastern Kentucky and the Lexington region where the use of aluminum compounds in the water supply is rare.[63] Thus at least one dispute about

aluminum toxicity being the source of Alzheimer's disease has been set-
tled.

All of the scientific community did conclude that Alzheimer's-disease
dementia is associated with several factors such as age, environmental
effects, and the presence of toxic metals in the affected individual's metabolism. The neurotoxicity of aluminum is increased by the dietary intake
of various metallic ions such as insufficient concentrations of zinc[30] and
excessive intake of arsenic, cadmium, iron, lead, manganese, mercury, or
additional toxic metals.[31] There is an age-related increase in the concentration of aluminum in many tissues, and this has an obvious bearing on the
relationship between aluminum and Alzheimer's disease.[64]

Does aluminum taken repeatedly in the diet, medication, or water supply
predispose one to being the eventual victim of dementia? In an important
study, the aluminum content of all food, water, medication, urine, and feces
was determined for a group of patients. When the aluminum intake was less
than five milligrams per day, the element was in a slightly negative balance
in the bodies of these individuals. Yet, when the patients' diet was supplemented with common, over-the-counter, aluminum-containing antacids, the
toxic metal was retained in the patients' metabolism. It is certain that the
potential storage effects of aluminum must be considered when anyone takes
antacids for long periods. Also, while there are no acute neurological effects
after ingesting the metal as part of the food or medicine supply, a lifetime
exposure probably will lead to progressive alterations of brain cells and
eventual serious neuronal damage.[65]

RESEARCH AND ANIMAL RIGHTS ACTIVISTS

The coauthors are animal rights adherents, but we are aware of the need
to employ laboratory models for purposes of research. Since Alzheimer's
disease must not be experimentally-induced in human beings, there is no
other way to come to conclusions about Alzheimer's disease except by use
of animal models.

Much of the laboratory research for Alzheimer's disease is carried out
on three-month-old rabbits, rats, or mice. Young rabbits are the animals
used most often for experiments because they are so susceptible to the toxic
effects of aluminum. Advancing the cause of medical research on behalf of
middle-aged and older people everywhere, the baby bunnies aid mankind.

Still, in human tissues there is this definite age-related increase in the
concentration of aluminum. With Alzheimer's disease being age-related,
this experimentation factor has been neglected in the search for a model of

the neuropathology of Alzheimer's disease. The continuing choice of young rabbits or their fetal material for the induction of neurofibrillary change actually is slowing the search for a species with more closely-related pathological features.

A simple means of performing more accurate research on Alzheimer's disease could prevail. If laboratory animals must be used at all, older animals should be studied so as to determine whether age does affect the lesion induced by aluminum. It is always difficult to make age-for-age comparisons between different species, but the maximum lifespan of the rabbit is over six years, the mouse and rat about 3.5 years, and that of the human about 120 years. Alzheimer's disease develops in middle life so that it would be more appropriate and more advantageous to study the neuropathological consequences of aluminum toxicity in animals of a corresponding age. A flaw in research to this point is that the different states of maturation being dealt with gives rise to misleading results as to the susceptibility of different species and to the type of lesion produced. This is part of the reason for controversy in coming to conclusions about the aluminum connection with Alzheimer's disease.

The general consensus among scientists is that aluminum intoxication is not a primary event in the Alzheimer's syndrome, but most certainly it is a secondary feature. Dr. McLaughlan therefore postulates that some pathological occurrence, which is unrelated to aluminum, selectively alters the blood-brain barrier to be more receptive to the metal and allows aluminum deposits in the victim's brain cells.[37]

The reputed, aluminum-neutralizing, metalloprotein that ordinarily protects the brain against metal toxicity does not get synthesized by the affected patient. The toxic metal gains access to neuronal chromatin and lethal effects result. Assuredly, the association of aluminum with neurons bearing the neurofibrillary lesion in humans makes it foolish to ignore the obvious aluminum/Alzheimer's connection.

Part III
The Heavy Metal Connection

A heavy metal is any metallic mineral with a specific gravity of five or more times that of water. Aluminum, for instance, while definitely toxic, is not classified in the group of heavy metals because its specific gravity is 2.7. All of the heavy metals, when given in large enough concentrations, produce symptoms and signs of poisoning in animals and humans. But some of them, in just trace quantities, are necessary to sustain good health. The heavy metals are:

Antimony	Cobalt	Manganese	Thallium
Arsenic	Copper	Mercury	Tin
Bismuth	Gallium	Nickel	Uranium
Cadmium	Gold	Platinum	Vanadium
Cerium	Iron	Silver	Zinc
Chromium	Lead	Tellurium	

None of these metallic elements is biodegradable, but rather accumulate until they leach from the soil and enter the sea. In oceans they tend eventually to fall to the bottom; however, during the process of traveling to great bodies of water the heavy metals can enter the bodies of humans. There they do immense harm by the nature of their poisons, which produce metabolic dysfunctions.

Believing that you cannot do much about it, ordinarily one might shrug away the effects of heavy-metal toxicity. But the high technology of our Western industrial society is making heavy metal an integral part of everyday living. Hence, all of us are are in greater danger of exposure to the pathology caused by metallic poisons. For example, organized dentistry is probably the most dangerous of all the human healthcare professions. F. Fuller Royal, M.D., H.M.D., of Las Vegas, Nevada, points out in his article, "Are Dentists Contributing to our Declining Health?" in the May 1990 issue of the *Townsend Letter for Doctors*, "The role the dentist plays is directly or indirectly related to the etiology of a large number of diseases, some occurring at sites far distant from the teeth. This role is becoming more significant as dentists continue to fill teeth with amalgam and alloy materials. I, along with members of my family, have had all of the toxic metals removed from every tooth and replaced with safer, non-toxic metals or materials."

A few of the heavy metals are especially hazardous to your health, and these are the ones that we describe in this section.

CHAPTER 10

Dental-Amalgam Dementia and Other Mercury Poisons

Amid the continual discovery of new, manmade, health hazards in our changing environment, the material used for filling dental cavities has proven itself poisonous. Mercury, a toxic heavy metal, is packed into over four-fifths of all dental cavities that 98 percent of the North American population develops. The result is subclinical illness (illness that is not readily apparent) with vague indications of mercury toxicity. Signs and symptoms of mercury poisoning are similar to the symptoms experienced with arthritis, getting drunk, premature aging, immune system breakdown, cardiovascular disease, gastrointestinal disturbances, allergies, and numerous conditions whose causes until now have been labeled "unknown" or "psychosomatic." However, the worst effect of mercury poisoning that we have come across is dementia, and in particular, Alzheimer's disease.

Many chronically ill patients have returned to the dental chair for removal of silver-mercury dental amalgams, following clinical studies and disclosures of research results by a few courageous physicians and dentists during the past twelve years. There have been exposés by members of the media—in particular, a segment of the *60 Minutes* television show hosted by Morley Safer—that have alerted people to the danger of their silver dental fillings. The implications of dental-filling toxicity in Western industrialized nations across the world is staggering. Such exposés are fated to shake all of the dental profession to its very roots.

What if it becomes generally established that senile Alzheimer's disease is triggered by so-called "silver" mercury amalgams? Such a possibility is not at all remote. In fact, two western industrialized countries—Germany and Sweden—already acknowledge this fact and have banned the use of mercury as dental filling material. The powerful Swedish Health and Welfare System demanded in July 1993 that the Swedish government submit a five-year plan for discontinuing the use of amalgam permanently because of environmental pollution and disease development in dental patients.[1]

ARE MOST OF US FATED TO BECOME MAD AS HATTERS?

Among the earliest of occupational injuries by chronic exposure to toxic agents were British workers in the hat trade, who used quicksilver (mercury) in the hat-making process. After long-term exposure to direct skin contact and inhalation, the hatters developed symptoms of mental deterioration on an industry-wide basis. Many were locked into insane asylums for life. The expression, "mad as a hatter," was derived from the symptoms of severe mental illness among persons in this trade.

Mirror makers and goldsmiths who handled mercury also became as mad as the hatters.

Dentists, their assistants and hygienists, and dental workers in laboratories are exposed to inhalation or skin contact with mercury. One of the frequent violations of the U.S. Occupational Safety and Health Administration (OSHA) regulations arises from unsafe storage and usage procedures for mercury in various aspects of dentistry.

It is a scientific and sociological truth that suicide among dentists is the highest of any learned profession. Not only do dentists destroy themselves most frequently, but they disrupt their marriages more often than any other professional people. Of all occupational groups, the divorce rate for dentists is the highest. Psychiatrists and sociologists have traced such antisocial behavior for dental workers to their handling of mercury.

In modern times, thousands of other workers in hazardous situations are exposed to mercury every day. As with dentists, their occupations preclude that they are going to get mercury poisoning. Here are some of the jobs people do that have them at continuous risk of dementia and death from mercury poisoning:[2]

- artifical flower workers
- cap loaders
- cartridge makers
- chemical workers that make: acid aldehyde, acetic acid, acetone, alcohol, chlorine, cyanogen, disinfectant

- cosmetic workers
- dental laboratory workers
- dental technicians
- detonator cleaners & fillers
- dry battery makers
- dye makers

- electroplaters
- embalmers
- embalming fluid makers
- engravers
- explosive makers
- felt hat makers
- file makers
- fulminate amalgam workers
- fur handlers
- gold refiners
- hair workers
- incandescent lamp workers
- ink makers
- lead platers
- lithographers
- manometer makers
- mercury boiler workers
- mercury bolt makers
- mercury bronzers
- mercury miners
- mercury salt workers
- mercury smelter workers
- mercury solder workers
- mercury switch makers
- mercury vapor lamp makers
- metal refiners
- mirror silverers
- motion picture machine operators
- painters & paint makers
- pharmaceutical workers
- photographic workers
- physicians
- pottery decorators
- printers
- radio tube makers
- storage battery makers
- thermometer makers
- welders
- wood preservers
- zinc electrode makers

Worse still are the millions of people—dental patients—with mercury amalgam fillings in their teeth. There are 235 million of them in the United States alone. As they chew, microscopic particles of the toxic agent float as a gas into their brains to steadily set out conditions for dementia. (Think about it! Are you numbered among those many millions of unfortunates?)

As we have implied in the previous paragraph, every time the amalgam filling is chewed upon, mercury vapor escapes into the brain tissues to bring on its destruction. Some amount of memory loss or outright dementia must be the eventual result.

THE DEADLINESS OF MERCURY

Mercuric compounds are the potential sources of the mercuric ion that, at the worst, kills all living things, or, at the very least, causes cellular damage and organ dysfunction. When ingested in any form mercury produces destructive changes in the mucous membrane linings of the gastrointestinal tract. It enters the blood circulation, travels to the tissues, and then damages literally every cell with which it comes into contact. Mercury molecules, no matter how tiny the amounts that enter the body, cause destruction, particularly in cells of the kidneys, liver, and brain.

When workers in the occupations that we listed above handle a mercuric component during product manufacture, they are affected first with abnormal physiological function and then later with outright pathology. The cells of their bodies and brains undergo numerous chemical alterations. Over time, and even long after they have discontinued the use of mercury in their routine activities, the uninformed unfortunates will experience the following series of abnormal physiological events:

- The blood sugar elevates, remains high for a time until insulin is dumped into the blood stream by the islands of Langerhans in the pancreas.

- Then the level of sugar drops precipitously and remains low.

- Hypoglycemia sets in with its depressive set of symptoms consisting of physical weakness, headache, hunger, problems with vision, loss of muscle coordination, anxiety, personality changes, memory loss, irregular reasoning, delirium, coma, and the potential of death.

- The blood-potassium level increases because of leakage of potassium ions out of the damaged cells.

- There is seepage of the mineral components of cells into surrounding cellular fluids, because mercury alters the permeability of individual cell walls.

- The entire ion transfer of minerals gets disrupted at any site where mercury has touched.

Mercury salts are pharmaceutical-like diuretics that were sometimes used in the past for medicinal purposes by physicians. When mercurial compounds get into the circulatory system they cause rapid liberation of calcium from the soft tissues and bones. This calcium liberation brings on an excess of calcium over sodium in the cellular fluids, as well. Sodium and water get driven from the spaces around cells and into the general circulation. There will be a resulting increase in fluid (plasma) level of the blood, which will call the kidneys into action. The kidneys may eliminate the excess of water into urine, but it is at a price. The tissues lose necessary mineral ions that ordinarily are required for other physiological purposes.

Because it has a strong affinity for sulfur, mercury tends to neutralize enzymes containing sulfur in the body. The sulfur enzymes are damaged or destroyed, which ends with the body's vital enzymes becoming useless when needed for normal physiological functioning. There is no more destructive mechanism for human enzymes than this toxic metal.

SYMPTOMS OF MERCURY POISONING

We have mentioned a few of the signs and symptoms of mercury toxicity, but there are many more we might cite. Chief among them are affectations of the cerebral spinal fluid, central nervous system, and the brain. For instance, symptoms of the danger often are related to actual nerve or brain damage—all close to or duplicating the indications of Alzheimer's disease being present in a person. Some of the dementia symptoms show themselves sooner, others later.

Among those many symptoms and signs of the mercury toxicity syndrome are:

Mental

- depression
- fearfulness
- frequent bouts of anger
- hallucinations
- inability to accept criticism
- inability to concentrate
- indecision
- irritability
- loss of memory
- metallic taste
- persecution complex
- slight tremors of hands, head, lips, tongue, jaw, or eyelid
- weight loss

Physical

- anemia
- anorexia
- chronically low body temperature
- constriction of the visual field
- drowsiness

- excitability
- headache
- hypersensitive reflexes
- insomnia
- loss of energy

Alzheimer's disease from prolonged mercury exposure is likely to make itself distinctly known toward the end of a person's life. When the brain becomes involved with mercury poisoning, often there will be additional signs and symptoms, such as trembling of the hands and fingers, stuttering and stammering speech, reduced energy, depression, irritability, temper tantrums, and constant complaining about circumstances and situations.

Certain signs can be recognized in the mouth too—forms of dental disease—such as receding gums, bleeding gums, bone loss in the dental arch, foul breath, leukoplakia (precancerous, raised, thickened, white patches), stomatitis (any inflammation of the mouth), ulceration of the gums, palate, or tongue, burning sensation around the inside of the cheeks or in the throat, tissue pigmentation, tooth mobility, and a blue mark at the gum line near to the mercury-amalgam filling itself.

Other systemic effects relate to the cardiovascular system such as feeble and irregular pulse, alterations in blood pressure, pain or pressure in the chest area, and irregular heartbeat with either tachycardia (rapid heart rate) or bradycardia (abnormally slow heart rate).

Or you could have respiratory symptoms consisting of persistent cough, emphysema, or shallow and irregular respiration.

Immunological weakness may be manifested by allergies, asthma, rhinitis, sinusitis, and lymph node enlargement, especially of the cervical nodes.

Endocrine dysfunction might be present, which takes the form of low body temperature, excessive perspiration, and cold and clammy skin, especially of the hands and feet.

If you are the one affected by mercury, you may feel dizziness, hear ringing or noises in the ears, sense fatigue, muscle weakness, inability to catch your breath, apathy, numbness and tingling of the extremities and lips, hearing difficulty, speech disorder, neuromuscular incoordination, emotional instability, joint pains, and general central nervous system dysfunction.

Finally, you could experience vague swellings, kidney damage, skin eruptions, loss of memory, paralysis, loss of vision, decline of intellect, hallucinations, manic-depression, coma, and eventually death.

Here is a summary listing of signs and symptoms to alert you to the syndrome associated with mercury toxicity:[3]

anemia	flu-like discomforts	mouth sores
anxiety	forgetfulness	nervousness
a sensitive tongue	gingivitis	numbness
bad breath	hallucinations	nutritional
bleeding gums	high blood pressure	disturbances
bronchitis	insomnia	paralysis
chills	irregular gait	shaking
colitis	irritability	sore throat
coughing and nausea	joint pains	stomach pains
depression	loss of appetite	trembling
drowsiness	low blood sugar	urinary frequency
erratic behavior	loosening of the teeth	or irregularity
fatigue	mental disturbances	visual changes
fever	metallic taste	vomiting

WHAT PREVENTIVE MEASURES SHOULD BE PURSUED WITH MERCURY?

Simply put, the most effective treatment for chronic exposure to mercury is to remove the mercury from the affected person's environment. If it is at all possible, quit any job that involves the handling of this toxic metal.

It is certainly vital to remove mercury in the form of "silver" dental amalgams (which contain almost no silver at all) from one's mouth. This book's coauthors both have had all forms of mercury removed from their mouths, including fillings, root canals, bridges, etc.

New York dentist Dr. John Miller has not filled a tooth with amalgams in nearly 15 years.

Throughout his practice, Iowa family dentist Dr. Carl W. Svare was steadily replacing his patients' amalgam fillings with gold.

New York allergy specialist Alfred V. Zamm, M.D. has had all silver fillings removed from his own mouth too.

Colorado dental researcher Dr. Hal A. Huggins—author of *It's All in Your Head*, an exposé on the dangers of mercury amalgams—is traveling across the North American continent to lecture about the dangers amalgam fillings present.

Massachusetts dentist and physician Dr. Victor Penzer has lost his license to practice dentistry because he has gone to the public with warnings about mercury amalgams. The Massachusetts Dental Association, which brought charges against Dr. Penzer, fears that it—along with the American Dental Association—will be in jeopardy of class action suits for malpractice if dental amalgams are shown to cause dementia and/or other degenerative diseases.

These courageous health professionals are taking actions against mercury in our mouths. The toxic metal content in fillings of silver-mercury amalgam could possibly cause conditions ranging from diarrhea and insomnia to multiple sclerosis and Alzheimer's disease. Informed dentists and physicians advise that they are detecting mercury toxicity in their patients, and they urge those who test positive for the metal to have their dental amalgams replaced with some other material as soon as possible.

"Silver" fillings are really amalgams of mercury, copper, silver, tin, zinc, and occasionally nickel. (Nickel is poisonous too.) Mercury, which is added to harden the mixture, makes up one half of the amalgamated metals. Mercury that is ingested or that even touches the skin is poisonous. When it is combined with the other metals in the dental amalgam it does not poison the patient immediately. Instead, mercury vapors are released in the mouth in low-level concentrations when fillings are subjected to the pressure and abrasion of chewing. The mercury vapors escaping from the fillings do some of the gradual poisoning.

Recent scientific studies show that there is a correlation between silver-mercury fillings and higher levels of mercury gas in the mouth. This allows some of the metallic toxin to enter the bloodstream, go through the blood-brain barrier, and damage neurons. Studies done at the University of Calgary and at Oral Roberts University, reported in *The Journal of Dental Research*, found that the level of mercury in the breath after chewing was more than fifteen times greater in people with silver-amalgam fillings than in those who did not have the fillings.

Dentists who warn against mercury also say that as many as 25 percent of people they test are allergic to the toxic substance in silver-mercury amalgams. Furthermore, some people with metallic fillings have electromagnetic fields develop around their teeth—the equivalent of batteries—presenting them with many illness symptoms, including tuning into local radio stations in their heads.

RECOVERY FROM MERCURY INTOXICATION

In the fall of 1979, 57-year-old Phillip K. of Lakeland, Florida, developed a kind of erratic behavior that caused him to talk to himself, hallucinate on and off, and generally give the impression to people around him that he was acting abnormally. Phil lived alone and there was no close relative who took an interest in his welfare. But he had friends, others who lived in the same trailer park as this lonely fellow. He seemed unable to manage by himself and began to lose weight from malnourishment. Eventually the neighbors around Phil's trailer called in paramedics from the Lakeland Municipal Hospital, and they transported the man by ambulance to that facility's outpatient clinic. There, diagnostic tests were performed and it was discovered that among other health difficulties, Phillip's overriding illness was mercury poisoning.

He had been a house painter for years and then changed his occupation to working for a mortician as an apprentice embalmer. His job was to mix the embalming fluids, which contained quantities of mercury. Moreover, when the progressive hospital resident on duty at the Lakeland hospital looked in Phil's mouth, he counted twenty-seven silver dental amalgams, most of which were disintegrating from excessive wear. It turns out that the man's mouth had not been worked on for nearly fourteen years.

The patient was transferred from the outpatient clinic for entry directly into the hospital where he spent ten days undergoing tests and therapy and then fourteen days recuperating at home. It was noted that he suffered from dementia, liver damage, and failing kidneys. It is known that these three major disabilities may result from mercury toxicity.

Since the patient was actually showing the results of mercury poisoning and his mouth was loaded down with all those amalgams packed into dental cavities, Phil was taken to visit another physician rather than a dentist, Roy Kupsinel, M.D., of Oviedo, Florida. Dr. Kupsinel specializes in testing for and treating mercury toxicity from amalgam fillings.

Dr. Kupsinel determined with diagnostic tests that silver-mercury amalgams had something to do with the dementia, liver disease, kidney malfunction, and other symptoms Phillip had sustained. (For more information on the diagnostic tests, see Chapter 11.) Thereafter, the unlucky fellow consulted silver-mercury amalgam opposition dentist Michael F. Ziff, D.D.S., of Orlando, Florida. Dr. Ziff is director of the Foundation for Toxic-Free Dentistry (P.O. Box 60810, Orlando, Florida 32860; 800–331–2303). The patient had his amalgam fillings removed and restored with plastic substitutes by Dr. Ziff. Moreover, he underwent chelation therapy for the heavy-metal toxicity.

Immediately the fellow got rid of the headaches that had been plaguing him on a daily basis, yet had never been considered as a symptom. These headaches had been such a normal occurrence for Phil that he had not even mentioned them to the hospital resident who had recorded his health history at Lakeland. While his liver and kidneys remained damaged, their dysfunction lessened.

The most dramatic result, however, was the improvement of his mental capabilities. Phillip's reasoning recovered and his memory came back. His behavior could no longer be considered erratic or isolationist. He became conversational, friendly, and sociable with everyone, whereas before his approach to society had been hermit-like.

Dr. Kupsinal examined the mercury content of Phil's body tissues again and found it to be greatly reduced. This result came about merely from the man's discontinuing an occupation that had him in touch with mercury on practically a daily basis. Also, because the amalgams were removed, he was no longer exposed to the mercury vapors from chewing. He became mentally normal once again. Twelve years later he still shows no signs of dementia. He remains sane, active, and a productive member of the community in Lakeland, Florida.

MINAMATA DISEASE

Cats that have been fed fish containing methyl mercury show significant brain atrophy and Alzheimer's-type lesions. Laboratory experiments with such cats cause severe neurological symptoms akin to Alzheimer's disease. The neurological poisoning the animals exhibit is called "Minamata disease," named after contamination in Minamata Bay, Japan during the period of 1932 to 1968 that resulted in one of the two largest outbreaks of methyl mercury poisoning ever recorded. (The other serious mercury poisoning episode took place in Iraq between 1956 and 1972.)

In Japan, the Chisso Factory of Minamata used mercury as a catalyst for making acetic acid (acetaldehyde). From this they manufactured vinyl chloride, to turn into floor tiles and artificial leather. During the fifty-six years of acetic acid production by Chisso, the factory dumped an estimated 100 tons of mercurial wastes into the coastal bay of Minamata. This caused a poisoning of the bay's fish from which the unknowing local Japanese made three meals a day. By 1982, 1,773 residents of the Minamata Bay province had been declared victims of severe methylmercuric poisoning resulting in serious brain damage, and 456 had died.[4,5,6,7]

Our research, performed recently among Japanese scientists, turns up that 5,000 more people suffering from Minamata-related neurological deficits await processing. There is no known means of correcting their conditions except the chelation techniques we describe in Part III. Chelation therapy is an ongoing detoxification process, and just fifty Japanese per month are able to receive treatment at present because of a lack of facilities. Biotoxicologist Bruce Halstead, M.D., Medical Director of the World Life Research Institute (23000 Grand Terrace Road, Colton, California 92324; telephone (714) 825–4773, teleFAX 714–783–3477) was employed by the World Health Organization to uncover the toxicological ramifications of Minamata disease and arrive at a method of treatment. Dr. Halstead discovered that the methyl mercury produced by the Chisso factory was the source of poisoning and declared that chelation therapy was its remedy.

Minamata disease is just one illustration of the prevalence of mercury in the food chain as being the reason for periodic bouts of catastrophic poisoning. Epidemics have arisen in Sweden in the late 1950s; Iraq in 1956, 1960, 1970, and 1972; Nigata Province in Japan in the mid-1960s; Northwestern Ontario and Quebec, Canada from 1961 to 1970; Pakistan in 1963; Guatemala in 1966; and the United States in 1970. A main cause of these outbreaks was the use of methyl mercury in agriculture as a fungicide. Its application to seed corn for planting makes the corn a potential threat of mercury poisoning to both livestock and people. Methyl mercury has since been banned in the United States as a fungicide, but it is still in use in third-world countries. If it is ingested by domestic animals such as cows, it becomes part of their beef or milk that, in turn, is consumed by humans.

In Iraq this antifungal treatment was used on seed corn that was used for the making of bread by illiterate Iraqis. They could not read warning the labels on the packaging. Eventually the poisoned bread was eaten, causing 6,530 people to be admitted to hospitals with neurological disease and brain dysfunction. There were 459 Iraqi deaths attributed directly to this methyl mercury poisoning.[8,9]

In the periodic table of elements, mercury is number eighty of the eighty-one stable elements in the universe. It is omnipresent on earth but need not be dangerous if it is not in close proximity to man. Unfortunately, however, the commercial use of mercury is increasing. You may be getting your disabling dose even now as you munch down on amalgam dental fillings. In the next chapter we advise about the disabilities from mercury toxicity that affect the body and brain and how to counteract them.

CHAPTER 11

Body and Brain Pathology
of Mercury Toxicity

On June 11, 1983, Tom Warren, a successful insurance agent living in Olympia, Washington, was diagnosed as the victim of Alzheimer's disease. He was fifty-four years old. His diagnosis resulted from a series of laboratory and psychological tests that left no doubt of the patient's Alzheimer's disease. The CAT scan performed at St. Peter Hospital in Olympia, for instance, actually showed that Tom suffered from atrophy (shrinkage) of the frontal and temporal lobes on both sides of his brain. The radiologist reported that the two clefts usually present on the brain's surface (the sylvian and interhemispheric fissures) were abnormally widened within the body of the patient's neurological tissue. With such an unmistakable diagnosis, the man's fate was sealed.

The family physician who attended him sadly pronounced the sentence that Tom had but seven years to live. Most of that time, the doctor implied, would be a waking death with loss of short-term memory and a steadily diminishing long-term memory. He would deteriorate into a vegetable-like existence until the loved ones around him eventually would welcome death for the non-person he had become. It was horrible to contemplate!

Modern medical technology had nothing to offer as treatment. None of the so-called "wonder" drugs worked for Alzheimer's disease. Internists, geriatricians, neurologists, and other medical experts could not even pinpoint the cause of the dementia connected with Alzheimer's disease.

Yet Tom Warren reversed his pathology and went on to author a book about his experience, *Beating Alzheimer's* (Avery Publishing, 1991). The book describes how he came back from the living dead by shifting his lifestyle to a more natural mode. He rid himself of food allergies, avoided environmental substances that brought on sensitivity reactions, eliminated subclinical vitamin and mineral deficiencies with nutritional supplements, took chelation therapy, and, most important of all for him, he sought dental care to remove from his mouth those toxic silver-mercury fillings that for decades had been poisoning him every time he chewed. Perpetually, silver dental fillings were vaporizing and sending off minute quantities of mercury gas into his brain. It is true that chelation therapy removes residual mercury and other heavy metals, but the treatment works many times more effectively when the metallic source of poisoning is removed first.

As part of the book's foreword, the dentist who eliminated mercury from Tom Warren's mouth, Russ Borneman, D.D.S., of Anacortes, Washington, writes:

> I have been a dentist for over twelve years. During the last six years, I have not placed a silver-mercury filling into any tooth. The reason is simple; mercury is a poison that should not be used in a person's mouth. The scientific research overwhelmingly supports my stand. However, the American Dental Association believes that not enough mercury comes out of fillings to be a problem. I have a Mercury Vapor Analyzer that accurately measures the mercury-vapor release from fillings in the mouth. Daily, I get readings that are above the Occupational Safety and Health Administration's standards for an occupational-setting exposure. This means that many people are walking around breathing mercury vapors at levels that would shut down industries.

So the patient had mercury removed from where it had been implanted at multiple sites in his teeth, from childhood onward. He also enhanced his lifestyle with healthier practices than before Alzheimer's disease came upon him. He also did an immense amount of study work with the assistance of his loving wife Louise, who is a career pharmacologist. In following a stringent program of self-improvement for body and brain, within four years, when a second series of CAT scans were taken, Tom Warren's brain was no longer atrophied. Cells that had been dysfunctional did restore themselves. Dead neurons did not come back to work again, but those that were merely damaged did. On April 30, 1987, the imaging report was negative for Alzheimer's disease. The St. Peter Hospital radiologist's report read "CT OF THE HEAD without contrast shows normal sized unshifted ventricles. Cavum septum. No atrophy appreciated. IMPRESSION: Negative CT."

Since X-ray films do not lie, this laboratory/clinical finding is not anecdotal evidence in any way. The patient's dementia had reversed itself and he was completely lucid once again. He accomplished this by eliminating the daily doses of mercury he was getting from his environment.[1]

WHY IS MERCURY ALLOWED IN DENTAL FILLINGS BUT NOT IN PAINT?

During the summer of 1990, the United States Environmental Protection Agency permanently banned mercury from being incorporated as an ingredient of interior latex house paints. Compliance with the ban since then has eliminated the dangerously high levels of mercury vapor that had been present in recently painted homes. Still, dentists continue to put toxic mercury into the mouths of Americans when it has been verified as being harmful to us in our homes.

Just as lead-based paint is known by most persons to be poisonous for children who ingest paint chips from their apartment house walls, mercury-based paint is even more toxic. People living in houses recently decorated with latex-based paint laced with mercury as coloring matter, or for another purpose, invariably show urine-mercury levels as high as 118 micrograms (mcg) per grams of creatinine. (Creatinine is a substance found in blood, urine, and muscle tissue that can be used as a measure of kidney function.) The urine-mercury elevates to such dangerous levels because of vapors escaping from the structure's newly painted walls. Mercury gas is extremely toxic. Disease symptoms from inhaled mercury vapor, in fact, begin at the urine level ranging from about 50 micrograms to 100 micrograms.

The risk grows with increasing exposure. For example, at 50 micrograms of mercury in the urine there will be an early indication of finger tremor on testing. Subclinical illness (subtle changes on some tests, but no overt signs or symptoms as yet) develops in the form of decreased response on examination for the patient's nerve conduction, brain-wave activity, and verbal skills. At 400 micrograms of mercury contamination there will be mild to moderate nerve and brain disease. Symptoms experienced by the victim take the form of depression, irritability, memory loss, minor tremors, and other nervous-system disturbances. Also there will be early signs of disturbed kidney function.

By the time mercury has permeated the patient's full body system at the 750 micrograms urine-mercury concentration, pronounced symptoms will have been exhibited. The poisoned person experiences severe inflammation of the kidneys, swollen gums, pronounced tremors, and other nervous-system disturbances. Thus the risk from mercury vapor depends on the amount and duration of exposure to it. An individual's chronic exposure from all sources is reflected in the concentration of mercury excreted in the urine. Physicians can order a standard test for urinary mercury. As stated, the results of such testing are expressed in micrograms of mercury per gram of creatinine. While no amount of mercury in human urine is acceptable, 4 micrograms per gram is the upper limit of passability in our industrialized and polluted society. How much mercury in urine is burdening your kidneys can be checked with the creatine clearance test. If the readout is high, your source may be mercury present in dental fillings.

Every time you chew for ten minutes, 4 micrograms of mercury escape from each of your dental amalgam fillings. That works out to 0.4 micrograms of poison gas per minute escaping from each filled dental cavity. Chew up a twelve-ounce steak and you will have poisoned yourself into illness.

The mercury-vapor detector, an instrument that Dr. Borneman referred to as a Mercury Vapor Analyzer, measures the amount of mercury fumes in the mouth, sucks up a small volume of air, and multiplies the mercury level to estimate the quantity of toxic gas present in a cubic meter of air. This measurement allows dentists to compare the amount of mercury detected in a patient's mouth with permissible levels in the workplace. Honest dentists who deliver services with integrity become alarmed at the amount of mercury gas coming off of silver dental fillings. Those dentists who parrot the party line disseminated by the American Dental Association (ADA) and who are more interested in the silver in a patient's pocket than that in his or her mouth, just do not care. Because it is convenient for them and conforming to accepted practice, the dentists continue to pack toxic metal into their patients' cavities.

If mercury is banned in house paints, then, why has it not been eliminated from that very intimately attached part of a person's jaw-bone anatomy, dental fillings? All of us have every right to put this question to the profession of dentistry, especially to its trade organization, the ADA. Financial needs and power plays among ADA politicians have kept mercury fillings in place. In the end, however, such mistreatment could be exceedingly costly for patients. If the 98 percent of the American population who are sporting amalgams in their mouths suddenly become aware that dentists have been a source of degenerative diseases and potential death, a class action could very well be brought against dentists everywhere, or at the very least against the ADA.

It is an enigma that makes conventionally-practicing dentists the most destructive healthcare professionals who lay hands on, or inside of, live patients. Anybody suffering from, or involved with, someone having chronic, baffling illness, such as rheumatoid arthritis, multiple sclerosis, Alzheimer's disease, or another degenerative disease could hardly ignore the possibility that mercury might be the key to the health problem—or resist the hope that a simple cure was now possible.[2]

In 1979, dental researchers at the University of Iowa, using the sensitive new measurement techniques, found that chewing does release tiny amounts of mercury vapor from fillings. This finding ran counter to the prevailing belief that no vapor escapes once amalgam has hardened. When scientists took a closer look, they discovered that people with amalgam fillings had more mercury in their blood and urine than did those without. The fluid levels correlate with the size and number of fillings, too. Autopsy studies showed, as well, that there is more mercury in the brain tissue of corpses with amalgams.[3] These are clear indications that mercury liberated from fillings finds its way into body tissues. It brings about toxic effects in the brain and nervous system.[4]

An excellent reference text for the health professional or the victim of mercury toxicity is *Chronic Mercury Toxicity* (Queen & Company, 1988) written by H.L. Queen, M.A., who is a health care educator, secondary researcher, and an investigative medical writer. In this book he describes the insidiousness of the dental amalgam problem and, more importantly, outlines protocols for proper use of intravenous vitamin C and other treatment modalities such as chelation therapy.[5]

DENTAL AMALGAMS ARE HAZARDOUS WASTE

The Environmental Protection Agency (EPA), in 1988, labelled scrap dental amalgam as a hazardous waste. It is highly dangerous for anyone to come in contact with the amalgam material in any way. The EPA declared that scrap amalgam, the portion that remains, after most of it is placed in your cavity as a filling, must be handled with extreme care. According to the Materials Safety Data Sheet for mercury, that the Occupational Safety and Health Administration (OSHA) orders be present in every dental office, it is mandatory for the dentist to handle scrap amalgam in the following manner:

1. Store in unbreakable, tightly sealed containers, away from heat.
2. Use a "no touch" technique for handling amalgam.
3. Store under liquid, preferably glycerin or photographic fixer solution.

Moreover, once a dentist removes a used amalgam filling from your mouth and places it on the tray, it once again becomes a hazardous waste material and must be handled in the same manner described above. If this scrap amalgam or the used amalgam that just came out of your old cavity finds its way into the ground, the dentist who has been less than careful with such amalgam handling may be fined thousands of dollars and face the anger of his professional peers.[6]

Question: Why is dental amalgam less dangerous when packed into the tooth of a living person than when it comes out of that tooth and remains loose on the tray? Answer: It is not less dangerous but offers the same liability to injury. There is no difference, for silver-dental amalgam offers similar poisoning whether vaporizing in someone's mouth or lying inert before a person who comes in contact with its mercury content.

PATHOLOGY CONNECTED TO
MERCURY AMALGAM TOXICITY

Sandra Denton, M.D., former medical director of the Huggins Diagnostic Center, a specialty laboratory devoted almost exclusively to toxicity from mercury amalgams, is certified by the American Board of Chelation Therapy for the treatment of heavy-metal poisoning. Dr. Denton is now in private practice in Anchorage, Alaska. She warns her patients that the mercury in dental fillings is even more dangerous than lead, cadmium, and arsenic. "It has been stated by world regulatory agencies," she advises, "that the smallest amount of mercury that will not cause damage is unknown! How then can we be so certain that the amount coming out of our dental fillings is insignificant?"[7]

The world's foremost researchers on mercury toxicity, Thomas Clarkson, D.D.S., John Hursh, M.D. of the University of Rochester School of Medicine, Magnus Nylander, D.D.S., and Lars Friberg, M.D., of Karolinska Institute in Stockholm, Sweden, concluded from their research that "the release of mercury from dental amalgams makes the predominant contribution to human exposure to inorganic mercury, including mercury vapor in the general population."[8] Therefore, vapor escaping from dental amalgam fillings offers more mercury poisoning than eating contaminated fish, being exposed to latex wall paint, and drinking polluted water.

The International Conference on Biocompatibility of Materials (ICBM) was held in November 1988 in Colorado Springs, Colorado. At this conference most of the world authorities on mercury discussed dental amalgams and other materials commonly used in dentistry (audiotapes of these proceedings are available for your purposes from the Huggins Diagnostic center. You can receive them by telephoning the Huggins laboratory at

(800) 331–2303. The attendees at this biocompatibility conference drafted and signed their official findings that read: "Based on the known toxic potentials of mercury and its documented release from dental amalgams, usage of mercury-containing amalgam increases the health risk of the patients, the dentists, and dental personnel."[9]

Upon their being tested by Joel Butler, Ph.D., professor of psychology, University of North Texas, mental problems were found to be present among 90 percent of all those dentists who use amalgam filling materials. The mercury vapors they inhale at work are affecting their brains adversely. Dr. Butler's abstract of his findings that he presented to ICBM reads as follows:

> Areas of suboptimal function were evident in shifting tasks—attention span, ability to concentrate—recent memory deficits—visual recall, control dyspraxia—tremor and perceptual accuracy in judgment. The dentists' psychological problems were concentrated in the areas of irritability, impatience, tension, frustration, and conflict. Notably absent was calmness for these doctors. Observation of data suggest that the longer a dentist practices, the less ability he or she has to pass the entrance examinations into dental school.

Dr. Butler is alarmed at the implications of his studies. He is informing dentists of the damage that has undermined their personalities and motor skills. Continued use of mercury dental materials by the dental profession is likely to increase the already elevated number of divorces and the high rate of suicide among dentists. Foolishly, the politicians who comprise the profession's bureaucracy are ignoring that admonition. Spouses of dentists beware. Dental personnel take heed for your own safety, for you are exposed to mercury vapors as well.

Multiple sclerosis patients are found to have eight times higher levels of mercury in the cerebrospinal fluid compared with neurologically healthy controls. Inorganic mercury is capable of producing symptoms that are indistinguishable from those of multiple sclerosis.[10]

PATIENT INFORMATION RESEARCH

In Victorville, California, Mark S. Hulet, D.D.S., a dental professional who does research on amalgam materials, has concluded that putting the poisonous metal into his patients' mouths is not only unethical behavior but is also a crime against humanity. Dr. Hulet distributes information to his patients so as to justify his going against the mainstream and using filling materials such as porcelain, composite, and gold rather than amalgam.

In brief, Dr. Hulet's pamphlet states that pathological reactions to mercury leaching out of dental fillings have been categorized by toxicologists, concerned dentists, and physicians who must treat increasing numbers of people suffering from mercury poisoning. The five categories of pathology they have identified include:

1. Neurological disease (referring to abnormalities of the nervous system) which is divided into two subdivisions;
   a. emotional (especially as the symptoms relate to depression, irritability, suicidal tendencies, and inability to cope);
   b. motor (as involuntary movements of the body structure pertaining to muscle spasms, facial twitches, seizures, and multiple sclerosis).
2. Cardiovascular diseases (referring to alterations of heart performance such as unidentified chest pains or rapid heart beat).
3. Collagen diseases (referring to problems with the cementing substances of the cells such as scleroderma, arthritis, systemic lupus erythematosis, and bursitis).
4. Immunological diseases (referring to how well one's body defense mechanisms are working).
5. Allergies (referring to food sensitivities, reactions to airborne vectors, and universal reactors). Mercury in combination with allergens tends to more readily rupture white blood cells to precipitate allergic responses.

There is a common demoninator to these five categories of adverse responses to mercury intoxication, says Dr. Hulet. All of the categorized physiological areas have manganese as one of their chief mineral activators, and mercury escaping from dental fillings blocks the action of manganese.

THE PATH OF DENTAL MERCURY VAPOR

Amalgam fillings act like small mercury-filled batteries lodged in the mouth. The 10 percent copper, 30 percent silver, 5 percent zinc, 5 percent tin, and 50 percent mercury standardly combined in one's dental filling join together to become a battery when bathed in saliva. An electrical current is generated from this battery. The chemical reaction that results sets up electrical charges, and they, in turn, produce mercury vapor as a by-product of the entire chemical/electrical reaction. Tiny portions of the battery metals get used up during the course of the steady chemical/electrical reactions. Thus, fillings only five years old are shown to have just 28 percent of mercury content left in the filling material. This means that nearly half the mercury has been released as a liquid chemical that escapes out into the body or as a vapor up into the head.

The neurons of the brain retain much of the mercury vapors as contaminants or implants in their organelles—the miniature chemical factories that run each brain cell. Organelles are damaged by these contaminants and become temporarily dysfunctional at first but later sustain permanent damage and eventually die. Once mercury enters the brain, its molecules combine with neurons and insert themselves in the organelles. Such mercury contamination from using the toxic metal in dental fillings is one of the prime sources for development of the symptoms of dementia in general, and Alzheimer's disease in particular.

Silver-mercury fillings that are present even longer than the five years, which we mentioned above, produce methyl mercury as a result of oral and intestinal bacteria working on the heavy metal. Methyl mercury is one hundred times more toxic than regular mercury, which is the most poisonous natural substance known to man.

Mercury vapor from the fillings also escapes into the nasal sinuses where axonal transport takes it into the brain through another pathway. The axons send nerve impulses from neuron to neuron, and mercury ions become part of the electrical transport mechanism. The vapor gets inhaled into the lungs, too. From there it directly enters the blood stream and spreads to every cellular structure of the brain and body.

If a pregnant woman has amalgam fillings in her teeth, the fetus temporarily protects this mother-to-be from mercury by absorbing most of the metallic poison. The newborn will emerge already contaminated. The red blood cell count in a fetus is often as much as 30 percent higher than its mother's, and mercury readily combines with this extra amount of red-blood cellular hemoglobin.

An adult's hemoglobin and hematocrit are elevated from ongoing exposure to amalgams while oxygen transport becomes reduced. The resultant blood test makes it look like the patient's blood cells are packed with energy, but the patient feels on the verge of collapse from fatigue. The new disease that has been striking millions of people in industrialized western countries called chronic fatigue/immune depression syndrome (CFIDS) is directly connected to amalgam fillings. The removal of these fillings can greatly improve the patient's ability to escape from chronic fatigue. Positive response against CFIDS is experienced by the patient and witnessed by the dentist within two weeks of amalgam removal.

The single most important factor for success in the mercury intoxicated patient is the sequential removal of amalgams. A meter is used by the informed dentist to determine what sequence to follow in removing the amalgams. Negative fillings must be removed first, followed by the high current positives, and finally the low-current positively charged fillings. As the second most important factor in curing mercury toxicity, biochemical coverage (taking free-radical "quenchers," such as high-dosages of garlic, and various antioxidants) should be started before the removal of amalgams. When these parameters are followed, chances for a successful outcome for degenerative disease symptoms, and especially dementia, are in the vicinity of 80 percent.

When the guidelines for sequential removal of dental amalgams are violated, however, the risk of failure increases by about 10 percent. The lesson here is not to just run out and have all your amalgams removed indiscriminately. Rather, the coauthors recommend that an affected person should go to a dentist who has studied the procedures required. We suggest that you or your acquaintance should question that dentist first before engaging his or her services.

Be assured that the ADA's continued assertion that silver-mercury amalgams are perfectly safe, may be left in place, and may be added to your mouth is a falsehood issued for the organizations own purposes. You are paying for belief of this assertion with your health and longevity.

CHAPTER 12

Dental Amalgams and Alzheimer's Disease

Clutching a teddy bear and a bag of diapers, an incontinent old man sat in a wheelchair near the men's rest-room door of the dog racing track where he was abandoned in Post Falls, Idaho on March 21, 1992. Post Falls, with a population of 8,000, is a quiet community on the banks of the Spokane River in Kootenai County, northern Idaho. Dropped off here like misplaced luggage, the old man could not walk and obviously was an Alzheimer's patient in need of care. A typewritten note pinned to his chest falsely identified him as "John King."

The elderly but amiable fellow was wearing bedroom slippers and a sweatshirt that said "Proud to Be an American." All labels on his new clothing had been cut away and any identifying markers on his wheelchair had been removed—an effort to disguise where he had come from, said the police.

Eighty-two-year-old John Kingery looked lost and helpless. He was identified later by administrators of the Laurelhurst Care Center in Portland, Oregon from which he had been taken three weeks before. The administrators recognized his picture on television where the police flashed it for assistance with identification. The patient had been transferred out of the Laurelhurst Care Center three weeks before to another nursing care facility, the Regency Park Living Center of Portland. His daughter, Sue Gifford of Portland Oregon, checked her father out of this second nursing home about ten hours previous to when he was found abandoned at the Idaho dog track.

It was a sad situation. The father's face, that of an elderly person who does not even know his name and was left on society's doorstep, could readily become the look of our future—the abandonment of elderly people who suffer with Alzheimer's disease. Certainly it has been the face of the past among some Americans who are showing the results of their multiple dental amalgams. John Kingery's facial appearance was clearly that of someone suffering from heavy-metal poisoning of the brain.

In the next thirty years, the number of Americans over the age of eighty-five is expected to grow 500 percent, to a population of 15 million. People over eighty-five years old make up the fastest-growing segment of the elderly. The number of people over age sixty-five is anticipated doubling also, from 30 million now to 60 million by the year 2030. At the same time the number of people suffering from Alzheimer's disease is expected to triple from 4 million today to 12 million by the year 2020.

Mr. Kingerly, who suffers simultaneously from mercury toxicity and Alzheimer's, was another victim of "granny dumping," as the increasingly common practice of abandonment of elderly parents is euphemistically labeled. In large measure, those martyred by dementia are showing the results of toxicity from mercury, aluminum, lead, cadmium, arsenic, and other heavy metals. Their neurons have been poisoned. They are turned into Alzheimer's victims directly through the efforts of dentists who blindly follow the party line of their trade organization, the American Dental Association (ADA). The ADA's party line advises the use of dental fillings containing amalgams of mercury and other metals that increase the toxin's effectiveness. Dentists who practice using conventional methods are the largest combined group of individuals in our society who cause exposure to heavy-metal toxins. A trip to the dentist may be hazardous to your health!

A STUDY OF EWES

Dentists commit the crime of filling patients' cavities with dental amalgams that allow mercury toxins to be readily absorbed into the internal organs. The dentists know this but find it convenient to ignore the vast amount of documentation from medical and scientific research that has been presented during the past decade. These dentists—current practitioners and even those long since retired—recognize that if they admit to their scientific failing, they will open themselves to multi-billions of dollars of legal liability for the diseases and death for which they must take responsibility.

A direct correlation between amalgam and mercury absorption was established in sheep, in 1989 and again in 1990, when radioactive mercury was used in amalgams inserted into twelve molars in each of a number of pregnant ewes, following intubation and general anesthesia. Radioactivity was detected in all of the sheep's jaw bones, lungs, and intestines within two days, even though maximum precautions had been taken to prevent amalgam particles from entering the stomach.

The mercury absorption was followed by the transfer of the metallic toxin to the animals' livers, kidneys, spleens, pituitaries, thyroids, and other tissues over the ensuing 140 days. Mercury was detected in the lambs that were born, and the mercury levels were eight times higher in the ewes' milk than in the blood. The sheep were fed only twice each day and although their chewing could be said to be more prolonged than in humans, it was considered that this would not be more than many habitual human gum chewers.

The amalgams implanted in the ewes were just 850 milligrams in weight, much smaller than those used frequently in humans, and only involved the occlusal surfaces of the teeth. Thus, these female sheep had less surface area covered with amalgam than humans.[1]

THE UNIVERSITY OF KENTUCKY STUDY

University of Kentucky researchers evaluating eighteen elements in the autopsied brains of ten Alzheimer's disease patients, compared with eighteen age-matched, non-diseased controls, found increased mercury/selenium and mercury/zinc ratios in the examined brains. Most significant was the increase in mercury in the Alzheimer's disease brain samples, especially in the cerebral cortex, compared with controls.

Alzheimer's patients also had an elevation of mercury in the nucleus basalis of Meynert (an oval mass of protoplasmic cells in the brain ventricals), which is the major cholinergic projection to the cerebral cortex. This section of the brain retains memory and is severely degenerated in Alzheimer's disease patients. The elevated mercury/selenium and mercury/zinc ratios of this University of Kentucky autopsy study are of importance because selenium and zinc are physiologically used by the human brain to protect against mercury toxicity.

The leaching of mercury from dental amalgams is the main means of human exposure to inorganic mercury and vapor in the general population. Scientists have shown that there is a direct correlation between the amount of inorganic mercury in the brain and the number of tooth surfaces furnished with amalgams in patients with Alzheimer's disease. Mercury from dental amalgam is passed rapidly and directly into body tissues and accumulates in patients' bodies with time.

This book's coauthors believe that no exposure to mercury vapor escaping from dental amalgams can be considered harmless, since the heavy metal has no known toxic threshold in the body. Dental amalgams that allow mercury vapors to escape into the facial tissues, body, and/or brain cannot be excluded as a primary potential source of Alzheimer's disease.[2]

Indeed, there is no question that mercury vapor escapes with time from the surfaces of amalgams, as shown by the laboratory study cited above. The mercury from amalgams was absorbed into the internal organs and brain of the sheep. There is definite evidence that mercury is shunted quickly from the blood and deposited in all organ tissues around the nervous system and brain.

THE WENSTRUP GROUP STUDY

A year earlier than the University of Kentucky study, another investigation had been carried out by three psychiatrists, Drs. Wenstrup, Ehmann, and Markesberry, to determine the trace element imbalances in isolated subcellular factions of the brains of Alzheimer's disease patients. In this first study, the brains from ten autopsied Alzheimer's disease patients who had died between the ages of 59 and 93 and twelve control patients who had died between 59 and 83 years were analyzed for concentrations of thirteen trace elements, including bromine, cesium, chromium, cobalt, iron, mercury, potassium, rubidium, selenium, silicon, silver, sodium, and zinc. An instrumental neutron activation analysis (INAA) was carried out on all of the brains examined. The clinically diagnosed Alzheimer's disease patients had met the criteria for the diagnosis of Alzheimer's disease (DAT).[3]

The most significant imbalance of metals found in these DAT patients was an elevated mercury level, and then some elevation of bromine. Fractional portions of the body down to the tiniest size (microsomal fractions) were examined. Considerable alterations in element ratios found were the following: increased mercury/selenium mass ratio in nuclear and microsomal fractions; increased mercury/zinc mass ratio in microsomal fractions; and increased zinc/selenium mass ratio in mitochondrial organelle fractions. All of these mineral ratios were abnormal and definitely present in the Alzheimer's-affected brains.

The three authors of the study concluded "that the elevation of mercury in DAT brains is the most important of the imbalances we observed." Previous investigations by the authors demonstrated a significant increase of mercury in DAT brain samples, especially in the cerebral cortex, compared with age-matched controls. They had found further that the largest trace element imbalance ever discovered was the elevation of mercury in the nucleus basalis of Meynert (nbM) of DAT patients, the same as in the study already reported on in the previous subsection. The implication is that memory loss occurs from mercury poisoning a primary center of memory retention.

Several mechanisms of pathology are at play when mercury leaches from amalgam fillings as vapor. These three investigators proposed that the brain of of a DAT patient alters from toxic reactions to mercury in the following ways:

1. A decrease in protein synthesis and ribonucleic acid (RNA) and deoxyribonucleic acid (DNA) levels takes place. RNA and DNA are the carriers of genetic information for the growth of new brain cells. Such a decrease has been demonstrated already in animal studies. The significant elevation of mercury found in the microsomal fraction in DAT causes inhibition of protein synthesis and may be a specific reason for brain cell degeneration and death in Alzheimer's disease. No new neurons develop.

2. Mercury binds to tubulin, a protein subunit of microtubules that is composed of two globular polypeptides, alpha-tubulin and beta-tubulin (see the next subsection). Excess mercury in DAT interferes with the normal assembly of microtubules and causes cytoskeletal (neurofilament supportive elements that strengthen the little chemical factories in neurons) abnormalities in DAT. Thus the tiny tubules that run between brain cells get clogged.

3. Cell membranes of neurons become bound up with mercury so that sodium- and potassium-ATPase (two enzymes) function get interfered with. Mercury-related alteration in cellular membranes makes them more permeable or "leaky" and leads to an altered ability to regulate the flow of elemental or molecular ions, morphological changes, or cell death. A selective leaky-membrane phenomenon permits cations of other heavy metals such as aluminum, lead, and cadmium to enter the cell, bind to sulfhydryl groups on the nuclear envelope, and deteriorate biochemical processes.

4. The interaction of mercury with the essential trace elements selenium and zinc, which diminish in the presence of mercury, result in deficiency of these two essential elements and lead to additional cellular dysfunctions.

The scientists who conducted this sophisticated clinical investigation point to two environmental sources of mercury poisoning: seafood and dental amalgams. They stated, "This and our previous studies suggest that mercury toxicity plays a role in neuronal degeneration in Alzheimer's disease. The extreme elevation of mercury in Alzheimer's disease could relate to the severe degeneration of the nucleus and to cholinergic deficit in DAT."

RATS AND ALZHEIMER'S DISEASE

Rats have been most helpful in studying the process of mercury on tubulin synthesis. Tubulin is a protein substance that is essential for the formation of neurofibril matrix between neurons. This matrix consists of finger-like projections from brain cells called dendrite spines, that are 100 to1,000 times narrower than a human hair. They are believed to play a critical role in the formation of long-term memories. For more than three decades, scientists have focused on electrical impulses flowing through brain cells as they attempt to explain how some memories can remain indelible throughout life.

Without tubulin, neurofibrillary tangles, the predominant feature of brain tissues found in Alzheimer's disease, will result. The rate of tubulin synthesis is determined by analysis of the radiolabeled precursor (a marker used to show brain-blood flow or nerve-impulse transfer). In human DAT brain tissue, tubulin synthesis is impaired compared with controls. There is less tubulin in the brain tissue in the areas of the autopsied brain where researchers have repeatedly found high accumulations of mercury. The addition of mercury (in the same amounts, proportional to the size of the rats' brains, as they found in the human brain tissue of DAT victims) to the brain tissue of rats caused a blockage of tubulin synthesis. This study was conducted over a long period of time by highly qualified medical scientists, and a large number of rat brain samples were analyzed. The researchers firmly established the connection of mercury to Alzheimer's disease. They concluded that dental amalgam fillings were a primary potential source of the high levels of toxic mercury found in the brain tissues of victims of Alzheimer's disease. Their definite findings were that mercury from amalgam fillings induces GTP-tubulin interactions in rat brains similar to those observed in Alzheimer's disease.[4]

BANNING SILVER-MERCURY AMALGAMS

On February 1, 1992, the German Ministry of Health declared a ban on silver-mercury fillings, to become effective March 1, 1992. The ban was put into effect on medical grounds because of adverse health occurrences in patients exposed to mercury released from amalgam fillings.

German scientists have found that chronic exposure to mercury from vapors thrown off by fillings while people were chewing made these people ill with a variety of pathologies. These individuals suffered from damage to the kidneys, poisoning of unborn babies due to passage of mercury through the placenta, increased resistance to the therapeutic effects of various antibiotics, increased incidence of cardiovascular disease, and the most disturbing connection of all: a definite relationship of mercury exposure to elevated occurrences of Alzheimer's disease.[5]

Research findings also showed that prenatal exposure of a mother-to-be to mercury vapor caused learning deficits and behavioral problems in the newborn. These effects are similar to those causing great medical concern about lead levels in children (see Chapter 13 for more information on lead poisoning).

The results of another German study showed reduced fertility in dental assistants who are occupationally exposed to mercury vapor. This new investigation corroborates a recently completed and newly published study indicating harmful effects of mercury on male fertility.

The German announcement and the German studies that brought about the ban contradict the pervasive and fraudulent pronouncements by the American Dental Association and the National Institute of Dental Research. These two organizations blatantly lie when they state that silver-mercury fillings are harmless to patients. Their further claims that amalgam fillings are safe repeatedly get declared in this way merely to protect American dentists from legal assault by an angry public. Such lies are contrary to existing scientific evidence and clearly not in the best interests of the public's health and welfare.

Silver-amalgam is used for dental fillings strictly for the convenience of the dentist and not for the welfare of the patient. Silver-amalgam remains the cheapest, most durable, and most extensively used restorative material in dentistry for repair of decayed posterior teeth—even though it breaks down immune systems, deteriorates brain cells, and generally poisons patients.

THEY BANNED LEAD, SO WHY NOT AMALGAMS?

Because of lobbying by politicians representing the American Dental Association, even the U.S. Food and Drug Administration came out in support of continuing with amalgam as a dental filling material. Despite safety reassurances from the dental profession and the federal agency, leading toxicologists said evidence still points to mercury in amalgam dental fillings as a serious health threat. Then there was a confession breakthrough. Dr. Donald Galloway, a scientist with the FDA's Center for Devices and Radiological Health in Rockville, Maryland, speaking at a Seattle meeting of the Society of Toxicology, drew parallels between the evidence against lead poisoning twenty years ago and the evidence against mercury today. Lead has since been proven harmful to humans and removed from paint, pipes, and many other materials.

"New evidence indicates a need for more vigorous study of the possible risk posed by the release of mercury vapor from 'silver' amalgam fillings," Dr. Galloway said. Thereafter making that analogy to lead poisoning, he added that the rule of thumb for safety in lead exposure used to be the point at which exposure caused obvious physical symptoms. But studies have since shown that chronic exposure to even low levels of lead, especially in children, can cause significant developmental and neurological damage.

"Lead was removed from paint in 1971," the FDA scientist advised. "Mercury was removed from paint in 1991. There are some striking similarities in the history." He said that he would prefer his children receive alternatives to amalgam fillings when possible. Common alternatives are plastic composites or porcelain fillings.

Another toxicologist at the meeting said the dental profession and the U.S. regulatory system are choosing to ignore the data implicating amalgams as the source of mercury poisoning of the brain. "These were preordained conclusions of safety," said Dr. Fritz Lorscheider from the University of Calgary in Alberta. Dr. Lorscheider and his colleague, Dr. Vimy, are the two primary scientists who conducted the experiments described earlier. Their earlier 1989 study, and then a second 1990 publication, of a study on sheep fitted with amalgam fillings was featured on the CBS television program *60 Minutes.*

Dentists from the ADA attacked the second study, which implicated amalgam toxicity as a source of multiple sclerosis, kidney damage, and Alzheimer's, by noting that sheep chew much more than humans. Other dental critics from the ADA also noted that the sheep received their twelve fillings at one time, which would be atypical in humans. The dentists following their ADA party line are looking for any excuse to justify the poisoning of patients.

But at The 1992 Seattle Conference of Clinical Toxicologists, Dr. Lorscheider reported finding similar data in monkeys, which chew like humans. Both sheep and monkeys having amalgam fillings, he said, show poisoning of their internal organs, as well as of the brain. Dental amalgams assuredly cause pathology.

Other evidence turned up by Dr. Lorscheider indicates that the standard methods used by dentists for measuring mercury exposure give inaccurately low readings. Most obsolete studies of exposure to mercury have based their measurements on blood and urine concentrations. New studies conducted by this renown toxicologist indicate that much of the mercury is retained in tissue, especially in the kidneys, liver, and brain, he said. "There is an impairment in kidney function in animal studies. And certain regions of the brain absolutely do concentrate mercury."

If silver-mercury amalgams were to be proposed today as a new medical or dental device, Dr. Lorscheider advised, the scientific evidence of potential risk would be enough to prevent them from ever reaching the market. "Dental amalgam is a major source of mercury poisoning in the general population," he concluded.

Other toxicology specialists—speakers at the Seattle panel on amalgams—generally supported the contention that dental amalgams do pose a health risk. For example, an epidemiological study by a researcher at the National Institutes of Environmental Safety and Health showed reduced fertility in both male and female dental assistants with high exposure to mercury.[5]

HOW REMOVAL OF AMALGAMS CAN EFFECT YOUR HEALTH

The medical puzzle of dental amalgam toxicity is not limited to North America or Europe. It has stretched around the world to New Zealand, Australia, Asia, and Africa, as well. For example, there is the case of Pauline B., a thirty-nine-year-old mother of four children, who currently resides in New Zealand. She had experienced a seven-year history of increasing debility, eventually resulting in admission to a hospital for clinical and laboratory investigations, including CAT scan. At the time, the diagnoses being considered for Pauline were multiple sclerosis, stroke, or cerebral tumor. She was manifesting multiple symptoms and signs of illness that caused her physicians to suspect one of these disorders. None of these turned out to be causing her problems.

The most troublesome syndrome of symptoms for Pauline was mental irregularities. She was depressed and irritable, showed sudden unreasonable anger, had suicidal thoughts, and even had failed at suicide once. Her loss of short-term memory became quite apparent many times throughout her daily routine—lost keys, credit cards and time schedules, losing her way in familiar neighborhoods, and more. While Pauline remained unaware of her mental failings, dementia was upsetting her family.

She also had paresthesiae (abnormal feelings of numbness, burning, pricking, tickling, and tingling), muscular twitching, intermittent tremor of facial muscles, tinnitus (ringing in the ears), blockage of her peripheral vision, headaches, constipation, difficulty with swallowing, and chronic fatigue syndrome with devastating weakness, especially in the left lower leg. The patient additionally complained of cold hands and feet, metallic burning sensation in the mouth, rhinitis with sinusitis, excessive salivation, chronic bleeding gums, recurrent left-sided sore throats, non-specific chest pains, itching, undiagnosed rashes, nocturia (excess urination at night), and urinary frequency during the day. She was experiencing discharge from the vagina, and her vaginal candidiasis had been with her from age sixteen. Pauline had experienced recurrent herpes simplex infection since the age of thirteen.

Pauline's first exposure to mercury amalgam fillings took place when she was only five years old. Frequent amalgam insertions took place after that, since they were disintegrating often and had to be replaced regularly. Amalgam replacements were stopped eventually, as she became too ill within hours afterwards with acute symptoms of nausea, breathlessness, and giant hives. To avoid such symptoms, several teeth were extracted instead of being filled—all this occurred without her physicians ever recording that the patient actually suffered from amalgam hypersensitivity and potential mercury toxicity.

After her marriage and the subsequent birth of several children over five years time, major aggravations of these same symptoms and signs recurred following extensive amalgam replacements prior to and during a fourth pregnancy. One week following the last amalgam replacement she was temporarily admitted to the hospital due to reappearance of the various signs and symptoms of breathlessness, nausea, marked weakness, and giant hives. The patient's onset of such difficulties frightened her husband, and he traveled with her for a long distance in New Zealand to consult with a physician who specializes in environmental toxicity and preventive medicine. Private family practitioner Michael E. Godfrey, M.B., B.S. of Willow House, Tauranga, New Zealand, is a member of the American College of Advancement in Medicine, administering chelation therapy, preventive medicine, and orthomolecular nutritional therapy.

Dr. Godfrey examined the patient and discovered that she still possessed fourteen amalgam-filled teeth. The amalgam was found in a total of eighteen surfaces, three root-filled teeth, and three teeth with metal pins in them. In his clinical journal article, Dr. Godfrey reports: "There was a marked weakness of the left leg with the patient having to be helped up stairs. The patient had cold hands and feet but was otherwise physically normal on examination. . . . Still, at the time of this initial consultation the patient had been either wheelchair bound or walking with crutches or sticks for over a year."

After examining her body fluids with laboratory tests, he discovered "that many of the nutrient minerals were below normal, notably selenium, cobalt, chromium, manganese, zinc, copper, potassium, sodium, and magnesium." Dr. Godfrey concluded that mercury hypersensitivity derived from the amalgam dental fillings was the source of health difficulties being experienced.

"Following discussion with the patient," the consultant wrote, "total amalgam removal was performed in four sessions according to a prescribed protocol that protected the patient from exposure to mercury.[6] Three months after amalgam removal this patient was able to walk for two hours and climb stairs with ease. Two months later she was enjoying seven hours of aerobics a week to regain her former fitness. During those five months her family doctor had been monitoring her progress. All of her previously reported symptoms and signs, except for tinnitus, some parasthesiae, cold hands, and constipation, had remitted and even these were improving. For the previous seven years she had had to be on continuous oral and intranasal medication for chronic rhinitis that had been diagnosed as hay fever. After her amalgams were removed, she no longer needed these medications."[7]

Pauline's husband, who balked at first since he saw no sense in his wife redoing so much dental work, was delighted with the result of the woman's amalgam removal. He reported that his wife's marked depression and dementia-like memory loss stopped disrupting their family life. Her mind simply came back to normal, he said. He was no longer fearful of Alzheimer's disease taking over the mind of someone he loved.

Pauline has recovered now from a kind of Minamata disease similar to the syndrome suffered by fishermen and their families around Minamata Bay, Japan. The only difference between the fishermen and Pauline was that the source of her neurological poisoning was amalgam dental fillings rather than eating fish contaminated by mercury.

Reviewing chronic mercury poisoning in Minamata, you will recognize that Pauline exhibited many aspects of the syndrome. Its main symptoms are irritability, insomnia, forgetfulness, inability to concentrate, parasthesiae, dysphagia (difficulty in swallowing), tremors, ataxia (staggering walk and poor balance), and visual disturbances (characteristically a concentric narrowing of the visual fields).[8] Short-term memory loss is the most common complaint, and in this regard other researchers have found high levels of mercury in those portions of the human brain labeled the hippocampus, amygdala, and nucleus basalis of Meynert, which are the sections of the brain that control memory.[9]

CHAPTER 13
Lead Poisoning

Throughout 1993, every time two-year-old Iola G., of Augusta, Georgia sucked her thumb, she was poisoning herself with the toxic, heavy metal, lead. The child was coming closer to eventually getting Alzheimer's disease. The metallic particles this toddler took into her mouth were carried in the dust she breathed, the soil she played in, and the paint chipping from walls in her family's rundown apartment.

"Her mama got lead poisoning so bad when she was little, that she's brain damaged," said Carol, Iola's grandmother, the girl's caregiver. "I never dreamed I'd have to go through that again with this baby. It's just a nightmare. My daughter's lead level reached 107 micrograms (mcg), and the teachers and doctors said that lead killed her memory. Iola's lead got to 52 micrograms, and I hope to God she won't be as bad."[1]

No amount of lead ingestion is safe, and any blood level above 10 micrograms per 100 milliliters (ml) of blood is dangerous for all people, but especially for children.[2] A blood level of 60 micrograms/100 milliliters is considered definitely indicative of lead poisoning.[3] In the same way that lead has damaged the brain of Carol's daughter, little Iola is at serious risk of having her mentality adversely and permanently affected, for assuredly chronic exposure to lead affects brain cells and the nervous system. Damage to these sensitive tissues reduces intelligence, produces memory loss, promotes neuropathy, and deteriorates thinking equivalent to dementia.

According to official statements put out by the National Centers for Disease Control and Prevention (CDCP) in Atlanta, Georgia, brain damage and subsequent dementia begins early in life from the subtle consumption of lead. Today, lead poisoning of the brain is found among an estimated three million American children, like Iola G., who are in danger of having stunted intellectual, behavioral, and emotional development.

In the past, pediatricians and other medical scientists waited until children turned up with lead poisoning and then pulled the toxin from their bodies and brains by administering intravenous chelation therapy. New studies have now prompted physicians and public health authorities to warn parents that even tiny amounts of the toxic metal kills brain cells. The public health authorities want children protected from the merest exposure to lead.

"Lead poisoning is the number one environmental threat to children, but it's preventable," said CDCP director William Roper, M.D. Maybe so, but Carol declared in frustration, "Nobody tells you anything in time to stop the poisoning." Her own doctor finally had to help to remove the lead paint from her dilapidated home.

Children breathe lead in the dust of pollution and in houses and apartments previously decorated with lead-based paint before it was banned by the government in the early 1970s. Lead tastes sweet, tempting little ones to nibble on the paint flakes. These lead-ingesting babies probably become the early-onset victims of Alzheimer's disease. Symptoms are liable to appear when they reach their middle years, starting around age forty-five, and certainly beyond.

Adults are at minimal risk of immediate lead poisoning because their bodies absorb only 10 percent of the metal to which they are exposed. But children absorb 50 percent. Those under age seven are most at risk because their nervous systems and other organs are still developing and are acutely vulnerable to absorbing even minute amounts. Because lead poisoning presents no discernible symptoms in its early stages, and because often parents do not know the dangers, children are seldom routinely tested for contamination with the heavy metal. The result is lead poisoning of the brain that remains undetected until Alzheimer's disease takes hold.

SOURCES OF LEAD POLLUTION

Lead occurs naturally in the earth's crust, averaging 12.5 parts per million (ppm). Natural or background levels are insignificant when compared with the amount of lead broadly disseminated into the environment by the careless practices of mankind's product-manufacturing techniques. Over four million tons of lead are mined each year and existing environmental lead levels are at least 500 times greater than prehistoric levels.[4]

Lead contaminates the land, particularly near foundries, gasoline stations, and highways. It is present in drinking water in the 20 percent of American homes still fitted with old plumbing and with new dripless faucets made of metal alloys containing lead.[5,6,7,8]

Lead is one of the most widely used nonferrous (not made of iron) metals in the manufacture of metal products, pigments, chemicals, batteries, and numerous other items. Lead contamination comes from the manufacture of the following products:[9]

Bearing metals	Insecticides	Paints
Cable covering	Lead shot and bullets	Pigments
Certain plastics	Lead wires	Pipes
Cisterns	Lead-containing	Porcelain enamel
Containers for sulfuric	products	Pottery glaze
acid	Lead-pigment-colored	Products painted with
Electric cable insula-	products	lead paint
tion	Linotype metal	Roof coverings
Flint glass	Litharge rubber	Solder
Gasoline additives	Metal alloys	Storage batteries
Heavy-duty greases	Noise barriers	Varnishes

From these processed products and their polluting methods of manufacture, even the most remote areas of the earth are now contaminated by airborne lead, found in areas as distant as the Arctic icecap and Greenland snows and in the blood of the New Guinea aborigines living far from any man-made source of lead exposure. Of all the metallic contaminants, lead is the most widely spread around the world.[10,11]

WHERE LEAD TRAVELS IN THE BODY

Protoplasm is the living substance of each cell. It is made up of water, minerals, and animal and vegetable compounds. Lead is a protoplasmic poison with affinity for the grey matter of the brain. Thus, the toxic metal invades the neurons and damages them. It damages the nerve synapses and dendrites, too, and severely reduces the number of a person's red blood cells.

Upon entering the body and combining with tissue fluids, the lead usually forms a soluble diphosphate compound. That is, lead in molecular form combines with two molecules of a phosphorous salt in much the same way that calcium does. In fact, it eventually follows the calcium metabolic pathways to precipitate in bones as a tertiary (three-molecule) lead phosphate. But that deposition comes later, upon the lead splitting into its molecules so that the actual molecular lead element proceeds to enter the blood stream.

Here is the pathway for lead in the body and brain: Immediately after absorption, most of the lead molecules show up in the spleen, the liver, and the kidneys. After a few days of being metabolized, however, lead moves to the bones and remains locked there unless the exposed individual eats a diet low in phosphates. Phosphate deficiency is a main factor in the development of lead-poisoning symptoms and signs (for more information on the signs and symptoms of lead poisoning, see pages 177–180). The lead-contaminated person's poor eating habits will have him or her getting insufficient phosphorus from foods.

Poor nutrition leads to heightened lead pathology. Someone who consumes too little phosphorus as part of his or her diet will liberate the toxic lead from the bones. From there it flows through the lymphatics and blood stream to elevate the content of blood elements and soft tissues so that excess lead leached from one's own bones is poisoning other tissues. Anemia develops.

With a high intake of calcium, and without a corresponding elevation of nutritional phosphates, there will be a physiological tendency to elevate the levels of lead molecules in blood and tissue by causing lead to leave the bones. That is when the relatively small lead molecules force their way through the blood-brain barrier, the mechanism whereby one's circulating blood is kept separate from the tissue fluids surrounding the brain cells. The blood-brain barrier actually exists as a semipermeable membrane allowing solutions to pass through it but excluding solid particles and large molecules.

Vitamin D in the food supply also helps to promote the safer deposit of lead in the bones, provided there are sufficient amounts of phosphate available. As we have stated, if one's mineral phosphorus is lacking from food intake, then the dietary calcium gets deposited instead of the lead. An intake of calcium is important because insufficient amounts of this mineral, the most voluminous in the human body, substantially increases the toxicity of lead. This finding has been observed in laboratory animals that have undergone investigations for the effects of lead contamination on living organisms.[12,13,14,15,16]

THE INCIDENCE OF LEAD POISONING
BEFORE ITS GOVERNMENT BAN

The only way to detect lead in the body is by having a doctor check for it in one's hair, blood, or urine and observing the symptoms of the metal's toxic effects. Hair analysis works best to determine an individual's long-term contamination.

Self-Applied Home Water Tests for Lead Contamination

Here are two self-administered tests to apply to your private well drinking water that is entering the home:

1. *Take a two-part sample—the first draw from a kitchen tap that has not been used for several hours, and the second draw after running the water for a minute or so. Lead coming from indoor plumbing would not be expected to show up in the second sample.*
2. *Go to the water-holding tank and take a sample there after briefly running the water to determine if your water pump is the source of lead.*

Take your marked samples to a water-testing laboratory and get the results interpreted within a few days. You may have to replace your water pump with one that contains no lead parts. Or, much worse is that you may have to abandon your well altogether because it is too contaminated with lead or some other toxic metal.

In 1972, before tetraethyllead was banned—a highly toxic compound that, when added in small proportions to gasoline, increased the fuel's antiknock quality—more than 220 million pounds of lead were discharged into the atmosphere by automobile exhausts. Another 3 billion pounds were projected into the environment by industrial sources—factories with smoking chimneys. All that lead entered our lungs as particulates of the air, as well as settling into our drinking water and onto our vegetables growing in the fields. Even the meat or milk of domestic animals was not safe to eat or drink. Someone drinking milk or eating beef, for instance, received lead pollutants because the lead molecules became part of the cattle's fluids and flesh.

We must emphasize that the CDCP deems the dangerous level of lead 10 micrograms of lead per deciliter (dl) of blood (one deciliter is equal to 100 milliliters)—an amount the size of a pencil tip. Before the United States Government cracked down on industrial polluters of lead and eliminated lead from gasoline, children registered lead levels in triple digits, like Iola's mother. Yet, for two decades the CDCP had considered a lead blood-level of 60 micrograms the danger zone. Those children growing up twenty,

How to Remove Lead
From Drinking Water

The most common source of lead ingestion is drinking water. In fact, lead in water is a growing health concern, especially among infants and young children. To minimize your family's exposure, take these simple precautions:

- *Never use the first water drawn from the kitchen tap in the morning. Let it run for at least three minutes before use.*

- *Use cold tap water instead of hot, especially to reconstitute powdered infant formula. Hot water allows lead in pipes to leach into water.*

- *Let the water run until cold any time you use it.*

- *Do not boil water any longer than necessary—five minutes is enough. Boiling concentrates contaminants in water, including lead.*

- *For the name of a laboratory that will test your water for lead, contact the American Council of Independent Laboratories at 1629 K Street NW, Suite 400, Washington, DC 20006; telephone (202) 887–5872.*

thirty, or forty years ago with the high lead concentrations in the environment are the likely Alzheimer's patients of today and tomorrow.

New studies show even 10 micrograms of lead can lower a child's intelligence quotient several points, resulting in their becoming semi-retarded or slow-thinking adults with lessened mental capacities. Once lead levels exceed 25 micrograms, a child may suffer chronic memory loss and be deprived of motor coordination; levels above 50 micrograms can cause kidney problems and iron deficiencies; levels over 100 micrograms can kill.[1]

Federal health officials are beginning to build a national system to track dangerous levels of lead in children's blood. The CDCP told the electronic and press media on August 27, 1992 that doctors do not know just how many children are being harmed by lead poisoning because only twenty-eight states and the District of Columbia currently require testing for lead exposure. And most of those states do not supply all the data researchers need to come to educated conclusions about the extent of the problem in the United States.

Private Wells and Lead Poisoning

People drinking water from private wells with water pumps containing lead alloys such as leaded brass or bronze are advised by the United States Environmental Protection Agency (EPA) to have their water supplies tested. The EPA warns that any water testing out at fifteen parts per billion or higher of lead is unfit to drink without facing the risk of poisoning. Since there are no EPA regulations on private well water, only municipal water supplies, it is strictly up to individual well owners to make the determination of safety. The EPA's acknowledged goal for lead exposure in order to maintain health is zero.

In 1993, the Food and Drug Administration proposed rules limiting the lead in bottled water to five parts per billion. Many laboratories use milligrams (mg) per liter, rather than parts per billion to measure contamination. Fifteen parts per billion is the same as 0.015 milligrams of lead per liter of water, and five parts per billion equals 0.0005 milligrams per liter.

Dr. Philip Landrigan, chairman of the environmental health department at Mount Sinai Medical Center in New York City said, "If I could not get the lead level down below ten, I would go to bottled water. If it were below ten, I would relax."[21]

The CDCP has begun to send funds to state health departments so they can set up systems to track lead exposure. Any child who has a blood test from now on will get his or her lead levels checked, as well, and the results will be sent along with the child's name, address, age, race, and income level to that state's health department. The departments, in turn, will report them to the CDCP. Federal health officials will then compile the nation's first official count of childhood lead poisoning, determine what areas have the biggest problem, and devise solutions. The process is probably going to take several years, the federal officials said.

"Many people believed that when lead paint was banned from housing and lead was cut from gasoline, lead-poisoning problems had disappeared, but they're wrong," said Dr. Suzanne Binder, an official with the Center for Disease Control and Prevention. "We know that throughout the country children of all races and ethnicities and income levels are being affected by lead."[17]

The last time health officials calculated the extent of childhood lead poisoning was 1984, when they estimated that three million to four million children had dangerous levels of lead. But that number is now considered to be incorrect, because it came from incomplete data. The level may be lower now because the amount of lead in use in the United States has decreased, Dr. Binder said. Elimination of lead-based paint was first talked about in 1971, but it actually was not prohibited in housing until 1978. Lead in gasoline was gradually eliminated beginning in the late-1970s, too. But the lead that has already been released into the environment will remain there indefinitely to work its deterioration on the brains of susceptible children. It is likely, therefore, that Alzheimer's disease caused by lead poisoning will be with us for decades to come.

ANALYSIS OF FIVE TOXIC METALS AFFECTING THE BRITISH

In London, Dr. Stephen Davies, M.A., B.M., BCh., F.A.C.N., medical and laboratory director of the Biolab Medical Unit, has performed statistical analyses of toxic-metal measurements in the tissues of 23,583 British patients. The elements measured were aluminum (or aluminium as the Brits spell it), mercury, arsenic, cadmium, and lead. All five of these metals were looked for in hair; just the four elements aluminum, cadmium, mercury, and lead were traced in whole blood; the three metals aluminum, cadmium, and lead were found in sweat.

A statistically, highly significant, age-related increase in all toxic-metal levels for all three tissues—hair, blood, and sweat—was observed by the Biolab Medical Unit staff. British males have slightly higher levels of all the metals than British females. Good correlation was found between toxic-metal levels in hair and whole blood, hair and sweat, and sweat and whole blood. As a distinctive finding for the study, Dr. Davies and his associates, Drs. John McLaren Howard, Adrian Hunnisett, and Mark Howard, concluded that toxic-metal exposure and subsequent absorption—at least in Great Britain—is greater in quantity and speed of absorption than the human body possesses as a capacity to excrete such contamination. Consequently, much toxic metal is retained in the bodies of the British.

The Davies study was carried out between January 1985 and December 1991, for assessment of the patients' nutritional and toxic status. The vast majority of these referrals were suffering some form of ill-health for which they were seeking medical care. Only a small minority without evident health problems came for hair, whole blood, and sweat testing in order to acquire medical advice for the sake of preventing illness.

A retrospective computer analysis was undertaken of the age-sex relationships of toxic-metal levels in the three tissues. No discrimination was made between patients with regards to ethnic origin, place of residence, occupation, clinical symptoms, signs, diagnoses, medication, nutritional supplementation, dietary habits, or lifestyle habits. Tissue samples were obtained without reference to time of day or timing of the last meal. All analyses were performed on a machine called the Pye Unicam PU9000 atomic absorption spectrophotometer, according to the manufacturer's instructions.

Hair was collected from the nape of the neck, measuring no more than 4 centimeters (cm) in length, and cut as close to the scalp as possible. Whole blood was taken from the vein in front of the elbow (anticubital vein) and collected in a Vacutainer heparin tube (a tube used to collect human blood), with or without a tourniquet, which can be used to speed up blood collection. Sweat collection was by means of passive sweating onto sterile blotting paper.

The increase with age in all toxic elements measured in the three tissues indicates that there are increasing body burdens of aluminum, cadmium, mercury, lead, and arsenic throughout life. The level of exposure definitely exceeds the capacity to excrete; this has broad implications for ill health, especially causing deterioration of a contaminated person's brain function from the "normal" after the age of forty.

We have placed the study of Dr. Davies and his colleagues in our current chapter on lead poisoning because of another of the researchers' important findings. Studies of lead stored in bone are well-established in the medical literature and show an absorption rate in the modern era of 50,000 percent more than the amount of lead stored in the bones of prehistoric man. Similar studies have not been conducted for other toxic metals. The levels in fetuses is much lower than babies already born because the placenta acts as a barrier to toxic-metal exposure.

Dr. Davies, providing us with a copy of his research group's paper before publication, writes:

> Statistically negative correlations have been found between placental cadmium and lead concentrations and birthweight, head circumference, and placental weight. Thus, these toxic metals are worthy of consideration in relation to reproductive capacity. The choroid plexus is involved in the active transport and facilitated diffusion of essential brain nutrients from blood into the cerebrospinal fluid (CSF), and brain tissue. The choroid plexus has been shown to be a sump [cesspool] for toxic metals where they are preferentially concentrated, presumably to prevent the brain from

receiving toxic insults. Aluminum, lead, cadmium, and arsenic are known to act as enzyme inhibitors and, therefore, by being concentrated in the choroid plexus, may compromise transport of essential nutrients in to the CSF and brain with consequent impairment of the central nervous system and mental function.

In children, following electroencephalographic and other studies, it is considered that there is no observable threshold for lead exposure; we do not know whether or not this same phenomenon applies to other toxic metals considered in this report. . . . A previous study showed that sweat lead increases with blood lead in occupationally exposed workers. Toxic metals are known to act antagonistically to essential elements, for example lead with cadmium and zinc and then mercury with selenium.

Dr. Davies additionally furnished us with analyses of the five toxic metals in the hair, whole blood, and sweat of 25,483 patients who consulted the Biolab Medical Unit in London. Of that number, 23,583 of the evaluations were deemed to be valid for participation in the listings.

THE SOIL TEST

A growing concern about lead poisoning among informed Americans is renewing interest in a ten-dollar test for lead levels in soil, says a scientist at the Agricultural Research Center of the United States Department of Agriculture (USDA) in Beltsville, Maryland. Rufus Chaney of the USDA said he expects the number of states offering soil testing to increase steadily, now that "public awareness of the potential for soil to contribute to lead poisoning of children is rising."

Maryland's Cooperative Extension Service soil testing laboratory joined similar laboratories in Minnesota, Texas, and Wisconsin in furnishing the established soil test to homeowners for ten dollars or less. Children can get lead poisoning from playing in lead-contaminated soil and putting their fingers in their mouths, Chaney confirmed. Where states do not offer a test, he added, homeowners have to rely on private laboratories, some of which charge two hundred dollars or more for the same type of soil analysis. "The high price makes a test impractical for most people," the USDA agriculturalist said.

The soil test was developed in the late 1970s by Chaney and his colleague, Howard Mielke of Xavier University in New Orleans. The United States Public Health Service offices and industries whose workers are exposed to lead have adopted the test, based on scientific papers written by the two agricultural scientists. Chaney advised us that the test has become fairly standard with researchers in the United States, Great Britain, and other European countries.

A state can run the Chaney-Mielke soil test for homeowners at a low cost since this procedure has fewer steps and does not need the safety procedures that are required for other types of soil tests, which use strong acids at high temperatures. For example, one such test boils soil samples in volatile acids, one of which is explosive.

In contrast, soil samples in the Chaney-Mielke test are passed through a strainer and placed in a mild solution of nitric acid at room temperature. That solution is placed next in a mechanical shaker for only one or two hours before being analyzed for lead content, usually with an atomic absorption spectrometer, which measures the emission of electromagnetic radiation lead atoms. Another test that gets similar results demands the time-consuming procedure of soaking the soil sample in hot nitric acid for sixteen hours.

Robert Munter, the director of the soil testing lab at the University of Minnesota, agrees that the Chaney-Mielke test does a good job of measuring the fraction of soil lead that could enter the bloodstream of a child who habitually eats soil. Why does a youngster do that? Quite simply, because there is likely to be a mineral deficiency in its metabolism and instinct has the child seeking minerals wherever they might be found. Unfortunately some of the minerals may be toxic, such as lead.

"Shaking the soil being tested in nitric acid approximates what happens to similar soil in a person's stomach," Robert Munter said. "In the stomach of a child, for example, the soil is churned in gastric juices, which are acidic. The acid juices free the lead from the soil, allowing it to move into the bloodstream rather than pass out through the intestinal tract."

In a 1991 report from the USDA, it was stated that Chaney found lead levels as high as 5,000 or more parts per million (ppm) in tests of gardens in Baltimore, Maryland. Soil with more than 500 parts per million of lead is considered hazardous waste by the United States Environmental Protection Agency (EPA). Lead occurs naturally in all soils, generally in the range of 15 to 40 parts per million, but studies have shown that many soils in older cities have accumulated much higher lead levels from years of deposits of airborne paint-chip dust and dust contaminated by auto exhaust.

For more specifics about the Chaney-Mielke soil test, contact Rufus L. Chaney, agronomist (Environmental Chemistry Laboratory, Agricultural

Research Service, U.S. Department of Agriculture, Beltsville, Maryland 20705; telephone (301) 504–8324.)

HAIR ANALYSIS FOR LEAD

Hair analysis is found to be superior to blood analysis or urine analysis as an indicator of the level of lead in the body. Acute lead toxicity not involving body burden is an exception, and in that case testing of the body's fluids is more accurate. In 1979, the United States Environmental Protection Agency (EPA) reviewed over fifty references and found that hair was excellent as a biological monitor for lead.

During the last five years, the level of hair-lead has decreased and the level at which lead significantly affects an individual has been found to be lower, possibly as a result of more sophisticated testing becoming available. Hair is sensitive to contamination as a result of exposure to hair-darkening agents such as Grecian Formula. There is some suggestion that part of the lead in the hair dye is absorbed into the scalp.

Pediatrician L. Kopito, M.D. and his associates, as quoted from the *Journal of the American Medical Association* (JAMA), wrote of a family affected by lead poisoning:

> The present study describes the cases of a family of four children and their neighbor-cousin in whom the diagnosis of mild lead intoxications was initially suspected because these children had increasingly elevated lead content in their scalp hair. The initial patient had been previously hospitalized with plumbism [lead poisoning]. With the exception of one child, none of the other patients had overt symptoms of plumbism and none were ill. We feel that under conventional circumstances these children would have escaped detection and would not have come to medical attention in time to be treated for plumbism. [Hair analysis made the diagnosis.] The determination of lead in scalp hair is a valuable diagnostic aid in chronic or mild lead intoxication particularly when the other clinical or laboratory evidence is of questionable diagnostic quality. This continuously growing tissue accumulates and stores lead for long periods and may be used for estimating the time and duration of the exposure.[18]

Doctor's Data Laboratories, Inc., a medical research and scientific hair analysis laboratory in West Chicago, Illinois, reported on a study performed by Robert W. Tuthill, Ph.D., Professor of Epidemiology, School of Public Health at the University of Massachusetts at Amherst. Dr. Tuthill obtained specimens from 277 of 532 first graders enrolled in the eight public elementary schools of a small western Massachusetts city. For each child, teachers had completed the eleven-item abbreviated Boston Teacher Questionnaire rating classroom attention behavior. Hair-lead concentrations, reflecting average lead excretion over the recent four- to five-month period, ranged from 1 to 11.3 parts per million (micrograms/gram) in the children. There was a striking and highly significant linear dose-response relationship between seven increasing levels of lead concentrations and negative teacher ratings. The more lead found in a child's hair, the greater was his or her attention deficit. The relationship was further validated by the finding of an even stronger association between physician-diagnosed attention deficit disorder and increased hair lead concentrations in the same children.

To acquire an accurate hair analysis to check for lead poisoning or for toxicity readings on other heavy metals or minerals, we suggest that you or your physician contact Doctors Data Laboratories, Inc., P.O. Box 111, 30 West 101 Roosevelt Road, West Chicago, Illinois 60185-9986; telephone nation-wide (800) 323–2784, in Illinois (708) 231–3649, teleFAX (708) 231–9190. The hair analysis will usually show the presence of lead if the patient's body is actively trying to excrete it.

THE SIGNS, SYMPTOMS, AND ILLNESS
OF LEAD POISONING

Walter J. Crinnion, N.D., who operates the Northwest Healing Arts Center in Bellevue, Washington, specializes in the treatment of chemical toxicity and provides a "tissue cleansing and restoration program" for lead intoxication. Dr. Crinnion advises:

> The initial symptoms of lead toxicity are often attributed to something else. These symptoms are fatigue, irritability, abdominal pain, constipation, and lack of hunger. The neurotoxic effect of lead exposure in-utero, through breast-feeding, and during childhood causes developmental problems and neurological deficits in the child. It will reduce nerve cell development in the cerebral cortex, and has been specifically shown to reduce nerve cell size in the optic nerve.
>
> Lead toxicity also delays growth, impairs motor skill develop-

ment, and alters the level and utilization of the all-important brain chemicals: dopamine, norepinephrine, serotonin, and gamma-aminobutyric acid (GABA). [GABA, an amino acid, inhibits cells from overfiring, and 750 milligrams of it can be taken to calm the body in much the same way as valium, librium, and other tranquilizers without the fear of addiction. GABA is being recommended by wholistic health professionals in place of many drugs. With niacinamide and inositol, it prevents anxiety and stress-related messages from reaching the motor centers of the brain by filling its receptor site. It functions as a neurotransmitter in the central nervous system by decreasing neuron activity.[19]]

Lead toxicity has also been linked to sudden infant death syndrome. In 1943, one study showed that children exposed to lead made unsatisfactory progress in school due to sensorimotor deficits, short attention span, and behavioral disorders. Even relatively low levels will cause a reduced I.Q. The higher the lead level, the lower the I.Q., and the worse the school performance as demonstrated by increased absenteeism, lower vocabulary and grammar scores, poorer hand-eye coordination, and slower reaction time. Children with the highest lead levels had the greatest risk of being drop-outs.

This lowered intelligence quotient never improves but is a sign that brain tangles potentially will give rise to future dementia of Alzheimer's disease. "Lead toxicity can also be a causative factor in developing osteoporosis for adult women," Dr. Crinnion concluded.

Sometimes only one or two of these symptoms are present. As the poisoning progresses, it can manifest in any of the following ways:

- bone pain

- gout

- high blood pressure

- iron-deficiency anemia

- neurological problems (such as dullness, poor attention span, headaches, muscular tremors, hallucinations, memory loss)

- numbness or tingling in the extremities

In the case of anemia of plumbism among young children, there will be a decreased play activity and irritability, that may be labeled as behavior disturbances. One of the dangers of lead poisoning (plumbism) is that the metallic poison causes anemia. Acute abdominal colic hits with loss of appetite (anorexia), apathy, irritability, refusal to play, episodic vomiting, and constipation.

In adults, acute abdominal colic due to lead poisoning strikes, as well, but it is preceded by headache and generalized muscle aches. Constipation, attacks of cramping, and diffuse abdominal pains come next, followed by vomiting, anorexia associated with weight loss, increasing fatigability, and a complaint of a "bad taste in the mouth."

Most of all, exposure to lead produces clear-cut progressive mental deterioration (chronic encephalopathy) in children. This is most noticeable in children over three years of age. Upon examination these children show severe hyperkinetic (grossly excessive levels of activity) and aggressive behavior disorders, a poorly controlled convulsive disorder, and excessive absorption of lead to the point of being poisoned with resulting brain deterioration.

The main clinical feature of lead poisoning in adults is motor abnormalities (peripheral lead neuropathy), typically involving the extensor muscles of the hands and feet. Wrist drop or foot drop may develop.

For people with a history of one or more episodes of acute lead encephalopathy, there is progressive and apparently irreversible degenerative change in kidney tissue, leading to kidney dysfunction. It can appear many years after toxic exposure to lead, hence the medical term *late* or *chronic nephropathy* (meaning *kidney damage*).

Intravenous infusion of ethylene diamine tetraacetic acid (EDTA) chelation therapy is the recognized standard treatment for heavy-metal toxicity. Lead poisoning also may be eliminated with the first oral medication ever approved by the FDA. It is succimer (produced by Chemet Laboratories), which is being used to treat children whose blood-lead levels are above 45 micrograms/deciliter. In one clinical study, 15 children with lead poisoning received 350 milligrams/square meter of succimer (10 milligrams/kilogram) every eight hours for five days. Blood-lead levels dropped an average of 78 percent, compared with a lesser drop with lower doses or with 1,000 milligrams/m² of calcium-sodium EDTA, the usual injectable treatment.

As with other chelators, a rebound rise in blood-lead levels was found two weeks after a five-day course of therapy with succimer. Further clinical trials to deal with this problem showed that continuing the therapy with 350 milligrams/m² every twelve hours during the ensuing two weeks effectively eliminated rebound during the treatment period and reduced the rebound after therapy ended. The recommended treatment course lasts nineteen days. It is also recommended by the FDA that patients have their blood-lead levels monitored at least once weekly after therapy until they are stable, to determine whether a repeat course of therapy is indicated.

This lead-removal drug is new and essentially untried. The FDA reported that clinical experience with succimer was limited to about 300 patients, so the full spectrum and incidence of adverse reactions, including the possibility of allergic reactions, had not yet been determined. Common adverse reactions found so far included gastrointestinal symptoms and rash; increases in blood enzymes (serum transaminases) have been observed in about 10 percent of patients. The safety of uninterrupted treatment with succimer lasting more than three weeks had not been determined as yet, and such treatment is not generally recommended as a substitute for usual EDTA chelation therapy.

Succimer was approved for the treatment of lead poisoning by the FDA on January 30, 1991 and is marketed by McNeil Consumer Products of Ft. Washington, Pennsylvania. Therapy with succimer should always be accompanied by the identification and removal of the source of the lead exposure, since the drug will not prevent further lead intoxication.[20]

In summary, lead poisoning can and often does produce brain syndromes that cause Alzheimer's-like symptoms of dementia. These mental difficulties probably are accompanied by physical signs and symptoms such as abdominal pain, anorexia, anxiety, constipation, chronic fatigue, headaches, impaired coordination, indigestion, irritability, malaise, muscle pains, poor concentration, poor memory, restlessness, and/or tremors.

CHAPTER 14
Cadmium Poisoning

In January 1993, a seventy-six-year-old, retired high-school algebra teacher, named Marjorie M., arrived at her physician's office in Allentown, Pennsylvania for a routine biannual examination. She was accompanied by Corliss, her fifty-year-old daughter. For over a quarter century the physican had cared for this patient and the three children she had raised. Two years earlier, a kidney stone had sent Marjorie to the hospital emergency room, but fortunately it passed without requiring surgery. X-ray examination had revealed a mass of such stones lodged in her right kidney. Ultrasound therapy for disintegrating the stones was discussed at the time but no follow-up care occurred, because the closest ultrasound device was located in Philadelphia, and Marjorie considered that too far a distance to travel.

A year before the kidney stone incident, degenerative joint disease had necessitated a total hip replacement for Marjorie, but with physical therapy (and under her daughter's watchful eye) the patient had recovered uneventfully. She regained her ability to perform daily activities. Today, she was visiting with her physician again because Corliss insisted that a checkup was in order.

As the two women were being escorted to the examining room, the daughter pulled the doctor aside and confided that over the past couple of years she had seen a decided decline in her mother's memory. Corliss explained that at first her mother had become gradually more forgetful during conversations. She was now forgetting the names of former associates and pupils, often in their presence. Also, almost daily, Marjorie forgot appointments with friends. She misplaced common objects like keys and books as well. Most disturbingly, she had recently lost her way in the shopping mall where she had regularly shopped with Corliss since it was built over twenty years ago. She was unaccompanied and she panicked. Security guards had attempted to calm her, in a commotion embarrassing to all.

When questioned about her apparent difficulties with memory, the patient was baffled. Marjorie admitted that she had missed appointments but stated that her memory was as sharp as ever. However, just from her halting speech pattern, it was obvious to the physician that some mental irregularity had taken hold of his longtime patient. It was two years since he had last examined her and he found quite a number of physical discomforts and malfunctions troubling the woman. Marjorie suffered with other illnesses besides her degenerative joint disease such as an itchy rash on her chest, high blood pressure, loss of appetite, and impairment of the ability to smell, as if she had olfactory anesthesia.

Marjorie's inheritance of a strong constitution was no longer standing her in good stead. Each of her parents had died peacefully in their late eighties without any history of serious degenerative diseases, such as cancer, diabetes, or heart trouble. But where Marjorie had once been naturally healthy, she was now displaying physical deterioration with reduced weight, dry, scaly skin, and thinning hair. Marjorie's main complaint, though, was sore joints throughout her body.

The Allentown physician became really disturbed by his patient's admission that despite his numerous warnings in years gone by, she had increased her consumption of vodka to about a pint every day. She also confessed to smoking a minimum of two packs of cigarettes daily, too. "Marjorie," he admonished her, "you are taking advantage of your genes perhaps overly much. They are not always going to keep your body and mind functioning normally."

Still, her prior health history was relatively uneventful except for those hospitalizations for hip surgery, kidney stones, and three childbirths. Previous X-ray examinations had revealed that she was affected by osteoporosis, but the only treatment that had been recommended was that she drink more milk and take nutritional supplementation with calcium. Her current medications consisted of daily oral estrogens, in modest dosage, and an occasional aspirin, for frequent aches and pains. Although Marjorie did feel weak and looked malnourished, the diet her daughter described seemed to be adequate.

Marjorie had sat quietly and attentively, smiling brightly during the physical examination. Her blood pressure was 190/100 (hypertensive), her pulse rate was 92 (bordering on tachycardia) and irregular, her respiratory rate was 19 (too fast) and labored, and her temperature was 97.3 degrees.

These abnormal results were suspicious-looking for some type of ongoing and chronic, low-grade pathology. The physician also noticed, upon examination, that Marjorie's liver was enlarged, he could hear abnormal sounds in her heart and lungs, and her pulse was abnormal. In contrast, Marjorie's vision and hearing, her abdomen, extremities, pelvis (except for the liver), head and neck, and palpable thyroid tissue appeared to be normal.

SCREENING FOR DEMENTIA

Marjorie's detailed neurologic physical examination was normal, too, except for a *Mini-Mental State Examination* with a score of 22 out of 30 (see Table 5.2, page 65). She additionally scored poorly on *The Short Portable Mental Status Questionnaire* (see Table 14.1, page 184). The patient missed the day of month and week, the season, and the year. She could recall only one of three objects after three minutes. She executed only two steps in a three-step command, and she could not copy a double pentagon correctly.

The Mini-Mental State Examination and The Short Portable Mental Status Questionnaire evaluate a broad range of cognitive functions, including orientation, recall, attention, calculation, language manipulation, and constructional praxis. In The Mini-Mental State Examination a score of 30 is normal, and in general a score of less than 24 signifies dementia or delirium. When 24 is used as a cutoff, the examination functions with a sensitivity of 87 percent and a specificity of 82 percent in hospitalized patients. That is, 87 precent is the best score for home-based people, and 82 percent is the best score for hospitalized patients. The test is not particularly sensitive for mild dementia, and scores are spuriously low in persons with a low level of education, poor motor function, or impaired vision. Since none of these problems pertained to Marjorie, her score of 22 created a high index of suspicion for the possibility of dementia—perhaps of the Alzheimer's type—but that diagnosis was yet to be determined.

The Mini-Mental State Examination took about seven minutes to complete, as did a follow-up with The Short Portable Mental Status Questionnaire. The Short Portable Mental Status Questionnaire had some advantages over The Mini-Mental State Examination, in that it partially adjusted for age, sex, race, education, and motor or visual impairment. The sensitivity of The Short Portable Mental Status Questionnaire is 82 percent and the specificity 92 percent. In checking for mild dementia, the figures change to 55 percent and 96 percent, respectively. This means that the top score will be 82 percent and will focus on the probelm with a 92-percent accuracy.

Table 14.1 The Short Portable Mental Status Questionnaire

Questions and Commands:
1. What is today's date?
2. What day of the week is it?
3. What is the name of this place?
4. What is your telephone number (or, if no telephone, the patient's home address)?
5. How old are you?
6. When were you born?
7. Who is currently President of the United States?
8. Who was President just before him (or her)?
9. What was your mother's maiden name?
10. Subtract 3 from 20 and keep subtracting downward.

Scoring*:
0–2 errors: Normal
3–4 errors: Mild intellectual impairment
5–7 errors: Moderate intellectual impairment
8–10 errors: Severe intellectual impairment

*Allow scores to range one error higher if subject had no grade-school education. Allow one less error if subject had education beyond high school.

Both of these brain tests have an inherent feature that all physicians appreciate—their ability to yield diagnostic information immediately.

Since these screenings suggested the presence of dementia, Marjorie's physician requested that blood, urine, and hair specimens be obtained from her for laboratory testing. He suspected that some external source of pathology was causing her variety of complaints and mental symptoms.

Most persons being evaluated for dementia, like Marjorie, are elderly outpatients and not hospitalized. In this elderly outpatient population, about 70 percent of those in whom dementia is detected by screening examinations will be affected by Alzheimer-type dementia. Another 5 percent will have Alzheimer-type dementia in association with Parkinson's disease. A third group of 17.5 percent will be suffering from multi-infarct dementia or alcohol-related dementia. Much of the remainder of dementia patients (about 7½ percent) will have cognitive impairment due to medication side effects or depression without true dementia.

In elderly outpatients, other illnesses affecting the central nervous system such as brain tumors, paraneoplastic (malignant tumor) syndromes, normal-pressure hydrocephalus, subdural hematoma (blood clot under the skull), transient ischemic attacks (ministroke), and central nervous system vasculitis (inflammation of the blood vessels to the nerves) are rare as causes of dementia. They are even less common than the various metabolic abnormalities such as hyperparathyroidism (overactive parathyroid gland), hyponatremia (abnormally low sodium ions in the circulating blood), hypothyroidism (underactive thyroid gland), hypoglycemia (low blood sugar), vitamin B12 deficiency, and folate deficiency, that together are implicated in 3 percent of cases. At least 8 percent of demented elderly patients have more than one illness capable of producing dementia and are judged to have mixed dementia, usually consisting of Alzheimer's disease plus some other cause such as multi-infarct dementia or alcohol-related dementia.

It turns out that Marjorie was the victim of mild dementia related to drinking too many vodka gimlets, a dementia related to her alcoholism. She also suffered from severe dementia connected with cadmium poisoning that arose directly from her excessive cigarette smoking. Cigarette tobacco and its 1001 additives contain an immense amount of cadmium.

CADMIUM POISONING AROUND US AND IN US

Cadmium is a toxic heavy metal that is becoming known as a more serious pollutant than lead. Cadmium inhibits the formation of many enzymes and the action of nutrients within the human body. It accumulates in the kidney with age, has no known biological function, and produces high blood pressure, metabolic dysfunction of the kidney, liver damage, anemia, and other problems we will mention later. The impairment of calcium metabolism that occurs in cadmium toxicity can contribute to bone disorders such as osteoporosis and osteomalacia in women of child-bearing age over forty with dietary deficiencies (a condition variously known as igai-igai or itai-itai). Osteomalacia is abnormal softening of the bone with loss of calcium, along with debilitating weakness, broken bones, pain, loss of desire to eat, and loss of weight. Osteomalacia brings on, and makes worse, many other diseases, such as dementia.

In fact, cadmium, like mercury, is toxic to every body system of adults and children whether ingested, injected, or inhaled and tends to accumulate in body tissues. From chronic cadmium poisoning, as occurs in cigarette-smoking, people experience symptoms of chronic fatigue syndrome, forgetfulness, mental abberations of different types, iron-deficiency anemia, emphysema, yellow coloring of teeth, renal colic with passage of calcium stones (calculi) from the kidney, excessive calcium stone formation in the ureters, hypercalcuria (excessive calcium excreted in the urine), pain in the lower back and legs, pain in the sternum, and the condition some-times referred to as "milkman's syndrome" (named this because milkmen who made home deliveries used to experience the tearing of membranes around certain bones—the scapula, femur, and ileum). Cadmium toxicity also shows up as too much phosphorus salts in the urine, rheumatoid arthritis, decreased production of active vitamin D, a lessening of pulmo-nary function, prostate cancer (in workers exposed to cadmium oxide), and early death. There are complications for pregnant women too. Mothers who pass cadmium toxicity to their fetuses through the placenta will give birth to low birth-weight babies that are cadmium-toxic.

An overweight person is less likely to show the symptoms of cadmium poisoning because fat deposits tend to store the cadmium ions and hold them back from circulating to internal organs. Overly thin people, such as the somewhat malnourished Marjorie, are more easily struck by cadmium toxicity.

People poisoned by cadmium will show miscellaneous groups of symp-toms or outright disease, such as decreased appetite,[1,2] sore joints,[3] mouth lesions,[3] dry and scaly skin,[4] loss of hair,[3] loss of body weight,[2] lung damage,[5] shortened life span,[6] hypertension from increased cadmium-zinc ratio,[4,7,8] blood-vessel pathology in the kidneys,[8] sodium retention and swelling,[9] increased concentrations of cadmium, zinc, and calcium in the liver and kidneys,[10] interference with zinc metabolism and magnification of symptoms of zinc deficiency,[4] decreased body temperature due to inter-ference with zinc,[4] decreased growth,[3] malabsorption of iron, copper, and manganese,[11] diminished blood hemoglobin levels,[3,10] antibody suppres-sion,[12] reduced testosterone activity and marked impotence,[13] decreased milk production in lactation,[14] aminoaciduria (amino acids in the urine) and enzymuria (enzymes in the urine),[2] proteinuria (protein in the urine),[2] anemia,[2] and glycosuria (sugar in the urine),[2] cadmium edge on teeth,[10] loss of sense of smell (anosmia),[10] accelerated erythrocyte sedimentation test,[10] pneumosclerosis with structural changes in bone tissue,[10] kidney and liver disease,[10] and neurasthenic syndrome.[10]

Nearly every bit of any cadmium that is ingested is absorbed. Low doses of cadmium seem to provide a tolerance to a lethal dose.[15] Excess trace minerals in the diet as well as other nutrients can decrease or eliminate some of the toxic effects of the metal.[11] High calcium can partially protect against cadmium uptake, accumulation in the liver and kidney, and thus lessen the heavy metal's toxicity.[16,17] Taking supplemental doses of copper, iron, zinc, and selenium can lessen the toxicity of any input of cad-mium.[3,18,19,20,21,22] A high-protein diet also reduces the retention of cadmium.[23] Popping down pills of iron and vitamin C tends to lessen the adverse effects of the poisoning by decreasing the absorption of cadmium.[24]

SOURCES OF CADMIUM

The toxic effects of cadmium are kept under control in the body and brain by the presence of zinc, which is its neutralizer or antidote. However, refining processes used for manufactured food disturb the important cadmium-zinc balance. In natural whole wheat, for example, cadmium is present in proportion to zinc in a ratio of 1 to 120, but in denatured white bread the cadmium to zinc ratio is 1 to 12. Thus cadmium toxicity is acquired from confining oneself to eating refined foods such as white flour, white rice, and white sugar which contain reduced quantities of zinc. Cadmium is present in the air as an industrial contaminant. In addition, soft water usually contains higher levels of cadmium than does hard water. Soft water, especially if it is acidic, leaches cadmium from metal water pipes.

Certain other sources give rise to cadmium toxicity. Smoking cigarettes is the worst contaminant, for cadmium is the most voluminous metal found in cured tobacco. It is sprayed on the tobacco plant as a fungicide. In each cigarette, the residual concentration of cadmium averages 1.4 micrograms. Smoking one of these white sticks of death increases the body's burden. Passive cigarette smoke contains substantial amounts of cadmium, too, meaning that non-smokers who breathe in the smoke of others are being poisoned with the toxic heavy metal. Cigarette smokers are each partially responsible for the 3,300 annual deaths that take place in the United States from passive tobacco smoke. One pack of cigarettes deposits at least four micrograms (mcg) of cadmium into the lungs of a smoker, which is ten times the amount able to be assimilated by the body in one day. Thus, the patient we have discussed, Marjorie, invariably poisoned herself with twenty times the allowable physiological amount of cadmium. The cadmium had to go somewhere so it moved into her kidneys, blood vessels, and brain. Eventually it must be the source of her death.

When other cigarette smokers meet one or more of their inevitable fates—lung infections, lung cancer, or emphysema—cadmium is the most likely source for their demise. Cadmium weakens the immune system so as to allow for the growth of bacteria, viruses, fungi, worms and other parasites, and malignant tumors. Additional environmental contributors to cadmium poisoning are the following:

Black polythylene
Black rubber
Burned motor oil
Cadmium alloys such as those used
    for dental prosthetics
Cadmium vapor lamps
Ceramics
Copper refineries
Drinking water
Dust
Electroplating
Evaporated milk
Fungicides
Marine hardware rustproofed
    with cadmium
Organ meats such as kidney
    and liver
Oysters and other seafood
Paint pigments

Pesticides
Plastic tapes
Polyvinyl plastics
Processed foods
Refined wheat flour increasing
    the cadmium/zinc ratio
Rice irrigated by cadmium-
    contaminated water
Rubber carpet backing
Rubber tires
Sewage sludge and effluents
Silver polish
Soft drinks from vending machines
    with cadmium piping
Soft water, causing uptake of
    cadmium from galvanized pipes
Soil containing cadmium
Solders
Superphosphate fertilizers

INDUSTRIAL SOURCES OF CADMIUM TOXICITY

The American ore-smelting industries that process and refine cadmium-bearing ores release 3.1 million pounds of cadmium into the air every year. Probably much of the so-called "iron-deficiency anemia" is really cadmium poisoning caused by this pollution. Cadmium is estimated to contain more lethal possibilities than practically any other of the metallic elements because it is hardly looked at as a toxic agent. For another example of its subtle toxicity, one need merely look at the incineration of cadmium products. Disposal of cadmium-galvanized metals in zinc compounds and the waste from electroplating iron and steel products with cadmium are just two sources that distribute huge amounts of cadmium into the environment. No effort is made to recover the cadmium released as vapor. No records are kept on the cadmium content of metallic scrap. Control of just this double source of airborne cadmium would substantially reduce the total remitted in the United States each year and save untold numbers of middle-aged and elderly people from Alzheimer's disease.

Cadmium is used to color and stabilize motor oil and plastics, such as polyvinyl chloride containers, automobile seat covers, furniture, and floor coverings. When such items are burned, the toxic metal gets released into the atmosphere. Environmental poisoning from cadmium also comes from fungicides such as those sprayed on apples, tobacco, and potatoes. Serious occupational exposures to cadmium toxin do occur, too, and some of the most dangerous of them are listed below:

Cadmium alloy manufacturing
Ceramics manufacturing
Electroplating metals
Fungicide manufacturing
Jewelry making
Marine hardware manufacturing
Nickel-cadmium battery
  manufacturing

Paint manufacture using
  cadmium pigments
Painting with cadmium pigments
Process engraving
Rustproofing tools
Soldering
Tetraethyl lead manufacturing
Zinc or polymetallic ore smelting

Daily intakes of cadmium have been estimated at 0.2 to 0.5 milligrams (mg), with considerable variation according to sources and types of food and exposure in the environment. Cadmium's toxic effects may stem from its being stored for use in the body in place of zinc, when the proportion between the two metals is unfavorably out of balance. Zinc is the natural antagonist to cadmium; subsequently, nutritional supplementation with zinc in the amount of 30 milligrams daily (in split doses with breakfast and dinner) would be advantageous as a preventive measure for cadmium toxicity.

Henry A. Schroeder, M.D. (now deceased), former Professor Emeritus of Physiology at Dartmouth Medical School, and Director of Research at Brattleboro Memorial Hospital, did vast amounts of research on trace minerals. He developed a theory about cadmium that has proven to be true. It is now a medical fact: the heavy toxic metal is a causative factor in hypertension and related heart ailments. Dr. Schroeder found that regular administration of high doses of cadmium to rats, because of their biological similarity to humans, caused increased tension of their blood vessels. When he stopped giving cadmium to the rats, normal tension returned to their arteries and veins.

In humans, the urine of hypertensive patients contains up to 40 percent more cadmium than does the urine of normotensive persons. This finding lends credibility to Dr. Schroeder's concept that excessive cadmium leads directly to high blood pressure.

According to Dr. Schroeder, cadmium is a perfect example of an accumulative abnormal, and subtly toxic, trace metal in the environment causing widespread and serious human diseases, most of which are fatal. As such, cadmium is the worst of the bad actors among all metals.

Cadmium poisoning does exist to some extent in nearly everyone around the globe, but especially those residing in industrialized countries. It is present around us and in us. A main manifestation of its presence is the growing number of patients exhibiting symptoms associated with Alzheimer's disease. Therefore, therapeutic procedures must be accomplished to eliminate the heavy metal from our bodies through the use of intravenous chelating agents, which we will discuss at length in our book's Part IV. Chelation therapy detoxification is mandatory as a way to save the minds and lives of anyone who aspires to reaching the full complement of mankind's years.

CHAPTER 15

Iron and
Alzheimer's Disease

Arthur G., a seventy-eight-year-old retired family physician from Ocean City, New Jersey, was referred for evaluation of heart palpitations and paroxysmal atrial fibrillation to a renown internist of his acquaintance. John F. Hagaman, M.D. examined Arthur and found that he had been struck by "sick sinus syndrome." This syndrome involves the sinus node, an area of special heart tissue that generates the cardiac electric impulse and is in turn controlled by the autonomic nervous system. It is also called the sinus pacemaker. Accompanying his sick sinus syndrome, Arthur also suffered from slowing of the heart rate (bradycardia), right bundle branch blockage, and fluttering of the atrial valve.

As it happens, Dr. Hagaman's routine chemistry screening includes a readout of the amount of iron concentration in any patient's blood. The test revealed an extremely elevated serum iron which then prompted him to measure Arthur for serum ferritin concentration. Ferritin is an iron compound found in the intestine, spleen, and liver. Ferritin, too, was elevated so that Dr. Hagaman ordered that his patient undergo a liver biopsy, which showed, in turn, grade four stainable iron in hepatic (liver) paraenchymal cells. The sum of these laboratory examinations indicated that Arthur was the victim of hemochromatosis or iron overload, a rare disease in which iron deposits build up throughout the body.

As you will learn in this chapter, enlarged liver, skin discoloration, diabetes mellitus, and heart failure are the potential complications of iron overload. It is a disease most often developing in men over forty years of age.

Dr. Hagaman affirms, "This case illustrates the importance of routine iron screening during laboratory examinations. Had measurement of serum iron concentration and transferrin saturation not been a standardized part of the chemistry profile, it is likely that the diagnosis of hemochromatosis would have been missed. The patient's heart condition would have continued to progress, perhaps even to complete heart block, necessitating pacemaker placement."[1]

Iron is a common metallic element needed by the body to make hemoglobin, and it is supplied as a mineral nutrient from the ingestion of food. Hemoglobin is a complex protein-iron compound in the blood that carries oxygen to the cells from the lungs and carbon dioxide away from the cells to the lungs. Each red blood cell contains two hundred to three hundred molecules of hemoglobin. Every molecule of hemoglobin contains several molecules of heme, any one of which can carry a single molecule of oxygen. (The iron-containing compound, *heme*, combines with protein globin to form hemoglobin.)

IRON NUTRIENT DISORDERS

Iron deficiency and iron overload are both heavy-metal nutrient disorders. Each of these nutrient imbalances represents a misunderstanding of dietary iron by the public and those vast numbers of attending physicians untrained in nutritional therapy. Indeed, massive amounts of nutritional misinformation is derived from the uninformed medical community and even the United States Government.

The 1990 Dietary Guidelines for Americans (DGA), for instance, emphasizes the eating of greater amounts of fiber foods when they state: "Choose a diet with plenty of vegetables, fruits, and grain products." The 1990 DGA recommendation is laudatory and a generally healthy suggestion. Yet, too much fiber in the diet tends to render available nutritional iron unabsorbable; thus, physicians may well be diagnosing more iron deficiency as a result of consumers' overreaction to such federal guidelines.

Advocating indiscriminate intake of nutritional iron supplements can, conversely, have dire consequences. Only one in 500 adult American men has iron deficiency anemia but twice as many suffer from iron overload disease. In fact, approximately 10 percent of white Americans—male and female—are carriers of the hemochromatosis gene, making this the most common genetic disorder in the country. (*Hemochromatosis* is a disease in which iron deposits build up throughout the body to cause enlargement of the liver, skin discoloration, diabetes mellitus, and heart failure. This rare disease most often develops in men over forty years of age.) A person homozygous (inheriting two identical genes, one from each parent) for hemochromatosis, amounting to one in every 250 Americans, will pass on the iron-overload disease gene to 100 percent of his or her offspring.

Clearly, too little or too much body iron is detrimental to one's health.

Brain biochemical imbalance of iron tends to deteriorate mental health and exists as a potential source of Alzheimer's disease.

The first stage of negative iron balance (too little iron) is inadequate absorption from the food supply, due to either insufficient intake of dietary iron or a defect in intestinal digestion. This imbalance results in depletion of the body's iron stores, also known as reserve iron. Loss of reserves is followed by biochemical, and then clinical, iron deficiency. Stages of pathology for positive iron balance (too much iron) progress in similar ways through stages, resulting in failure of overloaded iron-storage organs (liver, spleen, and small intestine).[1]

THE USE OF NUTRITIONAL IRON SUPPLEMENTS

Iron is different from most other minerals. It is not easily lost from the body through the kidneys or via the stool, such as are other minerals like magnesium, potassium, and calcium. Iron absorption is tightly regulated by the body according to need. The average Western diet contains about 20 milligrams (mg) of iron each day, but only 3 to 5 percent of dietary iron in plant foods is actually absorbed. Spinach, for example, a vegetable high in iron, has only 1.5 percent of its iron content absorbable. The absorbability of iron contained in red meat, fowl, and fish averages 15 percent.

Men absorb a minimum of about 0.6 to 1.00 milligrams of iron daily. Women absorb slightly more than the male minimum. This inadequate rate of absorption just about balances the daily iron loss, which is usually less than 1.00 milligrams. So a reasonable amount of supplemental nutrient iron, say 20 milligrams of elemental iron, is not toxic. What is unneeded by the body is simply not absorbed. Still, in the United States and most other Western industrialized countries, iron deficiency does exist in a considerable proportion among the populations.

Nutritional supplementation with liquids, tablets, capsules, or spansules of iron would be useful for correcting iron deficiency. What happens, however, if an individual continues to take, say, 200 milligrams of iron sulphate when there is no bodily requirement for such an excess? (Some weightlifters take up to 600 milligrams daily, mistakenly believing they are doing good for their body-builds by "pumping iron.")Eventually iron overload must develop. The body's regulatory mechanisms break down and excessive quantities get absorbed to induce a toxic condition.

This iron overload can also occur during certain medical conditions in which red blood cells are destroyed too rapidly by the spleen, releasing the iron in the hemoglobin and also producing a yellow skin discoloration due to the excessive production of bilirubin, the substance released when red blood cells are destroyed.

The other adverse effect of taking too much iron as a food supplement is that it competes with zinc for uptake into the body. This can be dangerous during early pregnancy and is a good reason for carefully monitoring iron levels during pregnancy. Even so, the mother and growing fetus need extra iron. Blood tests, urine tests, and hair analyses of the mother should be part of her regular pregnancy evaluations.

Infants and children require a plentiful supply of nutritional iron, because with growth comes an increase in the volume of blood. Parasites, such as hook worm, in children can be a hidden source of blood loss and should be looked at if a child seems anemic or is not functioning well at school. Similarly, a diet that is devoid of animal products is usually low in iron and may not supply adequate quantities of the nutrient for normal growth.

Here is the answer to the question we posed above: high dose iron supplements should be taken only when there is a nutritional or medical need. And then the dosage should range at around the "optimal" daily allowance of 15 to 25 milligrams for men and 20 to 30 milligrams for women. Iron should not be part of any multisupplement formula. It should be ingested separately if supplemented and may be omitted if no deficiency exists.

One more item to consider: large quantities of iron supplementation will most likely cause gastrointestinal side effects if taken over a long period of time. The most common form of supplement is iron sulphate, which is inexpensive but can be irritating to the digestive tract. Much less irritating supplementation is acquired from the use of iron fumarate and/or iron gluconate. Both are less likely to cause the constipation produced by iron sulphate. Unless iron deficiency anemia has been diagnosed by a physician, thus requiring a high therapeutic dose of iron, it is best to take only a low-dosage iron supplement each day that is easily assimilated by the body.

Ferrous lactate (iron lactate) is another type of supplement that is quite safe. For best compliance in children, one of the newer, pleasant tasting liquid preparations is preferred. These liquid forms are easier to swallow than tablets.

As with the other minerals, look for the "elemental" iron content when buying supplements at the health food store.

IRON FOR VEGETARIANS

Vegetarians, who restrict their diets to vegetables, grains, beans, nuts, fruits, and seeds exclusively, have to compensate for those nutrients found primarily in the meat, fish, dairy, and poultry which are eliminated. Otherwise, health problems are certain to result, as they often do when diets are limited. For this reason, it is imperative that vegetarians know the nutritional components of what they are eating. If haphazard consumption is followed, iron deficiency or overload (among other nutrient irregularities) could follow.

Iron is available from plant foods but some vegetable-based foods such as uncooked grains, like muesli, contain phytates that bind up necessary minerals, including iron, like a magnet, and let them pass out of the body unused. Iron phytates are unabsorbed and pass out with the stool. One way around this problem for vegetarians is to eat only cooked, baked, or sprouted grains. The cooking and sprouting destroy phytates. Vitamin C counteracts binding properties of phytates, so that iron can be absorbed. If a vegetarian diet is already low in iron, the small amounts present will be easier to absorb if the diet is rich in vitamin C and if there are few phytates present.

Dairy products, too, are a poor source of iron. In fact, eating dairy products increases the dietary intake of calcium which then competes with iron for uptake inside the body. Calcium-rich foods may decrease iron absorption by up to 50 percent. This can be a significant factor for children with low immune function who tend to come down with colds and flu all the time. These immune-suppressed children need optimal stores of iron.

Unfortunately, animal products such as fish, poultry, and meat are the best sources of iron and zinc. Children who live on wheat and dairy products with no fruit, vegetables, or meat are the most likely to be deficient in iron and zinc. Therefore they have a less than optimal immune function. Such children probably exhibit adverse behaviors also as a result of dysfunctional brain cells. Our discussion in the next section points up the value of iron for normal neurological response. Iron imbalance in the brain is a suspected source of dementia of the Alzheimer's type.

There are some vegetables, fruits, and grains that are high in iron. The list below gives some suggestions for vegatarian options that are high in iron. (These are listed in order from highest content to lowest.)

Kelp	Sunflower seeds	Jerusalem artichokes
Brewer's yeast	Millet	Brazil nuts
Blackstrap molasses	Parsley	Beet greens
Wheat bran	Almonds	Swiss chard
Pumpkin seeds	Dried prunes	Dandelion greens
Squash seeds	Cashews	English walnuts
Wheat germ	Raisins	Dates

Cooked dry beans	Green Peas	Broccoli
Sesame seeds, hulled	Brown rice	Whole wheat bread
Pecans	Ripe olives	Cauliflower
Peanuts	Artichokes	
Tofu	Mung bean sprouts	

IRON METABOLISM AND ALZHEIMER'S DISEASE

"Iron irregularity is a factor both in aging and Alzheimer's disease," says James R. Connor, Ph.D., assistant professor of anatomy at the Penn State College of Medicine, Milton S. Hershey Medical Center. "Iron is vital to the functions of the brain and the entire body. If you robbed the body of iron, you would see symptoms much like those of Alzheimer's disease, such as motor impairments and psychological disorders."

As early as 1953, Dr. L. Goodman, another anatomist writing in the *Journal of Nervous and Mental Diseases,* described iron accumulation in the brains of people with Alzheimer's disease.[2] Building on this finding, Dr. Connor has discovered through his research, which is supported by the American Federation for Aging Research, the Alzheimer's Disease Research Program of the American Health Assistance Foundation, and the National Multiple Sclerosis Society, that large amounts of iron are normally transported to and from the brain. He has recent evidence that transferrin, the protein that transports iron, dysfunctions in people with DAT. Moreover, transferrin bends and transports the toxic metal aluminum, which has long been thought to have a role in Alzheimer's disease (see Chapters 6, 7, 8, and 9).

"When iron is digested in the stomach," Dr. Connor continued, "it bonds with transferrin that acts as an iron taxi. Transferrin carries the iron through the blood to its destination in the brain, the oligodendrocyte neuroglial cell. The oligodendrocytes are the predominant cell type to contain ferritin [iron] in the human brain. Normally, another transferrin taxi comes along to pick up the iron and take it through the rest of the brain. As a result of physiological malfunction, the second transferrin taxi never arrives to pick up its passenger.

"This finding holding true," conjectures Dr. Connor, "we will have a better understanding of why such a range of neurological deficits are associated with Alzheimer's Disease. We can go on to correct the problem and alleviate some of the symptoms of Alzheimer's. The relationship between iron, aluminum, and transferrin presents scientists with a focal point from which to pursue aluminum neurotoxicity. There is evidence that aluminum increases lipid peroxidative damage in the brain possibly through an interaction with iron."[3,4,5]

IRON REQUIREMENTS IN THE BRAIN

Iron imbalance (not just iron deficiency but also excess iron) influences changes seen in DAT. Iron imbalance decreases the formation of some mitochondrial enzymes, (the main source of cellular energy) which result in lessened brain cellular activity.[6] There will be susceptibility of cholinergic neurotransmission, a well-known Alzheimer's disease defect, to impairment of oxidative metabolism.[7] Nerve fibers release a signal carrier, called acetylcholine, at the connection of muscles and nerves. Iron imbalance interferes with this signal (cholinergic neurotransmission) and impairs or stops the use of oxygen to break down nutritional components. This pathology is known to occur in DAT. Neurons and glia, as do all cells, require iron for many aspects of their cellular physiology.[8] More specifically, iron is involved in the function and synthesis of the nuerotransmitters dopamine, serotonin, and gamma-aminobutyric acid (GABA).[9] Iron is also involved in the synthesis and degradation of fatty acids[10] and cholesterol.[11] These latter substances are important components of cell membranes and are especially high in myelin, the lipid-rich substance that insulates nerve axons and forms the white matter of the brain.[12] Recent reports in the medical literature indicate that cholesterol is decreased in the brains of Alzheimer's disease patients.[13] Moreover, the brain is reponsible for synthesizing its own cholesterol.[12]

By virtue of its reactive ability with hydrogen peroxide and oxygen, free iron is known to initiate lipid peroxidation (the burning of fat in arterial walls),[14,15] leading to membrane damage and ultimately brain cell death. Because of its high lipid content, the brain is especially susceptible to oxidative injury.[16] Iron is a critical factor in the induction of events leading to lipid peroxidative damage in the brain.[17] Consequently, iron must both be available to cells and stringently regulated. An imbalance of iron and/or the iron regulatory proteins in the brain could result in substantial damage to neurons and glia leading to neurodegeneration and neurological dysfunction.

HOW IRON DEFICIENCY AFFECTS BRAIN BIOCHEMISTRY

We saw in Chapter 13 how lead poisoning of the brain induces behavioral abnormalities in children that include lowering of the intelligence quotient

(IQ), reduction of learning ability, and depletion of the cognitive processes. Exactly the same situation occurs in a child with chronic iron deficiency.

The brain has a great tendency to retain iron, and its slow loss over time is matched by a reduced rate of recovery. This finding was uncovered by experiments on laboratory rats and mice. The animal studies showed how in iron deficiency the content of non-heme iron in the brain is reduced by over 40 percent. In iron-depleted children who receive iron supplementation, there is only slow recovery of learning and behavior or in some cases no recovery at all.

The amount of iron actually present in the brain exceeds the normal requirement of all the biochemical systems present by 90 percent. No one knows why there is such an excess. It has been postulated that the organ of thought needs a "functional pool" of brain iron of about 80 percent of the normal level for adequate brain function. Without it, the most prominent feature of iron deficiency is a slowdown of neurotransmission or nerve signals in dopamine neurons in various parts of the brain. It is caused by a reduction in the number of dopamine D_2 receptors responsible for replaying the nervous impulses. Iron does form an integral part of these important dopamine receptors.

Iron deficiency in humans is usually observed in the first decades of life. This is also the most crucial time for brain development and differentiation to take place. The consequence of diminished dopamine-related neurotransmission is an alteration in behaviors and the body's biochemical reactions related to dopamine, the most important of which is the reduction in learning processes.

In laboratory rats, the first weeks of life are when there is the largest increase in iron concentration and dopamine D_2 receptor numbers. Very young rats (aged 10 days) who were experimented on and made iron deficient showed highly significant reductions in brain iron and dopamine D_2 receptor numbers as compared with adult rats (aged 48 days).

Another consequence of early iron deficiency in immature animals is that sustained iron therapy for more than six months does not fully restore the brain iron, dopamine D_2 receptor activity, proper behavior, or normal learning processes. The startling susceptibility of the young, immature animal brain to iron deficiency suggests that there is an accompanying irreversible damage with long term consequences in their adult lives.

For humans the consequence is likely to be Alzheimer's disease. The major portion (80 percent) of iron that is found in the adult brain is deposited in the first years of life. But this process can be inhibited by poor nutrition during those early years. There is irreversible damage induced by this very early iron deficiency, a truism indicated by children who fail to respond to iron therapy when it is administered later in life.

During iron deficiency, the blood-brain barrier (BBB), that sensitive protective membraneous layer surrounding the brain and spinal cord in animals and humans, is significantly altered. Additional animal experiments show that the BBB allows an increased uptake of iron when iron-deficient animals are supplemented with nutritional iron. Unfortunately, extra iron uptake by the BBB allows the influx of other potentially damaging molecules, such as insulin, that are not normally permitted entry into the brain. Such a finding stresses the seriousness of preventing iron deficiency in early childhood. Because of the lack of brain iron arising from childhood deficiencies, medical scientists have been forced to seek an answer to the question: to what extent do maladaptive behavior and learning reflect iron deficiency-induced changes to the BBB and its subsequent pathological disruption of the brain? So far, they have found no answer!

IRON DEFICIENCY AND DOPAMINE

Dopamine is known to play an inhibitory role in the attention span and random, exploratory actions of animals and humans. Such a conclusion was arrived at by behavioral research with laboratory animals using this main chemical message transmitter through the dopaminergic nerves in rat brains. Experimental stimulation of the rats' dopamine pathways led to a decrease in diffuse exploratory behavior and a reduction in the variety of behaviors. Further stimulation of the same animals led to grossly restricting their range of behavior to a single behavioral sequence.

From these experiments it was concluded that deficits in the dopaminergic neuronal pathways underlie attention deficit disorders in children or those with so-called hyperactive behavior. Those children displaying hyperactive behavior are shown to have a high turnover of dopamine in the cerebrospinal fluid and a high concentration of noradrenaline in the urine. Noradrenaline, unlike dopamine, produces a more diffuse nonspecific form of behavioral activation. It should be noted that high levels of urinary noradrenaline also have been observed present in iron deficient children, but it has been argued that the hyperactive child's problem is not just an excess of activity but activity that is not directed by adequate attentional control. Hence, iron is especially important for the correct functioning of dopamine-dependent, attentional modulatory systems in the brain. Iron deficiency and depletion of dopamine receptors and/or dopamine may explain the attentional problems associated with behavioral disability, cognition, and problems in iron deficient children.

If a child is to be successful at school, it is probable that his iron status is especially important for left hemisphere arousal. The left hemisphere contains more grey matter than the right hemisphere, and iron is more heavily concentrated in the grey matter. Iron is necessary for sequential, analytical, and verbal cognition in a school-age child. Measures of a major dopamine metabolite are shown to correlate with cortical arousal only in the left hemisphere of the brain.

IRON DEFICIENCY IN THE ELDERLY

Anemia caused by the ratio of too little iron to hemoglobin in the blood is called *iron deficiency anemia*. It is marked by pallor, fatigue, and weakness. The iron deficiency may be caused by insufficient dietary iron, poor absorption of iron, or chronic bleeding. Chronic bleeding is the most common cause, and in women this usually occurs because of heavy menstrual flow. After menopause, one would imagine that women should be almost immune to iron deficiency anemia, but this is not the case. The condition becomes increasingly more common with advancing age in both men and women and shows up in as many as 8 percent of elderly women.

So what is the most likely reason for iron deficiency to be common in elderly women who show no sign of frank bleeding? The main cause discovered by hospital investigations is that specific gastrointestinal lesions such as gastric erosions, gastric or duodenal ulcers, ulcerative esophagitis, gastric or intestinal carcinoma, and ulcerative colitis are present. Hospital-based surveys of anemia in the elderly consistently highlight the iron deficiency problem. One study of 1,094 patients aged over sixty revealed that 103 had iron deficiency anemia.[18]

At Leicester General Hospital, Leicester, England, 60 patients with unexplained anemia were referred to the geriatric assessment unit. They underwent gastrointestinal endoscopy or sigmoidoscopy or barium enemas and were diagnosed as suffering from benign upper gastrointestinal lesions. The source of such difficulties for 64 percent of the patients turned out to be their regular swallowing of nonsteroidal anti-inflammatory agents (NSAIA) such as aspirin. NSAIA are known to cause gastric ulceration with concomitant internal bleeding. In fact, when the reasons for anemia for the entire Leicester General Hospital geriatric group were identified, 88 percent of the patients were found to have bleeding gastrointestinal lesions.[19]

Elderly patients with rheumatoid arthritis are also prone to anemia. Their anemia is not connected with any internal bleeding problems but rather comes from the inflammatory process itself. The anemia arises from either a shortened red blood cell survival time, an impaired response of iron from tissue stores, or an impaired response of bone marrow (the source of red blood cells) to anemia. Of all patients with rheumatoid arthritis, the reported frequency of anemia has ranged from 16 to 65 percent.[20,21] Over 50 percent of these cases are due to iron deficiency anemia as defined by the absence of bone marrow iron stores.

Intramuscularly-injected iron dextran (a drug containing concentrated iron) is the most frequently used form of parenteral iron to treat the iron deficiency anemia of rheumatoid arthritis. Sometimes its administration leads to oxidative damage from free radicals, increased inflammation of the membranes enclosing joints, and pain. According to physicians attending The Inflammation Group at the Bone and Joint Research Unit located in the London Hospital, "Oral iron is the preferred way to treat iron deficient rheumatoid patients." Their declaration is based on the fact that iron should be delivered to the blood stream quite slowly in order to prevent the "flare" reaction that commonly occurs with the more rapid intravenous (IV) infusion. Slow administration of iron prevents further joint inflammation resulting from a high dose of iron supplementation.[22]

Apart from the more obvious reasons for iron deficiency, such as an imbalanced diet or malabsorption, it is now clear that inflammatory gastrointestinal problems and rheumatoid arthritis can be associated with iron deficiency anemia in a significant number of elderly people in our society. A low dose, palatable, liquid iron supplement like Floradix Formula Herbal Iron Extract or Floradix Iron + Herbs Liquid Extract Formula for such elderly people may lead to a great improvement in the general fatigue they experience.

IRON DEFICIENCY AND LEARNING

Iron deficiency numbers among the most prevalent nutritional disorders in the world. It induces behavioral changes in middle-aged and older adults that include unusual depths of lethargy, fatigue, irritability, listlessness, apathy, short attention span, inability to concentrate, and pagophagia (a pathological craving for ice). In children, the same condition offers the additional possibility of decreased intelligence quotient (IQ), reduction in the learning process, and adverse changes in behavior, including hyperactivity.

These conclusions were established by animal studies with iron-deficient rats. The studies have shown that the learning capacity of iron-deficient rats is significantly inferior to that of control iron-replete rats, animals which have no deficiency disease. The longer the rats are kept on iron-deficient diets, the greater the deficit in learning. Their learning deficit was evident even when the level of hemoglobin was not significantly below normal. What is more, iron supplementation failed to produce a rapid restoration in learning and/or memory. Indeed, these deficits remained, affecting the animals even after two months of treatment with copious amounts of nutritional iron.

Findings in studies on humans support the results obtained from animal models. A placebo-controlled, double-blind, clinical trial was conducted in Thailand to assess the importance of iron treatment on the intelligence quotient and educational attainment among 1,358 children, ages nine, ten, and eleven. The children who received diets containing sufficient nutritional iron showed significantly higher IQ scores than did iron-deficient and anemic children. Moreover, iron treatment administered for a period of fourteen weeks was insufficient to correct the variance in the deficient children.

In contrast, another study conducted among 130 iron-deficient, rural Indonesian children showed that extra iron supplementation for three months not only corrected anemia but also resulted in an improvement in their learning achievement scores.

Similar to the Indonesians, studies among Indians around Bombay involving iron supplementation for school children of various ages, both anemic and non-anemic, demonstrated significant improvements in cognitive function scores compared with anemic children who received a placebo and no iron. Improvements were demonstrated in visual recall and digit-span cognitive function tests, as well as clerical tasks.

IRON SUPPLEMENTATION

To get maximal iron absorption, take an iron supplement with meat or fish and foods containing vitamin C (such as citrus fruits, which contain higher amounts of ascorbic acid). You might use vitamin C supplementation to accompany iron supplementation, too. Vitamin C ensures conversion of dietary iron in the usual ferric form to the ferrous form that is necessary for absorption through the gut wall. Ascorbic acid reduces the chance of dietary iron binding up to other dietary components that render it poorly soluble and non-bioavailable. As we have mentioned at the beginning of this chapter, such poor solubility occurs when iron reacts with phytates in raw cereals, polyphenols (wrongly referred to as tannins) in tea, and phosphate ions. For this reason, raw cereals should be cooked, baked, or sprouted. The European mueslis, containing raw grains, are high in phytates and when eaten as a breakfast cereal, make iron insoluble in the balance of that day's diet by binding the mineral to them.

In fermented foods such as bread, the main phytate component, called inositol hexaphosphate, is partially broken down. The fermentation of vegetables may also induce a formation of iron absorption to promote compounds since sauerkraut markedly enhances iron absorption. On the other hand, vitamin C strongly counteracts the ability of phytates to inhibit iron absorption. Knowing this, the fact suggests that citrus fruits, which are high in vitamin C, will enhance iron absorption.

Calcium and iron are antagonists and interfere with each other's absorption from the diet. Calcium tends to overshadow iron's antagonism. A 600-milligram calcium supplement inhibits the absorption of an 18-milligram iron supplement by only 50 percent, especially if the supplements are taken with a meal and even more so if the meal is low in animal protein.

Iron and zinc are usually obtained from the same food sources, such as animal products. Because of this, a deficiency of iron may well be accompanied by a deficiency of zinc. Iron-deficient subjects also tend to absorb more lead and cadmium. In children ages one to twelve, the higher the blood-lead levels, the lower the percentage of iron bound to transferrin, its blood carrier-protein.

IRON OVERLOAD

Corwin Q. Edwards, M.D., professor of Medicine at the University of Utah School of Medicine, and his colleagues advise, "There are only two ways a person can become overloaded with iron: by increased intestinal absorption of iron, or by parenteral [injection] introduction of iron via red blood cell transfusions or injection of an iron preparation. . . . Normal adult men absorb 1 milligram of iron per day and menstruating women absorb 2 milligrams. Patients with hemochromatosis absorb 2 to 5 milligrams of iron per day, even though they are iron overloaded, and urinary tract epithelial cells contain excess iron, they also shed more iron than normal, but not enough to compensate for increased iron absorption. By the time symptoms appear, a patient with hemochromatosis may have accumulated as much as 20 to 40 grams of iron in storage organs. . . . In normal adults, storage iron totals 1 gram in men and 0.5 grams in women, with a total body iron content of 3 to 4 grams."[23]

Too much iron in the diet, such as from excessive intake of iron supplementation, can account for the increased intestinal absorption remarked upon by Dr. Edwards. With every tenth white American being a heterozygous carrier of the hemochromatosis gene and each 250th adult American male being a homozygous carrier, the storage of excess iron is quite a common occurrence. Where does this extra iron get stored? In the liver, pancreas, pituitary, adrenals, heart, and skeletal muscle. When the extra iron leaches into the general blood circulation, which organ tissues are most sensitive to the effects of abnormal iron metabolism? The answer becomes obvious from our earlier chapter statements; the most iron-sensitive tissues are the neurons of the brain.

To prevent or arrest brain damage, excess body iron should be removed as quickly as possible in all patients with the relatively common condition of hemochromatosis, regardless of the presence or absence of symptoms or signs of iron overload. There are two available treatment methods to accomplish this mandatory requirement: chelation therapy and phlebotomy therapy.

The first treatment, chelation therapy, is the administration, under the supervision of a physician, of a protein-like substance, combined with other nutrients, into a vein of your body. It is a process that takes several hours, so that the nutrients slowly circulate through the 60,000 miles of blood vessels that feed your body's organs, tissues, and cells. Chelation therapy, by ridding your body of potentially deadly poisons, can, more than any other therapeutic agent, give you the gift of longer life.

The chelating substance, particularly the protein (a man-made amino acid), grasps certain minerals, usually metal atoms such as lead, mercury, cadmium, iron, manganese, and others with two available bonds, or valences. The metal atom becomes locked in by the encircling amino acid, which, since it does not combine with any part of the human body, has nowhere to go—except out of the body.

Most of the toxic material passes out through the kidneys as part of the urine during the first twenty-four hours following the administration of chelation therapy. And with the amino acid travels the captured metallic ions that may very well have been producing toxic effects in your body.

By the chelation of toxins from the cells, the life of those cells is extended. Your body gets rid of accumulated devastation from metallic pollutants, destructive free radicals, radiation particles, and assorted foreign elements that cause cellular breakdown.

A hemochromatosis patient may suffer from angina or bone marrow suppression, in which case the other treatment, phlebotomy, cannot be performed. Such an individual will do much better physiologically from receiving intravenous or subcutaneous infusions of ethylene diamine tetraacetic acid or deferoxamine, either of which are excellent iron chelators. The infusion of either of these chelating agents deplete iron stores more slowly than phlebotomy.

The second treatment, phlebotomy therapy, is entry into a vein with a needle and syringe, to release blood in order to remove an excess of red blood cells containing iron. "Most hemochromatosis patients tolerate the removal of two 500-milliliter units of blood per week. At this rate of phlebotomy therapy, taking into account the amount of iron absorbed from the diet, hemochromatosis patients lose about 50 milligrams of iron per day, or 18 grams a year," wrote the Utah University researchers. "Massive iron stores of 20 to 30 grams can be normalized in 12 to 18 months of twice-weekly phlebotomy. Because the time-dosage toxic threshold of iron that results in irreversible organ damage is known, iron stores should be depleted completely and quickly. Phlebotomy performed at a rate of less than 500 milliliters every month may be counterproductive, as the rate of iron absorption from the diet may exceed the rate of iron depletion."[23]

The effect of chelation therapy or phlebotomy therapy on the amount of iron coming out of the body's storage areas may be monitored by measuring blood concentrations of hemoglobin or hematocrit. Treatment should continue until iron-limited erythropoiseis (red blood cell production) develops. At that time, the volume of packed red blood cells, the average red-cell volume, percent saturation of transferrin, and serum-ferritin concentration will be very low. After iron stores have been depleted, maintenance treatment using chelation therapy or phlebotomy should be carried forward four to six times each year to prevent reaccumulation of excess storage iron. Lifelong maintenance treatment is recommended, because a person who is homozygous for hemochromatosis whose maintenance therapy is neglected may become iron overloaded again over a period of a few years.

In 1976 it was reported that brain-syndrome patients with hemochromatosis whose iron stores were depleted by such therapy lived an average of 63 months after diagnosis, whereas untreated patients had an average survival of only 18 months.[24]

Another scientific investigation carried out in 1985 on 163 hemochromatosis patients demonstrated that those who did not have diabetes or cirrhosis at the time of diagnosis and treatment experienced a normal life expectancy. Cumulative survival of all hemochromatosis patients who underwent iron depletion therapy was 92 percent at five years, 76 percent at ten years, 59 percent at fifteen years, and 49 percent at twenty years.[25]

According to tabulations from a membership survey conducted by the

Table 15.1 National Origins of 892 Patients With Hemochromatosis

Irish	288	Welsh	9
German	176	Chinese	8
English	168	Russian	8
Scottish	55	Belgian	7
French	38	Portuguese	6
Italian	25	Finnish	4
Swiss	16	Czechoslovakian	4
Polish	16	Austrian	2
Danish	15	Luxembourgian	2
Swedish	10	Armenian	2
Norwegian	10	Syrian	2
Dutch	10	Greek	1
American Indian	10		

The survey shown is a tabulation done by the 1988 membership of a national organization, The Iron Overload Diseases Association. Roberta Crawford was organizational president at that time this survey was taken.

Iron Overload Diseases Association, iron overload from the presence of the hemochromatosis gene may be considered a killer disease of both the body and the brain among numerous patients of variable national origins (see Table 15.1).

CHAPTER 16
Manganese

On a warm July afternoon in 1984, James Oliver Huberty opened fire with an automatic assault rifle at a busy McDonald's restaurant in San Ysidro, California. He killed 21 customers and wounded 19 other innocent bystanders. A police sharpshooter's bullet finally managed to stop the slaughter. Among other tests, the city's medical examiner performed a special analysis of Huberty's hair. He found it to contain extraordinarily high levels of the toxic elements lead and cadmium, and an even greater elevation of the essential mineral manganese. In fact, the killer's hair-mineral analysis exhibited a "trace metal pattern previously observed only in violent sociopaths," read the medical examiner's report afterwards.

In January 1989, Patrick E. Purdy also sprayed automatic assault rifle fire, only he aimed at attendees of the Cleveland Elementary School in Stockton, California. He killed five children and wounded thirty others. Then this violent madman stuck the rifle's muzzle in his mouth and pulled its trigger using his thumb. Purdy also had a postmortem mineral analysis performed on strands of hair and was found to possess an exceedingly high amount of manganese in his body tissues.

As it happens, both killers had been preoccupied with guns and were members of the "old boy" network, belonging to their local chapters of the National Rifle Association. Moreover, their daily work schedules were identical too. They were welders laboring at jobs in which they applied heat either electrically or by means of a torch to metals in order to join them into alloys. Among the metals that the killers were working with regularly were lead, cadmium, iron, and manganese.

THE GOTTSHCALK STUDY

California State Senator Robert Presley has requested in California Senate

207

Bill SB107 that a five-year research project be authorized to determine if there is a correlation between violent conduct and abnormal, excessive levels of certain vitamins and minerals—especially heavy-metallic minerals—in the body systems of criminals and other people exhibiting antisocial behavior. The question to which this legislation seeks an answer is whether normalizing the levels of heavy metals in the body and brain would cut down abnormal, violent, criminal, and generally antisocial behavior in the United States.

Senator Presley said, "Preliminary studies in California and elsewhere, including a study involving youths in five states, have shown that a high percentage of violent offenders have substandard levels of essential nutrients, or high levels of such substances as iron, cadmium, manganese, or lead. This does not prove one causes the other. But examining this premise will be the aim of the project. If there is a correlation, this could be landmark research since we do not have much luck at present in reducing violent conduct in our society."

"It is not far fetched to suggest that we examine possible tie-ins between abnormal substance intake of vitamins and toxic chemicals and the possible impact on the brain as regards violent behavior," added Senator Presley. "It's serious research that needs to be done."[1]

This same California legislative medical research project, having been undertaken by Professor Louis A. Gottschalk, M.D., Ph.D., and his colleagues in the Department of Psychiatry and Human Behavior, at the University of California, Irvine, was financially underwritten by Everett L. "Red" Hodges of Tustin, California, an independent oil producer. Mr. Hodges offers grants toward such research because, he revealed in a personal interview, his son has had such difficulty with the law. The young man has exhibited antisocial behavior which Mr. Hodges indicated was probably due to physiological tissue overload with heavy metals like manganese.

Some of this chapter's educational material is excerpted from the four University of California researchers' pre-published paper, "Abnormalities in Hair Trace-Elements as Indicators of Aberrant Behavior." Out of tribute to his political support and financial contributions, Mr. Hodges has been added as the paper's fifth author. Mr. Hodges has furnished the information for additional publication by this book's authors.

In a January 31, 1991 letter to Red Hodges from the Director of the California State Department of Corrections, James Rowland, the director states: "The research dealing with the relationship between manganese toxicity and violent behavior may very well represent a significant breakthrough in understanding and possibly reducing the incidence of violent behavior. Through your good offices, we are accumulating an archive in the Department's Research Branch on the effects on behavior of toxic levels of trace materials in the body. Included in the archive is the very important tape containing the testimony on manganese toxicity presented by Dr. John Donaldson [whose research we shall cite later] at the hearing conducted by the Environmental Protection Agency. I want to congratulate you and Dr. Gottschalk on the success of your six-year effort."

Phase I

Dr. Gottschalk and his team conducted their study in three phases of time and technique that took place in 1984 (Phase I), 1987 (Phase II), and 1988 (Phase III).

In Phase I, the team acquired hair samples from 104 male criminal offenders, convicted felons lodged in a class III prison (maximum security) at the Deuel Vocational Institute, Stanislaus, California. Prior to this study phase, Alexander G. Schauss, M.A., Director of the American Institute for Biosocial Research, Inc. of Tacoma, Washington, had performed a similar study that, according to Alex Schauss, "There was association between significant declines in the levels of toxics [the heavy metals copper, lead, and cadmium] in subjects and subjective and psychometric reports of behavioral improvements [when the metals were reduced in the subjects' body tissues]."[2]

As in the Gottschalk investigation, Schauss used hair-mineral analysis as his evaluative tool.[3] Hair is collected without trauma to the individual, and can be analyzed relatively easily. Trace elements are accumulated in hair at concentrations that generally appear higher than those present in blood or urine.[4] Minerals once situated in the hair are no longer in dynamic equilibrium with the body since hair is a metabolic end product.[5,6] Inasmuch as this tissue grows at the rate of approximately 1.0 centimeter per month,[7,8] it provides a record over time of the status in the body of past toxic minerals.

A number of concerns have been raised by the conventional medical community about the utility of hair as a diagnostic tool. These concerns mainly center around the manner of collection, preparation, analysis of hair samples, interpretation of data, and hair that is contaminated by permanent waving solutions, dyes, or bleachings. If the hair sample is washed in the standard manner as preparation for its analysis procedure, however, such potential shortcomings may be effectively controlled.

The prisoner group in the Gottschalk team Phase I study consisted of thirty-nine whites, thirty-three hispanics, and thirty-two blacks who had been incarcerated for no less than one year prior to the hair sampling, and therein lies the flaw in this first phase study. Seeing the investigators' conclusions, critics validly questioned whether artifacts from manganese present in the prison's cooking utensils, shampoos, soaps, and other items might not have colored hair-mineral analysis results among prisoners who had been incarcerated for such a long period of time.

The prison inmates had been convicted of serious felonies, mainly murder, rape, armed robbery, and assault with a deadly weapon. Their average age was twenty-nine years old. A control group of ordinary people from the towns of Tracy and Stanislaus, California, and a second control group, the Deuel Vocational Institute prison guards themselves, were tested as well.

In the Phase I study, the Gottschalk team could not duplicate the published 1981 Schauss findings, despite hair tests being conducted for twenty-three different minerals, including aluminum, arsenic, beryllium, cadmium, calcium, chromium, cobalt, copper, iron, lead, lithium, magnesium, manganese, mercury, molybdenum, nickel, sodium, phosphorous, potassium, selenium, silicon, vanadium, and zinc. What he found, instead, was that there is a correlation between high levels of managanese and antisocial behavior.

The convicted felons had an average level of 2.20 parts per million manganese. The town controls had a mean level of 0.30 parts per million. The prison guard controls had a mean level of 0.55 parts per million. The differences between the prisoners and the two control groups were statistically significant; yet, since the prison population had been incarcerated for longer than 12 months, another study was thought necessary to be conducted and Phase II of the eventual three-part test was scheduled for the near future.

Phase II

Gottschalk and associates recruited sixty prison inmates awaiting trial on charges of violent crimes from the Los Angeles and San Bernardino California county jails for their Phase II study. In custody during part of 1987 for an average period of twenty days, there were twenty whites, twenty hispanics, and twenty blacks. As controls for comparison were forty-two conviction-free subjects matched for age, sex, and race. The only unusual metal pattern for hair content significantly different between the two groups was in manganese. The imprisoned group possessed an average manganese level of 1.39 parts per million; whereas the control group of citizens in good standing with society had an average level of 0.41 parts per million.

Phase III

The third phase of the Gottschalk three-part study was undertaken in 1988 at the San Bernardino County Jail. Here, twenty nine white males, ranging in age from eighteen to thirty nine (average age of twenty seven), and charged with violent crimes, were recruited for hair-mineral analyses. The control group of fifty nine noncriminal, white, male subjects had an average age of thirty three. Any subject who had used dyes, bleaches, or other hair chemical treatments was excluded from the study. Each subject was paid ten dollars for his participation. Studies of the metals in these hair samples were performed by Doctors Data Laboratories, Inc. of West Chicago, Illinois.

As with Phases I and II, in Phase III of the study, a retired Superior Court Judge held the sample codes while the hair samples were being analyzed. Only after the data were tabulated were the codes broken to determine who had what tissue levels of which mineral. This third phase of the study along with the other two, therefore, was double-blinded.

In Phase III, the average manganese level in hair for the jailed group was 0.71 parts per million and for the control group was 0.33 parts per million. The difference was statistically significant in Phase III.

When all three phases are grouped together, we can observe that the average manganese level in the hair samples from 197 prison inmates was 1.62 parts per million as compared with all of the controls who had an average level of 0.35 parts per million. These levels certainly were significantly different and suggested that abnormal trace-mineral metabolism is a factor associated with abnormally aggressive, criminal-like, and generally antisocial behavior. Hair samples taken from violent, criminal-type individuals who exhibit abberant thinking possess a metal pattern that can distinguish them from law-abiding individuals. Their criminal behavior, aggressiveness, or tendencies toward serious violence are predictable.[2,9]

MANGANESE MADNESS

An essential trace metal, manganese acts as a cofactor for the enzymes hydrolase, kinase, decarboxylase, transferase, and the free-radical scavenging enzyme superoxide dismutase. Such a mineral cofactor, also referred to as a coenzyme, is needed for the proper composition of body fluids, the formation of blood and bone, the maintenance of healthy nerve function, and for other purposes related to enzymatic function. Gross deficiencies of the trace metal produce a variety of diverse signs and symptoms, among them are weight loss, dermatitis, nausea, and the slow growth of hair.[10] It has been noted by medical scientists that epileptics have lower than normal manganese levels in blood and hair.[11]

Toxicity from an overload of manganese in the brain causes a depletion of dopamine, the well-recognized brain nerve-impulse transporter (neuro-transmitter).[12,13,14] The first symptoms of manganese overload are fatigue, a hypnotic-like state or trance, irritability, and erratic behavior that has been euphamistically labelled by toxicologists as "manganese madness" (*locaura manganica*). An individual suffering from manganese madness exhibits various antisocial acts, violent behavior, and involvement with "stupid" crimes such as actions taken on impulse, which often occur in domestic violence.[15,16]

Also the antisocial individual with manganese intoxication will engage in minor compulsive acts, emotional instability typified by easy laughter or crying, and hallucinations, as when one behaves erratically from being constantly drunk.[13] Moreover, there is generalized muscular weakness, followed by difficulty in walking, headaches, impaired equilibrium, and slurred speech. Most of all, elevated manganese levels have been found associated with dementia and extrapyramidal brain signs.[17] (Extrapyramidal brain signs are indicated by poor coordination and control of movements from abnormality of nerves and fibers.)

The only inconsistency in the three-phase study cited above was that manganese levels found in the hair samples of prisoners tested by Dr. Gottschalk and his team were somewhat lower than those in persons known to have toxic exposure to manganese.[18] Still, it was obvious that these prisoners were manganese-toxic, because their response to subclinical elevation made them perform antisocial acts that resulted in their imprisonment.

MANGANESE NEUROTOXICITY

Two researchers at the *Institut de Recherces Cliniques de Montreal*, Montreal, Quebec, Canada, John Donaldson, Ph.D., and Andre Barbeau, Ph.D., uncovered the ability of manganese ions to considerably destroy dopamine. Such destruction by auto-oxidation can result in the production of hydroxyl free radicals that possess the ability to destroy cells, in turn, for discrete brain compartments like the substantia nigra.[19,20] Free radicals wreak considerable havoc among the catecholaminergic nerve cells localized there.[21,22] Since this region of the brain contains the pigment neuromelanin, which is derived from dopamine, neurointoxication by manganese increases dopamine oxidation and the formation of cytotoxins.[23]

The syndrome of manganism (manganese poisoning) looks exactly like the signs and symptoms of Parkinson's disease and is clinically indistinguishable from it. There is damage to brain cells that causes tremors that occur while at rest, "pill rolling" movements of the fingers, and a masklike face. Other indications are a shuffling gait, a slightly bent over posture, rigid muscles, and weakness. The victim of manganese madness may drool, have a heavy appetite, be unable to stand heat, have oily skin, be emotionally unstable to the point of dementia, and have judgment problems. The syndrome is made worse by tiredness, excitement, and frustration. As with parkinsonism, manganese madness is a progressive neurological disease that results from destruction of the cells of the basal ganglia in the brain.[24]

From the Department of Psychiatry of Queen's University and Kingston Psychiatric Hospital in Kingston, Ontario, Canada, James A. Owen, Ph.D., along with Dr. Donaldson, confirmed "that environmental exposure to high levels of manganese results in a clinical neurological syndrome of manganism."

Manganese toxicity is the result of dopamine depletion caused by manganese-induced oxidative damage to dopamine-containing neurons.[25,26] The researchers added, "Symptoms of manganese toxicity span a continuum from mild features such as extreme fatigue, somnolence [the trancelike state], and irritability, to severe characteristics including extrapyramidal symptoms (Parkinson's disease-like syndrome), hallucinations, emotional instability, compulsive acts, involvement in 'stupid crimes' and [irrational] violent behavior (manganese madness)."

In a protocol dated January 29, 1991 put forth to Everett L. "Red" Hodges, which sought his financial backing for another scientific study, Dr. Owen and Dr. Donaldson offered their valid, albeit startling hypothesis that recidivistic (habitual and repeated relapse to crime) and violent behavior are the result of the interaction between high endogenous (originating from within the individual) levels of manganese and reduced metabolic detoxification activity. They wrote that there is a striking relationship between levels of the brain chemical, serotonin metabolite 5-HIAA, and high manganese levels in abnormally aggressive individuals, such that both of these biochemical markers identify the same type of patients exhibiting erratic behavior.

The scientists said, "Exposure to manganese may increase the generation of neurotoxic compounds, such that, in poor metabolizers, these toxins overwhelm the metabolic detoxification systems, and neuronal damage ensues with the accompanying behavioral changes. This suggests that although many individuals in the population may have increased levels of manganese through exposure to manganese-containing compounds, or deficient physiological mechanisms for manganese homeostasis, only those individuals with deficient detoxification systems would develop symptoms of manganism."

A LOOK AT GROOTE EYLANDT

As reported in 1988 by Dr. Donaldson, abnormally aggressive, erratic, and otherwise violent behavior has been associated with manganese toxicity on Groote Eylandt, an island in the Northern Territories of Australia. It happens also to be the singular site of the world's largest manganese mine. In addition to clinical symptoms of psychiatric excitement and motor neuron disease, the island population has the highest record of crimes, arrests, and incarcerations in Australia.[27]

Dr. Donaldson wrote, "Analysis of scalp and pubic hair manganese concentrations in the aboriginal population associated with the manganese mine of Groote Eylandt has revealed manganese levels approximately 20 times higher than those observed in a control group from Sydney, Australia." However, among the aboriginal population surveyed on Groote Eylandt, Dr. Donaldson added that hair manganese levels remained elevated for everyone, not only those with impaired coordination, but also those with no symptoms.[28]

The association between manganese overload and aggressive or antisocial behavior has been established only recently, so little data is available on the biochemical mechanisms underlying manganese-induced aggression. More medical research work is needed on heavy metals with special emphasis on manganese as a neurotoxic agent. There should be multi-center studies examining the relationship of manganese levels and metabolizer status as a source of antisocial, aggressive, and erratic behavior in those criminal-type subjects who are at war with peace-loving normal people and all others.

Although not usually recognized as such, violence arising from heavy-metal toxicity is the world's most serious health problem. Because of the unrecognized metallic source of mental derangement and antisocial behavior, innocent people are maimed and killed daily. The violence from toxic individuals interrupts and interferes with everyday lives of more normal persons by robbing them of loved ones, homes, food, medical care, education or jobs, and too often the opportunity to grow up. The riots in Los Angeles and other cities during 1992 were dramatic examples of the fear and misery inflicted by violence on ordinary people who are just trying to live their lives as best they can.

As we have seen already in the two previous sections on metal connections, the whole problem of metal pollution in its many ramifications appears so huge as to seem hopeless of solution. We live in an age of toxicity, and we can hardly change that on an individual level. Nor will such circumstance ever be modified drastically unless the human race goes backward to wood and stone in a hippie-like existence. We want the conveniences that are supplied by high technology too much and too often.

However, when we view each problem making up the whole individually, we do see glimmers of light. For violence, as an example, hair mineral analysis should be standard procedure during the indictment process for any criminal act. Finding an overabundance of metallic abnormality in a person's hair, nails, or other body tissues, treatment with chelation therapy would be a far better solution than imprisonment. Chelation therapy, as we shall note in the next section, is an established technique for restoring an impaired individual to society, who will greet him or her with open arms of welcome.

Part IV
The Chelation Connection

Chelation therapy curbs the flow of metallic minerals through the blood vessels of the body and brain so that their cellular storage is prevented and even reversed. Its protein-like chelating material (EDTA) binds with or "chelates" multiple minerals such as metastatic calcium. The most advantageous effect of chelation therapy is that all toxic metals, including aluminum, mercury, lead, cadmium, iron, manganese, plus others, are extracted and expelled from normal physiological systems. The body excretes such toxic metals through the urinary tract and/or bowel. Chelation therapy is the most sophisticated form of cellular detoxification known to medical science.

CHAPTER 17
What Is Chelation Therapy?

Suppose you have concluded that there is no way your elderly mother can remain at home unsupervised. You see that her mind is gone. Her short-term memory seems nonexistent.

While you remember how a few years ago she had been so mature and level-headed, alert and vivacious, always joking, clear thinking, and physically active, now the woman is forgetful, depressed, argumentative, childish, lethargic, and terribly weak. She has frequent accidents, such as spilling hot cooking oil down her legs. She loses things, like the time her house keys were misplaced permanently and all the locks had to be changed. She usually gets lost, including her disconcerting inability to find the bathroom in her own home. Consequently, she has reverted to infantilism by wetting her bed and at times defecating in her clothes. To the woman's embarrassment, frequent bouts of diarrhea force her into showers or the bathtub many times through the day. Only she is unable to bathe herself, and you must give assistance. The entire process of keeping the woman clean is time-consuming and counterproductive to your own obligations to work and immediate family. A home-care assistant has had to be hired but the home health-care agency's fee of $12 per hour for an eight-hour day is draining your mother's funds. She has less than enough funds to sustain her at home for one more year.

After much testing and neurological evaluations, the diagnosis for your much-loved mother has become the heartbreaking one of senility with Alzheimer's disease.

The term *senility* is often applied to those mental and emotional difficulties that sometimes appear in old age. They may include symptoms of extreme irritability, anxiety, loss of memory, depression, and an inability to maintain proper feeding, hygiene, and dressing habits. In its most extreme form, senility is sometimes diagnosed as Alzheimer's disease. Since dementia has the Alzheimer's patient exhibiting erratic behavior, he or she may require constant supervision, with attendant 24-hour nursing care. Medical treatment to reverse the condition, until now, has been unavailable simply because it did not exist.

Possibly you have come to a decision about your elderly mother. She needs to enter a nursing home, where, unless the nursing personnel and their numerous volunteers are unusually caring and conscientious, she will probably vegetate until she dies. You are distressed with this decision, but the "experts" have said that there is nothing else to be done.

Then, while arrangements are being made for mother's entry into a convalescent hospital, you stumble upon a book that describes a marvelous treatment that acts like a kind of gentle deblocking agent for clogged blood vessels in the body and brain and for removing toxic metals that contribute to production of pathological tangles and amyloid plaques among the affected person's neuronal cells. This book explains how *chelation therapy* (pronounced *key-lay'-shun*) potentially reverses the senile dementia of Alzheimer's disease.

CHELATION THERAPY IS NOT PART
OF THE MEDICAL MAINSTREAM

Of course, you bring this book to your mother's physician and inquire about the procedure. "Will it work?" you ask. The doctor, an honorable person, but one who has failed to do his homework on alternative or complementary methods of healing, feels threatened by medical questions he cannot answer. Such a doctor usually turns out to be a conventionally-trained *allopath* or *osteopath*—a doctor who strictly practices drug therapy in the medical mainstream. He aspires to follow the policy lines of the American Medical Association or the American Osteopathic Association, and chelation therapy has not been part of the medical mainstream.

The world scientific literature contains almost 2,000 clinical journal articles attesting to the multiple human and animal benefits—more than twenty-one physiological and biochemical actions—of the standard chelating substance used in treatment in the body and brain. Yet it is exceedingly difficult for the average physician to obtain most of these scientific references because they are seldom listed or even hinted at in the *Index Medicus*—the reference tool used by 95 percent of allopathic and osteopathic doctors. Journals that publish these articles are of the open-minded, wholistic-type that seldom are peer-reviewed and thus fail to get listed in the *Index Medicus.* The published articles or any reference to them, in fact, often are not available for a computerized literature search either.

It is even harder to educate conventional physicians about chelation therapy due to the many different names it can be found under in various world literature. The therapeutic substance itself is variably referred to around the world as (alphabetically) Antallin, Aquamollin, Calex, Calsol, Celon, cheladrate, Chelaplex, Chelation, Comlexone, Disodium edetate, Disotate, Distal 8, Edathamil disodium, Endrate disodium, Havidote, Indranal, Iminol-D, Irgalon, Kalex, Komplexon, Metaquest, Mosatil, Nervanaid-B, Nullapon, Permakleer, Pharmex Cheladrate, Sequestrene, Syntes 12a, Tetracemin, Tetrine, Titraver, Trilon-B, Triplex III, Tychrosol, Tyclarosol, Unithiol, Versene, Warkeelate, and some other names.

As is human nature, when ego gets involved, the physician, when asked about chelation therapy, is likely to come down on what he or she is not familiar with. Unfortunately, this medical conventionalist commits a kind of medical malpractice by erroneously declaring that such a treatment is "nonsense." Or, the allopath/osteopath possibly will label it "quackery" and turn a deaf ear to entreaties that it be tried.

MELINDA'S CASE

These are the exact circumstances met by a woman named Elsie M. in Oklahoma, in 1991. She was sadly arranging the permanent transfer of her senile parent to a nursing home when she came across the information in the book *The Chelation Way* (Avery Publishing Group, 1990) by Morton Walker, D.P.M.[1] Intrigued with the chelation-therapy concept, she sought the advice of the family doctor, who was himself elderly, a geriatrician who had tended to Elsie's mother, seventy-nine-year-old Melinda, for more than forty years. The old-timer, mired in medical orthodoxy, used some colorful language regarding the nontraditional treatment that Elsie described. He thought it was ridiculous to consider, and declared outright, "There's no such thing as treatment for Alzheimer's disease."

But the daughter pursued the subject and contacted another physician who was listed in the book's appendix along with colleagues around the world who provide chelation therapy. As it happens, Charles H. Farr, M.D., Ph.D., of Oklahoma City, Oklahoma, is a Diplomate in Chelation Therapy of the American College of Advancement in Medicine and former Chairman of the American Board of Chelation Therapy, the medical specialty organization that trains, tests, and certifies medical doctors and osteopathic physicians to give the treatment. On her own, with no financial assistance from governmental health insurance, Elsie brought Melinda to Dr. Farr for chelation therapy.

Melinda received 130 intravenous-chelation injections plus quantities of oral-chelating agents, which where administered by Dr. Farr. Her period of treatment lasted from June 5, 1991 to July 11, 1992. Dr. Farr is an expert on the administration of chelation therapy.

Elsie reported that within weeks of treatment she began to witness improvement in her mother's behavior. After ninety days (which is when chelation effects begin to maximize themselves), Melinda began to experience more beneficial reactions, too. She recognized loved ones and friends. Since at night she was able to navigate from her bedroom to the bathroom, she became continent during the day and stopped urinating in bed. Instead of lingering in her night clothes, she rose in the morning and got dressed for the day. Her personality turned cheerful, and her short-term memory returned, so that she began once again to speak of recent events, people she had met, and current holidays to celebrate. She even resumed telling jokes. Cooking and recipes became her occupation once more. Elsie took Melinda on drives and on shopping excursions to the supermarket—the first time in two years that Melinda had engaged in this sort of activity or, for that matter, had exhibited an interest in any outside pursuit.

Today, Melinda is functioning alertly. Chelation therapy, which she has now received over two hundred times, has her lively and conversational with family and friends. It has also kept her feeling well, with no particular physical ailments.

At least 50 percent of elderly people with senility problems are documented as showing mental keeness, greater memory retention, increased intelligence quotients, and other improvements after receiving intravenous-chelation therapy.

Chelation treatment is not only known for reversing the effects of senility, but also for reducing the severity of symptoms seen with certain conditions, like multi-infarct dementia and Alzheimer's disease. Some of these conditions are thought to come from arteriosclerosis and some are due to excessive amounts of toxic metals that have been lodged in the brain. Chelation therapy has the ability to help in both of these cases. But there are cases where, unfortunately, brain cells have actually been destroyed and replaced by scar tissue, such as after a stroke. Chelation treatment cannot help such problems of brain scarring, but it is useful in preventing further difficulties, such as the onset of another stroke.

Certainly chelation therapy stops the crosslinking pathology that occurs in the brain by taking hold of the ions of toxic metals. The metals that penetrate the blood-brain barrier (BBB) are instrumental in producing the pathological, neurofibrillary tangles and amyloid plaques that are indicative of Alzheimer's disease. Numerous administrations of chelation therapy remove toxic metals, such as aluminum, mercury, lead, cadmium, iron, manganese, and other pollutant molecules from the brain cells. To the detriment of medical consumers, what chelation therapy is and does has been overlooked or ignored by the organized medical community. Such neglect is a crime against humanity.

WHAT CHELATION THERAPY IS AND DOES

Chelation therapy consists of injections of a synthetic amino acid—a protein—whose actual generic name (aside from all of the other complicating labels) is ethylene diamine tetraacetic acid (EDTA). When introduced into the body through an intravenous infusion, EDTA locks onto a prevalent mineral or metal floating in the bloodstream or brain fluids and passes out of the body, taking the mineral or metal with it. Its chemical formula is:

$$
\begin{array}{cccc}
O{=}C{-}OH & & & HO{-}C{=}O \\
| & & & | \\
H{-}C{-}H & H \quad H & H{-}C{-}H \\
| & & & | \\
N{-}\!\!-\!\!-\!\!-\!\!-\!\!C{-}C\!\!-\!\!-\!\!-\!\!-\!\!N \\
| & & & | \\
H{-}C{-}H & H \quad H & H{-}C{-}H \\
| & & & | \\
O{=}C{-}O{-}N_a & & N_a{-}O{-}C{=}O
\end{array}
$$

According to world-famous gerontology researcher Johan Bjorksten, Ph.D., chelation therapy prevents the onset of Alzheimer's disease and holds great potential for extending anyone's life expectancy by at least twenty years. We believe in the truth of Dr. Bjorksten's findings. The coauthors have each received extensive numbers of chelation treatments themselves.

Diagnostic tests, conducted among literally hundreds of thousands of patients, performed before and after they received chelation therapy, reveal that areas of impaired circulation are restored to normal. Metallic pollutants are grasped by the EDTA, as if this amino acid is the claw of a lobster seizing its prey. The EDTA surrounds the metallic particle and takes it out of the blood stream and sends it as a waste product to the excretory and urinary systems, thus rendering a variety of physiological benefits.

Chelation therapy reduces muscular spasm of the artery that has caused blockage of blood flow. It also removes the blood stream's clogging material from the arterial wall. Such arterial clogging comes from deposits of junk material, such as fats, collagen, fibrin, mucopolysaccharides, cholesterol, foreign proteins, and other assorted garbage that people eat. All of this clogging matter is held together by a body glue comprised mainly of calcium. EDTA removes the calcium so that no more binding glue remains to hold the junk together. It goes into bloodstream solution and leaves the body as waste. A widened or unblocked, more flexible blood vessel passage is left behind. Therefore, blood can circulate without obstacles, and nourishment bathes the cellular structures.

Chelation treatment is absolutely safe when the protocol of the American College of Advancement in Medicine (ACAM) is followed. In contemporary chelation treatment there have been no documented fatalities as a result of its use. Rather, chelation therapy is effective for restoration of blood flow and removal of heavy metals from all body and brain tissues.

EDTA-chelation therapy has been used in the United States to relieve hardening of the arteries since 1952. Prior to this date, the treatment was employed almost exclusively for detoxification in cases of heavy-metal poisoning involving lead, mercury, and cadmium, and even for radioactive-metal toxicity. It is approved for such purposes by the United States Food and Drug Administration (FDA). Now we are recommending its application for removal of all other excessively concentrated, toxic, or unnecessary minerals, as a viable treatment for stopping the advance of most forms of dementia, and Alzheimer's disease in particular. As you will read in the chapters to follow, the intravenous (IV) procedure of chelation therapy has proven itself for this purpose.

Metallic ions play significant roles in two particular life-threatening formations within the body and brain: the first being atherosclerotic plaque formation, and the second, neuronal tangles with amyloid plaques. Ethylene diamine tetraacetic acid, when infused into the blood stream—whether an individual takes the treatment as therapy to correct existing pathology or as a prophylaxis to prevent its occurrence—removes those metallic ions with relative safety and without surgery or other drugs.

THE SIDE EFFECTS OF CHELATION THERAPY

The Food and Drug Administration (FDA) has made an extensive search of the medical literature for reports of adverse or poor results, including serious side effects, stemming from EDTA chelation therapy. The FDA could find no evidence of any kind that indicates that chelation therapy is detrimental to humans in any way. An official request was sent from the FDA to state health and regulatory agencies across the United States looking for any information relating to untoward results, poor results, or patient complaints about EDTA chelation therapy. No reports of that type were ever forwarded to, and none were received by, the FDA in response to the agency's request.[2]

The FDA, in fact, has accumulated a large body of published research showing that intravenous infusions with EDTA are safer than most other approved therapies used for any purpose in medicine. The agency, indeed, affirms that intravenous chelation therapy is the best, and perhaps only effective antidote for heavy-metal toxicity. In the United States, EDTA was first applied against lead poisoning in workers employed by a battery factory. Lead, being a toxic heavy-metal, was removed from the blood stream and other body storage areas of workers by application of intravenous EDTA. The United States Navy also expresses an interest in EDTA chelation therapy for their sailors who are in danger of lead poisoning. These sailors regularly scrape, chip, and then repaint the Navy's ships and dock facilities. The therapy is still used for that purpose.

The medical potential of EDTA was demonstrated dramatically in 1951 when it saved the life of a child suffering from lead poisoning (see an issue of *Scientific American* published in June 1953, the article titled "Chelation" by Harold F. Walton).

The most current use of chelation therapy is for necessary body detoxification for radioisotope saturation, which amounts to poisoning of the body with free-radical particles of radiation. This tragedy is likely to happen from the irradiation of food products at places like Vindicator, Inc., one of the nation's main food irradiation facilities. Opened in December 1991 in Mulberry, Florida, the company is counting on poultry and meat irradiation to breathe life into its bleak financial outlook. On May 6, 1992, the United States Department of Agriculture (USDA) gave preliminary approval to use irradiation to control the organisms salmonella, campylobacter, and other bacteria in raw poultry. This means that all of us have entered the era of being served "Hiroshima hens" by the use of a food processor's toxic technology to clean up contaminated chickens. Zapping food with deadly gamma rays derived from cesium-137, cobalt-60, or electron beam sources is fated to furnish radiation poisoning for workers in irradiation plants who unfortunately become exposed to excessive doses of the rays when they bypass safety precautions.

WHAT EDTA DOES

EDTA binds ionic-metal catalysts, making them chemically inert and removing them from the body and brain. The metallic ions may be of the toxic types or they could be essential ingredients required for usual physiological functions. In either case, introducing EDTA by infusion into the human blood stream activates its affinity for concentrations of metallic ions with the ability to catalyze lipid peroxidation (combustion of fat deposits). The metallic ion attraction of EDTA is so great that even homeopathic traces of ions (which are so small as to be considered trace) remaining in distilled water can initiate such chelating reactions.

Intravenous EDTA has long been accepted in medicine worldwide as the treatment of choice for metallic toxicity. Poisonous metals such as lead, mercury, cadmium, and aluminum react avidly with the EDTA type of sulfur-containing amino acids. Enzymes inhibited by the presence of heavy-metal ions become reactivated by intravenous EDTA chelating (grasping) the ionic particle and removing it from the enzyme's vicinity.

In chelation, a chemical reaction takes place in which a metal combines with another chemical such as EDTA or deferoxamine or penicillamine to form a ring-shaped molecular complex known as a *ligand*. Chelating agents such as ethylene diamine tetraacetic acid, deferoxamine, and penicillamine, therefore, form complexes by binding the metallic ions within these rings of the ligand. The metal is bound to the chelation agent and excreted, usually safely and uneventfully, through the urinary and/or excretory tract.

Besides those three chelating agents we have already mentioned, there are a minimum of twelve more generic chelating agents applicable for human administration. The more common chelating substances that have been used in medicine are the following:

- Bis (-aminoethyl) ether tetraacetate (BAETA)

- Cyclohexane trans 1, 2-diaminetetraacetate (CDTA)

- Di (hydroxyethyl) glycine (DHEG-N, N)

- Diethylenetriaminepentaacetate (DTPA)

- Ethylenediamine di (0-hydroxyphenylacetate) (EDDHA)

- Isopropyllenediaminetetraacetate (IPDTA)

- Nitrilotriacetate (NTA)

- 2,2-dimethylthiazoladine-4carbodylic acid (DTAC)

- 2,3 dimercaptoproponol (BAL)

- (2-hydroxycyclohexyl) ethylediaminetetraacetate (HCDTA-N)

- (2-hydroxyethyl) ethylediaminetetraacetate (HCDTA-N)

- (2-hydroxyethyl) imminodiacetate (HEIDA-N)

The earliest medical therapeutic use for which the chelation principle was applied was with dimercaprol or *British antilewisite* (BAL), discovered during World War II by Professor R.A. Peters and coworkers in Oxford, England. BAL is an antidote against the vesicant poison gas lewisite. (A vesicant gas is one that causes blisters.) Chelating the three arsenic atoms in the lewisite molecule BAL renders the gas harmless and easily removable from the skin by water or from the body tissues in the urine. BAL became the first chelating agent used in the routine treatment of arsenic and other metal poisons during the 1940s. Unhappily, BAL's own irritating effects upon living tissues, such as burning, itching and vomiting, severely limited its widespread employment. Subsequently, other chelating agents were sought that could be used internally with fewer undesirable side effects. This is the reason EDTA came into common usage for therapeutic purposes. When the EDTA chelation protocol of the American College of Advancement in Medicine is followed, almost no side effects develop. (For chelation therapy protocol, see Appendix 2.)

Along with the intravenous infusers, many orally administered anti-oxidant nutrients have chelating properties.[3,4] We will discuss these oral chelating agents, such as selenium, coenzyme Q_{10}, and vitamins E and C.

THE EDTA ORDER OF ATTRACTION TO METALS

At a normal body pH, EDTA has a natural attraction to various metals in order of decreasing stability. From highest affinity to lowest, the following is the order of inclination for this amino acid to bind with metallic ions:

chromium2+
iron3+
mercury2+
copper2+
lead2+
zinc2+
cadmium2+
cobalt2+

aluminum3+
iron2+
manganese2+
calcium2+
magnesium2+

In the presence of a more tightly bound metal, EDTA releases other metals lower in the electromotive series and will chelate the metal for which it has a greater affinity.[5] Thus, looking at the order of metallic attraction, EDTA has the greatest inclination to bind with the next hightest metal on the list.

In brief, then, EDTA grasps metals with a claw-like action and encircles them within a complex ring. The metals lose their physiologic and toxic properties and in this way are rendered ineffective by becoming trapped and removed. Therefore, when chelation takes place, the toxic metal comes in contact with EDTA, or some other chelating agent, and becomes imprisoned by the ring. The sodium part of the EDTA molecule is never dropped and so the sodium is apparently not toxic. The sodium portion is simply excreted by the body intact with the EDTA. Excess lead, mercury, cadmium, aluminum, arsenic, iron, manganese, or other toxic metals are excreted from the system along with the EDTA. The "poisonous" element is trapped by the chelator, like the claw of a crab holding something in its pincers. In fact, *chele* comes from the Greek language, meaning "the claw of a lobster or crab."

As potential users of this life-extending treatment, for ourselves or our loved ones, we should be aware that chelation is as old as life on this planet. All biological processes are involved in the phenomenon. It is only in recent years, however, that chelation therapy has emerged as a very valuable therapeutic technique for improving health and reversing Alzheimer's disease by the removal of toxic metals from the brain, bone, blood vessels, and other body tissues.

SUCCESSFUL CHELATION THERAPY FOR LEAD POISONING

Stephen K., a 35-year-old farmer, from a rural farming community around Portland, Oregon, was arrested at 6:30 in the morning by the local sheriff's department. He was charged with the residential burglary of a house located less than one mile from his home. He had no prior arrests or convictions.

At the time of his arrest, Stephen had no recollection of entering anyone's house other than his own. He did admit that he had been intoxicated the night before and may have entered somebody else's residence, thinking he was walking into his own home.

An investigation by sheriff's deputies into the breaking and entry found nothing missing from the premises. However, mud tracks from Stephen's shoes were found throughout the entered house and the tire tracks of his pickup truck in the driveway, together, had led to his arrest.

Since the farmer was practically impoverished, the case was referred to a public defender who arranged to have Stephen tested by the former chief medical officer for the state prison system, who had recently retired from the position followed by his return to private practice as a board certified psychiatrist. By means of a hair mineral analysis, the examining physician discovered that Stephen had a highly elevated hair-lead level—41 parts per million (normal is less than 10 parts per million). His blood levels for lead were determined, too, confirming evidence of systemic lead poisoning. It was decided that intravenous, EDTA chelation should be the treatment of choice.

Just before chelation therapy was begun, Stephen underwent psychological testing, by an Oregon clinical psychologist, as well. The psychologist found the detainee had an intelligence quotient (IQ) of only 72, considered to be borderline retarded.

After four months of being aggressively administered chelation therapy for lead toxicity by the Oregon state public health service, Stephen's court case arrived on the county calendar. It is recorded in the court record that the prisoner's appearance was "remarkably improved since the time of his arrest." The man's demeanor was cooperative and friendly. His alertness was quite apparent, especially to the arresting officers. And Stephen's responsiveness to questions was surprisingly open, verbal, and accurate. The first witness in his jury trial was the psychologist, backed up by the psychiatrist, both of whom testified that the prisoner's most recent I.Q. test had shown a gain of 28 points so that his present intelligence quotient had elevated to 100.

Other witnesses from throughout the rural community were presented by the public defender, and they further attested to "dramatically improved" behavior exhibited by the defendant since the beginning of his chelation treatment. By the end of the second hour of testimony from defense witnesses, the judge called a brief recess. After a private discussion in chambers with the prosecuting attorney and the public defender, the case was dismissed with prejudice. The judge thanked the jury for their service to the court. The detainee went free under supervision.

Eight months after the date of his arrest, Stephen's hair was once again tested by the psychiatrist, who found that the lead level had declined to a relatively low 8 parts per million. The source of the farmer's lead levels was never determined. There was some suspicion that it may have been due to his repeated handling of leaded gasoline during frequent repairs to his farm equipment and pickup truck. At any rate, chelation therapy had saved him from conviction, serving time in jail, and a continued life bordering on mental retardation.[6]

CHELATION THERAPY AND CHILDREN'S IQS

Stephen's improved mental status would come as no surprise to Holly Ruff, M.D., a developmental psychologist and professor of pediatrics at the Albert Einstein College of Medicine in the Bronx, New York. On April 7, 1993, Dr. Ruff published a study in *The Journal of the American Medical Association* that reported on reversal of intelligence decline when steps are taken to reduce blood-lead levels. Reducing lead levels in adults and children who have no obvious symptoms of lead poisoning causes marked improvement on standardized tests for cognitive development. This increased intelligence quotient occurred six months after children were treated by Dr. Ruff and her research team to reduce the levels of lead in their blood. In addition, their homes were cleaned to reduce exposure to the heavy metal. The I.Q. elevation was in direct proportion to the drop in blood-lead levels, suggesting that cleansing the children's blood of lead with chelation therapy (using edetate calcium disodium) directly results in better intelligence-test scores.

154 children, ranging in age from one to seven years, had been diagnosed with what is called moderate lead poisoning, with levels between 25 and 55 micrograms of lead per deciliter of blood. In children, 10 micrograms is a matter of concern to the Centers for Disease Control and Prevention (CDCP) in Atlanta, Georgia. Outward signs and symptoms occur at much higher levels. Above 15 micrograms, the CDCP recommends initiating measures to reduce children's exposure to lead. Adults are able to sustain slightly higher levels before intravenous EDTA needs to be administered.

Noteworthy was that the average drop in lead levels over six months was 7 micrograms per deciliter of blood. On average, the Albert Einstein College of Medicine researchers found that for each 3-micrograms drop in lead there was a corresponding one-point improvement in the children's performance on I.Q. tests. In the group of children who responded best to treatment, a drop of up to 30 micrograms of lead was noted, which would correspond to a 10-point increase in intelligence scores.[7]

For children, the elderly, middle-aged adults, or anyone else, intravenous infusions with EDTA is safe and effective. It is a viable therapeutic agent for stopping the advance of Alzheimer's disease. If administered as a preventive technique, it may defer Alzheimer's disease from making its appearance at all. EDTA has been applied as a heavy-metal detoxifier—tested for safety and proven effective—in more than six million IV drips administered to upwards of one million patients by over 1000 American physicians and another approximately 550 medical and osteopathic doctors who have been practicing internationally for the past forty-two years.[8]

CHELATING FATS AND OILS

Free-radical pathology is accepted by followers of Dr. Denham Harmon's free-radical theory of aging as a causative factor of Alzheimer's disease.[9] EDTA chelation therapy has been shown to improve, and in some cases stop, the effects of Alzheimer's disease in 50 percent of patients.[8] Another significant percentage of patients with Alzheimer's dementia has been reported to show improvements in thinking following treatment with deferoxamine, an iron chelating agent.[10] Iron is a potent catalyst of lipid (fat) peroxidation. Lipid peroxidation actually is a "turning" or rancidity of fats and oils (by means of combustion or oxidation) when they become exposed to air, and such oxidative damage is catalyzed by metallic ions of the types we are discussing here.

Unsaturated vegetable oils containing heavy metals, such as iron and copper, are routinely exposed to heat and oxygen in the cooking process. This is especially apparent when frying hamburgers, chicken, shrimp, and French fries at fast-food restaurants. Eating foods prepared in this manner gives the consumer a substantial dose of Alzheimer's disease, as well as ample exposure to heart disease and cancer. The oils used in the manufacture of salad dressings, such as mayonnaise, are probably just as bad for the brain. The poor-quality oil content of these dressings, with their everpresent rancidity, gets masked by the heavy amounts of seasoning included. High concentrations of lipid peroxides are their chief ingredients.[11]

Peroxidation and hydrogenation of vegetable oils during the manufacture of margarine and shortening brings about changes from healthy *cis* fats to brain-deteriorating *trans* fats. Cis molecules are formed naturally and perform certain functions in the body. Trans molecules are not natural, take longer to break down, and can inhibit the actions of essential-fatty acids. Such formation of trans molecules, such as occurs in hydrogenated peanut butter, alters the three-dimensional configuration of the dietary fatty-acid constituents from their normal, coiled, cis chains to toxic, straightened, trans chains. Trans-fatty acids are incorporated into cell membranes of the brain in the place of naturally occurring cis forms, causing pathological changes in membrane structure. There will then be impairment in function of phospholipid-dependent enzymes contained in the pathology-ridden neurons.[12,13,14,15,16] Substrate recognition by enzymes that synthesize cell membranes is inadequate to distinguish between cis and trans stereo isomers. Chelation therapy can remove the detrimental iron and copper ions from the body, so that they cannot assist in the transformation of cis fats to trans fats.

THREE SYNERGISTIC TREATMENTS FOR DEMENTIA

There are three treatments for dementia which seem to work cooperatively, each one enhancing improvements created by the other. Chelation therapy, hyperbaric oxygen, and dietary fat limitation show great advantages when instituted together.

Research on senility, dementia, brain ischemia, stroke, and spinal cord injury incriminates free-radical damage as one of the most important sources of brain cell dysfunction. The brain and spinal cord contain the highest concentration of fat of any human organ. Central nervous system fats are rich in highly unsaturated arachadonic and docosahexanoic acids. For these two fatty acids, the rate of lipid peroxidation increases exponentially with the number of unsaturated double-bonds per fatty acid molecule. Docosahexanoic and arachadonic acids peroxidize many times more readily than other lipids.

Unsaturated double bonds are encountered in fatty acids derived from food oils with minimum units of hydrogen in their chemical structures. They have more useful roles in human nutrition and are exemplified by linoleic, linolenic, and arachidonic acids. They are found in such lightly processed seed and vegetable oils as wheat germ, sunflower seed, safflower, and sesame.

Three treatment mechanisms, when jointly administered, work synergistically for reversing Alzheimer's disease: chelation therapy, hyperbaric oxygen, and dietary fat restriction. These therapies can slow the progression of, or actually reverse, the dementia resulting from free-radical pathology. Then, when these treatments are further combined with intravenous infusions of dimethyl sulfoxide (DMSO, a solvent derived from wood), the ultimate in free-radical scavenging takes place, and the destructive particles running rampant are gathered up and flushed from the body and brain.[17,18,19,20]

For in-depth information on the use of DMSO for treatment of the brain, including raising the intelligence of victims affected by Down's syndrome, read *DMSO, Nature's Healer* by Morton Walker, D.P.M. (Avery Publishing Group, 1993).[21]

CHAPTER 18

The Case Studies on EDTA Chelation Therapy

Gertrude N., a sixty-five-year old Illinois homemaker, was suffering from depression and recurrent memory loss. Her son, Phillip, brought her to see Dr. Cal Streeter, a physician who specializes in nutritional intravenous treatments, including chelation therapy.

Gertrude's depression, according to Phillip, had been a part of her personality for as long as he could remember, and he was thirty-five years old. Gertrude admitted that during this entire period she had been prescribed numerous medications, and at the time of her visit to Dr. Streeter she was taking Tofranil, lithium, Trilofon, and chlorpromozine, which are nerve and brain reactants. Previously the patient had consulted over a dozen doctors, of various specialties, including neurologists and psychiatrists, but nothing seemed to improve her ability to think clearly or to remember for any length of time. Phillip explained (and brought records to show) that two years earlier, his mother had been diagnosed by the staff of a medical institution specializing in neurological conditions as being in the early stages of Alzheimer's disease.

Dr. Streeter's physical examination of the patient failed to reveal any significant pathology that might give a cause to her memory loss and depression, except that he found she was hypothyroid (had an underactive thyroid gland) and hyperlipidemic (had excess fat in the blood).

In her case report to the authors, the Indiana physician described his treatment procedure for Gertrude. Dr. Streeter wrote, "I placed her on supplemental thyroid and a few appropriate nutritional supplements. After finding her to have an abnormal EKG [electrocardiogram], and knowing she had hypertension [high blood pressure], I recommended that she take chelation therapy." These physical conditions respond quite well to intravenous injections with EDTA. As discussed in Chapter 17, chelation therapy is an infusion technique that is very effective in reversing hardening of the arteries, which subsequently brings elevated blood pressure back to normal and frequently corrects an irregular cardiac rhythm.

"She almost immediately showed improvement in her memory retention and a reduction in mental depression too," Dr. Streeter said. While chelation therapy was administered to improve his patient's physical health, it reduced her abnormal mental symptoms as well. This is not an uncommon occurrence, and it is frequently reported by chelating physicians.

"She has taken 59 chelation treatments in the past seven years, with little or no signs of memory loss or depression returning, as long as she keeps up with her treatment boosters yearly," said Dr. Streeter. "Her hypertension has not responded to the chelation therapy as well as her mind. None of her previous nerve and brain medications are required anymore. I am not sure she needs to continue chelating on a monthly basis but may be able to receive three to four treatments a year to maintain her mental capacity. She is fearful of becoming totally forgetful and deeply depressed and is comfortable with the present program of chelation therapy." It is necessary that systolic blood pressure be 140 or below; otherwise, antihypertensive drugs may be required in addition to EDTA chelation treatments.

CHELATION THERAPY FOR "SENILITY"

Brain disease, one of the leading causes of death among all people in the industrialized West, is actually a myriad of disorders caused by different sources. The most common of its associated pathologies is cerebrovascular disease, and its highly prominent manifestation, stroke. Not only do strokes cause death, they may bring on abnormally severe signs and symptoms, including permanent paralysis, transient ischemic attacks (TIA), memory loss, personality changes, and "senility."

All cases of senility are not due to cerebrovascular disease. Recent innovative research in the United States and Canada, upon which we reported in Part II, has shown increased concentrations of aluminum and other toxic metals in the brains of patients with dementia.[1,2,3,4,5]

The Alzheimer's type of dementia does respond rather well to chelation therapy. Fifteen Alzheimer's disease patients, in a private clinical setting, were tested first, then administered chelation therapy, and were observed by loved ones to have returned to normal, or near normal, functioning. It was a gratifying experience for everyone involved with the testing and treatment: diagnostitians, clinicians, health care technicians, the patients, plus their family and friends.

EDTA binds aluminum and other metallic elements and carries the toxic agents out of the body and brain. Functional brain-cell improvement definitely does occur in patients with early-stage Alzheimer's disease after they have received chelation therapy. Although until now no documented studies ever before focused on such evidence, we advise that brain-blood flow measurements, using radionuclide evaluative studies, sharply improved for people victimized by Alzheimer's disease after receiving chelation therapy.

Let us be clear and specific: the isotopic before-and-after measurements we made of the brains of those fifteen patients who had been diagnosed with Alzheimer's disease, stroke, or transient ischemic attacks (TIAs) indicate that some forms of dementia (including schizophrenia), at least in the early stages, respond positively to intravenous chelation therapy. The information we are supplying here is the pivotal point of this book.

Conventional medical science has little or nothing to offer most patients with brain disorders, especially those with cerebrovascular disease. It is because of prior observations we had made in medical practice, reviewed with considerable amazement, that our presently reported clinical and nuclear-medicine study was carried out. Our use of radionuclide techniques is sophisticated nuclear medicine. Consistently successful results were achieved in individuals who had been struck by some form of senile dementia, Alzheimer's disease in particular. All fifteen patients evaluated experienced enhancement of memory retention and mental abilities after having received chelation therapy.

Every one of those people who received intravenous injections with EDTA in a series of twenty or more treatments discovered, and then enthusiastically praised, how they felt symptomatically and physically better than before accepting the infusions. Because subjective responses such as these are insufficient to satisfy the research-oriented medical community, we sought an objective method of measuring the patients' mental restoration. Thereafter, those people seeking medical consultation at the Casdorph Clinic and exhibiting definite manifestations of brain disorders underwent radioisotope brain blood-flow studies before, and at the end of, the approximately twenty intravenous treatments with disodium EDTA.

BRAIN BLOOD-FLOW STUDIES

We carried out investigations on blood flow in the brain using a nuclide with radioactivity. A nuclide exhibits the ability to last for a measurable amount of time in human tissues so that its presence in blood flow offers a picture inside the brain.

The radioactive studies about to be described were performed in the Nuclear Medicine Department of Long Beach Community Hospital, Long Beach, California, U.S.A. These were evaluations performed on hardcopy printouts evolving from the data recorded on floppy discs after use of a scintillation camera attached to a microprocessor manufactured by Searle Radiographics, Inc. for purposes of creating a brain blood-flow study of fifteen individuals who had consulted at the private practice Casdorph Clinic in Long Beach.

We followed a previous sample of successful gamma isotope camera studies of chelation therapy administered for the relief of brain disorders. The initial studies measuring cerebral blood flow before and after chelation treatment were described to the spring 1979 semi-annual medical science meeting of the American College of Advancement in Medicine (ACAM) by Philadelphia psychiatrist Lloyd A. Grumbles, M.D.[8] As compared with our use of the Searle Radiographics scintillation camera, Dr. Grumbles had employed the Baird System 77 Multicrystal Computerized Radioisotope Camera. This allowed him to measure and show the blood as it flowed through the brains or hearts of twenty patients with color photographs.

In Dr. Grumbles' tests, very short-lived radioisotopes were injected into the patients before and after they received chelation therapy for their infirmities. His multicrystalline camera took four pictures per second in a series of multiple photographs. Following just one second of photography, the individual patient's internal carotid arteries were outlined. In three more seconds the entire brain came into view, outlined in brilliant red and yellow colors. At five seconds an observer was able to see the individual's blood coming in and rushing out of his brain tissue.

Of the twenty people tested by Dr. Grumbles, over 80 percent of them had symptomatic relief of their heart or brain problems, including the near-total reversal of Alzheimer's disease. Being a psychiatrist, Dr. Grumbles was most keenly interested in the cerebral symptom improvements, but he also was amazed by the elimination of heart trouble in his chelated patients. He showed these improvements by verified measurements supplied by the Baird System 77 camera. We viewed his films, and they set us thinking about conducting our own measurements of brain-blood flow by radionuclide studies.

At nearly the same time Dr. Grumbles was performing his investigations, biotoxicologist Bruce W. Halstead, M.D., of Colton, California, performed before-and-after brain studies on thirteen chelated patients in the neurosurgical department at Loma Linda University School of Medicine. Dr. Halstead documented his results at the spring and fall ACAM science

conferences in 1980. His studies indicated about an 82-percent improvement in the blood transit time—the period it takes a labelled red blood cell
to get into the brain and out again. Together, these two studies gave
impetus to our enthusiasm for adopting chelation therapy as a treatment
for brain disorders.

Dr. Casdorph, an internist with a specialty in cardiology, had practiced
conventionally until he came upon the excellent health-enhancement effects
afforded by chelation therapy. Dr. Casdorph followed the results from his
colleagues' chelation treatment for four years before he decided to incorporate
it into his own cardiovascular practice. To prove to himself that the treatment
was not producing improvements through any placebo effect, he elected to
perform studies similar to Drs. Grumbles and Halstead on fifteen patients
with well-documented impairment of cerebral blood flow.

DR. CASDORPH'S STUDY

At the time of his brain blood-flow studies, Dr. Casdorph was Assistant
Clinical Professor of Medicine at the University of California Medical
School, Irvine. He had been Chief of Medicine at Long Beach Community
Hospital and held close ties to the Nuclear Medicine Department at that
institution.

In the radioactive brain blood-flow studies conducted at Long Beach
Community Hospital, nuclear scintigraphy was conducted using the agent
technetium 99m. (Tc99 is a uranium/plutonium fission product used in
medical diagnosis in order to trace blood flow through tissues.) Each
patient served as his or her own control. The blood flow to the individual's
brain was studied before and at the end of the prescribed course of chelation therapy administered by Dr. Casdorph. Unless indicated, no other
change in treatment or drugs affecting the brain occurred during the course
of study.

Figure 18.1 depicts an artist's rendition of a computer printout pattern
of normal and abnormal graphs of blood brain-flow studies using technetium 99m performed on patients.

As shown in the illustration, the curve on the left shows the normal brain
flow curve. The upstroke of wave "A" indicates blood flowing into the
brain followed by a normal decline to point "b" as the washout effect of
fresh blood, containing no radioactivity, reduces the level of technetium
99m to the baseline at point "b." This is followed by a slight recirculation
of blood wave "C" and a subsequent baseline or steady level of radioactivity.

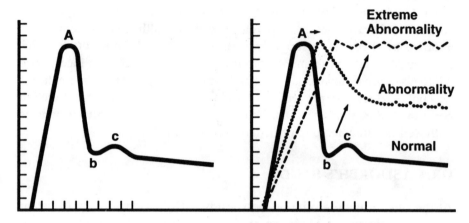

BRAIN FLOW STUDIES WITH TECHNETIUM 99M.

Figure 18.1. This artist's rendition shows the computer printout pattern of brain flow studies performed on patients injected with the isotope technetium 99m. With the rise of the heavy solid line to point "A" as shown on the left, we see blood flowing into the brain. As the line descends to point "b," the isotope carried by the blood is leaving the brain. Point "C" indicates a recirculation wave of blood and then the radioactivity in the brain levels off. In contrast, the dotted and dashed lines shown on the right, separately show abnormal and extremely abnormal blood flow to the brain that invariably manifest themselves in patients as dementia of the Alzheimer type (DAT). Central nervous system abnormalities associated with delayed blood flow into and out of the brain cause a delayed rise in point "A," shown by a shift to the right. Delayed outflow of blood out from the brain is shown by a rise of point "b," as indicated on the right side of the illustration.

The curves on the right of Figure 18.1 indicate changes that occur to cerebral blood flow with progressively more severe cerebrovascular occlusion. As brain blood-flow becomes impaired there is a delay of flow into the brain, causing the peak of wave "A" to move to the right. This is associated with a decrease in the washout phase inasmuch as fresh blood flows less readily into the brain to wash out the existing radioactivity. Point b is what is used to measure the degree of occlusion in the brain. If point b is relatively high, there is a greater amount of occlusion, if point b is relatively low, then there is relatively little blocking the brain-blood flow. By performing these tests on patients before and after chelation therapy, a doctor can observe if there is any benefit to the patient, point b should eventually get lower.

The sequence of twenty infusions with EDTA (ethylene diamine tetraacetic acid) was considered to be the basic course of therapy. Occasionally, however, for reasons such as individual need for hospitalization, some patients were studied before the completion of twenty intravenous treatments. In the case of one patient, the repeat brain blood-flow study after she had taken twenty infusions indicated no change, although the patient was markedly improved from a clinical standpoint. Her husband remarked on how his wife had resumed her household duties and was so much more pleasant to be with. Then, a third brain blood-flow study was performed on the same after she had received twenty-six EDTA infusions and her brain blood-flow pattern showed significant improvement to the point of normality.

EDTA was administered as a dose of 3 grams disodium EDTA in 250 milliliters or 500 milliliters of Ringer's lactate solution. Two hundred milligrams of lidocaine was added to each solution in order to prevent local pain from occurring at the vein injection site.

All patients had a complete physical evaluation and appropriate laboratory studies prior to beginning the therapy. In addition to customary laboratory testing, particular emphasis was placed on kidney function, inasmuch as the urinary tract is the primary mode of excretion for EDTA. The biologic half-life of EDTA in the body, following intravenous administration, is approximately one hour, at which point nearly all of the drug is recoverable in the urine.

The intravenous infusions were ordinarily administered once a week, over a three-hour period, on an outpatient basis. During the course of chelation therapy, vitamin and mineral supplements and other supplements—such as coenzyme Q_{10}, carnitine, and garlic—were administered orally. Aside from this supplementation, there was no change in the patients' usual program of drug therapy.

RESULTS OF CHELATION THERAPY
BRAIN BLOOD-FLOW STUDIES

As mentioned, the normal brain blood-flow curve that is obtained over each side of the cerebral cortex, as shown in Figure 18.1, depicts upstroke of wave "A." This indicates that blood is flowing into the brain; it is caused by a rise of gamma ray counts detected by the scintillation crystal. The curve falls during the washout phase of cerebral circulation, leading to the lowest point "b," followed by a slight rise or recirculation at wave "C." The count then levels off with recirculation as radioactivity assumes a constant baseline level.

In the presence of occlusive cerebrovascular disease, such as impaired inflow to the brain, the peak of wave "A" shifts to the right, indicating a greater time required for blood to flow into the brain. This is associated with a delay in the washout phase resulting in an elevation of point "b," or baseline of the curve. For the purpose of this study, an elevation of point "b" above the normal is considered an index of the degree of cerebrovascular insufficiency and is used as an objective measure of the apparent benefit of the infusions of EDTA. The evaluations of point "b" are measured before and after chelation therapy, and the results are shown in Table 18.1.

As explained, the normal brain blood-flow curve seen in Figure 18.1 represents a computer printout of the cerebral blood flow study. Along the horizontal and vertical axes are arithmetic scales, and the point "b" of the normal curve is usually found four units above the horizontal axis. The degree of elevation of point "b" is considered a measure of the degree of cerebrovascular insufficiency. (Here is a note for physicians: this point "b" elevation may be compared to ST segment elevation in an electrocardiogram that indicates myocardial injury.)

When point "b" returns to, or toward normal, as a result of chelation therapy, it is interpreted to be an index of improvement or normalization of brain-blood flow. When on the graphic illustrations the curve is marked with an "R," that indicates blood flow was to the right side of the brain. And "L" indicates that blood flow was to the left side of the brain.

Table 18.1 includes the results of the study of fifteen patients, as mentioned. All patients showed clinical improvement as a result of receiving chelation therapy, and all except one experienced improvement in the degree of elevation of point "b." That is, a point "b" that was elevated returned toward normal following the patient's treatment.

One patient (Patient 8) who showed no change in point "b" did, however, improve clinically. Her transient ischemic attacks (TIA) that were occurring prior to therapy disappeared entirely during and after treatment, although coumadin anticoagulant therapy was also added to her program as another means to prevent TIA.

Elevation of the "b" segment is measured by units along the vertical axis. The points are part of the computer printout and are approximately two millimeters apart.

The advantage of this type of radionuclide study is that each patient serves as his or her control and no single- or double-blinding is required. The results are highly significant. Here, statistically significant improvement in the patients' brain wave "b" occurred. The probability of error is quite low. The average improvement in wave &b" for the fifteen patients, as illustrated in Table 18.1 (on page 244), was 2.29 millimeters with a range of 0–5.

In referring to Table 18.1, since the average elevation of point "b" in Figure 18.1 was 6.1, which returned to a mean of 3.87 after treatment, this represents a 71-percent return toward normal of point "b," inasmuch as in a healthy brain 3 is the normal level for point "b." The brain responses to chelation therapy from patients affected with Alzheimer's disease truly are impressive. This is a treatment mechanism that demands further investigation and more general usage for degenerative diseases connected with interruption in blood flow, heavy metal toxicity, and, in particular, the senile-type dementias.

EXAMPLES OF BRAIN BLOOD-FLOW CURVES

The technique of objective measurement of brain-blood flow utilizing technetium 99m radionuclide scintigraphy that we are presenting here is new and unprecedented in applications. Its use is tantamount to going inside the brain as in autopsy to analyze the status of blood flow. As you will read near the end of this chapter, medical researchers at the University of Texas Southwestern Medical Center have declared the measurement of live patient brain-blood flow by radionuclide studies a valid alternative to autopsy to definitively diagnose Alzheimer's disease.

The normal brain wave curve, including our description of the "A," "b," and "C" portions of the brain-blood flow graph that we provide, is being discussed for the first time. This chapter, predicated on research performed by chelating physicians in 1979, 1980, and 1981, is offering to the scientific community an objective method for quantifying abnormalities and for measuring health or pathology status of the brain.

Our described technique also evaluates improvement as a result of treatment with intravenous disodium EDTA chelation therapy. Invariably general mentality—thinking, memory retention, intelligence quotient, and nearly all other aspects of brain function—get better when IV chelation therapy is received by patients who are impaired. Indeed, there is no reason to hold the therapy in abeyance, awaiting pathology to manifest itself. Chelation therapy has medical prevention value. We, the authors, have taken many dozens of

Table 18.1 Brain Blood-Flow Study Results

Patient	Age	Diagnosis	Wave "b" move Before/After	Change	No./IVs	Clinically Improved
1	80	Stroke	R Brain 7/4	+3	13	yes
			L Brain 7/4	+3		
2	51	Schizo-phrenia	R Brain 7/3.5	+3.5	13	yes
			L Brain 7/3.5	+3.5		
3	72	Cerebral Atrophy	R Brain 8.7/7	+1.7	26	yes
			L Brain 8/6.5	+1.5		
4	62	TIA	R Brain 6.5/3.5	+3	20	yes
			L Brain 6.4/3.4	+3		
5	57	Stroke	R Brain 5/2.8	+2.2	20	yes
			L Brain 5/3	+2		
6	65	TIA	R Brain 5/3.5	+1.5	20	yes
			L Brain 4.5/3	+1.5		
7	66	Diabetes ASO	R Brain 6/3	+3	20	yes
			L Brain 5.5/3	+2.5		
8	66	TIA	R Brain 4/4	0	20	yes
			L Brain 4/4	0		
9	67	TIA	R Brain 6/3	+3	20	yes
			L Brain 6/3.2	+2.8		
10	72	Cerebral Atrophy	R Brain 5.5/3.8	+1.7	20	yes
			L Brain 5/3.1	+1.9		
11	76	Cerebral Atrophy	R Brain 6/4	+2	20	yes
			L Brain 6/3.2	+2.8		
12	92	Cerebral Atrophy	R Brain 9/7	+2	20	yes
			L Brain 8/5.2	+3.8		
13	68	ASHD	R Brain 6/4	+2	20	yes
			L Brain 5.8/3.8	+2		
14	52	CVD	R Brain 4/3	+1	20	yes
			L Brain 4.5/3	+1.5		
15	80	ASHD	R Brain 9/4	+5	20	yes
			L Brain 7/4	+3		
Mean Brain Scores			6.1/3.87	+2.3	(P = 0.0005)	

IV infusions with EDTA, not for the correction of any dysfunction but simply because the treatment program with chelation improves mentality, extends life, and creates a general body and brain betterment for daily living. Chelation therapy delivers these benefits without adverse side effects when the protocol of the American College of Advancement in Medicine is followed (see Appendix 2 for the full protocol).

MORE ABOUT THE "CASDORPH METHOD"

The technique of brain blood-flow imaging developed by H. Richard Casdorph, M.D., Ph.D., in 1980 and described in this chapter was reperformed at the University of Texas Southwestern Medical Center at Dallas. This medical facility comprises the Southwestern Medical School, the Southwestern Graduate School of Biomedical Sciences, the Southwestern Allied Health Sciences School, affiliated teaching hospitals, and various outpatient clinics. The University's Office of Medical Information announced on December 4, 1992 that Dr. Casdorph's method for diagnosing Alzheimer's disease is an accurate tool. The Casdorph method has won tacit approval from the University's diagnostic and treatment facilities by UT Southwestern Medical Center personnel duplicating the technique and praising it mightily.

Up to now only biopsy or autopsy of the affected patient's brain had been accepted as definitive confirmation of Alzheimer's disease. But in a study of eighteen patients, Professor Frederick Bonte, M.D., and colleagues, applied the Casdorph method and found that brain blood-flow imaging correlated almost 100 percent with autopsy verification of Alzheimer's disease. (Dr. Bonte is professor of radiology and director of the Nuclear Medicine Center at UT Southwestern. He also holds the Effie and Wofford Cain Distinguished Chair in Diagnostic Imaging.) He presented his group's findings to the Radiological Society of North America's 78th scientific assembly and annual meeting in Chicago on November 30, 1992, more than a decade after Dr. Casdorph's paper describing the method and how chelation therapy improved brain function, appeared in the *Journal of Holistic Medicine*.[7]

Besides describing his brain blood-flow imaging technique, Dr. Casdorph wrote: "The results of treatment of fifteen patients with this form of chelation therapy are presented. All patients improved and in all but one patient there was objective evidence of significant and sometimes dramatic improvement in cerebral blood flow.... Intravenous infusions of disodium EDTA are shown to be an effective form of therapy for various states associated with abnormal cerebral blood flow. This is particularly noteworthy in view of the fact that medical science has no other effective treatment for most of these conditions."

Recently, in a follow-up investigation, Dr. Bonte and his associates used more up-to-date and elaborate equipment called single-photon emission computed tomography (SPECT) to study the regional brain-blood flow of eleven men and seven women between the ages of forty-two and eighty-four. Fourteen were diagnosed with Alzheimer's and three with other disorders of dementia. One was found normal.

Fifteen of the UT Southwestern patients were studied with Xe-133 SPECT, two with Tc-99m (technetium 99m) HM-PAO 3-camera SPECT, and one with both. Diagnosis of patients imaged with the Xe-133 was made by visually interpreting the computer scan of each patient's brain-blood flow and by quantifying flow ratios of brain-blood flow in areas thought to be involved in the disease process and comparing them with results in elderly, normal volunteers. Tc-99m HM-PAO studies were interpreted visually. All were compared with normal subjects.

UT Southwestern researchers now have completed a total of 24 brain blood-flow imaging comparisons with brain tissue samples. "To really test brain blood-flow imaging as a diagnostic tool for Alzheimer's, we need a sampling of 50 to 100 patients," Dr. Bonte said. Talks are under way with the University of California, Berkeley, scientists about working together to study more patients faster using the Casdorph method.

"We are fortunate to have a busy Alzheimer's Disease Research Center at UT Southwestern, which gives us an opportunity to study and evaluate large numbers of patients," Bonte said. He added that UT Southwestern would be able to complete the sampling alone in about two years.

The technique—not the machine—is what matters, Dr. Bonte affirmed, so there will be no problem combining data from patient studies at UT Southwestern with those done at another institution. "Even primitive equipment in a small hospital [such as the 1981 studies performed at Long Beach Community Hospital] can show abnormal brain blood-flow patterns if the physicians know how to interpret them," he said.

UT Southwestern researchers in the Alzheimer's Disease Research Center see the greatest promise for the technique in hard-to-diagnose cases since its cost makes routine use impractical.

Dr. Bonte and his associates are excited about the results of their first study and continue to look at brain-blood flow with larger patient groups. He concluded, "Some of our researchers think if you live to be eighty-five, you have an almost 50-percent chance of developing Alzheimer's disease. If that's true, we all need all the help we can get."

CHAPTER 19

The Administration and Effects of Chelation Therapy

When Margot S. was sixty-two years old, she asked her daughter Constance to drive her to the Celebration of Health Center in Bluffton, Ohio, in order to consult with the clinic's medical director, L. Terry Chappell, M.D. Margot was aware of certain personal mental and physical inabilities that were slowly but steadily creeping into her life. Constance, indeed, confirmed them when she participated in helping to give details of her mother's medical and behavioral history to Dr. Chappell.

The problems were multiple for Margot, and they had not responded to the medical care she was receiving from the physician who had been the family's long-established doctor and friend for three generations. "I been doctorin' with my troubles for a long while and take all kinds of pills for them," explained Margot. "You see, I got sore muscles here and here and all over the rest of my body. The pain is real bad at my tail bone where I sit down. I'm worried about my heart too, 'cause my mother and her mother both had severe heart problems and high blood pressure. In fact, my grandmother died at age fifty-three after suffering with over a dozen small strokes. It's got me anxious that the same thing could happen to me."

"There is something else wrong, Dr. Chappell, that is necessary to bring up and make it a part of my momma's history," added the daughter.

"For about six years, now," Constance recounted, "my momma's memory has been deteriorating. At first it started with little things—an inability to remember recent events or to place names with the faces of people she has known for many years. Then she began to misplace things, such as items of clothing, her eyeglasses, her wallet, and three years ago she left behind forty-eight dollars worth of food items in the supermarket parking lot. She just drove off without taking her bags of groceries from the shopping cart and putting them in the car trunk.

"This sort of thing doesn't happen anymore simply because Momma stopped driving the car after that," continued the daughter. "Also, I do her food shopping for her."

With a nod of her head and a sad face, Margot verified that Constance was correct. Then she added, "I thought at first the mistakes were from my bad eyesight. I've been diagnosed with macular degeneration, but now I'm not so sure. I've been workin' on an assembly line for a small manufacturing plant, and more frequently than I'd like to admit I misassemble little parts more than is acceptable by the shop manager. I just lose them washers, nuts, and screws—yeh, they keep getting lost—either dropped on the floor or misplaced somewhere around my bench. I'm amazed at where I might find them. He doesn't want to fire me, but the boss said it's time for me to retire. And I do believe that he is right."

"Our family doctor, who knows about Momma's lack of coordination and forgetfulness, suggested that I take her for psychological testing," Constance added. Later she whispered to Dr. Chappell out of earshot of her mother, "The doctor thinks she could be affected by an early stage of Alzheimer's disease."

After taking note of the daughter's remark, Dr. Chappell gave Margot a thorough physical examination. Among the body systems that he checked were her eyes. They were evaluated for the extent of her macular degeneration—the gradual decay of a spot at the rear of the eye chamber owing to the diminished blood supply sometimes associated with senile changes. Margot's diagnostic tests were positive for the disease.

Several abnormalities made their appearance in Margot's initial clinical and laboratory workups, too, including an abnormal stress electrocardiogram and reduced blood flow in her legs. Her serum cholesterol was high at 230—normal is less than 200. Her iron level was also high at 339, and her fibrinogen level was high—fibrinogen is the protein found in the blood that causes clotting.

Not only was Margot's fibrinogen blood-chemistry level elevated too much, but a study of how her platelets stuck together showed that she had a marked tendency to form blood clots in the presence of adrenaline. Her reaction to life's daily stress on the job and at home caused excess hormone secretion from her adrenal glands. Such a release created the potential for the formation of atherosclerotic plaques in arteries, capillaries, and veins throughout the woman's body. In effect, then, this means that increased stress was a precursor source for her to form blood clots easily. Just like her grandmother, as she suspected, Margot was at high risk for strokes and other vascular problems. So, she was correct in taking her mother's and grandmother's health histories as warnings that she was in danger of developing similar symptoms of heart and blood-vessel disease.

As a Diplomate of the American Board of Chelation Therapy, Dr. Chappell is a leader among the wholistic physicians who utilize chelation therapy. After examining Margot, he recognized that the best course of treatment was for Margot to undergo a minimum of thirty intravenous chelation infusions with the mineral-protein combination product, magnesium disodium ethylene diamine tetraacetic acid (Mg-EDTA).

The first symptom that improved was her overall muscle aching, which disappeared entirely after the first four chelation treatments. The patient's laboratory platelet studies before and after therapy showed that chelation made her blood much less likely to clot. Even her vision improved, for macular degeneration is one of those conditions that readily responds to chelation therapy. After the infusion series was completed over a period of fifteen weeks, the patient noticed great improvement in how she felt and reacted to life's situations.

More than that, the patient expressed the feeling that a mental fog had lifted from her. "I can think more clearly," Margot said. "I even speak better with less slurring of my words. I'm making fewer mistakes at work too. Recently I discovered a new placement method for the parts assembly in order to speed up not only my production, but the production of everyone else on the assembly line as well. It was so effective that our shop manager adopted the way I was doing things for the assembly lines all over our factory. My boss was so happy to get me back to an efficient work level. Many at work thought that something or somebody had been sabotaging the line—an unknown enemy. That unknown enemy actually turned out to be me when I was wearing a head that didn't work so well."

Near the end of her mother's series of chelation treatments, Constance confirmed to Dr. Chappell that Margot was like a new person. "I have to tell you, in all honesty, four months ago I was awfully worried. Before she started treatment, my mother did not appear to have a healthy, well-functioning brain. I think that maybe our family doctor could have guessed right. Alzheimer's disease was a potential danger to her, but no more."

"Besides causing a great amount of inconvenience for those who love her or who worked with her, the mistakes she was making then were obviously putting her life and limb in jeopardy. Today it's different," added the daughter. "My momma is her old self again. Her grandchildren find her fun, like before, and she remembers obligations, dates, places, people, and appointments, like before. She doesn't lose things anymore. Her car was taken down from blocks that had propped it up in the garage, and she has resumed driving it."

Margot decided she would continue working for the manufacturing plant for several years more now that her confidence was restored. Assembling errors would not occur, she assured herself. But she also began making plans for a vigorous retirement, with a lot more to be accomplished as a senior citizen. Periodically she returns to the Celebration of Health Center in Bluffton, Ohio for booster treatment with chelation therapy. "It's necessary for me to do that," Margot told us, "so that I can keep my head on straight and not go around the bend into some sort of craziness. I realize that I've been saved from progressing into some kind of senile brain disease, and I'm grateful."

(For answers to some of the most common chelation-therapy questions, see the inset on pages 251–253.)

METAL-LIGAND BONDING

In Chapter 17 we stated that British Anti-Lewisite (BAL) was the first chelating agent utilized for therapeutic purposes. BAL was applied as an antidoting mechanism against arsenic toxicity from poison gas during wartime. That was true for the 1940s, but the initial work on the chelation process or the bonding of metals was performed by the Swiss Nobel Laureate, Alfred Warner. Dr. Warner propounded his theory of metal-ligand bonding in 1893 and thus provided the foundation for all of modern coordination chemistry.

The present, most commonly used chemical foundation substance to achieve a chelation effect in human beings, EDTA, binds metallic ions to itself. It is approved for that medical purpose, among other applications, by the United States Food and Drug Association (FDA). The earliest clinical application of intravenous infusions with EDTA was for offsetting lead poisoning. It works exceedingly well for the detoxification of lead from the body, and this was confirmed as far back as 1961 during the "Federation Proceedings on the Biological Aspects of Metal Binding."

The State University of New York, Downstate Medical Center, College of Medicine, has used calcium EDTA to treat hyperactivity of children, with excellent results. The medical authorities there believe that these children may have benefitted because their hyperactivity represented an increased susceptibility to lead toxicity.

METAL POISONING AMONG THE BRITISH

Metallic toxicity with aluminum, antimony, arsenic, Beryllium (berylliosis), cadmium, iron, lead, mercury, manganese, nickel carbonyl, tellurium,

Dr. Chappell's Chelation Questions

Dr. Chappell has written the answers to a series of one hundred questions often asked by patients undergoing chelation therapy. He has titled his series "Questions From the Heart," which he compiled with the assistance of literature professor Phillip O'Connor of Bowling Green University, who had been receiving chelation therapy for his coronary artery disease at the Celebration of Health Center in Bluffton, Ohio. (Questions From the Heart *will be a quality paperback issued in the fall of 1994 by Hampton Roads Publishing Co., Inc. of Norfolk, Virginia.) The following is contributed by Dr. Chappell:*

Question (Q): When is a patient too old to take chelation therapy?

Answer (A): Remarkably, I have seen patients in their nineties respond very well to treatments with EDTA chelation. I don't believe that any one is too old to take chelation therapy.

Q: Will chelation therapy help to allay Alzheimer's disease?

A: Chelation therapy improves blood circulation to the brain and, to whatever extent the problem is due to a circulatory deficit, chelation may have a significant benefit. It is very difficult to tell in advance which patients are going to be helped, but I have certainly witnessed a good number of cases in which dramatic improvements in memory and mental function occur in those who carry the diagnosis of Alzheimer's disease. I tell my patients that the chances of success are probably no more than 50 percent, but if it helps, chelation therapy may improve brain function dramatically.

Q: Will chelation therapy relieve the symptoms of arthritis?

A: By its antioxidant enhancing effects, EDTA can reduce inflammation and possibly ease the damaging effects of arthritis. However, the results are not as predictable as they are with vascular disease. I would try oral antioxidants and other nutritional treatments first for osteoarthritis, especially if vascular disease is not also present.

Q: Is chelation applicable for Parkinson's disease?

A: There have been reports in the literature about its applicability, and I have seen some patients who have improved from the use of chelation therapy for their Parkinson's disease. Chelation treatment is not nearly as effective with Parkinsonism as it is with vascular and brain diseases.

Q: Can chelation therapy help with multiple sclerosis (MS)?

A: EDTA chelation infusions have not been shown by themselves to help multiple sclerosis. It's possible, though, for intravenous (IV) EDTA to be used alongwith a number of other modalities in reducing the symptoms of MS in an experimental treatment design. The benefit would arise from EDTA's antioxidant characteristics and its reduction of metastatic soft tissue calcium. [As with the toxic metals, excess mineral calcium is removed by IV chelation therapy.]

Q: Do EDTA infusions have some side benefits that may treat cancer or arthritis?

A: By the reduction of heavy metals, including excessive iron, EDTA is a great help to the body in controlling free-radical reactions. These free radicals increase the likelihood and speed of development of cancer or arthritis if the predisposition is there for those conditions. Therefore, EDTA theoretically could have a free-radical benefit for arthritis and cancer.

Q: How do I find out if I have heavy-metal toxicity, and can I use the results of those findings as a diagnosis?

A: Probably the best way to detect heavy-metal toxicity is to take an EDTA challenge dose and have the doctor's laboratory measure the amount of heavy metals that come out into one's urine. If there is a high level of metals or a significant increase in metallic urine content from the baseline level, then you have a good indication that too many heavy metals are built up in the body. Whether this evidence will be enough to convince your health insurance company that the chelation treatments should be covered because of heavy-metal toxicity is uncertain. Some health insurance carriers accept the diagnosis if shown in this way, but others have much stricter criteria that involve finding an elevated blood level of heavy metals. Unfortunately the blood level criterion is very inaccurate because most heavy metals pass quickly out of the blood into the fat, bones, and other storage tissues of the body soon after they accumulate.

Q: Following up on this health insurance inquiry, if I do have an excess amount of heavy metals in my urine, will a health insurance policy that I carry pay for my chelation treatment?

A: It is possible that health insurance will cover chelation therapy if a large amount of heavy metal is detected in the patient's urine. The best procedure is to measure the level of metals in the urine before and after an infusion of EDTA. Even a small amount of toxic metals may be harmful. However, the level of heavy metals detected in urine rarely is enough to be defined as "heavy metal toxicity," according to industrial standards. Most physicians do not want to spend huge efforts to convince health insurance companies that an industrial level of heavy-metal toxicity exists because usually this is fruitless. My main efforts to get intravenous

EDTA infusions covered by health insurance are directed towards doing research in proving that EDTA is an effective therapy for vascular disease and dementia, so that it can be widely used to the benefit of humankind.

thallium, radioactive metals, or others is much more prevalent throughout the world than is commonly recognized.[1] Stephen Davies, M.A., B.M., B.Ch., is the Medical Director of the Biolab Medical Unit in London, England. Dr. Davies showed during his presentation of the Annual Carlos Lamar Lecture to the American College of Advancement in Medicine (ACAM), on May 14, 1992, that concentrations of toxic metals comprise the body tissues of vast numbers of people in Great Britain. At any time, metallic poisonings in England burden the human body and brain with the potential for illness from cellular damage.

As we described in Chapter 13, in the United Kingdom, Dr. Davies measured lead, cadmium, aluminum, arsenic, and mercury over a seven-year period in the hair of 17,000 patients, the sweat of 15,000 patients, and the blood of 3,000 patients. He analyzed these tissue-saturated metallic toxicities in relation to age and sex to reveal that males generally have higher levels of the poisonings than females and that levels increase progressively with age. The implications for physical illness and dementia are enormous.

Elsewhere it has been written that heavy-metal poisoning is more effectively diagnosed with hair analysis alone[2] than with conventional blood and urine tests,[3] but Dr. Davies' methods and his statistical report are impressive. Obviously, the patients under review, as well as millions of other British subjects left out of the examination, will benefit from receiving courses of chelation therapy.

As well as relieving the body of heavy metals, chelation therapy can also alleviate other health threats. For instance, elderly patients with atherosclerosis who had been treated primarily for chronic lead poisoning showed a dramatic improvement in their atherosclerotic disease following chelation therapy.[4,5] This type of pathological atherosclerotic connection to heavy-metal poisoning is a primary area of interest for Dr. Chappell.

Previously accepted and erroneously determined so-called "safe levels" of heavy-metal exposure have been found to cause or aggravate many chronic diseases.[6] Hyperactivity in children,[7,8] myocarditis,[9] and neuropathy due to lead,[6] hypertension from cadmium, and Alzheimer's disease from aluminum[10,11] are among those heavy-metal toxicity diseases now finally recognized. After chelation therapy and adequate nutritional supplementation, repeated hair, blood, urine, or sweat analysis confirms the decrease in heavy metals as well as the improved trace-mineral levels. As we shall see in the dietary chapters of Part V, nutritional supplementation is an integral part of the full program for EDTA chelation therapy.

THE CHEMICAL PROPERTIES OF EDTA

Ethylene diamine tetraacetic acid, also known by chemists as *edetic acid* (EDTA), is a white crystalline solid with a molecular weight of 292.1 and an empirical formula of $C_{10}H_{16}N_2O_8$. In his book, *The Scientific Basis of EDTA Chelation Therapy*, eminent biotoxicologist Bruce W. Halstead, M.D., of Colton, California describes it as "a weak tetrabasic acid and only slightly soluble in water. . . . Each nitrogen atom has an unshared pair of electrons, in addition to the four acidic hydrogens, the EDTA molecule thus has six potential sites for bonding with a metal ion and may be considered to be a sexadentate ligand." (A sexadentate ligand possesses six available bonds to grasp hold of and surround metallic ions [see the paragraphs immediately below], which makes it an exceedingly powerful chelating agent.)

Similar to our definition of a *ligand* earlier in the book, Dr. Halstead confirms that it is any atom, radical, or molecule in a complex that is bound to a central atom, having at least one pair of electrons that can be donated to a metal ion.[5] Nearly every metal cation in the periodic table forms stable one-to-one complexes with the EDTA ion. It is the primary chelating agent used in medicine worldwide for detoxifying people affected by heavy metals, excessive mineralizations, radiation particles, digitalis intoxication, snake venoms, and assorted other poisons.

The coordination number of EDTA is the number of bonds formed by the central atom for creating the metallic chelate. Like the lobster's crusher claw clasping a dead fish, several complex groups within the molecule effectively surround and isolate the metallic cation. "In order for a complex ion to be formed from one or more ligands and a central atom," writes Dr. Halstead, "each ligand must possess at least one unshared pair of electrons, and the central metal atom must be able to accept an electron pair from each ligand. This results in a ligand sharing a pair of electrons with the central metal atom in the formation of a covalent bond. Because of the speed and precision with which this complexion process is accomplished by the EDTA molecule, it has become a useful tool in complexion titration in analytical chemistry."[5]

PRECAUTIONS IN THE IV PROCEDURE FOR EDTA

EDTA is administered intravenously in not less than three hours. The longer an IV drip takes to proceed with this chelating substance, the less chance of the patient experiencing any type of side effect. A small, 25-gauge butterfly needle is preferred for the IV procedure because it is easier and less painful to insert, and the tiny lumen prevents any excessive rate of infusion. Some people being treated do get impatient with the slow rate of flow of their infusions and may attempt to speed up the process on their own. However, it is difficult to infuse 500 ml of solution through a 25-gauge needle in much less than three hours.

The therapeutic benefit of IV infusions with EDTA is dependent on the total number of injections and not related so much to the interval between treatments. In no case should EDTA infusions be given more often than once in twenty-four hours. The accepted IV interval among chelating physicians to administer EDTA to any one patient is not closer than forty-eight hours between infusions and the generally acknowledged standard is a schedule of two to three weekly treatments. Each time, then, measurements are made to determine that the patient's serum creatinine and kidney function tests are within normal or satisfactory limits. If an individual is debilitated or has a preexisting kidney insufficiency, the delay of two weeks or more between infusions may be required. The doctor's judgment is a main determining factor here.

Renal function tests should be carefully followed in all patients receiving EDTA and the laboratory costs for such measurements figured into the estimated expenditures for chelation treatment. The ACAM protocol calls for repeated pre-infusion urine analyses. Then it recommends serum creatinine measurements before every third treatment. If pretreatment renal function tests are not completely normal or if treatments are taken by the patient more than once weekly, serum creatinine and urinalysis should be performed as often as before each infusion. An upward trend in serum creatinine is a reason for the doctor to discontinue therapy until the patient's creatinine reading returns to baseline levels. On its own, renal function will usually improve to pretreatment levels or better within two to four weeks.

"If a rising trend in serum creatinine is not detected early and if treatment is continued in the face of progressively impaired renal function," warns the ACAM *Protocol*, "more serious renal damage will result. Lasting renal impairment from EDTA has never ever been reported when the precautions described in this *Protocol* were followed."

In fact, renal function improves, on the average, after the chelating physician properly administers a series of EDTA infusions.[11,12,13,14]Admittedly there have been reports of lasting kidney damage occurring from excessively large doses of EDTA, administered too rapidly or too often for individual tolerance and without close monitoring of renal function.[15] Variable tolerance among patients who are unusually sensitive to EDTA makes frequent renal function testing imperative.

The total number of infusions for optimal therapeutic effect varies from one patient to the next. A series of twenty infusions is minimum for patients with symptomatic disease. It is not unusual for some people to take forty or more infusions before they feel any significant benefit. In cases of patients with early-stage Alzheimer's disease, positive brain-cell response is not likely to appear until twenty or more—perhaps as many as one hundred IV infusions with EDTA—are received by them. Be aware that full benefit from treatment definitely does not normally occur for up to three months following a completed series of infusions.

Follow-up chelation treatments may be taken once or twice monthly for long term maintenance, to sustain health improvement, and to prevent the recurrence of symptoms. Moreover, informed people, in particular chelating physicians themselves, take chelation therapy as a preventive measure against body and brain deterioration. It is the ultimate anti-aging therapy which assures longevity and an alert mind until the moment of physical death.

PROOF THAT EDTA CHELATES HEAVY METALS OUT OF THE BLOOD

Charles J. Rudolph, D.O., Ph.D., Edward W. McDonagh, D.O., and R.K. Barber, B.S., reported on results they achieved at the McDonagh Medical Center in Kansas City, Missouri in chelating away heavy-metal toxicity for one hundred and twenty-two patients who had been suffering from various chronic degenerative disorders. Brain dementia was among the most predominant. Included were seventy-three men ranging in age from 32 to 84 years and forty-nine women aged from 39 to 84 years. Over a seventeen-month period, the amount of iron in their blood was measured both before and then after each patient received thirty chelation treatments.

This experiment, performed at a private chelation practice facility, is illustrative of how EDTA chelates excessive heavy metals out of the blood and restores tissue cells to refunction in a normal manner.[16]

After the series of thirty EDTA infusions were completed, the decreases in serum iron concentrations were statistically significant for the men and women within the entire group. Their serum iron on average decreased overall by 17.15 percent. For the males, blood iron decrease was 14.14 percent. For the females, blood iron decrease was 21.69 percent.

In eighteen subjects whose initial values for serum iron were abnormally high, a 43.6 percent drop in the blood iron content occurred. In contrast, chelation therapy appeared to normalize twenty-one other subjects who were experiencing abnormally low concentrations of blood iron. The male patients who showed insufficiently concentrated iron in their blood before treatment eventually elevated toward normal with a 31.6 percent increase. Those females with low concentrations of serum iron had a healthy increase by 10.4 percent.

Serum iron has been clearly established as a catalyst for many forms of free-radical reactions.[5,17,18,19] Disorders such as chronic liver disease, congestive cardiomyopathy, neoplastic disease of the bone marrow (tumor tissue in the bone marrow), and Alzheimer's disease have been associated with high serum iron levels.[20,21,22] Iron chelators such as EDTA prevent artery trauma from the forced flow of blood (reperfusion injury) directly after the pathological process, which brings on acute tissue anoxia followed by rapid re-introduction of oxygen.[24] This pathological mechanism, particularly affecting brain cells, involves the generation of superoxide radicals (free radicals comprised of iron combined with oxygen ions) by free-tissue iron.

Iron in the brain becomes twice as harmful because it further catalyzes the breakdown of superoxide radicals into hydroxyl (OH) free radicals, which are even more devastating to the tissue than are superoxide radicals.[25]

Reducing tissue-iron concentrations, as with depleting any of the body's heavy-metal concentrations, is of paramount importance to reduce damage from free-radicals and brain-cell destruction. EDTA aids in control of excess iron. Reduction serves to retard lipid peroxidation and to diminish chain reactions of unwanted free radical reactions. Using iron as the illustrative heavy metal, the data presented by Rudolph, McDonagh, and Barber show how EDTA infusions remove heavy metals from the body and brain.[26,27]

Not only did EDTA infusions lower excess levels of serum iron in this study, they also raised them when required. It seems to be clinically desirable to lower serum iron in patients with established insufficient concentrations. When these subjects with low serum-iron levels were examined, it was found that their bodies increased blood iron so as to approach normal. EDTA raises the blood quantity of iron in accordance with the body's need.

CHAPTER 20

The Clinical Studies With Chelation Therapy

Seventy-one-year-old Rosalee N. was brought by her husband, Harry, to the Maulfair Medical Center in Mertztown, Pennsylvania. They had driven in the late morning on a windy day from their home in Allentown, Pennsylvania. It was mandatory that Harry bring Rosalee for medical attention, because he had come to the end of his rope with her complicated health problems.

Harry discussed his wife's difficulties with the clinic's medical director before she was examined by the doctor, Conrad G. Maulfair, Jr., D.O. Rosalee was obviously mentally incompetent, and unable to describe the many discomforts that kept her in a state of debilitation. She had been diagnosed by a university psychiatrist as being in the middle stages of Alzheimer's disease with many of its manifestations.

Additionally, the patient was discomforted by a variety of physical complaints including generalized pain and weakness around most parts of her skeleton. For nearly a decade Rosalee exhibited what Harry described to Dr. Maulfair as frequent and repeated bouts of "nerves"—shaking and tremors that went with her sharp tone of voice and an attitude of anger. Plus, she often squeezed her head in her hands because of severe headaches.

Harry explained that his wife suffered from apparent morning fatigue even directly after arising from a night's sleep. She drooled, too. And heart palpitations were an ever-present sensation for her. Because she felt that her heart was about to burst, Rosalee would let go of her head only to clutch at her chest. The poor woman's eyesight for far objects was decreasing, as well, and each year the optometrist was forced to increase the correction strength of lens diopters in her "Coke-bottle"-thick spectacles.

The reason for her shaking and tremors became apparent later, when during laboratory and clinical examinations Dr. Maulfair uncovered that Rosalee was, in truth, a victim of Parkinson's disease, among many other health problems. As is generally known, Parkinson's disease is a slowly increasing disorder caused by damage to brain cells. Symptoms include tremors that occur while at rest, "pill rolling" movements of the fingers, and a masklike face. Other symptoms are a shuffling gait, a slightly bent over posture, rigid muscles, and weakness. It is usually a disease of un-known cause (idiopathic), affecting persons over sixty years of age. Park-inson's disease patients do drool, possess oily skin, are unable to stand heat, are emotionally unstable, and exhibit misjudgment problems. The symptoms are made worse by the patient's confronting, either alone or in combination, tiredness, excitement, and frustration.

Because of a prior automobile accident, Rosalee additionally had under-gone a hip replacement operation approximately six years before. She felt an arthritic-type pain in the operated hip that seemed to radiate to other body joints.

Moreover, she was suffering from iatrogenic (doctor-caused) disease due to the excessive amount of drug therapy prescribed for her by at least four other physicians to whom the woman's loving and concerned husband had brought her for treatment. She was taking eleven drugs, which included Quinaglute Dura-Tabs for her heart palpitations. The palpitations arose from arrhythmia (an irregular heart beat). She also swallowed the ten additional drugs consisting of AlternaGEL liquid for the symptomatic relief of her stomach hyperacidity, Sinemet for reducing shaking and tremors, Lanoxin tablets for increasing her heart-pump output, Tranxene tranquilizer tablets to alleviate her anxiety and "nerves," Desyrel to lift her out of major episodes of depression, Imodium capsules for the control of a nonspecific diarrhea, Trili-sate tablets and liquid for her arthritic-like skeletal pains, Esgic capsules for overcoming tension headache arising from muscular contractions, Ascriptin analgesic against rheumatoid arthritis and osteoarthritis, plus Extra Strength Tylenol caplets as a pain reliever and sleeping aid.

"The patient was taking a minimum of twenty-four tablets, capsules, or liquids of various drugs every day on a regular basis and, as you mentioned in your introduction to this case, additional numbers of three other drugs on an 'as-needed' basis for diarrhea, skeletal pain, and headache," Dr. Maulfair told us in reiterating the woman's dilemma. "Certainly she was ingesting the Quinaglute for her heart irregularity, and then she swallowed AlternaGEL to control the diarrhea produced in her by the Quinaglute. The Imodium was also used for the diarrhea and was given to her by her husband on an 'as-needed' basis, depending on how severely the diarrhea came on after she took Quinaglute. Of course, the Sinemet was for reducing the Parkinson's disease-like symptoms from which she suffered.

"The patient was taking two tranquilizers, Tranxene and Desyrel. The

Lanoxin was useful for the heart, and the Trilisate, Esgic, Ascripton, and Tylenol were all anti-inflammatory and pain-relieving drugs for chronic joint pain. To say that this seventy-one-year-old woman was over-medicated would be as much an understatement as it would be to say that Hitler was *not* a nice person," Dr. Maulfair added with a smile.

What stimulated Harry to consult yet a fifth physician for his wife was information that came to him about chelation therapy. As were Drs. Casdorph, Streeter, Schachter, Farr, and Chappell in their individual states of California, Indiana, New York, Oklahoma, and Ohio, respectively, Dr. Conrad Maulfair was known around the eastern sectors of Pennsylvania to be an expert in chelation infusion treatment. He, too, is a Diplomate of the American Board of Chelation Therapy who uses the therapy on a regular schedule for his patients. Harry had heard from neighbors in Allentown that symptoms of Alzheimer's-type dementia were much reduced or even eliminated by this intravenous administration of a chelating amino acid.

Since the most disturbing series of symptoms for Rosalee's spouse was her ongoing state of confusion, memory loss, restlessness, problems with perception, speech trouble, poor coordination, anxiety, constant fear, loose bowels, loss of bladder control, and refusal to eat—all established as symptoms of Alzheimer's disease—Harry decided that chelation therapy was a treatment program worth trying.

Dr. Maulfair performed a number of laboratory and clinical examinations to determine if Rosalee was, in fact, a suitable candidate to receive chelation therapy. Most of her symptoms of degenerative diseases, the doctor judged, would reduce or reverse from administration of the treatment. First, however, it was necessary for him to build up Rosalee's inner strength and health with oral and intravenous nutritional programs. These were used to improve her general functional status, including her suppressed immune system. This was accomplished in a couple of visits, and she started chelation therapy."As chelation therapy continued, the patient's overall status slowly improved," Dr. Maulfair said. "After her tenth chelation treatment, Rosalee's numbers and dosages of drugs were decreased."

The quality of life for the couple improved. Rosalee was becoming mentally competent and began doing more toward fulfilling her personal needs. The patient grew in strength and vigor. Her skeletal pains left her and there was almost no more need for nonsteroidal anti-inflammatory drugs (NSAID)—even Tylenol was no longer required. Her headaches steadily diminished so that neither NSAID nor any other painkiller had to be taken for this symptom either.

By the time she had received fifty-seven intravenous chelation infusions

Rosalee was able to resume her own grocery shopping. She walked to the corner store without Harry worrying that she might not find her way home while carrying her packages. Her anger and anxiety subsided. The patient's spirits lifted to the point that Rosalee and Harry participated in a joyous little ceremony of flushing the tranquilizer drugs, Tranxene and Desyrel, down the toilet. As she approached her seventy-sixth year, the staff at the Maulfair Medical Center in Mertztown, Pennsylvania agreed on a prognosis for her future. They believed that the quality of life for Rosalee and her husband was excellent—wholesome, happy, and generally good to a point that was balanced with their ages and conditions.

As an aside, it should be observed that an outside medical expert took notice of the patient's progress, too. Early in their doctor/patient relationship, Dr. Maulfair had referred Rosalee to a neurologist so as to receive specialty treatment for her Parkinson's disease. During the ensuing four-year interval that he was being consulted by the patient, this nerve specialist remarked repeatedly, as did his office nurses, that they were amazed to see her progressing so well considering her advanced pathological condition. Most parkinsonian patients, they further stated, would have become considerably worse with debilitating symptoms over a similar period of time. This was not the case for Rosalee, because Parkinson's disease is one of the conditions that respond somewhat positively to chelation therapy. Her signs and symptoms of parkinsonism had leveled off and deterioration from the disease had stopped.

Dr. Maulfair advises us, "While the patient's tremor persists, overall it is much less than it was when she started chelation therapy more than four years earlier. The patient, now alert, lively, and conversational, freely states that if changes had not been made, she does not believe that she would be alive today. Whether or not this is true, of course no one can say. What we can say, however, is that the quality of her life has been improved immeasurably and for this we are both thrilled and grateful."

THE ACAM RESULTS

The American College of Advancement in Medicine estimates that around the world at least 500,000 patients have received EDTA chelation therapy—about 10 million intravenous treatments to date—administered under guidelines of the ACAM protocol. These infusions have been received by people without a single fatality attributable to ethylene diamine tetraacetic acid (EDTA). Undoubtedly this unsurpassed record makes EDTA chelation therapy one of the safest therapeutic modalities of modern medicine.

It's two most important uses are for the reversal of hardening of the arteries and for antidoting against heavy-metal toxicity. For heavy metals, as an example, experiments with silver-mercury fillings indicate that these amalgams emit enough toxic mercury to cause cell damage in laboratory animals. Such poisoning shows up quickly in the kidney and intestine but takes longer to manifest itself in the brain. About 300 million North Americans as well as myriad numbers of others around the globe have mercury amalgams packed into the cavities of their teeth. Such dental fillings are comprised of 50 percent mercury, which is a silver-white liquid metal that virtually is the most toxic substance on earth.

After much research, in the fall of 1990 the Swedish Health Administration declared dental amalgam "unsuitable and too toxic" to be put into people's mouths and recommended that its use be discontinued starting in 1991. Amalgam fillings are no longer used by dentists in Sweden. Now the United States Food and Drug Administration has embarked on emergency investigations to determine the deleteriousness of dental amalgams and whether they really do produce neurotoxicity of the Alzheimer's type. The American Dental Association has been resistant to the practice, but numbers of its nonconformist members are recommending to their patients that they have their amalgams removed while simultaneously undergoing courses of IV injections with EDTA. Chelation therapy is necessary, because the amalgam removal itself sends mercury vapors into the brain with at least temporary dementia symptoms developing.

Manganese, another heavy metal that we have already discussed, produces profound neurological dysfunction when associated with a person's excessive exposure to this mineral. Manganese intoxication is known to bring on rigid gaze, muscular stiffness, staccato-like gait, and liver malfunction along with extreme anti-social behavior of the criminal type. Medical researchers have lately been looking to manganese as a potential source of Alzheimer's disease. The only treatment for manganese poisoning is chelation therapy, mainly with EDTA.

Lead assuredly destroys the brain and nerve cells. It increases the permeability of tissues and raises the leakage of nutrients from out of tissue cells. Lead poisoning is an ancient disease, feared by man ever since he began to smelt, shape, and industrialize minerals. The Roman Empire is believed to have disintegrated partly because of it. Lead poisoning is rarely something one gets just yesterday. The manifestation of symptoms from lead toxicity is a result of a whole lifetime of exposure and accumulation. Yet chelation therapy remains as the life-saving method of removing lead from the bodies and brains of children, young adults, and the elderly.

Cadmium, a soft, silver-white, blue-tinged element that is chemically related to mercury in the atomic table of elements, is present in dust, fumes, and mists which are common byproducts during the refining of zinc, copper, and lead. Inhaling the metal's fumes produces pulmonary emphysema, kidney damage, excessive urinary excretion of low molecular weight proteins, low hemoglobin, kidney stones, and mental derangement. Be assured that cadmium toxicity brings on dementia. What is the treatment for serious cadmium exposure? Of course, it is EDTA chelation therapy.

These metallic poisonings are cited here merely as examples of the worth of EDTA chelation therapy to humankind and its medical community. Unfortunately the treatment is hardly utilized enough, as will be demonstrated during the course of our looking at the clinical investigations that already have been carried out. They show the well-established worth of chelation therapy.

ARTERIOSCLEROSIS TREATED WITH EDTA CHELATION

As stated, the other very important use of EDTA chelation is for the reversal of arteriosclerosis (hardening of the arteries). A flexibility of the arterial walls and an apparent clearing of atherosclerotic plaque occurs from IV administration of the treatment. Numerous clinical studies have been conducted by advocates of chelation therapy to examine the treatment's efficacy against arteriosclerosis. Not only have journal articles been published about chelation therapy's usefulness as an antidote for heavy-metal toxicity, but they have also confirmed the procedure's application for peripheral vascular disease, cardiovascular disease, arthritis, diabetic retinopathy, and many other diseases.

In 1988, ACAM compiled and made available abstracts of 3,539 published laboratory journal and clinical journal articles on EDTA and EDTA chelation therapy.

The information that follows in these next few sections, expounding on clinical studies that show the worth of EDTA chelation, is derived from a presentation made by ACAM past president Michael B. Schachter, M.D., of Suffern, New York, at the organization's semi-annual scientific meeting in Houston, Texas, May 6–9, 1993. For this book, we have merely selected highlights from Dr. Schachter's presentation. The paper from which he took his information, "Chronological History of EDTA Chelation Therapy," was a joint undertaking by Charles H. Farr, M.D., Ph.D., and Robert L. White, Ph.D., with revisions by Dr. Schachter made in April 1993.

HEART CONDITIONS AND EDTA CHELATION THERAPY

In 1960, medical doctors Lawrence E. Meltzer and J. Roderick Kitchell first reported on "The Treatment of Coronary Artery Disease With Disodium EDTA" in a book written by Marvin J. Seven, M.D.[1] This article stated, "Ten male patients with angina pectoris [periodic chest pain] were selected for evaluation and therapy with disodium EDTA, each patient receiving between 57 and 163.5 grams intravenously over a period of two to three months. At the end of this period, therapy was discontinued because of disappointing results [nobody indicated improvement]. Three months later, reevaluation showed that nine of the ten men had significant reduction in the number and severity of anginal attacks, five out of the nine patients' electrocardiograms revealed improvement, and all three patients with cardiomegaly [enlargement of the heart] showed a reduction in heart size. No significant toxicity was encountered."

This investigation by Drs. Meltzer and Kitchell was a completely positive and enthusiastic report with the body of the paper in harmony with its conclusion.

Then, Meltzer, Kitchell, and a third colleague, Dr. F. Palmon, Jr., again published a medical paper in 1961, that stated: "Two thousand consecutive infusions of disodium EDTA were given to 81 subjects in a study of the effectiveness of this therapy in coronary artery disease during a two-year period. We have found no serious side effects or toxicity with the use of disodium EDTA when administered as a 3-gm dose and infused as a 0.5 percent solution over 2½ to 3 hours. It is therefore our opinion that the drug can be used without danger over prolonged periods."[2]

Next, surprisingly, in a complete reversal of their encouraging stance on chelation therapy, Meltzer, Kitchell, and assorted other colleagues reappraised EDTA and set the science of chelation therapy on its ear, starting in 1963. It was the beginning of bitter controversy about the treatment that prevails even today. This "reappraisal" article frequently is cited by the treatment's opponents as proving the lack of efficacy of chelation therapy for cardiovascular disease.

In their "reappraisal" study, the authors added to their experiments. They took the original ten patients of the first-time 1961 investigations, then added twenty-eight more for a total of thirty-eight subjects.

Their article's summary states: "At the end of four years of treatment in ten patients and after one and a half to three years in twenty-eight others, a re-appraisal of the effect of EDTA therapy on arteriosclerotic coronary disease is reported. Whereas after three months of treatment, 66 percent of these thirty-eight patients exhibited improved anginal patterns (from the patients' own impressions plus measured exercise tolerance) and 40 percent showed improved electrocardiographic patterns, none of these effects were lasting. At the time of this report, twelve of the thirty-eight were dead of their original disease (32 percent), and only 40 percent remained clinically improved.

"At present we believe that chelation as used in this study did not benefit patients more than other commonly used therapeutic methods. It is not a useful clinical tool in the treatment of coronary artery disease."[3]

Upon analysis of what the investigators actually witnessed, it became apparent to any intelligent observer that something was very wrong with their method and motivation. Here is a clear case of misreporting. As we said, a careful reading of their erroneously concluded "reappraisal" article along with an attempt by chelation scientists to put this information into perspective forces evaluators to the opposite conclusion from the authors—namely, that EDTA is of much value for the treatment of coronary artery disease.

Analysis of the Kitchell/Meltzer data, for example, reveals that their patients were extremely high-risk coronary patients in which no form of therapy had helped. The majority of the patients were reported to have improved and to have maintained improvement following therapy.

After 18 months with no further therapy, and with no stated dietary or risk factor modification, 46 percent of a group of twenty-eight patients remained improved and even thriving.

Twenty-three of those twenty-eight patients had suffered previous heart attacks and were therefore at relatively high risk for cardiac complications or death.

Sixty-four percent of the twenty-eight patients improved after only 20 EDTA infusions, and 46 percent showed sharply improved electrocardiographic patterns. As pointed out in a 1982 review article, "These results were very impressive and did not support the author's negative conclusions. In retrospect, it appears that the authors' summary in the 're-appraisal article' was, to a great extent, responsible for the lack of subsequent funding for cessation of clinical trials with EDTA chelation therapy for occlusive arterial disease."[4]

Dr. L.E. Kitchell and J.R. Meltzer have done a disservice to myriad patients who could have benefited from taking chelation therapy but were kept from the treatment by their own primary care physicians and specialists who believed the published, erroneous "reappraisal" report.

As we had stated in an earlier chapter, at the Spring conference of the American Academy of Medical Preventics (AAMP) in 1979, psychiatrist

Lloyd Grumbles, M.D., presented radionuclide studies showing improvement of cerebral arterial blood flow after chelation therapy. Then, following biotoxicologist Dr. Bruce Halstead's 1980 investigations, Dr. Casdorph came out with two dynamic reports on the efficacy of chelation therapy.

In 1981, the two studies conducted by Dr. Casdorph indicated that EDTA caused an increase in cerebral blood flow and cardiac output as measured by technetium perfusion studies. Brain blood-flow and heart action both improved, but the patients also benefited even more from decreased peripheral vascular resistance in the limbs, increased blood flow to and from the heart, and increased cardiac ejection fraction (the pumping force of the heart) or cardiac output.[5,6]

Also in 1981, Donald R. McLaughlan, M.D. Professor of Physiology and Medicine and Director of the Centre for Research in Neurodegenerative Diseases at the University of Toronto, appeared before the fall semi-annual scientific convention of the AAMP. He advised the assembly that chelation therapy, using deferoxamine as the chelating agent, was helpful in treating Alzheimer's disease.[7] Dr. McLaughlan drew upon the clinical and laboratory research experience accumulated over at least a decade. His research was being conducted on Alzheimer's disease and its tie-in to human brain pollution with the toxic metal, aluminum. The renown Canadian neurotoxicologist cited from twenty-one research papers that he had produced from 1972 to 1980, all on the highly controversial Alzheimer's disease/aluminum/chelation connection.[8-28]

Dr. McLaughlan has gone on to investigate aluminum neurotoxicity as a source of brain dysfunction and, to date, he has turned out at least another twenty-one exceedingly significant research papers on the subject. No matter how much the aluminum industry denies it and how many medical scholars the industry's executives pay to speak against the aluminum/Alzheimer's connection, this causative relationship of brain cell invasion to dementia remains irrefutable.

In 1982, Edward W. McDonagh, D.O., Charles J. Rudolph, D.O., Ph.D., and Emanuel Cheraskin, M.D., D.M.D., evaluated fifty-seven patients objectively for cerebral vascular arterial occlusion before and after administering to them an average of twenty-eight intravenous infusions with EDTA. Measurements of arterial occlusion were made with noninvasive measurements of eye, brain, and arterial blood flows (oculocerebrovasculometric analysis). Arterial occlusion to the brain diminished by an average of 18 percent from an average of 28 percent to an average of 10 percent following therapy. Of these patients, 88 percent showed objective improvement in cerebrovascular blood flow.[29]

Next, Drs. Casdorph and Farr joined in 1983 to conduct a research project to measure the amount of improvement furnished by EDTA chelation for those patients acutely involved with peripheral vascular disease. The investigators reported significant improvement with EDTA infusions as an alternative to lower extremity amputation.[30]

In 1984, A. Gotto, M.D., reported on "The Status of EDTA Chelation Therapy in Texas."[31] He had just relinquished his position as the head of the American Heart Association. Until then, medical politics had dissuaded Dr. Gotto from, in any way, being associated with chelation therapy. However, as an honest cardiologist he was well aware of the benefits accrued by heart patients who took the treatment. He subsequently initiated a study on EDTA chelation therapy as the treatment of choice for peripheral vascular disease at Baylor College of Medicine. The report evolving from this study was positive for the treatment.

Keith W. Sehnert, M.D., A.F. Clague, and Emanuel Cheraskin, M.D., D.M.D., reported on thirteen subjects with chronic degenerative disease and abnormal creatinine clearances. They were given twenty EDTA infusions and following the treatment their creatinine clearance significantly improved.[32]

THE FRAUDULENT THIEMANN STUDY

In 1985, the first double-blind, placebo-controlled study ever performed on the administration of intravenous EDTA was funded by Thiemann Pharmaceuticals, the commercial manufacturer of a platelet-inhibitor prescription medication, bencyclan, which is marketed under the brand name *Fludilat*. This drug is widely prescribed in Europe for the treatment of atherosclerosis.

The scientific study, sponsored and owned by the Thiemann Pharmaceutical Company, was conducted at the University of Heidelberg in West Germany by Professor Doktor G. Schettler, M.D., and others who were active staff members in the clinics of the University Hospital there. Dr. Schettler held the very distinguished, double-positions of Chairman of the Department of Internal Medicine and President of West Germany's International Atherosclerosis Research Association.

Looking at the study as a whole, in summary, it showed a 250-percent increase in the average distance walked in patients receiving EDTA and only a 64-percent increase in patients receiving Fludilat. There were four individuals in the EDTA chelation-therapy group who walked 1000 meters more than their prechelation exercise capabilities would have allowed—an astonishing feat for any individuals possessed of so much pathology to start.

These dramatic results for the four patients that were highly in favor of chelation treatment, however, were dropped from the study by the German pharmaceutical manufacturer. Thiemann Pharmaceuticals held tight control over what would be reported. The elimination of these four patients, therefore, caused a serious alteration of the report. As a result of this exceedingly unusual and absolutely dishonest manipulation of the data, it was concluded by medical statisticians that EDTA was no better than the placebo, even though the placebo in this case actually was Thiemann's platelet inhibitor, Fludilat.

Another factor that was not reported was that EDTA chelation therapy patients continued to improve after thirty days following the treatment's conclusion. This was in contrast to the Fludilat group of patients who gradually reverted to their disabling pretreatment status. The information given here was never published in any scientific journal but rather was obtained from raw data on the study. After a lot of soul-searching, this information was supplied by Dr. Schettler and his colleagues at Heidelberg University. They were shocked at the fraudulent practices pursued by Thiemann Pharmaceutical Company executives.

For greater detail on just what occurred in that fraudulent 1985 study that masked the effectiveness of chelation therapy, we checked with the medical detective James P. Carter, M.D. Dr. Carter is Professor and Head of the Nutrition Section, the School of Public Health and Tropical Medicine, Tulane University Medical Center, New Orleans, Louisiana. He described some of what follows here in his 1992 book *Racketeering in Medicine: The Suppression of Alternatives.*

> In order to build sales for their commercial prescription product, the Thiemann Pharmaceutical Company executives wanted to compare EDTA chelation therapy with bencyclan. Thiemann company officials originally believed that with IV EDTA marked as the standard, intravenously-administered Fludilat would show up as a superior treatment. When it turned out that they had guessed wrong, they were shocked and resorted to research chicanery.[33]

Thiemann did not publish the results of its finding because, as we stated, it turned out that EDTA chelation therapy is a safer and far more efficient way to enhance arterial blood flow than anything else ever developed by scientific medicine.

Instead of allowing its publication through usual scientific channels of communication, Thiemann Pharmaceuticals buried it's officially sponsored chelation therapy study. Consequently, in order to get out the vital information, the study was presented secretly, and without Thiemann's permission, in 1985, to the Seventh Atherosclerosis Congress in Melbourne, Australia, by the same investigating scientists from Heidelberg who originally conducted it. Dr. Schettler and his colleagues were proud of their work and wished the world medical community to become aware of what they had uncovered. Therefore, the German researchers let it be known that chelation therapy far surpassed the Thiemann Pharmaceutical Company's commerical product.

A total of approximately 48 patients were treated, 24 in the Fludilat group and 24 in the EDTA group. Disodium EDTA was administered in a dose of 2.5 grams in 500 milliliters of ½ normal saline. Treatments were given five days a week for a total of four weeks. Each patient received twenty intravenous infusions. Only patients with peripheral vascular disease who could not walk 200 meters without feeling the discomfort of intermittent claudication were included in the investigations.

Intermittent claudication is a cramping pain, induced by exercise and relieved by rest, that is caused by an inadequate supply of blood to the affected muscles. It is most often felt in the calf and leg muscles as a result of blockage of the leg arteries. The leg pulses are often absent and the feet may be cold. As a means of monitoring the effects of the two treatments, pain-free walking distance was measured before, during, and after therapy on a treadmill running at 3.5 kilometers/hour with a 10-percent gradient.

The measured results showed a 250-percent increase in distance walked before onset of claudication pain in the EDTA-treated group after they had taken four weeks of chelation therapy. By comparison, there was only a 60-percent increase in the bencyclan group. Bencyclan, however, is a drug proven to be of benefit in this peripheral vascular disease and is widely prescribed in Europe for relieving it.

There were four patients in the EDTA group who experienced more than 1,000-meter-increases in the pain-free walking distance at the end of only 30 days of treatment. Highly favorable data from those four patients mysteriously disappeared when Thiemann officials were forced to officially make the final results public following the Australian Seventh Atherosclerosis Congress disclosure.

Thiemann had a legal right under terms of its contract with the researchers to edit the final results and to interpret the data in any way they wanted. Their final report contained data that reduced observed EDTA benefit by 72 percent. From a 250-percent increase in walking ability, the

Thiemann report reduced the patients' publicized progress report to only 70 percent. To this point, the community of physicians of organized medicine around the world has failed to look beyond the release of Thiemann's public relations information.

If it had not been for revelations by Dr. Schettler and the other Heidelberg scientists who possessed the actual tracings of the patients' treadmill readouts, no one would ever have learned the true results. The Heidelberg doctors were agitated by what they considered unethical scientific conduct by a pharmaceutical company. An attachment to the abstract of their Australian presentation contained a graphic plot of pain-free walking distance extending out to three months after the end of therapy. By that time, even using Thiemann's modified data, which the company was forced to make public, the increase in pain-free walking distance in the EDTA-treated patients had increased to 130 percent of the baseline, while the bencyclan-treated patients averaged less than half that much with no significant improvement after therapy was stopped at the end of thirty days.

Despite the study's great clinical significance in proving the effectiveness of EDTA chelation therapy, it fell to chelating physicians attached to ACAM to evaluate the data and discover the true residual benefit. The ACAM members announced that the Thiemann report analyzed data only to the end of thirty days, when the bencyclan and EDTA groups had responded equally. Chelation therapists acknowledge that full benefit from intravenous EDTA is often delayed for up to three months after therapy, when the maximum effect becomes apparent.

Moreover, the only patient death that occurred during this study was in the bencyclan group. No serious side effects were observed from EDTA; yet, encouraged by the Thiemann company's publicity people, negative effects for EDTA were reported in the news media. The press releases stated that "EDTA was no better than a placebo," without mentioning that the "placebo" actually was Thiemann Pharmaceutical's product, Fludilat, a so-called proven effective drug. Would you characterize such reporting as, at the very least, ironic?

By way of comparison, Dr. Carter described the praise received by another drug. Its study resulted in United States FDA approval of pentoxifyllin, brandnamed Trental, for the treatment of intermittent claudication in peripheral vascular disease. The walking distance for patients before their pain of claudication increased by an average of only 25 percent over baseline with Trental treatment. Nonetheless, that small amount of improvement was considered statistically significant, and Trental was approved for marketing by the FDA.

Even using Thiemann's false report as a hallmark, EDTA chelation therapy was almost three times as effective as Trental, but chelation therapy remains without FDA approval for the treatment of peripheral vascular disease. You might wonder why. The answer quite simply is that EDTA's patent protection ran out in 1958. It is an orphan drug treatment. But Trental is backed by a wealthy pharmaceutical company who has pursued its approval through the FDA process. Still, the potential for EDTA is that the situation is going to change for the better (see the 1986 study that is reported below).

MORE CLINICAL STUDY SUMMARIES SHOWING THE WORTH OF IV EDTA

In 1986, the American Institute of Medical Preventics and the International Chelation Research Foundation were granted IND (Investigational New Drug) #128.847 by the FDA to study the use of "Disodium EDTA With Magnesium" in the treatment of peripheral vascular disease (specifically for intermittent claudication pain).

Under this new drug application filed on August 15, 1986, the treatment protocol for heavy-metal detoxification and enhancement of blood flow endorsed by ACAM began to come under investigation at two United States government hospitals, the Walter Reed Army Hospital in Washington, D.C. and the Lederman Army Hospital in San Francisco. After completion of these two intricate studies, which were placebo-controlled and double-blinded, approval for national administration of chelation treatment was expected to be received for the public's medical welfare from the FDA.

Unfortunately, an obstruction in the ongoing four-year study's proceedings reared its ugly head unexpectedly. It was the fault of Sadam Husein. As a result of the Persian Gulf War with its transfer of large numbers of United States Army medical personnel to Saudi Arabia and the Gulf area during the 1990–1991 period, this first-time ever FDA approved study on EDTA chelation therapy at the two Army hospitals was slowed down and finally came to a halt.

Then, the Wyeth-Ayerst Pharmaceutical Company, which had helped to support the FDA chelation study, agreed to finance the rest of the necessary investigations to the tune of more than $6 million. Even so, another obstacle interfered. Following Wyeth-Ayerst's hiring of a new medical director, who had been a long time opponent of chelation therapy for use in cardiovascular disease, Wyeth-Ayerst renegged on its commitment to furnish the funding and complete the studies. This action has left the vital chelation therapy study in limbo. As of July 1993, the code had not been broken on the thirty plus patients who had completed the course of treatment.

Although, until now, the study codes are still unbroken, informed anticipation from the studies' administrators is that the metallic detoxification and increased peripheral vascular and cardiovascular blood circulation treatment is 200 times more efficacious than any other procedure as yet developed—that is 20,000-percent improvement over pathology that the Army personnel and veterans being treated had had before they started treatment. It is rather obvious who is getting chelation treatment and who is not. Some veterans are worsening steadily during the progress of their peripheral vascular disease and having their legs amputated. Others are dancing out of the hospital improved to the point of normality. Assuredly we need completion of the study to comply with FDA guidelines. Does anyone have a spare $6 million that he or she wishes to invest for the welfare of humanity?

In 1988, Efrain Olszewer, M.D., and Dr. Carter, of Tulane School of Medicine presented a retrospective analysis of 2,870 patients with various chronic degenerative diseases treated with disodium magnesium EDTA chelation therapy. To summarize, the two doctors evaluated patients' records and then reported on the results:

1. Individuals with ischemic heart disease showed 76.89-percent "Marked" improvement and 16.56-percent "Good" improvement of their heart conditions.

2. Patients with peripheral vascular disease and intermittent claudication showed 91-percent "Marked" improvement and 7.6-percent "Good" response in blood flow of their lower extremities.

The protocol followed by these ACAM researchers in administering chelation treatment for brain disorder, including Alzheimer's disease, was the one advocated by Dr. Casdorph. Drs. Olszewer and Carter analyzed the three patients suffering from cerebral vascular disease and found that they demonstrated an overall 24-percent "Marked" improvement and 30-percent "Good" improvement to changes in their dementia and associated brain symptoms from having undergone EDTA chelation therapy.[34]

To round out the Oszewer/Carter additional studies on chelation therapy conducted the next year, we furnish the following details: Their other significant study took place in Sao Paulo, Brazil, in 1990, at the International Institute of Preventive Medicine. Under the auspices of that organization, a controlled double-blind investigation on chelation therapy was conducted. The resultant paper, "A Pilot Double-Blind Study of Sodium-Magnesium EDTA in Peripheral Vascular Disease," discussed the subjects who suffered with intermittent claudication, but experienced no pain at rest or in the night, and no gangrene. They included eight former heavy cigarette smokers, all of whom had quit at least six months before the study began.

Altogether, ten male patients with peripheral vascular disease were randomly assigned in a double-blind investigation to receive either EDTA plus magnesium, a dosage of the vitamin B complex, and vitamin C. Or, the alternative group received a placebo of magnesium, B complex, and vitamin C in Ringer's lactate solution. A total of twenty intravenous infusions were planned for administration to each patient. Clinical and noninvasive laboratory tests showed dramatic improvements after ten infusions in some patients, and thus the double-blind code was broken, indicating who was receiving EDTA and who was receiving placebo. The group that improved had been receiving EDTA; there was no change in the placebo group. The trial was then completed in a single-blind fashion. Patients originally assigned to receive placebo then received ten EDTA infusions, while the group originally assigned to EDTA received twenty EDTA infusions. The patients who had formerly received placebo showed improvements comparable to those seen in the first EDTA group after ten treatments. This study has been ignored by both American organized medicine and the United States FDA merely because it was performed in a foreign country. [35]

Coming back to 1989, Edward W. McDonagh, D.O., Charles J. Rudolph, D.O., Ph.D., and Emanuel Cheraskin, M.D., D.M.D., published their study of 117 lower extremities in seventy-seven elderly patients with documented occlusive peripheral vascular stenosis (narrowing) by the Doppler systolic ankle/brachial blood pressure ratio. After approximately twenty-six infusions over sixty days, the ratios improved indicating significant arterial improvement in the patients' blood flow.[36]

Also in 1989, Dr. Rudolph, Dr. McDonagh, and Rhonda K. Barber reported on the benefits of EDTA chelation therapy for chronic lung disorders. Pulmonary function tests were performed on thirty-eight patients before and after they received thirty EDTA infusions. Significant improvements occurred in both the complete expansion of the lungs, or forced vital capacity (FVC), and the complete emptying of the lungs, or forced expiration volume, in one second (FEV1). The patients with the more abnormal tests presented a higher percentage of increase. Overall, thirty-four of the thirty-eight subjects (90.5 percent) improved in pulmonary function after EDTA infusions.[37]

In 1989, Walter Blumer, M.D., assisted in writing a published paper by

Elmer M. Cranton, M.D., that reported on an amazing finding relating to the possible role of EDTA chelation therapy in the prevention of cancer. A group of fifty-nine patients who lived next to a heavily traveled highway were given calcium-EDTA infusions because of lead exposure from automobile exhaust. A similar group of 172 people living in the same neighborhood and exposed to the same pollution were used as controls. During an eighteen-year followup, only one of the fifty-nine treated patients (1.7 percent) died of cancer while thirty of the 172 nontreated control subjects (17.6 percent) died. None of the patients or subjects had any clinical evidence of cancer at the start of the study. Exposure to carcinogens was no greater for the studied population than exists in most metropolitan areas throughout the world.[38]

In 1990, it was shown that average platelet volume was significantly reduced in a group of eighty-five patients receiving 30 or more EDTA chelation infusions over a period of 13 months. Overall, seventy-two people in the research group (85 percent) had increased average platelet volume after the infusions. A low platelet volume is associated with increased platelet accumulation which is related to an increased risk of a cardiovascular disease.[39]

In 1991, there was the repeat of clear evidence that the reversal of atherosclerotic plaque takes place in the carotid arteries to the brains of patients receiving EDTA chelation therapy. Here is what happened: the three participating Missouri researchers had been encouraged by the striking reversal of dementia in a single patient whose history and treatment effect was published the year before. During that time, Drs. Rudolph, McDonagh, and Ms. Barber observed that the severe carotid artery disease cleared. Visible evidence was left behind of shear motion in their female patient's right carotid artery. Her right internal carotid artery, before she received thirty EDTA infusions, was 98-percent blocked. After the infusions the occlusion was reduced to 33 percent and the shear motion that had been present initially was replaced by normal arterial expansion.[40]

This amazing 1990 result for this individual caused the three investigators to evaluate thirty more patients for stenosis of both internal carotid arteries at the bifurcation where they lead into the brain, using ultrasound imaging. Each patient underwent thirty EDTA infusions over a ten-month period. The reported results were striking and highly significant. Overall intra-arterial obstruction decreased 20.9 percent. Patients with more severe stenosis had an even greater reduction in the amount of arterial occlusion.[41]

In 1992, fifty-four patients who had received chelation therapy for a variety of heart and/or blood vessel problems were followed up in a survey. 92.6 percent of the treated persons indicated that they had noted some clinical improvement and 36 percent of those same fifty patients who had improved were totally asymptomatic. The asymptomatic group differed from the group having symptoms in two ways. First, they sought help with their symptoms within a year of onset. Second, unlike the symptomatic group, 100 percent continued to ingest supplements prescribed by the chelating physician who had been administering treatment. The conclusion was that patients should seek help early and continue to take supplements to enhance the benefits of chelation therapy.[42]

There are another hundred studies or so that we might have reported on in order to illustrate the great value of chelation therapy for Alzheimer's disease and other degenerative conditions. For example, the internationally respected cardiovascular surgeon, P.J. van der Schaar, M.D., of Leyden, Holland presented his paper, "A Cardiovascular Surgeon Looks at Chelation Therapy," to the 1983 spring conference of ACAM. Dr. van der Schaar has the unique position of practicing cardiovascular surgery both in his native Netherlands and at St. Luke's Hospital in Houston, Texas. He reported that he routinely sees improvements in his patients when he administers chelation therapy to them. Those who frequently improve most dramatically are patients with cerebral vascular disease who exhibit symptoms of transient ischemic attack, loss of memory, dementia, stroke, headache, hypertension, bad vision, and dizziness. Such symptoms disappear for most of these people when they receive IV chelation therapy. It is a therapy to be depended on for the treatment of Alzheimer's disease.

Part V
The Dietary Connection

As teenagers and young adults, people in the industrialized western countries tend to eat excessive amounts of processed foods with inadequate nutritional value. Then, adults tend to consume less food as they age, without increasing the nutrient density of what they eat. This situation, combined with pollutants invading the environment of our modern era, brings on increases in brain deterioration that we are witnessing worldwide. However, there are easily-employed nutritional antidotes to Alzheimer's disease in the form of additions to the diet.

Incorporating fatty acids of the omega-three, -six, and -nine types along with certain supplemental brain nutrients will assist the corrective/preventive programs, which are mandatory if we are to have societies free of Alzheimer's disease.

CHAPTER 21

The Anti-Alzheimer's Disease Diet

"Use it or lose it" is a fitness injunction that may apply to our minds as well as our bodies. Research by neuropathologist Robert Terry, M.D., an investigator at the University of California, San Diego (UCSD), indicates that the more mentally fit a person's brain is (as measured by its number of synapses, or chemical connections between cells), the longer it can function if Alzheimer's disease eventually sets in.

Over a two-year period, UCSD psychologists had tested Alzheimer's disease patients—measuring word recall and other mental skills—to gauge the extent of their obvious dementia. When Dr. Terry performed autopsies on the brains of fifteen of the patients who had died, his investigations revealed a loss of synapses in the part of the brain that controls higher functions such as memory. "The patients who had the fewest synapses were those who had suffered the severest dementia," said Dr. Terry.

Our assumption is that the more nutritionally nourished a person had been throughout life, using certain food and nutrient components that comprise the anti-Alzheimer's disease diet that we are recommending here, the less Alzheimer's disease has a chance to take hold.

"Possessing brain synapses may be a little like having money in the bank," remarked Dr. Robert Terry in a press report. "The more you have, the more you can afford to lose before you go bankrupt."[1]

MEMORY AND THE DIET

A condition exists in patients that may go unrecognized by attending physicians. The condition may presage warnings that vascular disease is developing in a patient. The following hypothetical situation illustrates a common happening in somebody's life: Upon a family doctor's viewing the results of a laboratory examination of his or her patient's blood, not uncommonly there may be the presence of a low level of high density lipoprotein (HDL) cholesterol against a normal-appearing, total cholesterol reading (i.e. indicated as the total Cholesterol/HDL ratio) that precursors the "sneaky" heart attack to come. If the attending doctor does not spot this irregularity, the patient may be in for heart attack difficulty.

This situation happened to a realtor who was supposedly healthy, named Lawrence M., who was then sixty-three years old, and living and working in St. Louis, Missouri. In June 1985, Larry visited the outpatient clinic of his local, private, St. Louis hospital to undergo a low-cost, routine, annual physical examination, as he had been in the habit of doing for the past twenty years. Usually, the intern on duty went through the checkup, and Larry felt secure with his good health report for another year. The serum cholesterol looked "OK" to the inexperienced eye of the examining doctor-in-training, but the next month, on an emergency basis, the patient was forced into hospitalization because of severe chest pain that had begun on the golf course even before he started to play.

It is true that Larry had been suffering with diabetes for the prior fifteen years and was taking insulin before breakfast and before supper daily. Now the sick man's electrocardiograms additionally showed poor circulation in the heart region but were negative for a myocardial infarct (an area of dead heart muscle tissue). Another diagnostic test, an echocardiogram, taken by the hospital's cardiologist, showed poor left-ventricular heart function. Corrective measures became necessary for this complication.

Larry requested that he be treated with medication as a trial procedure rather than undergo the recommended angiogram. He knew that angiography, no matter the result, invariably is accompanied with advice from the angiographer or from the cardiologist that a coronary artery bypass operation be undertaken. He wanted none of that kind of operation! So, instead Larry took the prescribed medication.

A month later Larry landed in the hospital again with a serious heart attack. Following this he did undergo cardiac catherization—the angiogram he had attempted to avoid—and it showed severe, three-vessel, coronary artery disease. His condition involved a reduction in power of his left ventricle with elevated left-ventricular-end diastolic blood pressure. In brief, his heart attack was really serious and required not one but four coronary-artery bypass graftings, which he finally underwent on August 14, 1985.

Two weeks later he was discharged from the hospital with four more prescriptions to take: Digoxin, Inderal, Dipyridamole, NPH insulin, and regular insulin as before. Still, these medications were not rehabilitating him well enough, and he knew very well that his life remained in danger.

Because Larry knew of Harvey Walker, Jr., M.D., Ph.D., as a chelating physician, he went to see the highly skilled doctor at his Clayton, Missouri clinic, Preventive Medicine, Inc., on December 9, 1985. In the case report that Dr. Walker provided us, he wrote: "L.M. was complaining of inability to work as hard as he used to or walk as far as he used to be able to walk or get as much done in a day as he was used to accomplishing. . . . I arranged for him to have carotid artery sonography which revealed left carotid artery plaques [the neck artery was clogged]. He also had posterior tibial artery [in both lower legs] insufficiency with intermittent claudication."

Larry loved to play golf, but the deep claudication pain in his calf muscles denied him that recreational pleasure. Also, and perhaps worse for those family members affected by his mental lapses, the bypass surgery had done nothing to improve the man's ability to remember necessary information. Seemingly, at any provocation, Larry's mind wandered. He was experiencing severe memory loss for faces, places, dates, business matters, and street routes when he was required to take a client to see one of the many properties his real estate office represented. To him, the bypass operation appeared to have affected his thinking and ability to remember. This type of short-term memory loss is a known common occurrence in post-bypass blood vessel grafting.

Larry's forgetfulness was troublesome to most of his family and friends, especially those close to him. For instance, Larry forgot what his wife sent him to buy in the supermarket—even one or two items. She had mumbled that she wished there were a similar surgery for her husband's brain as there had been for his heart. While the man did not possess a lot of mental agility before undergoing the bypass procedure, it had lessened markedly afterward.

His blood pressure was too high as well, at 140/105, which was putting a strain on the four sites of the blood vessel graphs. They were in danger of closing. The patient was a prime candidate for dietary improvements in his lifestyle along with taking a course of chelation therapy. Dr. Harvey Walker, Jr. did make those forms of therapeutic recommendations, for the sort of condition this man was exhibiting responds rather dramatically to the two programs of treatment, chelation and a new diet containing foods that work against dementia.

Still, Larry ignored the doctor's suggestion that would have benefited him so much. He failed to follow the anti-Alzheimer's disease diet and outright refused to accept treatment with intravenous (IV) EDTA. The result was that he could no longer play golf on a daily basis. Recurrence of a heart attack on the golf course became a very real danger. Moreover, his malfunctioning memory became a sort of "acquired dementia." He lived, it seemed to his wife and other close relatives, as if in a world of his own. Larry's wife and children recognized, even if Larry did not, that he required lifestyle improvement and chelation therapy or he would deteriorate steadily into Alzheimer's disease and then death. Dr. Harvey Walker, Jr. continued with his description of the case history: "Persuaded by his family, Larry finally decided to start diet management and chelation therapy on 15 May 1986, and was treated on a regular basis, twice a week at first, tapering to weekly, and finally to a twice-a-month program of visits. His diet became steadily more controllable as his loving relatives joined in with the meal-planning and, as part of their persuasive efforts, ate the required foods to show him and for their own health enhancements."

"The patient received a total of 51 chelation treatments. The chelating fluid consisted of 250 ml of D5W containing 2000 units of heparin, 1000 mg of magnesium chloride, 10 mg of potassium chloride, and 3 grams of EDTA. During the time of his treatments he had gradually improved exercise function too. He was able to walk for 45 minutes without leg pain or chest pain. He was able to play 18 holes of golf twice a week without any symptoms," wrote Dr. Harvey Walker, Jr.

Upon completing his fiftieth chelation treatment, Larry told Dr. Walker that he felt so alert, with no more memory problems, that he was enrolling in a college course just for the sake of learning something new. Then he added that, although he would continue following the anti-Alzheimer's disease diet, the next office visit in May 1987 would be his last. The man refused maintenance chelation therapy of a once-a-month visit but did agree to follow this ongoing preventive dementia/atherosclerosis eating program.

It is well known among members of the Amerian College of Advancement in Medicine (ACAM) that Dr. Casdorph successfully reverses or reduces the symptoms of Alzheimer's disease with a diet that he developed, along with EDTA chelation therapy. Many physicians who are members of ACAM recommend that their patients follow this particular diet. Dr. Walker is one of these members. Consequently, Dr. Walker gave Larry strict instructions to continue following Dr. Casdorph's anti-Alzheimer's disease diet, and the patient has done so.

Dr. Walker concluded, "L.M. was last seen in my office [for a routine checkup] 18 October 1990. He stated then that he had no chest pain, played golf twice a week—18 holes—all summer and into the fall and had no need for any medical services since last I saw him three years earlier. His blood pressure remained normal at 128/80. He was down to injecting 8 units of regular insulin mixed with 8 units of NPH twice a day. In checking with his wife, I was told that she no longer feels frustration with her husband's forgetfulness."

Larry earned a student grade of "A" in his college course and went on to enroll as a full-time student. This was proof enough that his short-term memory had been restored. By June 1993, he had completed all the necessary courses for the degree of Bachelor of Arts. At age seventy-one, in fulfilling a lifetime dream, the man finished his schooling by graduating from St. Louis University.

DIETARY OILS FOR THE BRAIN

The concept that what we eat influences the integrity of one's brain and its various functions, including memory, is new and poorly understood. This concept, however, was graphically portrayed in the spring of 1993 with the showing of the movie, *Lorenzo's Oil*, seen by millions around the world. Starring actors Nick Nolte and Susan Sarandon, the film portrayed a true family, Michaela and Augusto Odone, whose five-year-old son, Lorenzo, had developed the rare and fatal brain disorder medically known as *adrenoleukodystrophy* (pronounced a-dreen-o-luke-o-dis-tro-phee). This abnormality affects only boys, and causes a progressive deterioration of virtually all of the brain functions. It begins with irritability and emotional outbursts followed by muscular weakness, loss of vision, loss of hearing, and inevitable progression to death. This was the common medical situation for patients with adrenoleukodystrophy prior to the development of Lorenzo's oil antidote. This counteracting therapy was discovered by the persistence of two parents whose child had become the victim of the disorder.

The parents simply would not give up hope that some remedy might be found to help their child despite the negative responses from conventional medicine. The Odones defied the slow-moving medical establishment. They organized their own medical symposium and did a literature search for their own natural treatment for the condition. Then they experimented with nutrient oils for their child. Against all odds, and amidst vilification by representatives from organized medicine, they were successful. Their success with Lorenzo has proven advantageous for many other victims of adrenoleukodystrophy.

"The AMA is greedy and corrupt," said actress Susan Sarandon in a press interview that was cited by *USA Today* and *Newsweek*. "But we shouldn't blame them as much as [we must blame] people who simply hand their lives over to authority figures. . . . Michaela and Augusto are ordinary people who became extraordinary because of their refusal to bow down."[2]

By their hard work in personal research, Michaela and Augusto Odone ultimately found that the addition of extracts from two commonly used cooking oils—olive oil and rapeseed oil—stop the progression of adrenoleukodystrophy and actually reversed the disease in the case of their son. Indeed, since the time of its discovery, this remedial oil extract has become the only available treatment for children possessed of this relatively rare neurologic disorder. Although it may not work for all children with adrenoleukodystrpohy, it is used worldwide for the condition's treatment.

From a more technical reason why Lorenzo's oil works, you may wish to know that long-chain fatty acids are present in high concentration in the blood of individuals affected by adrenoleukodystrophy. These fatty acids are deposited in the neurons of the victim's brain and ultimately lead to a destruction of brain cells. Therefore, dysfunction of the brain develops. The simple, yet brilliant, discovery by Lorenzo's parents was that another fatty acid in olive oil (glyceryl trioleate) and a fatty acid obtained from rapeseed oil (glyceryl trierucate derived from the erucic acid in rapeseed) antidote the problem when ingested in a certain proportion. The corrective formula consists of one volume of glyceryl trierucate and four volumes of glyceryl trioleate. Taken in this combination, they nearly always lead to halting and often reversal of the brain disease process.

Thus, administration of these oils to afflicted individuals results in clinical improvement such as return of the ability to swallow, to speak, and to move the body's extremities after they have been paralyzed. These observed clinical changes have been correlated with the patient's laboratory test improvements. For instance, magnetic resonance imaging (MRI) of the brain before treatment compared with five months after therapy show significant improvement in the brain images as a result of the patient's consuming Lorenzo's oil.[3]

In a somewhat similar manner, a combination of fatty acids have been found to help brain function and memory of patients with Alzheimer's dementia. They are used as part of the dietary treatment of this disorder and are disclosed as part of the menu plan for this chapter.

For decades now, most medical authorities acknowledge that fish oil, in the form of fish-oil capsules, or the regular ingestion of salmon oil, or fish itself, on a daily basis has brought about dramatic reductions in the level of serum triglycerides and sometimes the reduction in serum cholesterol for patients who had been at risk of heart and blood vessel disease.

On a deeply felt basis, our grandmothers and their mothers before them had advised us to take cod liver oil each day, which contains essential fatty acids. "Cod liver oil is good for you," they had declared. We turned up our noses at their admonition but finally have learned that valid medical science does back up their declarations.

ESSENTIAL FATTY ACIDS

Essential fatty acids (EFAs), the main families of which are the omega-three (omega-3 or N-3) and omega-six (omega-6 or N-6) fatty acids, have precursors in the vegetable kingdom that can be further metabolized in animals to longer chain EFAs with more unsaturated bonds—double bonds between the two carbon atoms that comprise the fatty acid molecule. The N-6 essential fatty acids predominate in our basic land-based diet whereas the N-3 essential fatty acids are especially plentiful in marine creatures, such as fish. The N-6 and N-3 family of nutrients are both precursors for the eicosanoids and act as building blocks for some enzymes. Consequently increasing the proportion of one type of EFA in the diet can influence which products following the cyclo-oxygenase or lipo-oxygenase pathways are synthesized in the body. These products differ considerably in their biologic effects and can have clinical implications in the form of either being responsible for illness or for enhanced homeostasis.

There are three EFAs: (1) linolenic, (2) arachodonic, and (3) linoleic acids. Unofficially they are sometimes referred to as vitamin F. The body can make the first two if it has a sufficient supply of the third one; therefore, linoleic acid can be considered the ultimate essential fat for the human body. Of all the sources of linoleic acid, as well as of other fatty acids, flax seed oil contains the greatest amount and highest quality. Flax seed oil is not just rich in EFAs but it also contains greater quantities of the B vitamins, protein, and zinc.

Flax oil is sometimes called linseed oil, but it is really just another name for the oil extracted from the flax plant. Besides furnishing mankind with its deep amber oil, the flax plant has been useful since ancient times as a source of fibers for the making of linen thread. The plant has other uses, too. For example, flax meal left over after the oil has been expressed often is fed to livestock, and the oil incorporated for the production of most oil paintings is flax or linseed oil.

Orthodox medicine agrees that linoleic acid is essential as a nutrient (as mentioned, part of the vitamin F complex) and should provide at least 2 percent of the calories in the normal diet for adults. There is some concern among oncologists that ingesting too much linoleic acid could be hazardous for the health. Diets high in linoleic acid are said to increase the risk of cancer because they tend to generate oxidizing free radicals. Yet, not all medical authorities accept this caution or that we even get enough of the essential flax component.

In central Europe where some informed people prize the linseed plant's health-giving properties, cold-pressed, virgin, raw, and unrefined flax oil is exceedingly popular to consume. For a decade now, this product has been available for sale in American and Canadian health food stores. It probably should be utilized regularly for purposes of nutritional supplementation. Moreover, cold-pressed, unrefined flax oil could be applied, among other ways, as a salad dressing or as a spread on toast. Take note that unrefined, it requires refrigeration after being opened. Flax oil lasts only about three months before turning rancid, and consuming rancid flax seed oil is totally disadvantageous—even harmful)since it is loaded with free radicals and produces free-radical pathology that is carcinogenic.

It is well known by health professionals that cancer rarely develops in the small intestines. Why this is so has been one of the more pleasant mysteries to unravel in medicine. A University of California radiologist located on that school's Los Angeles campus has isolated a component of the intestinal lining of mice that seems to be reponsible for stopping such growth in experimental animals. Tests indicate that this anticancer substance is linoleic acid present in the mouse gut in a "surprisingly high concentration" and linoleic acid was "probably the major component responsible for this antitumor activity."[4]

Many nutritional researchers have studied the effects of flax seed oil, linoleic acid, and fish oil, which also is a source of the omega-three fatty acids. A particular study conducted in 1990 at the University of Illinois gave the appearance that flax seed oil was a more healthful nutrient than fish oil. Mice were given oil from corn, fish, or flax before receiving injections of breast cancer cells. Flax oil reduced the growth of breast cancers and metastases compared with the tumor growth in those animals receiving corn oil but fish oil did not. "Tumor growth was only inhibited by linseed oil," the Urbana-Champaign scientists said.

Other studies of fish oils have found them nontoxic and highly beneficial with the added advantage of antitumor activity.

Mice with lymphoma and thymoma (thymus gland tumor) were administered either soy bean oil, linseed oil, or fish oil as 4 percent of their diet. While none of the supplements brought about significant differences in tumor incidence or in mortality, the tumor size was decreased by diets supplying N-3 fatty acids from fish oil or linseed oil. For example, lymphoma tumor weight was markedly depressed by linseed oil. Thymoma tumor weight turned out to be lowest in mice receiving fish oil.

THE HYPE OR HOPE OF ALZENE

The latest entry into the dietary aspect of the treatment of Alzheimer's disease is the brandnamed product Alzene, which is mentioned in this section because it has a high composition of two fatty acids, alpha-linolenic acid and linoleic acid. Alzene, a mixture of fatty acids, will be discussed much more extensively in the next chapter as a so-called "smart drug" for Alzheimer's disease treatment.

The guiding force behind Alzene is the Canadian business man and physician, Morton Shulman, M.D. As one of its reportorial segments, Dr. Shulman and his deprenyl research were featured in May 1993 on the television show *60 Minutes*. Six years ago, while suffering from severe Parkinson's disease himself, Dr. Shulman traveled to Europe to procure a supply of deprenyl. He was so impressed with its benefit in his own therapy that he purchased the Canadian rights to the drug and founded Deprenyl Research Ltd., which is now a company with annual sales of over $30 million. Dr. Shulman is focusing his effort on Alzene, which he claims is not only the best drug available for the treatment of Alzheimer's disease but also appears to be the first real "smart drug."

Alzene was developed by the Israeli psychologist Shlomo Yehuda, Ph.D., and is composed of a special ratio of the two fatty acids that we have mentioned, alpha-linolenic acid and linoleic acid. Both EFAs are commonly present in vegetable oils such as soybean and safflower. Dr. Yehuda noted the cognitive-enhancing properties of this unusual combination when it improved the memory abilities of laboratory rodents.

A double-blind, placebo-controlled study performed on victims of Alzheimer's disease with his fatty-acid mixture produced a statistically significant improvement in cognitive function. These two fatty acids, therefore, are incorporated into the dietary aspect of this book's suggested dietary treatment program for Alzheimer's disease.

SCIENTIFIC BACKGROUND FOR DIETARY ALZENE IN ALZHEIMER'S DISEASE

Studies of laboratory animals have shown that manipulation of the type of fat they are fed influences their behavior. When groups of rats receive experimental diets that contain the same amount of 20-percent fat but the origin of fat is different (from an animal or vegetable source), they behave differently on the individual diets. The group of rats that are fed soybean oil in their diet show an improvement in learning capacity as measured by the Morse Water-Tank method (an animal education evaluation technique). Groups of rats that get fed dietary oils and fats from other sources do not exhibit these results.[5] Those rats fed diets containing a different source of vegetable oils, such as sunflower seeds, fail to show the beneficial effects that the soybean oil diet induces. Sunflower oil contains a higher percentage of linoleic acid; therefore, the effects of the soybean oil diet cannot be attributed only to the level of linoleic acid.

A hypothesis developed by Dr. Yehuda and others is that the site of action of dietary manipulation, such as soybean oil treatment, is the lipid constituent of the neuronal membrane. The sheath around nerve cells, this neuronal membrane, is modified by dietary lipids so as to alter the composition of the neuronal membrane with consequent changes in the membrane's "fluidity index." Also there is a functional change of status likely in certain membrane-bound proteins.

Since the sunflower-oil diet is not as effective as the soybean-oil diet toward influencing behavior, the hypothesis held is that the main factor in soybean oil is not the level of linoleic acid but the ratio of the level of linoleic acid to other unsaturated, essential fatty acids, such as linolenic acid. One particular ratio of these fatty acids singled out as the most effective in improving the learning capacity of test animals is marketed under the code name of SR-3, also identified as the above-described product Alzene.

Behavioral studies on animals include observations made on the effects of Alzene given to old rats that ranged in age from twenty to twenty-two months. The observations of Alzene administration made by researchers were for the purpose of answering the specific question: Do the old rats acquire an increased capacity for learning when given swimming tests? The conclusion was that Alzene-treated rats were able to learn the task of swimming faster than non-treated rats.

Biochemical studies include preliminary investigations on the effects of four weeks of Alzene treatment alone on the level of cholesterol and membrane-fluidity index. The results show that the level of neuronal-membrane cholesterol is decreased (a desirable effect) while the membrane-fluidity index is increased (another desirable effect).

In test animals there is no observation of any toxic effect of the administration of these fatty-acid mixtures. The level of blood lipids do not differ from the level of the control group. Rats that are treated with the Alzene dose thirty times the usual daily dose do not show any behavior or physiological toxic effect.

CLINICAL STUDIES OF ALZENE PERFORMED ON HUMANS

In view of the beneficial effects of the fatty-acid mixture on rats' learning and memory capacity, plus its affectation in small groups of old rats as well as its very low toxicity level, Alzene was then administered to humans. Investigators suspected that Alzene could exert beneficial results for patients affected by Alzheimer's disease. Two observations: the cognitive defects shown along with post mortem reports about the neuronal membrane of Alzheimer's disease patients being much harder than in the brains of controlled patients (dead but not from Alzheimer's disease) points to Alzene as a possible therapeutic agent for Alzheimer's disease patients.

In studies on humans with Alzheimer's disease, the experiments consist of each patient receiving one bottle of either SR-3 or placebo. The instructions are to take one cubic centimeter (cc) in the morning and 1 cc at bedtime. Each cc contains a mixture of linolenic acid and linoleic acid in a ratio of 1 part to 4.25 parts. The patients are advised to store the medication in a cold environment or in the refrigerator.

In one such clinical investigation, 100 patients between the ages of fifty and seventy-three years old were tested. Among them were 79 men and 21 women, of which 71 were diagnostically confirmed as having Alzheimer's disease for four years or longer. The scores on the Mini-mental test that we described in Chapter 5 were used to gauge improvement. Out of the 40 subjects receiving placebo, there was no change in test scores before and after the placebo's administration. Of the 60 patients receiving the SR-3, there was a truly significant improvement in the Mini-Mental State test scores in 49 responders plus a borderline-significant response in 11.

After a three-week period of treatment, no major side effects were found. One patient reported stomach upset and diarrhea. The researchers saw no other physical changes during this period, including the patients' blood pressures, which remained at the same level as before the study. Biochemical blood and urine laboratory tests did not show any significant changes either, comparing the patients' readings before and after treatment. There was no increase in total lipids in the blood. Yet, the level of blood cholesterol did not decrease enough to make a noticable difference.

Based on the animal and human studies conducted on ingredients in Alzene, it seems prudent to add an adequate amount of the essential fatty acids to the diet. By all means, a source of linoleic and linolenic acid should be included, such as soybean products and fish oils.

THE MOLECULAR MAKEUP OF FATTY ACIDS

An individual fat molecule is made up of a singular type of glycerin molecule and one, two, or three fatty acid-type molecules. As can be seen, then, fatty acids are among the main subunits of fats. Chemically they are characterized by containing a long hydrocarbon chain that ends in a carboxylic acid group that is made up of chains of carbon and oxygen. The hydrocarbon chain can be of variable length and chemists refer to the type of fat in its makeup by how many carbons are in its chain. If the fat molecule contains from two to six carbons, it is called a short-chain fatty acid; if it is eight to twelve carbons long, the fat is considered a medium-chain fatty acid; if it is fourteen to thirty carbons long, the molecule is labeled as a long-chain fatty acid.

Plants store both medium-chain and long-chain fatty acids; animals store predominantly long-chain fatty acids. Because oleic acid has only one double bond, it is called a *mono-unsaturated* fatty acid. Linoleic acid has two double bonds and standardly is referred to as a *poly-unsaturated* fatty acid (PUFA).

The chemical formula for linoleic acid contains eighteen carbons and two double bonds with a hydrogen, two oxygens, and a carbon at the end (HOOC). Therefore it is called 18:2 omega-six (N-6) indicating that along the line of its eighteen carbons, two double bonds start at the sixth carbon from the end (see the formula below depicting linoleic acid).

```
    H H H H H H H        H H     H H H H H
HOOC-C-C-C-C-C-C-C-C=C-C-C=C-C-C-C-C-C-H
    H H H H H H H H  H H H H H H H H H
```

Biochemically essential PUFAs have three or more double bonds. All of them can be made from linoleic acid by the action of enzymes called desaturases. Linolenic acid is found in two essential forms: alpha-linolenic acid (18:3 N-3), found in flax seed, walnut, and soybean oils, and gamma linolenic acid 18:N-6, which is found in evening primrose oil, borage oil, and black currant seed oils (see the formula below depicting linolenic acid).

```
    H H H H H H H      H       H       H H
HOOC-C-C-C-C-C-C-C-C=C-C-C=C-C-C=C-C-C-H
    H H H H H H H H   H H H   H H H   H H H
```

Alpha-linolenic acid can be further metabolized into eicosapentaenoic acid (EPA) and docosahexaenoic acid (DHA), both of which are found in high concentrations in mammalian brain membranes and cold water fish oils.

THE IMPORTANCE OF OMEGA-THREE FATTY ACIDS

The omega-3 fatty acids are well documented to have functional importance in learning ability and retinal physiology. Two scientists, Lampety and Walker, first reported poor discriminant-learning in rats deficient in omega 3, compared with control animals that had been fed a good source of omega 3 (soybean oil). More than ten years later, Yamamoto and coworkers confirmed those first findings when they determined the number of trials required by rats to learn that food pellets were available only at a specific light intensity. Almost twice as many trials were required by omega-3 deficient rats compared with controls. In yet another study of exploratory behavior, learning time was also increased in omega-3 deficient rats.

The rat was also the first animal species in which retinal physiology was studied in response to depletion and repletion of omega-3 and omega-6 fatty acids. Several researchers have found over time that diets deficient in omega-3 and omega-6 fatty acids reduced the electroretinogram A-wave. (An electroretinogram is a record of the retinal action currents produced in the retina of the eye by a light stimulus.) Omega-3 fatty acid compared with omega-6 fatty acid was more effective in improving the graphic feedback (the A-wave response) after depletion of these fatty acids.

Dr. William Connor and his associates at the Oregon Health Sciences University have studied rhesus monkeys that were given pre- and post-natal diets deficient in omega-3 fatty acids. These monkeys developed low levels of DHA (the derivative of omega 3) in the cerebral cortex and retina. This resulted in impaired visual function.

Dr. Connor's team discovered that this PUFA is an important component of retinal photoreceptors and brain synaptic membranes. The experimental monkeys were initially fed a diet low in omega-3 fatty acids; then they were fed a fish oil diet rich in DHA and other omega-3 fatty acids for up to 129 weeks. Their studies of the cerebral cortex indicating alteration in brain fatty-acid composition began as early as one week after fish oil feeding and stabilized at twelve weeks. The omega-6 fatty acid content of the cerebral cortex was abnormally high when the animals were fed a diet deficient of the omega-3 fatty acids. The half-life (T-$\frac{1}{2}$) of the omega-3 fatty acid DHA was estimated to be twenty-one days. The DHA content of plasma and erythrocyte (red blood cell) phospholipids also increased greatly with estimated half-lives of twenty-nine and twenty-one days.

The Connor team concluded that the monkeys' cerebral cortices, with an abnormal fatty-acid composition produced by omega-3 fatty acid deficiency, has a remarkable capacity to change its fatty-acid content after dietary fish oil supplementation. The biochemical evidence of omega-3 fatty acid deficiency was completely corrected by this dietary manipulation.

The point emphasized from the Connor research is that by the administration of a diet rich in omega-3 fatty acids, the composition of the brain membranes, as well as other cells of the body, is changed to a more healthful state. Vision is improved and mental functioning is improved.[6]

Thus the dietary omega-3 fatty acids are proven to be essential for normal function and development of the brain. Japanese researchers concur that a deficiency of essential fatty acids leads to an impaired ability to learn and to remember information.[7]

Supplementation with essential fatty acids must be made a part of any anti-Alzheimer's disease diet. Such membrane lipids constitute 50 to 60 percent of the solid matter of the brain. A major portion of brain phospholipids contain long-chain polyunsaturated fatty acids of the two essential fatty acid classes, omega-6 and omega-3. Normally omega-3 fatty acid DHA is the predominant polyunsaturated fatty acid in phospholipids of the brain and retina. The primate brain gradually accumulates its full complement of DHA while it is a fetus and during the first year after birth. DHA, or its precursor, omega-3 fatty acids, must be provided in the diet of the mother and infant for normal brain and retinal development.

OMEGA-3 FATTY ACIDS AND IMMUNITY

Books and published papers over the years have emphasized the importance of omega-3 fatty acids in boosting the strength of the immune system and giving one a feeling of natural health and well-being. One of the early books to make this statement loud and clear was *The Omega-3 Phenomenon*. Claims from the three authors are just now coming under scientific scrutiny and consistently are shown to be true.[8]

Although we affirm that scientific journal articles are a bit technical, the bottom line that you get from reading them is that the addition of a source of omega-3 fatty acids, such as from sardine oil, salmon oil, mackerel oil, or menhaden oil, enables animals as well as ailing humans to survive pathological processes when they otherwise might not be able to do so.

Dietary omega-3 fatty acids decrease mortality and liver Kupffer cell prostaglandin E_2 production in which a rat model is affected by chronic sepsis (blood poisoning). R.G. Barton and associates tested this hypothesis by substituting omega-3 fat for dietary omega-6 fat to see if the substitution would reduce mortality and decrease liver Kupffer cell prostaglandin E2 (hormone-like fatty acids) in the septic rat. When the sardine, salmon, or menhaden oil containing omega-3 was fed to the diseased animals, mortality for them decreased by 35 percent compared with other animals who were fed safflower oil and experienced a death decrease of only 16 percent.[9]

An improvement similar to the one seen in animals also helps in the survival of sick people residing in intensive care units. After undergoing extensive trauma, multiple organ failure syndrome (MOFS), hypermetabolism, septicemia, serious surgery, and other life-threatening health problems, most often there is accelerated breakdown in the tissues, the rapid onset of malnutrition, and immune system failure. Nutrients, such as the amino acid arginine, menhaden oil, and ribonucleic acid (RNA), have been found to have immune-stimulating properties. Follow-up by the researchers to check on the patients in six months and twelve months demonstrated no long-term, adverse effects.[10] Their immune systems were no longer stimulated.

FOODS FOR THE BRAIN

Long before the above-mentioned, sophisticated, essential fatty-acid studies were performed, fish has been considered "brain food." Today we know that fish and their beneficial oils literally are foods for the brain, since about one half of the weight of the brain is composed of fatty acids that line the membrane of each of the 100 billion neurons that make up the brain.

While seven days of menus for brain-function improvement tailored especially for people with memory disorders concludes this chapter, we have some supplemental suggestions to add to these menus as well. Our recommendation is that each day the anti-Alzheimer's diet be supplemented with one teaspoonful (5 ml) of cod liver oil. The best time to take cod liver oil is first thing in the morning on an empty stomach, but it may be mixed with fruit juice according to one's taste. Any good source of fresh cod liver oil should be adequate, and it is medically advantageous to take the oil unadulterated if you can get past the taste.

One preparation that is quite popular throughout the United States is Dale Alexander Emulsified Norwegian Cod Liver Oil manufactured by Twin Laboratories, Inc. (Ronkonkoma, New York 11779 U.S.A.) In this preparation the usual unpleasant cod liver oil taste is quite nicely disguised with mint flavor making the supplement quite palatable. It is a fine natural source of omega-3 polyunsaturates.

In addition, as a secondary source of omega-3 fatty acids we recommend that each day a tablespoonful of flaxseed oil be included as part of the diet. Flax oil may be taken as a supplement or used in place of butter when added to a baked potato. Or, flax oil may be incorporated into a tossed green salad as part of the dressing. Avoid the use of margarine under any circumstances because of the unhealthy trans fats with which the margarine is loaded.

Any time a fat of any variety is added to the diet for enhancement of memory or for any other purpose, periodic checks of blood lipids should be conducted by your physician. Part of any health care examination should include the monitoring of blood lipids, especially cholesterol, triglycerides, and high density lipoproteins (HDL) as well as low density lipoproteins (LDL).

In most cases a beneficial effect with a drop in the serum total cholesterol and the blood triglycerides will follow the ingestion of the omega-3 fatty acids. Such beneficial effects have been proven by the research of Dr. Connor, whose work on rhesus monkeys we discussed earlier. Dr. Connor utilized salmon and salmon oil as a source of omega-3 fatty acids. In general, the cold-water oily fish are rich sources of such omega-3 fatty acids. These fish include not only salmon and menhaden but also mackerel, tuna, sardines, and halibut.[11]

According to data obtained from the World Health Organization, residents of the Island of Okinawa, a Japanese possession, have the longest life expectancy of any people on earth. On average, Okinawan women exhibit 83.4 years of expectancy for living; Okinawan men live an average of 77.5 years. The Japanese also are known to be the longest lived peoples of any major nation; however, from the research of Helmut Hasibeder, M.D., a Munich-based physician who has spent much of the last decade studying Okinawan longevity, the residents of Okinawa outshine anyone else around the world.

The Island of Okinawa boasts an astonishing percentage of centenarians, which amounts to 12.47 people per 100,000 population compared with 2.54 people who live to be over 100 years old per 100,000 in Japan. In the United States, there is the miniscule figure of only one centenarian for every 1,750,000 persons in the population. Americans appear to bury themselves with their teeth by eating vast amounts of junk food from the fast food restaurants and from the junk processed into prepared foods. In contrast, Dr. Hasibeder believes that the Okinawans, like the Japanese, owe their long lives principally to eating a healthier diet of fresh and low-fat foods based on vegetables, fish, and almost no meat. Especially significant is that the Okinawans consume large quantities of sweet potatoes, turnip greens, and mustard greens, all three of which are among the best natural sources of vitamin E. Dr. Hasibeder says that vitamin E, in its role as an antioxidant, retards cancer, atherosclerosis, and aging.

In the Okinawan population there is a lessened amount of dementia and mental retardation because of lack of oxidation of the older population's brain-cell membranes. This same fortunate circumstance is characteristic of the Japanese people. Both the Okinawans and the Japanese consume a great deal of cold-water fish such as tuna, mackerel, and sardines, which are rich in the same omega-3 fatty acids we have been advocating. Although they are fats, the omega-3 fatty acids are acknowledged to protect against myocardial infarction and other forms of heart disease and against dementia.

In addition, the Japanese and Okinawans rely on rice and vegetables for their food supply, both high in fiber, which explains their low rate of prostate and colon cancer. It would be advantageous for Americans and Canadians to gradually assume this same dietary model without suddenly making drastic changes in their eating patterns. The North Americans need merely to increase their intake of pasta, rice, vegetables, and other complex carbohydrates, including whole grain breads, cereals, and all fruits. They should consider the protein of fish and meat and poultry more as side dishes and fat as a condiment. As authors of this book on mental fitness, we advise that these relatively painless changes in lifestyle alone could be beneficial to keep your heart strong, your brain clear, your body cancer-free, and your longevity increased with an improved quality of life.

We recommend supplementing the diet with vitamins, minerals, certain amino acids, herbal formulas, and a type of adjunctive health food substance with medicinal quality that lately has been designated by the health food industry as "nutraceuticals." Among the various nutraceuticals are CoEnzyme Q10, L-carnitine, dimethylglycine, choline, inositol, RNA, microflora, and numerous other substances. (See our recommended nutritional formulation in the next chapter.) Patients who are receiving intravenous EDTA chelation therapy in particular should be taking megadose supplemental nutrients. For anyone with a brain disorder, it is especially important that he or she receive adequate amounts of cobalamine (vitamin B12) and folic acid.

It is surprising to find from laboratory blood examinations of patients that a "normal" level of folate in the blood stream does not exclude the possibility of folate deficiency. This was pointed out in a lecture presented at the Spring 1993 Conference of ACAM by Derrick Lonsdale, M.D., of Cleveland, Ohio. Dr. Lonsdale stated that some people who are deficient in folate, even with their showing high levels of folic acid in the blood, are unmasked when they receive thiamine (vitamin B1). Taking thiamine results in a drop in the folate level.

The vitamin folate, of course, is an important cofactor in chemical reactions leading to the formation of choline and acetocholine. Both of these are essential neurotransmitter substances of the brain. Without them, thoughts do not get developed or memories retained.

MORE COMPONENTS OF THE
ANTI-ALZHEIMER'S DISEASE DIET

The final word on the optimal diet for all of us and specifically for individuals with memory loss and brain disorders has yet to be written. What is coming out of research studies, however, is that basically a vegetarian eating plan with added sources of omega-3 fatty acids is the way to eat. Fish is part of the appropriate eating program, perhaps served to one's family three times a week.

Inasmuch as unsaturated fatty acids comprise over one half of the weight of the human brain, the fat content of what is ingested must influence the composition of the membraneous walls of neurons. The average person needs to consume less than fourteen grams of fat to meet the daily requirements of essential fatty acids that our bodies utilize for a variety of important metabolic substances. Too bad that the average North American consumes over eight times that amount, which finally builds up on arterial walls as atherosclerotic plaque.

A recent study published in the English journal *Lancet* found a 29 percent reduction in mortality in men who ate fish three times a week after each had sustained a heart attack. So, from the foregoing, a series of summary statements could be the following: for the body and brain, eating chicken instead of meat is far healthier; eating fish rather than chicken is better yet; eating vegetarian as a total lifestyle is the best practice overall, if one eats sufficient plant foods that have a high iron content (see Chapter 15 for a list of iron-containing foods).

In 1985, three investigating internists, Drs. Castelli, Sax, and Ornish, studied groups of vegetarians living near Putnam, Connecticut. These doctors found that the ratio of total cholesterol to HDL was exceedingly low in these people, but it tended to increase or worsen in quantity as they added dairy products, eggs, or fish to their eating programs. It was recognized that even eating herbivorous fish (fish that only feed on vegetation) was healthier, since herbivorous fish allowed for lower cholesterol levels for a person than if he or she ate carnivorous fish (fish that only feed on meat).

POTENTIAL DISADVANTAGES OF EATING FISH

While fish is a great source for omega-3 fatty acids, it is better to derive this nutrient from vegetarian sources, like flaxseed oil and soybean oil. The healthy benefits received from eating fish rich in omega-3 fatty acids may not be worth the effort, if the fish has been living in contaminated waters. While you may not want to cut fish out of your diet altogether, there are some factors you may want to take into consideration:

- If caught in coastal waters, fish may be contaminated with pesticides, chlorinated hydrocarbons, and heavy metals.

- In patients with diabetes, fish oils may cause insulin resistance and elevation of blood-glucose levels.

- Because fish oils are higher in omega-3 fatty acids than the whole grains in soybean products, on a theoretical basis they may increase the risk of hemorrhagic stroke.

- Compared to the LDL-lowering effect of eating foods that are vegetarian, fish contain saturated fat and cholesterol so that they tend to increase LDL.

PROTEIN INTAKE

Most of us know that proteins as assimilated amino acids form the building blocks of our cells. There are twenty-two different amino acids that combine to form the protein components of our bodies and brains. The human body is able to synthesize thirteen of these amino acids, but it is essential that the other nine be gotten from the food supply. Consequently they are called "essential amino acids." Of these, three of them—lysine, tryptophan, and methionine—are absolutely critical since the others are plentiful in most foods.

Unlike animal products, no single plant source contains all of the essential amino acids but all of them do contain the three critical ones in varying proportions. By eating different plant foods anyone can obtain the necessary amino acids. Legumes such as beans are high in lysine but low in tryptophan and methionine. A meal of brown rice and beans provides a complete protein no different from the protein found in eggs or meat.

One good rule to follow for excellent nutrition is to eat any grain and any legume sometime during the same day. Here are some examples of complete protein combinations to consume as part of your meal planning for the anti-Alzheimer's disease diet:

• Brown rice and beans

• Tacos with beans

• Tofu with brown rice

• Whole wheat pasta and beans

• Black eye peas and brown rice

• Boston baked beans and brown bread

Another way to combine foods to make a complete protein is to join grains or legumes with small amounts of skim milk or nonfat yogurt. For example, make common use of these food combinations:

• Oatmeal with skim milk or nonfat yogurt

• Any nonsugared breakfast cereal with skim milk or yogurt

• Buckwheat pancakes made with nonfat milk or yogurt

• Meatless chili topped with a dab of nonfat yogurt

• Fried egg whites (egg yolk contains all of the unwanted dietary cholesterol)

BRAIN-ALTERING BEVERAGES

The caffeine content of a cup of coffee, black tea, a cola drink, cocoa, and hot or cold chocolate, chemically stimulates your sympathetic nervous system which, in turn, results in your body calling for high levels of adrenaline and other stress hormones. The stimulating beverage may pick up your energy level temporarily but it soon drops off—sometimes as soon as twenty minutes later—so that another cup of "java" makes its demand on your brain. Drinking cup after cup of stimulant this way is addictive because your sympathetic nervous system arrives at a state in which the beverage becomes a required inciter to action. You become a slave to the beverage in order to get motivated to move, perform, or even think. Continued use of quantities of these stimulating beverages could ulti-mately result in over-stimulation of the heart and could finally cause an irregular heart beat.

In contrast to caffeine's stimulating effect, alcohol can do more than just depress you. Neurons respond adversely anytime they come into contact with alcohol. Alcohol sedates the nerve centers one by one, until the brain can no longer perform properly to sustain proper bodily functions. Knowing this, it is only common sense for patients with brain disorders to eliminate the drinking of alcohol in any form from their lifestyle. From a cardiac standpoint, the French people who eat a high animal-fat diet do have a low incidence of heart attack owing to their ingestion of red wines. This is referred to in medicine as the "French paradox," attributed to phenols and other chemical ingredients in the wines that possess antioxidant properties. However, we suggest removing alcohol from the diet.

SEVEN DAYS OF SAMPLE MENUS FOR THE ANTI-ALZHEIMER'S DISEASE DIET

Cod liver oil should be taken daily without fruit juice, on an empty stomach.

DAY ONE

Breakfast

1 cup oatmeal
1 slice whole wheat toast, lightly sprinkled with safflower oil
8 ounces carrot juice
8 ounces non-fat milk

Lunch

Tuna fish sandwich on whole wheat toast (tomato, lettuce, and no-cholesterol mayonnaise optional)
1 cup tossed salad, lightly sprinkled with Italian dressing and flaxseed oil
1 cup mixed vegetables
Fresh fruit as desired
8 ounces tomato juice

Dinner

Veggie burger on a whole wheat bun (sliced tomato, lettuce, and no-cholesterol mayonnaise optional)
1 cup tossed salad, lightly sprinkled with Italian dressing and flaxseed oil
1 small baked potato, diced, with 1 teaspoon flaxseed oil
Dietetic gelatin, fruit salad, or fresh fruit as desired
8 ounces non-fat milk

Snacks (optional)

1 cup non-fat yogurt
Fresh fruit as desired
Crackers with one tablespoon peanut butter
Sugar-free protein drink

DAY TWO

Breakfast

2 slices whole wheat toast, lightly
   sprinkled with safflower oil
5 stewed prunes
8 ounces orange juice

Lunch

Filet of Turbot
1 cup tossed salad, lightly sprinkled
   with Italian dressing and
   flaxseed oil
6 asparagus tips
1 baked potato
1 pear
8 ounces non-fat milk

Dinner

1 large black bean burrito
1 cup tossed salad with light Italian
   dressing with flaxseed oil added
Brown rice as desired
1 cup non-fat yogurt with
   strawberries
8 ounces carrot juice

Snacks (optional)

1 cup non-fat yogurt
Fresh fruit as desired
Crackers with one tablespoon
   peanut butter
Sugar-free protein drink

DAY THREE

Breakfast

1 whole wheat or buckwheat waffle
½ cup non-fat yogurt
½ cup fresh strawberries
8 ounces carrot juice

Lunch

Vegetarian chili
1 cup tossed salad with light Italian
   dressing
3 toasted or heated corn tortillas
¼ cup guacamole
Fresh fruit as desired
8 ounces tomato juice

Dinner

1 personal size vegetarian pizza
1 cup tossed green salad
Sorbet with fresh fruit
8 ounces non-fat milk or fruit juice

Snacks (optional)

1 cup non-fat yogurt
Fresh fruit as desired
Crackers with one tablespoon
   peanut butter
Sugar-free protein drink

DAY FOUR

Breakfast

4 to 6 four-inch buckwheat pancakes
½ cup non-fat yogurt
½ large sliced banana
8 ounces orange juice

Lunch

Lentil soup
1 cup tossed green salad, dressing
   optional
2 slices whole wheat bread
Fresh fruit as desired
8 ounces tomato juice

Dinner

Wok-cooked vegetables with tofu
1 cup tossed salad, dressing
   optional
1 cup brown rice
2 cups string beans
1 pear
8 ounces non-fat milk

Snacks (optional)

1 cup non-fat yogurt
Fresh fruit as desired
Crackers with one tablespoon
   peanut butter
Sugar-free protein drink

DAY FIVE

Breakfast

Oatmeal with raisins and cinnamon
½ cup non-fat yogurt
Fresh fruit as desired
8 ounces orange juice

Lunch

Filet of salmon
6 asparagus tips
1 baked potato
Fresh fruit as desired
8 ounces non-fat milk

Dinner

Spaghetti with marinara sauce
1 cup tossed green salad
Mushrooms, braised with herbs
Broccoli
Italian bread (optional)
8 ounces fresh fruit juice

Snacks (optional)

1 cup non-fat yogurt
Fresh fruit as desired
Crackers with one tablespoon
   peanut butter
Sugar-free protein drink

DAY SIX

Breakfast

Corn bread with sugar-free
    preserves
½ cup non-fat yogurt
8 ounces carrot juice

Lunch

Spaghetti with marinara sauce
1 cup tossed green salad,
    dressing optional
Tofu cheese with fresh herbs
2 slices Italian bread or whole wheat
    bread
Fresh fruit
8 ounces orange juice

Dinner

Eggplant Parmesan
1½ cups split pea soup
Shiitake mushrooms
2 slices garlic toast, Italian bread,
    or whole wheat bread
Fresh fruit as desired
8 ounces non-fat milk

Snacks (optional)

1 cup non-fat yogurt
Fresh fruit as desired
Crackers with one tablespoon
    peanut butter
Sugar-free protein drink

DAY SEVEN

Breakfast

(Breakfast out)
3 Egg whites, cooked over easy
¼ cup non-fat cottage cheese
2 slices whole wheat toast
Fruit cup
8 ounces orange juice

Lunch

½ tuna sandwich on whole wheat
    toast (cholesterol-free
    mayonnaise, sliced tomato,
    and lettuce optional)
1 cup tossed green salad
2 cups mixed vegetables
Fresh fruit as desired
8 ounces fresh fruit juice

Dinner

Mock Chicken Salad
1 cup brown rice
½ cup string beans
Fresh fruit as desired
8 ounces carrot juice

Snacks (optional)

1 cup non-fat yogurt
Fresh fruit as desired
Crackers with one tablespoon
    peanut butter
Sugar-free protein drink

SUGGESTED READING

Books

Arrowhead Mills Cookbook, Vicki Rae Chelf; Avery Publishing Group, Garden City Park, New York, 1991.

Cooking For Life, Cherie Calbom and Vicki Rae Chelf; Avery Publishing Group, Garden City Park, New York, 1993.

Cooking With the Right Side of the Brain, Vick Rae Chelf; Avery Publishing Group, Garden City Park, New York, 1991.

Diet for a Small Planet, Frances Moore Lappe; Ballantine Books, New York, 1991 Edition.

The Farm Vegetarian Cookbook; The Book Publishing Company, Summertown, Tennessee, 1978 (available through People for the Ethical Treatment of Animals).

Guide to Natural Foods Cooking, Judy Brown; The Book Publishing Co., Summertown, Tennessee, 1989 (available through People for the Ethical Treatment of Animals).

The High Road to Health, Lindsay Wagner & Ariane Spade; Prentice Hall Press, New York, 1990.

Instead of Chicken, Instead of Turkey: A Poultryless 'Poultry' Potpourri, Karen Davis; United Poultry Concerns, Potomac, Maryland, 1991 (available through People for the Ethical Treatment of Animals).

Linda McCartney's Home Cooking, Linda McCartney (wife of Paul McCartney of the Beatles); Arcade Publishing, New York, 1989.

May All Be Fed, Diet for a New World, John Robbins (author of *Diet for a New America*); William Morrow and Company, Inc., New York, 1992.

A Physician's Slimming Guide for Permanent Weight Control, Neal D. Barnard, M.D.; The Book Publishing Co., Summertown, Tennessee, 1992 (available through Physicians Committee for Responsible Medicine—also by same author, *The Power of Your Plate*—more recipes).

Recipes for a Small Planet, Ellen Buchman Ewald; Ballantine Books, New York; 1992 Edition.

Slimming the Vegetarian Way, Leah Leneman (also *The Single Vegan*);

Thorsons Publishing Group, Northamptonshire, England, 1989 (available through Physicians for Responsible Medicine).

Sundays at Moosewood Restaurant—Ethnic and Regional Recipes From the Cooks at the Legendary Restaurant, by the Moosewood Collection, Simon and Shuster, Fireside, New York, 1990.

Whole Meals, Marcea Weber; Avery Publishing Group, Garden City Park, New York, 1993.

Whole World Cookbook, Editors of *East West Journal*; Avery Publishing Group, Garden City Park, New York, 1984.

Magazines

Good Medicine, from the Physicians Committee for Responsible Medicine, published quarterly by Physicians Committee for Responsible Medicine, 5100 Wisconsin Avenue, NW, Suite 404, Washington, DC 20016 (202) 686–2210. Distributed as a membership benefit to PCRM members.

Vegetarian Times, monthly 1–800–435–9610 (outside Illinois), 1–800–435–0715 (inside Illinois) or P.O. Box 446, Mt. Morris, IL 61054-9894.

CHAPTER 22

Dietary Brain Boosters and Memory Pills

The elderly are the fastest-growing age group in all of the industrialized western countries. Twelve percent of the world population is now over age sixty-five and this number is expected to double within the next four decades. Those persons older than eighty-five are the segment that is increasing most quickly.

According to a recent survey of health professionals specializing in elder care, malnutrition is a serious health problem among the world's elderly population. The survey of 750 physicians, nurses, and administrators of hospitals and other health care institutions found that every fourth geriatric patient is malnourished. One-half of all elderly hospital patients and 40 percent of nursing home residents do suffer from malnutrition. A coalition of more than thirty national medical, health, and aging organizations, the Nutrition Screening Initiative (NSI) of the United States, uncovered that Americans of middle and advanced age fail to get proper amounts of nutrients because of deficiencies, excesses, or imbalances in food or diet.

Alzheimer's disease is the most common type of dementia affecting the elderly in North America. Educated estimates advise that 47 percent of all persons older than eight-five years of age on this continent suffer from Alzheimer's disease.[1] Because of the increasing number of malnourished elderly people throughout the industrialized West—including not only North America but also Europe, Great Britain, Australia, and New Zealand—the prevalence of Alzheimer's disease is expanding in numbers.

Until now there has been no established cure for Alzheimer's disease. Albeit inadequate, the only conventionally-accepted treatments have included certain psychological and sociological types such as counseling and support for the patients' families, plus a general kind of support with the provision of safe and appropriately stimulating environments for the disease victims. More currently coming to be recognized is another program— the nutritional approach using various food supplements and drugs.

Dietary brain boosters and memory pills supplemented to one's daily menu plan are useful adjuncts to usual food intake. They are swallowed as preventatives or treatments for brain syndromes involving dementia, senility, and other mental malfunctions. Such nutritional supplements should accompany chelation therapy, which is the treatment program we have described as successfully employed to reverse Alzheimer's disease. As coauthors, both of us highly recommend intravenous infusions with ethylene diamine tetraacetic acid (EDTA). It is the treatment of choice for Alzheimer's disease. EDTA is also the primary available medical program of prevention for any kind of heavy-metal toxicity affecting the brain.

Now, added to chelation therapy, we are recommending another therapy, the anti-Alzheimer's dementia diet with its associated ingestion of certain complementary, nontoxic nutrients that are described in depth in this chapter.

THE NUTRITIONAL STATUS OF ALZHEIMER'S DISEASE PATIENTS COMPARED WITH CONTROLS

Dietary brain boosters and memory pills have been useful for the treatment of reversible dementia, dementia associated with reduced plasma/serum levels of nutrients, and brain tissue disease related to elevation or deficiency of certain minerals needed for metabolism. Melvyn R. Werbach, M.D., is a psychiatrist and author of two highly respected textbooks widely used as references in the wholistic movement, *Nutritional Influences on Illness* and *Nutritional Influences on Mental Illness.* Dr. Werbach, who is an assistant clinical professor in the Department of Psychiatry at the UCLA School of Medicine, states: "Patients with dementia are more likely than controls to be nutritionally deficient, although it is unclear if the deficiency is secondary to the effect of the disease on eating behavior."[2]

Dr. Werbach repeated to us the story of Tom Warren, which we had related in Chapter 11. Mr. Warren was a diabetic, and came from a family background of depression, schizophrenia, and senility. At age twenty he had been hospitalized for a severe mental breakdown. At age forty-two, he began to feel weak and irritable and eventually was unable to work. His diagnosis then was described as "depression." A few years later, the patient's mental faculties had gradually declined until he would spend weeks sitting in a chair looking at his shoes. A CAT (computerized axial tomography) scan, taken when he was 50 years old, showed brain atrophy. Three psychiatrists separately diagnosed him as suffering from Alzheimer's dementia and predicted that he would be dead in seven years.

On his own, Tom Warren began a water fast and after five days was able to think more clearly. Then he had his silver-mercury dental fillings replaced with an alternative material—a composite. Mercury gas could no longer leach from his teeth. He felt better! However, his sensitivity reaction to the replacement material was terribly severe, so he decided to have all of his teeth extracted. Ridding himself of the allergen substances and his dental amalgam fillings worked well, for his thinking improved even more. Finally, the man embarked on an extensive program of supplementing his food intake with vitamins, minerals, and adjunctive nutrients.

Dr. Werbach, who himself is an orthomolecular psychiatrist known to prescribe nutrients for successfully overcoming mental illness, reports that within a few months after starting the nutrient program, Mr. Warren felt so much better compared with how he had been feeling that he was able to resume a completely normal life. He beat Alzheimer's. "After two years, Tom was clearly in remission. Almost four years after the first CAT scan, a second scan showed definite improvement that was confirmed by several specialists," advised Dr. Werbach. "He subsequently recovered so fully that he was able to return to work as an insurance salesman. While he has returned to his former lifestyle, he must rigidly adhere to his dietary and lifestyle program to minimize symptoms."

An article published in the *Journal of Orthomolecular Medicine* puts forth four major arguments for the view that Alzheimer's disease is caused by malnutrition with or without digestive malabsorption. Orthomolecular medicine is the treatment and prevention of disease and the promotion of health by adjustment of the chemical components of the body, primarily by nutritional management. Here are the four orthomolecular concepts:

1. Alzheimer's disease is associated with malnutrition, and probably with digestive malabsorption as well.

2. Alzheimer's disease is the consequence rather than the cause of malnutrition.

3. Alzheimer's disease is connected with the neuropathologic changes of Down's Syndrome that develop slightly before the patient's fourth decade, and such patients suffer from malnutrition, probably due to malabsorption.

4. Alzheimer's disease is the source of clinical, anatomical, neurobiochemical, and other pathologies that are connected to metallic toxicities and/or malnutrition.[3]

Many elderly people experience a reduction in the transportation of most vitamins, minerals, and essential trace elements through the blood-brain barrier and, possibly, the large and small intestines (the gut). Such reduction causes deficiencies in the patients' brain cells that may be the primary cause of the formation of age pigment (lipofuscin) and neurofibrillary tangles standardly observed in Alzheimer's disease. Administration of missing nutrients could halt or slow the development of the pathological processes of Alzheimer's disease.[4]

The above thesis was confirmed by an important observational study of the nutritional status of twenty-three severely demented patients. They were compared with that of twenty-three similarly aged control people. With the possible exception of vitamin C, the poorer nutritional status of the demented patients could not be explained satisfactorily in terms of nutrient intake. They ate the same diets as the healthier controls, but the demented patients seemed to have poor metabolic absorption.[5]

In another similar clinical study, the nutritional status of twenty-nine patients with senile dementia (Alzheimer's disease) was compared with thirty-five other healthy elderly controls. Dietary intakes were below recommended levels for one-third of the controls and for a greater proportion of the patients. A higher proportion of Alzheimer's disease patients than the controls displayed evidence of nutritional deficiency for a number of vitamins.[6]

In a third clinical experiment, ten Alzheimer's disease patients and ten healthy elderly controls were given vitamin supplements daily for two months. Vitamin concentration differences in the blood of these two populations disappeared; then some of the Alzheimer's patients showed a startlingly apparent clinical improvement in their thinking and memory retention.[6]

SUPPLEMENTS TO THE ANTI-ALZHEIMER'S DISEASE DIET

The anti-Alzheimer's disease diet that we described in the last chapter has great efficacy as far as it goes, but certain nutritional elevations, dependencies, or deficiencies exhibited by patients must be corrected by means of additional nutrient supplementation. If nutrient quantities are deficient in older people, nutritional supplementation will likely be beneficial for those patients exhibiting dementia. There are numerous examples of successful nutrient treatment for Alzheimer's disease and other dementias.

Supplementation with the nutrient phosphatidyl choline tends to retard the progress of Alzheimer's disease and in some instances has been responsible for the elevation of intelligence and improved memory in affected people.

In other cases, total calcium elevation in the body and reduced levels of ionized calcium in the brain tissue tends to bring on dementia. Then it has been observed elsewhere that calcium deficiency in the blood is a source of dementia.

In Wilson's disease (an inborn defect of copper metabolism known medically as hepatolenticular degeneration), dementia or mental retardation is associated with elevated brain-tissue levels of copper. The only viable treatment for Wilson's disease is administration of the chelating agent, penicillamine, to grasp the copper in a molecular vise and remove it from the body and brain. Such chelation therapy being administered, the patient's mental and physical developments are improved.

Ginkgo biloba, an herbal extract of the ginkgo tree that we will discuss later in this chapter, helps to bring back clearer thinking for people with dementia.

Supplementation with massive doses of thiamine (vitamin B1) tends to improve perception.

Adding the two amino acid-derived substances L-tryptophan and D,L-5-hydroxytryptophan to an Alzheimer's patient suffering from tryptophan malabsorption helps that patient's brain to function.

VITAMIN SUPPLEMENTS AND MENTALITY

Folic acid (part of the B-complex of vitamins) deficiency is known to be associated with mental apathy, disorientation, poor concentration, and memory deficits, in addition to damage to the pyramidal tract of the brain.[7,8] If a person is deficient in folic acid, 10 to 20 milligrams of this B-vitamin should be taken daily for one week; then 2.5 to 10 milligrams daily of folate is the dose for maintenance.

Out of twenty-nine patients with senile dementia, a higher proportion displayed evidence of folate deficiency when compared with thirty-five healthy elderly control patients.[6]

Niacin (vitamin B3) dependency may require more of this vitamin B3 component for an elderly individual who has short-term memory loss or is otherwise mentally inept. (A person with a vitamin dependency, as compared with a vitamin deficiency, has a greater metabolic need for the particular nutrient in question than is usual for other humans.) Orthomolecular psychiatrist Abram Hoffer, M.D., Ph.D., of Victoria, British Columbia has reported on patients with dementia. Dr. Hoffer said, "I have found vitamin B3 very effective in restoring memory, in improving energy, in lessening the need for sleep, and in increasing alertness."[10]

Pyridoxin (vitamin B6) is often deficient in elderly Alzheimer patients as compared with healthy elderly controls.[11] Moreover, there is an age-related fall in dopamine receptors that parallels a decline in plasma vitamin B6 levels.[12] Without such elevated levels, memory impairment may ensue.

Thiamine (vitamin B1) is frequently lacking in the brains of Alzheimer's disease patients.[5] Additionally, the activity of thiamine-dependent enzymes in these people may be deficient. For instance, the activities of several enzymes dependent on vitamin B1 were deficient in the brain and in some peripheral tissues of Alzheimer's patients as reported in the *Archives of Neurology*.[13]

In a placebo-controlled, double-blind crossover study using thiamine, eleven Alzheimer's patients with an average age of seventy-two years received 3 grams/day of the vitamin for three months followed by niacinamide (derived from vitamin B3) 750 milligrams/day as a placebo for another three months. The clinical researcher reported that "global ratings" (meaning most aspects of mental improvement) for the patients receiving thiamine were significantly higher than with placebos.[14]

Cobalamin (vitamin B12) deficiency is associated with dementia, emotional and mental depression, confusion, memory losses, and general mental slowness along with neurologic deficits. Vitamin B12 deficiency is about four times (23 percent) more frequent in patients with senile Alzheimer's disease than in age-matched control patients or in those suffering with simple dementia that comes from vascular impairment to the brain such as that involving carotid artery disease.

The psychiatrist and president of the European College of Neuropsychopharmacology, Dr. C.G. Gottfries, reported that vitamin B12 deficiency itself, or other deficiencies of essential nutrients being discussed here, that are caused by certain atrophic changes in the gut, are important as causes of cobalamin deficiency in the central nervous system.[15]

There are numerous clinical studies published in the medical literature that prove the adverse effects of cobalamin deficiency on the human brain. They result in Alzheimer's disease and other brain syndromes.[16,17,18,19,20,21]

Ascorbic acid (vitamin C) intake frequently is lower in dementia patients than for healthy elderly. For instance, the nutritional status of 885 psychiatric patients revealed a much lower plasma level of vitamin C than healthy controls. Some of their blood test readings included a lessened 0.51/100 milliliters plasma level of vitamin C, that was 0.36/100 milliliters below the 0.87/100 milliliters vitamin C plasma level for 110 healthy control patients. The lowest values were found in patients with senile dementia and in females on iron therapy (which we know, from Chapter 15, can be a source of dementia).[22]

Alpha tocopherol (vitamin E) proved in an observational clinical study to be far below the accepted normal range of serum-blood levels of vitamin E for nearly 60 percent of Alzheimer's patients.[23]

People with Down's syndrome, who are prone to Alzheimer-like neuropathological change in middle age and are at high risk of clinical dementia, have increased superoxide activity. Such excessive superoxide—a free radical—damages cell membranes in the brain because of increased hydroxyl radicals.[24,25] Since vitamin E is a free-radical scavenger, supplementing with this vitamin may reduce cellular damage in the brain.[26]

MINERAL SUPPLEMENTS AND MENTALITY

Calcium, as we stated earlier, is elevated in brain-tissue levels of Alzheimer's disease patients. It is their total calcium that is increased excessively, while the demented patients' levels of ionized calcium (calcium ions floating in their blood) may be reduced. This was proved in autopsies of deceased Alzheimer's disease patients. These subjects revealed significantly elevated calcium levels in brain tissues as compared with deceased elderly who had been healthy comparison controls.[27]

In old age, low calcium and vitamin D intake showed up when there were short exposure times in the sun. Also decreased was intestinal absorption, plus kidney function failed with insufficient synthesis of vitamin D (1,25-dihydroxyvitamin D). All of these complications contributed to various health problems, including the complications of calcium deficiency in the blood, secondary hyperparathyroidism, bone loss, and calcium shift from the bone to soft tissues. Calcium mineral salts are known to move from the extracellular to the intracellular compartments of tissue cells, thus blunting the sharp concentration gap between these cellular compartments. The consequence often is senile Alzheimer's disease due to calcium deposition in the central nervous system. The patients experience cellular mineral overflow.[28]

The presence of aluminum silicates in the plaques found in the brains of Alzheimer's disease patients are probably secondary to calcium deficiency.[29]

Magnesium deficiency in the brain is not uncommon in Alzheimer's patients. Such magnesium lack may be attributable to low intake or poor retention of magnesium from body metabolism. Further, the presence of inadequate magnesium, an essential mineral, may be related as well to a high intake of some neurotoxic metal, such as aluminum, mercury, lead, or cadmium, that inhibits the activity of magnesium-requiring enzymes. Or, there could be impaired magnesium transport through the body with associated increased transport of the neurotoxic metal into brain tissue.

Alzheimer's disease may therefore involve a defective mineral transport process, characterized by both an abnormally high incorporation of aluminum and an abnormally low incorporation of magnesium into brain neurons.

An altered serum protein, probably albumin, is likely to have a greater affinity for aluminum than for magnesium, in contrast to the normal protein, which binds magnesium better than aluminum. This altered protein tends to cross the blood-brain barrier more efficiently than the normal protein and competes with it in binding to brain neurons.[30]

Selenium is deficient in the brain tissue of Alzheimer's disease patients, so it is likely, as well, that selenium supplementation would be advantageous.[27]

Silicon may contribute to the development of plaque seen in Alzheimer's disease. To illustrate, aluminum and silicon were found together in the central region of senile plaque cores and were identified as aluminosilicates (see Chapter 7). The distribution of these elements was similar in cores isolated from the cerebral cortex of patients with Alzheimer's dementia and in the cores *in situ* (studied at their origin) from tissue sections taken during autopsies from the cerebral cortex of presenile and senile patients with Alzheimer's disease.

The presence of aluminosilicates at the center of Alzheimer's plaque cores contrasts with the distribution of other inorganic constituents. It indicates that silicon is involved with aluminum in the initiation of early stages of senile plaque formation.[31]

Zinc, another essential mineral, often is reduced below normal in the brain tissue of Alzheimer's disease patients. This was shown in the autopsies of eleven Alzheimer's patients in different regions of the brain.[32]

With zinc reduced overall, invariably there is an increased amount of aluminum present in the brain and blood serum of Alzheimer's disease patients. Such a conclusion was arrived at from observing thirty-three subjects with a marked deficiency of zinc. They had elevated levels of blood-serum aluminum.[33]

Zinc supplementation may be beneficial in Wilson's disease to prevent the intestinal absorption of copper.[34]

Most enzymes concerned with DNA replication, repair, and transcription are zinc metallo-enzymes. If there were an age-associated loss of incorporation of zinc into these enzymes in neurons, such as with zinc replaced by other metal ions, then a loss of enzyme activity occurs and loss of neurons results.[35,36]

OTHER NUTRIENT FACTORS FOR ALZHEIMER'S DISEASE

Ginkgo biloba is an herb with diverse pharmacological, dose-related effects on attention span and alertness, which are well-demonstrated by electro-encephalographic (EEG) analysis. The ginkgo biloba extract (GBE) is manu-factured in both oral and injectable forms. In Europe, injectable GBE is produced under the code number EGb761. The oral dosage forms of the extract, provided as encapsulated powders and tablets, are more conven-ient to use. They possess antioxidant activity as shown in both laboratory and live organism experimental models. Flavonoid components of the extract scavenge free-radical superoxide ions. Non-flavonoid constituents are involved in the scavenging of hydroxyl radicals.

We are advocates of utilizing GBE for the treatment of early stages of Alzheimer's disease. The antioxidant properties of ginkgo flavonoids are found to break the chain of free-radical formation at a "high level"—that is, at the beginning of the chemical reaction, as opposed to a reaction occurring after the radical's formation. This unique antioxidant activity of the ginkgo extract is one mechanism that explains the reported brain-di-rected, vascular-system protective effect of ginkgo extract.

Administering oral GBE significantly increases the speed of memory scan-ning, too, without causing any adverse effect on the patient's performance. The ginkgo giloba extract increases cerebral blood flow and enhances glucose consumption while having a markedly beneficial effect upon the patient's sociability, alertness, mood, memory, and intellectual efficiency.[37]

An experimental double-blind study was carried out on fifty-four eld-erly patients with mild signs of impairment in everyday function that showed up on the Crichton Geriatric Rating Scale. They randomly received either GBE or a placebo. Cognitive efficiency was measured monthly using a battery of tests of mental ability, while the quality of life was assessed using a behavioral questionnaire administered before and after the study. Not only did the treated group's general accuracy on the tests improve with GBE, but the speed of performance also increased, indicating an improve-ment in their mental efficiency.

In addition, the patients in the treatment group reported an increase in their degree of interest in everyday activities. Results of the study sug-gested that GBE is effective in the treatment of the early stages of primary degenerative dementia.[38]

Another experimental double-blind study carried out one year prior to the one just reported was performed on sixty patients with mild to moderate primary degenerative dementia. They randomly received either GBE or a placebo. In comparison with the placebo's inaction, ginkgo biloba extract administered over a period of four to twelve weeks significantly improved the patients' clinical conditions and the results of their psychometric tests. By the end of four weeks, there were marked improvements in the psychometric tests of the treated group of patients. Subjective assessments from both the physician and his patients, plus the global scores of the clinical-geriatric adverse testing scales dropped by an amount of 30 percent. This precipitous drop demonstrated that patients on ginkgo biloba extract were better able to handle everyday problems. On the standard Number-Symbol Test and the Number-Repeat Test, initial test values for the GBE group increased a great deal compared with the placebo group, showing that short-term memory and vigilance are considerably improved.[39]

In 1986, 166 elderly patients with cerebral disorders that caused mild mental deterioration received either GBE or a placebo. After three months, the experimentally treated group began to demonstrate significant positive differences from the untreated control group. After one year, patients receiving the ginkgo biloba extract demonstrated immense amounts of improvement in their mental function when tested for memory, altertness, attention span, mood, and sociability. They improved more than twice that of the placebo group.[40]

Phosphatidyl choline is a cholinergic nutrient in its purest form of 95-percent concentration. Given in a dosage of 10 to 20 grams daily for six months or more, phosphatidlyl choline may be useful in restoring alertness to the Alzheimer's disease patient. Alzheimer's disease is recognized as a deficiency in the acetylcholine neurosystem, the system that stores and retrieves items supposedly held in memory.[41]

Acetylcholine is degraded by the enzyme cholinesterase. A cholinesterase inhibitor is the drug tetrahydroaminocridine that causes liver toxicity, yet it is frequently prescribed by psychiatrists. We therefore do not recommend tetrahydroaminocridine for increasing one's mental status.[42] Instead, it is best to supplement with phosphatidyl choline itself.

DRUG TREATMENT OF ALZHEIMER'S DISEASE

There are, of course, many pharmaceuticals (not nutrients) utilized for Alzheimer's disease, including a minimum of sixteen drugs that may improve cognitive function for people with Alzheimer's disease. Some drugs improve abnormal behaviors, others augment acetylcholine neurotransmitter function. A few are nootropics that affect neuron metabolism with little effect elsewhere. Another group improves brain vasculature so that more blood flows to the neurons. A fifth group of Alzheimer's drugs includes those that modify certain defects of the brain. Drugs that affect behavior include neuroleptics, anxiolytics, and antirage modifiers. Substances making up these groups are described below.

The employment of all drugs for brain syndromes is controversial and federal legislation has been enacted to offer strict guidelines on their use in nursing homes which are attendant to senior citizens. There is no consensus among health professionals on the drug applications for Alzheimer's disease.

To the dismay of the United States Food and Drug Administration (FDA), numbers of anti-Alzheimer's disease prescription pharmaceutical products are being ordered by mail from Mexico, the Bahamas, England, Switzerland, and Germany. They are collectively called "smart drugs" for the improvement of memory and often are unapproved by the FDA. Most of them are approved by the food and drug administrations of the countries from which they may be purchased. However, be warned that the U.S. Customs Service, working in unison with the FDA, is likely to seize these nonapproved drugs when they are spotted during shipment into the United States. As coauthors, we do *not* advocate the employment of non-FDA-approved substances.

Some of the smart-drug products produce a sense of heightened awareness and energy inasmuch as many contain caffeine or sugars or both. Users of the non-approved drugs comprise a few types of constituencies. Among them are forty-something professional people knocking back powdered nutrients mixed with fruit juice at so-called "smart bars" (especially popular in southern California) to maintain the energy to dance all night at clubs.

Acetyl-l-carnitine (ALC) is a nutrient with pharmaceutical characteristics that has implications in the treatment of Alzheimer's disease. Its cholinergic properties exert action on the central nervous system by blockading post-synaptic inhibition of the endoneural mechanism. It is suitable therapy in encephalic conditions such as the senile brain, which we have stated is characterized by a depression of the cholinergic systems. ALC is one of those rare drugs that does not have to be imported from overseas. It is available from Cardiovascular Research, Ltd. (1061-B Shary Circle, Concord, California 94518; 800–888–4585 or 415–827–2636).

Cognex (tacrine, tetrahydroaminoacridine, or THA) has been allowed by the FDA to be accessible for patients from physicians participating in a research program on Alzheimer's disease. For the first six weeks, patients receive a 40-mg daily dose, which eventually may be titrated up to 120 milligrams per day as tolerated. Close monitoring for the first eighteen weeks of treatment is mandatory, because of the side effect of reversible elevations of the patient's transaminases. (Transaminase is one of a group of enzymes that catalyze the transfer of the amino group of an amino acid to a keto acid to form another amino acid.) Of those Alzheimer's disease patients ages fifty- to sixty-years-old who tolerate tacrine, 30 percent respond to the treatment by showing improved cognition and greater function.[43]

Deprenyl (L-deprenyl) is currently recognized internationally for the treatment of Parkinson's disease. It is also a selective inhibitor of the type B cerebral monamine oxidases (MAO-Bs) that bring on defects of the brain's monoaminergic neurotransmitters. Thus 10 milligrams per day of L-deprenyl administered in split doses of 5 milligrams each, morning and evening, pharmacologically corrects the alterations of the cerebral systems of neurotransmission.[44,45,46]

The defect in cortical cholinergic transmission of the human brain caused by MAO-Bs plays a major role in neuropsychological disorders that are typical of Alzheimer's disease.[47]

A placebo-controlled, double-blind, crossover study of L-deprenyl conducted at Perugia University in Italy showed the drug's higher and statistically significant effects on cognitive brain function (attention span and memory improvement) as opposed to placebo.[48]

In some cases of early-stage Alzheimer's disease, oral administration of L-deprenyl seems to slow or even stop the progression of symptoms within four months. Improvement in middle- to late-stage Alzheimer's disease occurs in approximately 40 percent of cases. Deprenyl is not any sort of cure for Alzheimer's disease, but in conjunction with deferoxamine it is extremely effective in removing the aluminum content of brain cells and bringing about their rejuvenation.

Deferoxamine (DFO), developed, manufactured, and distributed by Ciba-Geigy Corporation of Switzerland, is in FDA-approved phase II clinical trials for the removal of aluminum build-up in the brain. As we have discussed in Chapters 6, 7, 8, and 9, aluminum is one of the primary metallic toxins that blocks brain cell function and causes brain cell death. Improvement is noted for varying degrees for Alzheimer's disease patients under treatment with DFO. The main investigators using DFO for Alzheimer's patients are Donald R. McLaughlan, and his coworkers.[49]

Deprenyl and DFO seem to work synergistically and quite effectively against Alzheimer's disease caused by aluminum toxicity. The Alzheimer's Association is playing down the fact on aluminum and its involvement in Alzheimer's disease. It makes no mention of deprenyl or deferoxamine anywhere in the treatment protocols it provides.

Nootropics, a new class of smart drugs that tend to improve learning, memory consolidation, and memory retrieval without other central nervous system effects, has low toxicity. These are not FDA-approved but are prescribed to millions of people in Europe, Asia, and South America. The nootropics hold promise for Alzheimer's victims. According to their derivations, the following are classified as nootropics:[50]

Piracetam enhances cognition in the presence of insufficient oxygen being transported through the blood-brain barrier. Brand names include Avigilen, Cerebroforte, Cerebrospan, Cetam, Dinagen, Encefalux, Encetrop, Euvifor, Gabacet, Genogris, Memo-Puren, Nootron, Nootrop, Nootropil, Nootropyl, Normabrain, Norzetam, Novocetam, Pirroxil, Psycoton, Stimucortex, and UCB-6215.

Aniracetam, patented by Hoffman-La Roche, Inc., is unapproved for distribution in any country.

Fipexide enhances fine motor coordination, immune function, motivation, and emotions by stimulating the neurotransmitter dopamine.

Oxiracetam, championed by SmithKline Beecham, Inc., there are attempts being made to win its approval for the treatment of Alzheimer's disease. It is presently sold in Italy under the brand names CT-848, ISF-2522, Nueractiv, Neuromet, and as the generic hydroxypiracetam.

Pramiracetam was developed by Parke-Davis, a division of Warner-Lambert Company. It is fifteen times more potent than piracetam.

Pyroglutamate (PGA) is an amino acid nootropic naturally occurring in vegetables, fruits, dairy products, and meat as a flavor enhancer. Its generic name is 1-oxo-pyrrolidone carboxylic acid and it passes through the blood-brain barrier to stimulate cognitive function with resultant increases in memory and learning.

Vinpocetine facilitates cerebral metabolism by building blood flow and stepping up cellular energy in neurons. The Gedeon Richter company of Hungary markets vinpocetine throughout Europe under the brand name Cavinton.

Centrophenoxine is not a nootropic but rather a mood elevator. While not specific for Alzheimer's disease, it reduces the incidence of hypoxia (oxygen lack in the brain) that may be speeding the development of the disease.

Dimethylaminoethanol (DMAE), is a nutritional supplement found in health food stores, and according to some reports increases intelligence, improves memory, extends the life span, cures insomnia, and increases physical energy.

Dehydroepiandrosterone (DHEA) protects brain cells from Alzheimer's disease because it acts as a safeguard against nerve degeneration. A substance naturally present in the blood stream, Alzheimer's patients have 48 percent less DHEA than healthy controls of the same age.

Hydergine, produced by Sandoz Pharmaceuticals Corporation, is an extract of ergot, a fungus that grows on rye. It offers a popular treatment for all forms of senility since it is reported to improve the brain's blood supply, increase brain cell metabolism, protect against free radicals, eliminate the age pigment lipofuscin, normalize blood pressure, reduce tiredness, ameliorate dizziness and tinnitus (ringing in the ears), lower elevated blood cholesterol, and increase memory, learning ability, recall, and intelligence.

There are numerous other drugs that can be considered useful as therapy for Alzheimer's disease because of certain beneficial side effects they display. Among them are *propranolol hydrochloride (inderal), phenytoin (dilantin),* and *idebenone.*

When the brain fails to function, its letdown can affect five particular areas of living—perception, thinking, feeling, behavior, and memory. Usually one area is bound to be more affected than others, and in this book we have been concerned mostly with memory malfunction.

From the various functional changes we derive syndromes. For Alzheimer's disease it is a dementia predicated on the etiological syndrome of toxic metals. The toxic metal syndrome presents an aggregate of signs and symptoms that together constitute the picture of Alzheimer's disease. For the patient with this exceedingly sad syndrome of living death, correct treatment entails ridding the brain of toxic metals. To achieve such a worthy goal, we must administer forms of chelation therapy and follow the anti-Alzheimer's disease diet. Additionally, the patient can take memory pills and brain boosters.

The thinking aberrations and memory loss of Alzheimer's disease are of a peculiar sort. At the midway point—about phase four of the condition—the Alzheimer's patient may be unable to remember recent events, not even what was eaten for breakfast that morning, or whether he or she had even eaten breakfast at all. Nevertheless, this middle-stage Alzheimer's patient could probably describe a memorable meal that was enjoyed decades before. It is standard symptomatology in this peculiar disorder.

Although society seemingly accepts the shadow of Alzheimer's disease, we do not believe it is inescapable, unpreventable, or irreversible. Others in the "healing" profession may do so, and they cannot be faulted too much. In little more than a decade, Alzheimer's disease has moved from an obscure and supposedly rare condition to the fourth most frequent cause of death in North America. According to the Gallup Poll, every third resident of the United States knows someone who has been victimized by Alzheimer's, and every second person is worried about developing it's symptoms.

Alzheimer's disease from toxic metal syndrome has become a familiar ailment for all of us. But there is a solution that we have discussed at length. Knowledge is only one step to solving a problem; now you must use it.

Recipes for the Anti-Alzheimer's Disease Diet

Mock Chicken Salad

A great dish for those in transition from meat to meat-free.

Yield: 4 servings

> *8 ounces tempeh, diced (tempeh is a fermented soybean product*
> *found refrigerated or frozen in health food stores)*
> *¼ cup egg-free mayonnaise (look for cholesterol free-70% fat free)*
> *2 tablespoons nutritional yeast (found in health food stores)*
> *1 tablespoon chopped dill pickle*
> *½ teaspoon prepared mustard*
> *1 teaspoon low-sodium soy sauce or Bragg's Liquid*
> *(found in health food stores)*
> *2 tablespoons chopped onion*
> *¼ cup chopped celery*

1. Place the tempeh in a steamer, and steam for 10 minutes.
2. Transfer the tempeh to a large bowl. Add the remaining ingredients, and mix.
3. Cover and refrigerate the tempeh mixture until needed. Use as a topping for rice cakes, as a filling for pita bread, or as a filling for traditional sandwiches.

Spicy Tomato Sauce

Yield: 4 servings

¼ cup extra virgin olive oil
1 clove garlic, minced
½ medium onion, chopped
¼ cup chopped fresh basil
1 teaspoon chopped fresh rosemary
1 teaspoon chopped fresh thyme
1 can (32 ounces) cooked tomato pears or Roma tomatoes

1. Place the oil in a large, heavy pot over medium-high heat. Then add the garlic, onion, basil, rosemary, and thyme, and cook until the onions are golden brown.
2. Add the canned tomatoes to the onion mixture, and simmer for approximately 30 minutes. Serve hot.

Quick Tacos and Speedy Burritos

Using the black bean instant soup mixes now available in most grocery, health, and natural food stores, you can whip up tacos and burritos with practically no effort and lots of taste.

Yield: 6 tacos or burritos

Premade taco shells or flour tortillas
1 package instant black bean soup mix
¼ cup chopped onions
¼ cup chopped lettuce
¼ cup chopped tomato

Tacos
1. Make the black bean instant soup mix using only half the amount of water indicated on the package instructions, to form a paste.
2. Spoon the mixture into the taco shells, and top with the chopped onions, lettuce, and tomato. Serve warm.

Burritos

1. To soften the flour tortillas, heat them between two towels in the microwave or place in a covered container in the oven at 250°F for 2 to 5 minutes.
2. Make the black bean instant soup mix using only half the amount of water indicated on the package instructions, to form a paste.
3. Spread the black bean paste on the warmed tortillas. Add the chopped onions, lettuce, and tomato, and fold in thirds to form a burrito.

Riccioli D'oro Al Tre Crostacei

Yield: 4 servings

¼ cup extra virgin olive oil
½ teaspoon minced garlic
Meat of 4 lobster claws
12 tiger shrimp, shelled and deveined
½ cup shredded Dungeness crab meat
½ teaspoon diced chili pepper
¼ cup white wine
1 pound angel hair pasta
2¼ cups Spicy Tomato Sauce (see below)

1. Place the oil in a skillet over medium heat. Add the garlic, lobster meat, shrimp, and crab meat, and sauté for 2 to 3 minutes, until the meat is pink.
2. Add the chili pepper and white wine. Simmer until the wine is reduced out.
3. Bring a large pot of water to a rolling boil, and add the pasta. Cook according to package directions, drain, and mix with the Spicy Tomato Sauce.
4. Place the pasta on serving plates, and arrange the seafood around the edges. Serve immediately.

"Instead of Turkey" Tofu Turkey

Bruce, our pet turkey, showed us what intelligent and charming birds
turkeys really are. This "turkey" is great at Thanksgiving, Christmas,
or any time you want a "roast" with stuffing.
It can even be used cold in sandwiches just like real turkey.

Yield: 8 servings

5 pounds firm tofu

Stuffing
1 cup diced celery
1 cup diced onions
1 cup diced fresh mushrooms, or ½ cup canned mushrooms, drained well
1–2 cloves garlic, minced (optional)
¼ cup vegetable broth or water
2 tablespoons sesame, flax, walnut, or peanut oil
1 tablespoon black pepper
½ cup low-sodium soy sauce or Bragg's Liquid, divided
½ cup ground nuts
4 cups cubed whole wheat bread
½ cup minced fresh parsley, or ¼ cup dried parsley
¼ cup minced dried sage
2 tablespoons each marjoram, thyme, savory, rosemary, and celery seed

1. Drain the tofu by mashing it and then placing it in a large colander lined with cheesecloth. Cover the colander with cheesecloth or a clean towel and a small plate. Place something heavy on the plate (about 5 or 6 pounds), and leave the tofu to drain for 2 to 3 hours. Be sure to leave a plate or bowl under the colander to catch the run off.
2. To make the stuffing, sauté the celery, onions, mushrooms, and garlic (optional) in the vegetable broth or water. Add the sesame oil, pepper, and ¼ cup of the soy sauce. Cover and cook five minutes until the vegetables are soft. Add the nuts, bread cubes, parsley, sage, and the remaining spices. Toss to mix well.
3. Remove the weighted plate and cheesecloth from tofu. Hollow out the tofu to leave a 1-inch lining all the way around the colander. Transfer the stuffing to the tofu-lined colander, and pack in firmly. Cover with remaining tofu, and pat down firmly.

4. Flip the colander over onto a nonstick baking sheet flat side down.
5. Baste the "turkey" with the remaining ¼ cup of soy sauce.
6. Cover with foil and bake 1 hour until golden, and then baste again.
7. Using two large spatulas, transfer the tofu turkey to a serving platter. Serve as you would serve turkey.

"Instead of Turkey" Gravy

Yield: 6 servings

2 cups water
1 cup diced fresh mushrooms, or ½ cup canned mushrooms, drained well
½ cup finely minced onion
3 tablespoons nutritional yeast
2 tablespoons vegetable oil
1 cube vegetable bouillon
Mrs. Dash seasoning to taste
Whole wheat or unbleached flour

1. Boil the water. Then combine all the ingredients except the flour in a large saucepan, and simmer for 4 to 5 minutes.
2. While stirring the mixture, slowly add the flour a spoonful at a time. Stir with a whisk or fork to avoid lumps until gravy reaches desired consistency. Serve warm over "Instead of Turkey Tofu Turkey or Stuffed Winter Squash.

"Instead of Meat" Balls

Great with spaghetti!

Yield: 24 "meat" balls

1 recipe Garden Burgers (page 000)

1. Form the Garden Burger mix into balls.
2. Place the balls on a nonstick baking sheet. Bake at 350°F, turning occasionally, until all sides are evenly browned. Serve over spaghetti with marinara sauce.

Cashew Nut Gravy

Yield: 4 servings

1 cup cashews
3 tablespoons low-sodium soy sauce, or Bragg's Liquid to taste
2 tablespoons cornstarch or arrowroot powder
2 tablespoons powder egg replacer
1 tablespoon nutritional yeast
1½ teaspoons onion powder
2 cups hot water
¾ cup liquid nondairy creamer, rice milk, or soymilk

1. Place all of the ingredients except the water and the nondairy creamer in a food processor and process until the mixture forms a paste. Add the water, and process to blend.
2. Pour the mixture into a medium-sized saucepan, and bring to a boil over high heat.
3. Remove the saucepan from the heat. Add the nondairy creamer, and stir. Serve with "Instead of Turkey" Tofu Turkey.

Mushroom Gravy

Yield: 4 servings

1 cup whole wheat flour
2 tablespoons sesame oil
2 medium onions, diced
6 cups sliced mushrooms
6–7 cups water

1. Spread the flour on an ungreased cookie sheet. Roast in a 250°F oven until golden.
2. While the flour is roasting, place the sesame oil in a large skillet over medium-high heat. Add the onions and mushrooms, and sauté until the onions are soft.
3. In a large bowl, mix the flour and water until smooth. Add the flour mixture to the onions and mushrooms, and simmer over low heat for 15 to 20 minutes, stirring to prevent lumps and burning. Serve warm.

"Veggie Burger"

Yield: 6 patties

1 cup cooked, well-drained beans
1 cup uncooked oats
¾ cup coarsely ground nuts
¼ cup minced celery
¼ cup minced onions
3 tablespoons finely grated raw beet
3 tablespoons finely chopped black olives
2 tablespoons low-sodium soy sauce or Bragg's Liquid
2 tablespoons sesame seeds
1 tablespoon vegetable seasoning mix
1 teaspoon basil
¼ teaspoon each thyme, sage, and mustard powder.

1. Combine the ingredients in a large bowl, and mix well.
2. Form the mixture into burger patties.
3. Grill the patties for 10 to 15 minutes, turning over at about 5 to 7 minutes for even grilling, until cooked through. Serve as you would serve hamburgers.

Easy Homemade 1000 Island Dressing

A good "secret sauce" for burgers.

Yield: 2 cups

1 cup egg-free mayonnaise
¾ cup catsup
3 tablespoons sweet pickle relish
½ to ¾ teaspoon Mrs. Dash seasoning mix

1. Combine all the ingredients in a medium-sized bowl.
2. Cover and refrigerate until needed. Serve on burgers or sandwiches.

Garden Burgers

Yield: 6 patties

1 cup TVP granules*
¾ cup hot water
1 tablespoon catsup
¼ cup chopped onion
2 tablespoons chopped olives
¼ cup chopped celery
1 teaspoon dried Italian seasoning
1 tablespoon dried parsley
1 tablespoon dried paprika
¼ cup mashed cooked rice, beans, or lentils
2 tablespoons powder egg replacer
¼ cup whole wheat flour
1 tablespoon nut butter or tahini to taste (optional)

1. In a large bowl, combine the TVP granules, hot water, and catsup. Stir and let sit for about 15 minutes.
2. Fold the onion, olives, and celery into the TVP mixture.
3. Add the Italian seasoning, parsley, paprika, and rice. Stir to mix.
4. Add the powder egg replacer and whole wheat flour. (If you can't find egg replacer, increase flour to ½ cup.)
5. Mix in the nut butter or tahini (optional).
6. Cover the mixture, and refrigerate for 1 hour.
7. Form the mixture into burger patties.
8. Cook the patties on a nonstick skillet until brown on both sides. Serve as you would serve hamburgers.

---

* Made from soybeans, this meat substitute has the texture of ground beef. Look for it in health food stores.

Heather's Easy-Baked Eggplant Parmigiana

*Baking the eggplant instead of coating it in batter and frying it
the traditional way means a lot less calories!
And this version is quicker and requires very little clean up.*

Yield: 6 servings

*1 or 2 medium eggplants
1 jar (30 ounces) marinara sauce
Soy or low-fat mozzarella cheese
2 cups sliced fresh mushrooms (optional)
Parmesan cheese (optional)*

1. Slice the eggplant into ½- to 1-inch slices.
2. Spread the eggplant slices onto a nonstick baking sheet in a single layer, and place under a broiler until browned. Then turn the slices over, and brown other side.
3. Spray a lasagna dish with vegetable oil.
4. Place the eggplant slices in a single layer across the bottom of the lasagna dish. Cover the slices with a layer of the marinara sauce and mushrooms (optional). Cover the marinara sauce and mushrooms with a layer of the mozzarella cheese.
5. Repeat this layering process until the eggplant slices are used up. Top with a layer of the Parmesan cheese, if desired.
6. Bake in oven at 350°F until the cheese is bubbly.
7. Remove from the oven and let sit for about 5 minutes. Then cut into serving size portions and enjoy. For a variation, follow steps 1 through 3, then use just one layer of the eggplant slices, topping each piece with a spoonful of the marinara sauce. Sprinkle the sauce with the mozzarella cheese, and broil on a nonstick cookie sheet until brown and bubbly. This makes a crisper Eggplant Parmesan.

No Fry Sweet Potato Fries

A wonderful change from French fried potatoes.
You can also use regular Russet potatoes.

Yield: 6 servings

4 medium sweet potatoes (about 4 pounds)
Vegetable coating spray or 1 tablespoon olive oil
Pepper or salt substitute to taste (optional)

1. Scrub the sweet potatoes, and cut lengthwise in ½-inch thick wedges.
2. Heat the oven to 450°F.
3. Spray a baking sheet with an even layer of the vegetable coating spray. Or rub ½ tablespoon of the olive oil onto hands, and then rub on half of the potato wedges, and then rub the other ½ tablespoon of olive oil into hands and onto the remaining potato wedges.
4. Place the wedges on the baking sheet, and bake for 30 minutes, turning occasionally for even baking. Bake until evenly golden or until they are tender to the touch of a fork.
5. Season with the pepper and salt substitute, if desired. Serve hot.

Crisp and Fruity Coleslaw

A refreshing coleslaw, chockfull of fiber.

Yield: 8 servings

1 container (8 ounces) vanilla low-fat yogurt
1 tablespoon chopped fresh mint, or 1 teaspoon dried mint
1 small pineapple, peeled, cored, and cut into 1-inch chunks, or 1 can (20 ounces) unsweetened pineapple chunks, drained
1 medium carrot, peeled and shredded
1 medium apple, cored and shredded
½ medium jicama, shredded (optional)
3 cups shredded green cabbage (1 small head)

1. In a large bowl, combine the yogurt and mint. Add the remaining ingredients, and toss gently to coat well.
2. Cover and refrigerate for at least 1 hour. Garnish with a sprig of mint, and serve.

Stuffed Winter Squash

This really looks good on the holiday table.

Yield: 2 servings

1 large acorn squash
1 medium onion, diced
2 stalks celery, sliced
¼ cup vegetable broth or water
2 medium apples, chopped (peeled, if desired)
½ cup prunes or raisins, chopped
½ cup chopped walnuts or pecans
1 teaspoon poultry stuffing seasoning
¼ cup chopped fresh parsley, or 1 tablespoon dried parsley
2 cups stuffing mix or dried cubed whole wheat bread

1. Cut the squash in half, and scoop out the insides.
2. To cook, either cover the squash with wax paper and microwave on high for 10 minutes, or place the squash in a pan with ¼-inch water, cut side down, and bake in the oven for 30 to 40 minutes at 350°F.
3. Place the onion, celery, and vegetable broth or water in a medium saucepan, over medium heat, and cook, stirring occasionally, until the vegetables are soft.
4. Add the apples and prunes, and cook for another 5 to 7 minutes covered, stirring occasionally.
5. There should still be liquid in the saucepan, if not, add ⅛ cup. Fold in the nuts, seasoning, parsley, and stuffing mix, until all are moist.
6. Fill the squash halves with the stuffing mixture, and return to the oven until the tops look crispy and golden. Serve immediately.

A COMPASSIONATE COOKOUT

You don't have to give up picnics and backyard barbecues just because you don't eat meat. Here are some helpful suggestions for a humane cookout.

- Veggie "burgers" and tofu "hot dogs" taste even better, and are easier on the body, than meat. You can find veggie burger mixes in the natural or gourmet food section of your supermarket (or you can try the "Veggie Burger" recipe on page 325, or Garden Burgers on page 326), and frozen tofu dogs in the freezer cases of health food stores.

- Harvest Burger has the classic flavor of an all-American burger without the meat. This product, along with Chili Fixins, Taco Fixins, and Sloppy Joe Fixins, are from Archer Daniels Midland Company and can be ordered from Harvest Direct, Inc. 1–800–835–2867 or by mail, P.O. Box 4514, Decatur, IL 62525-4514. They have a wonderful catalog called "Vegetarian Lifestyle." They offer a variety of products made from TVP.

- For a wonderful barbecue alternative, grill tempeh, tofu, eggplant slices, or sweet bell peppers. You can also baste vegetable shish-kabobs with Italian dressing or a barbecue sauce and grill until slightly blackened.

- Try grilled corn on the cob. Take fresh ears in the husk, and grill for 10–12 minutes, turning frequently.

- On a nonstick baking sheet, baste ½-inch slices of drained, firm tofu with olive oil, Italian dressing, or barbecue sauce, and bake at 450°F. After 10 minutes, turn slices over and brown on other side for 10–15 minutes. These slices can then be barbecued on shish-kabobs or on the grill, or used in a sandwich or burger bun.

APPENDIX 2

The Protocol for Administration of Chelation Therapy

Clearly stated in the *Protocol of the American College of Advancement in Medicine for the Safe and Effective Administration of EDTA Chelation Therapy* (1989) are the following words:

Alzheimer's disease will often improve or slow in its progression following a course of EDTA chelation therapy. Favorable results are more often seen in the earlier stages of that disease. If the degree of pretreatment dementia is fluctuating, mental status will frequently stabilize at the best point, and will occasionally become much improved. Results are usually poor in the treatment of far advanced dementias.

It takes a longer course of treatment to effect a reversal of DAT or other forms of senile dementia because EDTA and most of its derivatives do not pass readily through certain natural body and brain barriers such as cell membranes, endothelias, or the blood/brain barrier. In the treatment of lead poisoning, for example, EDTA rapidly clears any lead that is circulating from the blood, but it can only indirectly remove intracellular lead, particularly that in the central nervous system.[1] The chelation does work, but it takes a decidedly longer time in its administration with many more treatments required to restore short term and long term memories affected by the pathology of neurofibrillary tangles.

The protocol for administering chelation therapy calls for a particular formulation of ingredients to be used for intravenous (IV) infusion. They are:

- A *carrier solution* that is iso-osmolar (of equal pressure) of 250, 500, or 1,000 ml. The infusion bottle is mixed individually for each patient. Ringer's lactate (a clear colorless solution of sodium, potassium, and calcium chlorides having the same osmotic presure of blood serum), normal or one-half normal saline (salt solution), or 5 percent glucose may be used. The final solution will be hyper-osmolar which causes no adverse effects.

- *EDTA* in a dose of 50 mg per kg of lean body weight administered to patients with normal renal (kidney) function, to a maximum dose of 3.0 gm in a large patient. If creatinine clearance is less than 100 ml per minute, the dose based on body weight is reduced by multiplying the dose by a fraction equal to creatinine clearance divided by 100.

- *Magnesium* in the form of magnesium chloride (MgCl) or magnesium sulfate (MgSO4) to provide a 2-gram dose is added to each infusion bottle (10 ml of 20% MgCl solution). That amount of magnesium converts 3.0 gm of disodium EDTA (Na2-EDTA) to magnesium EDTA (Mg-EDTA). It is not necessary to reduce the dose of magnesium for lower doses of EDTA. Magnesium has two functions: First, it prevents pain from the EDTA, and second, magnesium is therapeutic for many conditions treated with EDTA. Most patients who enter EDTA chelation therapy have suboptimal amounts of body magnesium and many are deficient.

- *Sodium bicarbonate buffer* for intravenous use added in a ratio of 10 meq bicarbonate to 3 gm EDTA acts as a neutralizer of the acid formed from EDTA-releasing hydrogen ions that combine with the magnesium. The resulting acid pH of the infusion would cause localized pain and inflammation at the site of infusion with possible localized phlebitis if not for the buffering effect of sodium bicarbonate to raise the solution to a physiological pH.

- Local anesthetic such as lidocaine or procaine, even with the use of magnesium and bicarbonate buffer, prevents pain at the infusion site. Five ml of a 2% solution of either anesthetic agent added directly into the infusion bottle helps to prevent allergic sensitivity. The dose should not exceed 10 ml of a 2% solution given over three hours. Although rare, allergic reactions to these local anesthetics have occurred.

- *Heparin* in a dose of about 1,500 units tends to reduce the incidence of localized phlebitis proximal to the infusion site. This small amount will not cause much systemic anticoagulation, but it may be contraindicated for patients with bleeding tendencies or for those already receiving full anticoagulating doses of warfarin.

- *Ascorbate* as vitamin C, in a dose of 4 to 20 gm, may be added to the infusion bottle. Ascorbate makes a distilled water carrier solution iso-osmolar.[2] It is also a weak chelating agent and is synergistic with EDTA to enhance removal of lead from the central nervous system.

- *Miscellaneous* nutrients may be added to the solution such as vitamin B-complex, including B_1, B_6, and B_{12}. EDTA depletes vitamin B_6, which should be supplemented by the patient during IV therapy. B-complex vitamins are synergistic with antioxidant defenses. Potassium chloride may be added to the infusion for patients who are taking potassium-wasting diuretics or are otherwise found to be in need of potassium by laboratory testing.

- *Other ingredients*, while sometimes included in the infusion bottle at the discretion of the chelating physician, are not a part of the official ACAM protocol for EDTA administration. Efficacy of the resulting solution then becomes the responsibility of that prescribing physician.

PRECAUTIONS IN THE IV PROCEDURE FOR EDTA

EDTA is administered intravenously in not less than three hours. The longer an IV drip takes to proceed with this chelating substance, the less chance of the patient experiencing any type of side effect. A small, 25-gauge butterfly needle is preferred for the IV procedure because it is easier and less painful to insert, and the tiny lumen prevents any excessive rate of infusion. Some people being treated do get impatient with the slow rate of flow of their infusions and may attempt to speed up the process on their own. However, it is difficult to infuse 500 ml of solution through a 25-gauge needle in much less than three hours.

The therapeutic benefit of IV infusions with EDTA is dependent on the total number of injections and not related so much to the interval between treatments. In no case should EDTA infusions be given more often than once in twenty-four hours. The accepted IV interval among chelating physicians to administer EDTA to any one patient is not closer than forty-eight hours between infusions and the generally acknowledged standard is a schedule of two to three weekly treatments. Each time, then, measurements are made to determine that the patient's serum creatinine and kidney function tests are within normal or satisfactory limits. If an individual is debilitated or has a preexisting kidney insufficiency, the delay of two weeks or more between infusions may be required. The doctor's judgment is a main determining factor here.

Renal function tests should be carefully followed in all patients receiving EDTA and the laboratory costs for such measurements figured into the estimated expenditures for chelation treatment. The ACAM protocol calls for repeated pre-infusion urine analyses. Then it recommends serum creatinine measurements before every third treatment. If pretreatment renal function tests are not completely normal or if treatments are taken by the patient more than once weekly, serum creatinine and urinalysis should be performed as often as before each infusion. An upward trend in serum creatinine is a reason for the doctor to discontinue therapy until the patient's creatinine reading returns to baseline levels. On its own, renal function will usually improve to pretreatment levels or better within two to four weeks.

"If a rising trend in serum creatinine is not detected early and if treatment is continued in the face of progressively impaired renal function," warns the ACAM *Protocol*, "more serious renal damage will result. Lasting renal impairment from EDTA has never ever been reported when the precautions described in this *Protocol* were followed."

In fact, renal function improves, on the average, after the chelating physician properly administers a series of EDTA infusions.[3,4,5,6] Admittedly there have been reports of lasting kidney damage occurring from excessively large doses of EDTA, administered too rapidly or too often for individual tolerance and without close monitoring of renal function.[18] Variable tolerance among patients who are unusually sensitive to EDTA makes frequent renal function testing imperative.

The total number of infusions for optimal therapeutic effect varies from one patient to the next. A series of twenty infusions is minimum for patients with symptomatic disease. It is not unusual for some people to take forty or more infusions before they feel any significant benefit. In cases of patients with early-stage Alzheimer's disease, positive brain-cell response is not likely to appear until twenty or more—perhaps as many as one hundred IV infusions with EDTA—are received by them. Be aware that full benefit from treatment definitely does not normally occur for up to three months following a completed series of infusions.

Follow-up chelation treatments may be taken once or twice monthly for long term maintenance, to sustain health improvement, and to prevent the recurrence of symptoms. Moreover, informed people, in particular chelating physicians themselves, take chelation therapy as a preventive measure against body and brain deterioration. It is the ultimate anti-aging therapy which assures longevity and an alert mind until the moment of physical death.

North American Physicians Who Offer Chelation Therapy

Key to Worldwide American College
of Advancement in Medicine Physician's List

PROFESSIONAL LEVEL CODES

DIPL   Diplomate
D/C   Diplomate candidate
P   Licensed physician who follows the program now
put forth by the American College of Advancement
in Medicine.

SPECIALTY CODES

A	Allergy	IM	Internal Medicine
AC	Acupuncture	LM	Legal Medicine
AN	Anesthesiology	MM	Metabolic Medicine
AR	Arthritis	NT	Nutrition
AU	Auriculotherapy	OBS	Obstetrics
BA	Bariatrics	OME	Orthomolecular Medicine
CD	Cardiovascular	OPH	Ophthalmology
CS	Chest Disease	OSM	Osteopathic Manipulation
CT	Chelation Therapy	P	Psychiatry
DD	Degenerative Disease	PD	Pediatrics
DIA	Diabetes	PH	Public Health
EM	Environmental Medicine	PM	Preventive Medicine
END	Endocrinology	PMR	Physical Medicine & Rehabilitation
FP	Family Practice		
GE	Gastroenterology	PO	Psychiatry Orthomolecular
GER	Geriatrics	PUD	Pulmonary Diseases
GP	General Practice	R	Radiology
GYN	Gynecology	RHI	Rhinology
HGL	Hypoglycemia	RHU	Rheumatology
HO	Hyperbaric Oxygen	S	Surgery
HOM	Homeopathy	WR	Weight Reduction
HYP	Hypnosis	YS	Yeast Syndrome

American College of Advancement in Medicine (ACAM) Physicians—United States

ALABAMA

Birmingham

P. Gus J. Prosch Jr., MD (P)
759 Valley St.
Birmingham, AL 35226
(205) 823-6180
A,AR,CT,GP,NT,OME

ALASKA

Anchorage

Sandra Denton, MD (DIPL)
4115 Lake Otis Pkwy., #200
Anchorage, AK 99508
(907) 563-6200
Emerg. and Env. Medicine

F. Russell Manuel, MD (P)
4200 Lake Otis Blvd., #304
Anchorage, AK 99508
(907) 562-7070
CT,GP,PM

Robert Rowen, MD (DIPL)
615 E. 82nd Ave., Ste 300
Anchorage, AK 99518
(907) 344-7775
AC,CT,FP,,NT,PM,HYP

Soldotna

Paul G. Isaak, MD
Box 219
Soldotna, AK 99669
(907) 262-9341
RETIRED

Wasilla

Robert E. Martin, MD (P)
P.O. Box 870710
Wasilla, AK 99667
(907) 376-5284
AU,CT,FP,GP,OS,PM

ARIZONA

Glendale

Lloyd D. Armold, DO (DIPL)
4901 W. Bell Rd., Ste 2
Glendale, AZ 85308
(602) 939-8916
AR,CT,GP,MM,PM,OSM

Mesa

Wlliam W. Halcomb, DO (P)
4323 E. Broadway, Ste 109
Mesa, AZ 85206
(602) 832-3014
A,CT,GP,HO,OSM,PM

Parker

S.W. Meyer, DO (D/C)
332 River Front Dr.
P.O. BOx 1870
Parker, AZ 85344
(602) 669-8911
CD,CT,DD,FP,OS,RHU

Phoenix

Terry S. Friedmann, MD (DIPL)
2701 E. Camelback Rd., Suite 381
Phoenix, AZ 85016
(602) 381-0800
A, CT, FP, HGL, HYP, NT

Stanley R. Olsztyn, MD (P)
Whitton Place
3610 N. 44St., Ste. 210
Phoenix, AZ 85018
(602) 954-0811
A, CT, PM, DD

Prescott

John M. Hope, MD
831 Gail Gardner Way
Prescott, AZ 86301
(602) 778-9510
OPH

Gordon H. Josephs, DO (P)
315 W. Goodwin St.
Prescott, AZ 86303
(602) 778-6169
CT, GP, NT, PM, S

Scottsdale

Gordon H. Josephs, DO (P)
7315 E. Evans
Scottsdale, AZ 85260
(602) 998-9232
CT, GP, NT, PM, S

Tempe

Garry Gordon, MD (DIPL)
5535 S. Compass
Tempe, AZ 85283
(602) 838-2079
CT, NT, PM

ARKANSAS

Hot Springs

William Wright, MD (P)
1 Mercy Dr., Suite 211
Hot Springs, AR 71913
(501) 824-3312
A, CT, GP, IM

Leslie

Melissa Taliaferro, MD (DIPL)
Cherry Street, P.O. Box 400
Leslie, AR 72645
(501) 447-2599 FAX (501) 447-2917
AC, CT, DD, IM, NT, PM, RHU

Little Rock

Norbert J. Becquet, MD (DIPL)
115 W. Sixth St.
Little Rock, AR 72201
(501) 375-4419
CT, OPH, PM, RHU

John Gustavus, MD (D/C)
4721 E. Broadway
N. Little Rock, AR 72117
(501) 758-9350
FP

Springdale

Doty Murphy III, MD (P)
812 Dorman
Springdale, AR 72764
(501) 756-3251
CD, CT

CALIFORNIA

Albany

Ross B. Gordon, MD
405 Kains Ave.
Albany, CA 94706
(510) 526-3232 FAX (510) 526-3217
BA, CT, NT, PM

Beverly Hills

Cathie Ann Lippman, MD
8383 Wilshire Blvd., #360
(213) 653-0486
A, AC, PM, YS

Callahan

Kenneyh A. Wolkoff, MD
Box 180
Callahan, CA 98014
NO REFERRALS

Campbell

Carol A. Shamlin, MD (D/C)
621 E. Campbell, Ste. 11A
Campbell, CA 95008
(408) 378-7970
A, CT, GP, MM, OME, PM

Chico

Eva Jalkotzy, MD (P)
156 Eaton Rd., #E
Chico, CA 95926
(916) 893-3080
CT, FP, GP, NT, PM

Concord

John P. Toth, MD (D/C)
2299 Bacon St., Ste. 10
Concord, CA 94520
(510) 682-5660
A, FP, GP

Corte Madera

Michael Rosenbaum, MD (P)
45 San Clemente Drive, Suite B-130
Corte Madera, CA 94925
(415) 927-9450 FAX: (415) 927-3759
A, HGL, MM, NT, P, TS

Covina

James Privitera, MD (D/C)
105 No. Grandview Ave.
Covina, CA 91723
(818) 966-1618
A, CT, MM, NT

Daly City

Charles K. Dahlgren, MD (P)
1800 Sullivan Ave., #604
Daly City, CA 94015
(415) 756-2900
A, NT, RHI, S

El Cajon

William J. Saccoman, MD (P)
505 N. Mollison Ave., Suite 103
El Cajon, CA 92021
(619) 440-3838
CT, NT, PM

Encino

A. Leonard Klepp, MD (DIPL)
16311 Ventura Blvd., #725
Encino, CA 91436
(818) 981-5511 FAX: (818) 907-1468
CT, FP, PM, HGL, NT

Fresno

David J. Edwards, MD (P)
360 S. Clovis Ave.
Fresno, CA 93727
(209) 251-5066
GYN, PM, CT

Hollywood

James J. Jullian, MD (P)
1654 Cahuenga Blvd.
Hollywood, CA 90028
(213) 467-5555
AR, BA, CT, NT, PM

Joan Priestly, MD (P)
7080 Hollywood Blvd., Suite 603
Hollywood, CA 90028
(213) 957-4217
A, Env Med, FP, NT

Huntington Beach

Joan M. Resk, DO (D/C)
18821 Delaware St., Suite 203
Huntington Beach, CA 92648
(714) 842-5591 FAX (714) 843-9580
CD, CT, DD, OSM, NT, PM

Kentfield

Carolyn Albrecht, MD
10 Wolfe Grade
Kentfield, CA
RETIRED

La Jolla

Charles Moss, MD
8950 Villa La Jolla, #2162
La Jolla, CA 92037
(619) 457-1314
AC, FP, HGL, MM, NT, YS, Env.
Med.

Lake Forest

David A. Steenblock, DO (DIPL)
22706 Aspen, Suite 500
Lake Forest, CA 92630
(714) 770-9616 FAX (714) 770-9775
CD, CT, DIA, IM

Laytonville

Eugene D. Finkle, MD (D/C)
P.O. Box 309
Laytonville, CA 95454
(707) 984-6151 FAX (707) 984- 6151
CT, GP, GYN, MM, NT, PM

Long Beach

H. Richard Casdorph, MD, PhD,
  FACAM (DIPL)
1703 Termino Ave., Suite 201
Long Beach, CA 90804
(310) 597-8716 FAX: (310) 597-4616
CD, CS, CT, DIA, IM, NT

Los Altos

Robert F. Cathcart III, MD
127 Second St., Ste. 4
Los Altos, CA 94022
(415) 949-2822
A, AR, CT, DD, OME, PM

Claude Marquette, MD (P)
5050 El Camino Real, #110
Los Altos, CA 94022
(415) 964-6700
A, BA, CT, NT, PM

Los Angeles

Laszlo Belenyessy, MD (P)
12732 Washington Blvd. #D
Los Angeles, CA 90066
(213 822-4014
A, AC, BA, CT, GP, NT

M. Jahangirl, MD
2156 South Santa Fe
Los Angeles, CA 90058
(213) 587-3218
A, AC, CT, FP, GP

Byung Sun Park, MD
945 S. Western Ave., #102
Los Angeles, CA 90006
(213) 734-6684
IM

Manhattan Beach

Joseph Sclabbarrasi, MD
571-35 Street
Manhattan Beach, CA 90266
AC, HOM, NT

Monterey

Lon B. Work, MD
841 Foam St., #D
Monterey, CA 93940
(408) 655-0215
CT, DD, GYN, HGL, NT, RHU

Newport Beach

Julian Whitaker, MD
4321 Birch St., Suite 100
Newport Beach, CA 92660
(714) 851-1550 FAX (714) 851-9970
CD, CT, DIA, DD, NT, PM

North Hollywood

David C. Freeman, MD (P)
11311 Camarillo St., #103
North Hollywood, CA 91602
(818) 985-1103
CD, CT, END, HGL, NT, PM

Oceanside

A. Hal Thatcher, MD
2552 Cornwall St.
Oceanside, CA 92054
RETIRED

Oxnard

Mohamed Moharram, MD (P)
300 W. 5th St., Ste. B
Oxnard, CA 93030
(805) 483-2355
CT, CS, DIA, DD, GP, PM

Palm Desert

David H. Tang, MD (D/C)
74133 El Paseo, #6
Palm desert, CA 92260
(619) 341-2113 FAX (619) 341-2724
AC, CT, IM, MM, NT, PM

Palm Springs

Sean Degan, MD (D/C)
2825 Tahqultz McCallum, Suite 200
Palm Springs, CA 92262
(619) 320-4292
AC, CT, NT, PM

Porterville

John B. Park, MD (D/C)
200 North G St.
Porterville, CA 93257
(209) 781-6224
AN, BA, FP, GP, PM, S

Rancho Mirage

Charles Farinella, MD (P)
69-730 Hwy. 111, #106A
Rancho Mirage, CA 92270
CT, GP, PM

Redding

Bessie J. Tillman, MD (D/C)
2054 Market St.
Redding, CA 96001
((16) 246-3022
A, CT, DD, NT, PM, YS

Reseda

Ilona Abraham, MD
19231 Victoria Blvd.
Reseda, CA 91335
(818) 345-8721
CT, P, A, CD, AC

Sacramento

J. E. Dugas, MD
3400 Cottage Way, #206
Sacramento, CA 95825
RETIRED

Michael Kwiker, DO
3301 Alta Arden, Ste. 3
Sacramento, CA 95825
(916) 489-4400
A, CT, DIA, NT

San Clemente

William Doell, DO (DIPL)
971 Calle Negocio
San Clemente, CA 92672
NO REFERRALS

San Diego

Lawernce Taylor, MD (P)
3330 Third Ave., #402
San Diego, CA 92103
(619) 296-2952
A, CT, FP, NT, PM, YS

San Francisco

Richard A. Kunin, MD
2698 Pacific Ave.
San Francisco, CA 94115
(415) 346-2500
CT, DD, HYP, PM, P, PO

Russell A. Lemesh, MD
595 Buckingham Wy #320
San Francisco, CA 94132
(415) 731-5907
CD, END, GER, IM, MM, PM

Paul Lynn, MD (DIPL)
345 W. Portal Ave.
San Francisco, CA 94127
(415) 566-1000
A, AR, CT, DD, NT, PM

Denise R. Mark, MD (DIPL)
345 Portal Ave.
San Francisco, CA 94127
(415) 566-1000
CT, DIA, DD, IM, PM, YS

Gary S. Ross, MD
500 Sutter, #300
San Francisco, CA 94102
(415) 398-0555
A, AC, CT, DD, FP, NT, PM

San Leandro

Steven H. Gee, MD (DIPL)
595 Estudillo St.
San Leandro, CA 94577
(510) 483-5881
AC, BA, CT, GP

San Luis Obispo

Thomas A. Dorman, MD
171 N. Santa Rosa St., #A
San Luis Obispo, CA 93405
(805) 781-3388 FAX (805) 544-3126
IM

San Marcos

William C. Kubitschek, DO
1194 Calle Maria
San Marcos, CA 92069
(619) 744-6991
AC, FP, NT, OSM, PM, PMR

San Rafael

Ross Gordon, MD (DIPL)
4144 Redwood Highway
San Rafael, CA 94903
(415) 499-9377
BA, CT, NT, PM

Santa Ana

Ronald Wempen, MD
3620 S. Bristol St., #306
Santa Ana, CA 92704
(714) 546-4325
A, AC, MM, NT, PO, YS

Santa Barbara

H. J. Hoegerman, MD (DIPL)
101 W. Arrellaga, Ste. B
Santa Barbara, CA 93101
(805) 965- 5229
A, CT, CD, GP, DIA, FP, RHU

Mohamed Moharram, MD (P)
101 W. Arrellaga, Ste. B
Santa Barbara, CA 93101
(805) 965-5229
CT, CS, DIA, DD, GP, PM

Santa Maria

Donald E. Reiner, MD (P)
1414-D South Miller
Santa Maria, CA 93454
(805) 925- 0961
CT, GP, OME, PM, S

Santa Monica

Michael Rosenbaum, MD (P)
2730 Wilshire Blvd., #110
Santa Monica, CA 90403
(310) 453-4424
A, HGL, MM, NT, P, TS

Murray Susser, MD (DIPL)
2730 Wilshire Blvd., #110
Santa Monica, CA 90403
(310) 453-4424 FAX (310) 828-0281
A, CT, NT, OME

Santa Rosa

Terri Su, MD (D/C)
1038 4th St., #3
Santa Rosa, CA 95404
(707) 571-7560
AC, AN, CT, FP, NT, PM

Seal Beach

Allen Green, MD (P)
909 Electric Ave., #212
Seal Beach, CA 90740
(310) 493-4526
AC, CT, FP, NT, PM

Sherman Oaks

Rosa M. Ami Belli, MD
13481 Cheltenham Dr.
Sherman Oaks, CA 91423
NO REFERRALS

Clifford Fraser, MD
4910 Van Nuys Blvd., #110
Sherman Oaks, CA 91403
(818) 986-2199
DD, END, FP, MM, NT, PM

Smith River

JoAnn Hoffer, MD (D/C)
12559 Hwy. 101 North, (Mini-Mart)
Smith River, CA 95567
(707) 487-3405
CT, NT, PM

Lames D. Schuler, MD (DIPL)
12559 Hwy. 101 North, (Mini-Mart)
Smith River, CA 95567
(707) 487-3405
A, CT, DIA, PM, S, YS

Stanton

William J. Goldwag, MD (P)
7499 Cerritos Ave.
Stanton, CA 90680
(714) 827-5180
CT, NT, PM

Studio City

Charles E. Law Jr., MD (P)
3959 Laurel Canyon Blvd., Suite 1
Studio City, CA 91604
(818) 761-1661
AC, BA, CT, GP, NT, PM

Torrance

Anita Millen, MD (P)
1010 Crenshaw Blvd., Suite 170
Torrance, CA 90501
(301) 320-1132
CT, FP, GYN, NT, PM, DD

Van Nuys

Frank Mosler, MD (P)
14428 Gilmore St.
Van Nuys, CA 91401
(818) 785-7425
BA, CT, GP, HGL, NT, PM

Walnut Creek

Ingrid A. Bellwood, MD
106 Kendal Rd.
Walnut Creek, CA 94595
NO REFERRALS

Alan Shifman Charles, MD
1414 Maria Lane
Walnut Creek, CA 94596
(510) 937-3331
AC, CT, DD, FP, OM

Peter H. C. Mutke, MD (P)
1808 San Miguel Drive
Walnut Creek, CA 94596
(510) 933-2405
CT, HGL, HYP, NT, PM, YS

COLORADO

Colorado Springs

James R. Fish, MD (DIPL)
3030 N. Hancock
Colorado Springs, CO 80907
CT, HYP, PM

George Jeutersonke, DO (D/C)
5455 N. Union, #200
Colorado Springs, CO 80918
(719) 528-1960
A, AC, CT, HGL, NT, OSM, P

Englewood

John H. Altshuler, MD (P)
Greenwood Exec. Park, Building 10
7485 E. Peakview Ave.
Englewood, CO 80111
(303) 740-7771
HYP, IM

Grand Junction

William L. Reed, MD (D/C)
2700 G Road, #1-B
Grand Junction, CO 81506
NO REFERRALS

CONNECTICUT

Orange

Alan R. Cohen
325 Post Rd.
Orange, CT 06477
(203) 799-7733
FP, NT, PD, PM, YS

Robban Sica-Cohen, MD
325 Post Rd.
Orange, CT 06477
(203) 799-7733
A, AC, NT, PM, P, YS

Torrington

Jerrold N. Finnie, MD (P)
333 Kennedy Dr., #204
Torrington, CT 06790
(203) 489-8977
A, CT, CS, NT, RHI, YS

DISTRICT OF COLUMBIA

Washington

Paul Beals, MD (P)
2639 Connecticut Ane N. W.,
Suite 100
Washington, D. C. 20037
(202) 332-0370
CT, FP, NT, PM

George H. Mitchell, MD
2639 Connecticut Ave. NW,
Suite C-100
Washington, D. C. 20037
(202) 265-4111
A, NT

FLORIDA

Atlantic Beach

Richard Worsham, MD (D/C)
303 1st Street
Atlantic Beach, FL 32233
NO REFERRALS

Boca Raton

Leonard Haimes, MD (P)
7300 N. Federal Hwy., Suite 107
Boca Raton, FL 33487
(407) 994-3868 FAX (407) 997-8998
A, BA, CT, IM, NT, PM

Narinder Singh Parhar, MD (D/C)
7840 Glades Road, #220
Boca Raton, FL 33434
NO REFERRALS

Bradenton

Etri Meinikov, MD (D/C)
116 Manatee Ave. East
Bradenton, FL 34208
(813) 748-7943
CD, CT, DIA, GP, PM, YS

Crystal River

Azael Borromeo, MD
206 NE 3rd Street
Crystal River, FL 32629
(904) 795-7177
BA, GP

Fort Lauderdale

Stefano DiMauro, MD
1333 S. State Road 7
Tam O'Shanter Plaza
N. Lauderdale, FL 33068
(305) 978-6604
A, CT, DIA, FP, NT, PMR

Bruce Dooley, MD (D/C)
1493 S. E. 17th Street
Fort Lauderdale, FL 33316
(305) 527-9355
A, CT, GP, NT, PM, YS

Fort Myers

Gary L. Pynckel, DO (DIPL)
3940 Metro Parkway, #115
Fort Meyers, FL 33916
(813) 278-3377
CT, FP, GP, OSM, PM

Hollywood

Herbert Pardell, DO (DIPL)
7061 Taft ST.
Hollywood, FL 33020
(305) 989-5558
CT, DD, IM, MM, NT, PM

Homosassa

Carlos F. Gonzalez, MD (DIPL)
7991 So. Suncoast Blvd.
Homossasa, FL 32648
(904) 382-8282
A, CD, CS, END, PMR, RHU

Jacksonville

John Mauriello, MD
4063 Salisbury Rd., #206
Jacksonville, FL 32216
(904) 296-0900
AC, AN, GP, NT, PM, PMR

Juniper

Neil Ahner, MD (DIPL)
1080 E. Indiantown Rd.
Juniper, FL 33477
(407) 744-0077 FAX (407) 744-0094
CT, NT, PM

Lakeland

Harold Robinson, MD (P)
4406 S. Florida Ave., Suite 27
Lakeland, FL 33803
(813) 646-5088
CT, FP, GP, HGL, NT, PM

Lauderhill

Herbert R. Slavin, MD
7200 W. Commercial Blvd.,
Suite #210
Lauderhill, FL 33319
(305) 748-4991
CT, DIA, DD, GER, IM, NT

Maitland

Joya Lynn Schoen, MD (D/C)
341 No. Maitland Ave., Suite 200
Maitland, FL 32751
(407) 644-27 29 FAX (407) 644-1205
A, CT, HGL, OSM, Homeop.

Miami

Joseph G. Godorov, DO
9055 S. W. 87th Ave., Suite 307
Miami, Fl 33176
(305) 595-0671
CT, END, FP, HGL, NT, PM

Bernard J. Letourneau, DO (P)
6475 SW 40th Street
Miami, FL 33155
(305) 595-0671
CT, END, FP, HGL, NT, PM

Milton

William Watson, MD
600 Stewart St. N. E.
Milton, FL 32570
(904) 623-3836
BA, GP, S

New Smyrna Beach

William Campbell Douglas Jr., MD
2111 Ocean Drive
New Smyrna Beach, FL 32169
(904) 426-8803
FP, NT, PM

Martin Dayton, DO (DIPL)
18600 Collins Ave.
N. Miami Beach, FL 33160
(305) 931-8484
CT, FP, GER, NT, OSM, PM

Stefano DiMauro, MD
16666 N. E. 19th Ave., #101
N. Miami Beach, FL 33162
(305) 940-6474
A, CT, DIA, FP, NT, PMR

Ocala

George Graves, DO (P)
3501 N. E. Tenth St.
Ocala, FL 32670
(904) 236-2525 or (904) 732-3633
CT, DD, PM

Orange City

Travis L. Herring, MD (P)
106 West Fern Dr.
Orange City, FL 32763
(904) 775-0525
CT, FP, HOM, IM

Oviedo

Roy Kupsinel, MD
1325 Shangri-la Lane
Oviedo, FL 32765
(407) 365-6681 FAX (407) 365-1834
CT, DD, MM, NT, PM, TS

Palm Bay

Neil Ahner, MD (DIPL)
1200 Malabar Road
Palm Bay, FL 32907
(407) 729-8581
CT, NT, PM

Panama City

Naima ABD Elghany, MD (P)
710 Venetian Way
Panama City, FL 32405
(904) 763-7689
A, CD, IM, PUD, PH, PM

Pensacola

Ward Dean, MD (P)
P.O. Box 11097
Pensacola, FL 32524
NO REFERRALS
Pompano Beach

Dan C. Roehm, MD (P)
3400 Park Central Blvd. N.,
Suite 3450
Pompano Beach, FL 33064
(305) 977-3700 FAX (305) 977-0180
CD, CT, IM, MM, NT, OME

Port Canaveral

James Parsons, MD (D/C)
707 Mullet Dr., Ste. 110
Port Canaveral, FL 32920
(407) 784-2102
A, CT, MM, NT, PO, RHU

Port St. Lucie

Ricardo V. Barbaza, MD
1541 S.E. Port St. Lucie Blvd.
Port St. Lucie, FL 34952
(407) 335-4994
GP, NT, PM

Sarasota

Thomas McNaughton, MD (D/C)
1521 Dolphin St.
Sarasota, FL 34236
(813) 365-6273 FAX (813) 365-4269
CT, GP, NT, PM

Joseph Ossorlo, MD (P)
3900 Clark Rd., #H-5
Sarasota, FL 34277
(813) 921-6338
HYP, PM, P

St. Petersburg

Ray Wunderlich Jr., MD (DIPL)
666 6th Street South
St. Petersburg, FL 33701
(813) 822-3612
A, BA, CT, DD, HGL, MM, PO

Tampa

Donald J. Carrow, MD (P)
3902 Henderson Blvd., Suite 206
Tampa, FL 33629
(813) 832-3220 FAX (813) 282-1132
CD, CT, DIA, GP, HGL, NT

Eugene H. Lee, MD (P)
1804 W. Kennedy Blvd. #A
(813) 251-3089
AC, CT, NT, PM, GP, HGL

Venice

Thomas McNaughton, MD
540 South Nokomis Ave.
Venice, FL 34285
(813) 484-2167
CT, GP, NT, PM

Wauchula

Alfred S. Massam, MD (P)
528 West Main St.
Wauchula, FL 33873
CT, FP, PM

Winter Park

James M. Parsons, MD (D/C)
Great Western Bank Bldg.
#303 2699 Lee Rd.
Winter Park, Fl 32789
(407) 628-3399
A, CT, MM, NT, PO, RHU

Robert Rogers, MD (P)
1865 No. Semoran Blvd., Suite 204
Winter Park, FL 32789
(407) 679-2811
A, CD, CT, NT, PM

GEORGIA

Atlanta

Stephen Edelson, MD (D/C)
3833 Roswell Rd., #110
Atlanta, GA 30342
(404) 841-0088
CT, NT, FP, Env Med, PM

David Epstein, DO (P)
427 Moreland Ave., #100
Atlanta, GA 30307
(404) 525-7333
BA, CT, GP, NT, OSM, PM

Milton Fried, MD (DIPL)
4426 Tilly Mill Road
Atlanta, GA 30360
(404) 451-4857
A, CT, IM, NT, PM, PO

Bernard Miaver, MD (DIPL)
4480 North Shallowford Rd.
Atlanta, GA 30338
(404) 395-1600
CT, NT, PM

William E. Richardson, MD
1718 Peachtree St. N.W., #552
Atlanta, GA 30309
(404) 607-0570
CT, NT, PM

Camilla

Oliver L. Gunter, MD (DIPL)
24 N. Ellis Street
Camilla, GA 31730
(912) 336-7343
CT, DIA, DD, GP, NT, PU

Warner Robins

Terril J. Schneider, MD (P)
205 Dental Drive, Ste. 19
Warner Robins, GA 31088
(912) 929-1027
A, CT, FP, NT, PM, PMR

HAWAII

Honolulu

Frederick Lam, MD
1270 Queen Emma St., #501
Honolulu, HI 96813
NO REFERRALS

Kailua-Kona

Clifton Arrington, MD (P)
P.O. Box 649
Kealakekua, HI 96750
(808) 322-9400
BA, CT, FP, NT, PM

IDAHO

Coeur d'Alene

Charles T. McGee, MD
1717 Lincolnway, Ste. 108
Coer d'Alene, ID 83814
(208) 664-1478
A, CT, NT, OME, PM

Nampa

John O. Boxall, MD (P)
824 17th Ave. South
Nampa, ID 83651
(208) 466-3517
AC, CT, GP, HYP

Stephen Thornburgh, DO
824 17th Ave. So.
Nampa, ID 83651
(208) 466-3517
AC, CT, HOM, OS

Sandpoint

K. Peter McCallum, MD (DIPL)
2500 Selle Rd.
Sandpoint, ID 83864
(208) 263-5456
CT, NT, MM, PM, OME

ILLINOIS

Arlington Heights

Terrill K. Haws, DO (D/C)
121 So. Wilke Road, Suite 111
Arlington Heights, IL 60005
(708) 577-9451
CT, DD, FP, GP, OSM

William Maurer, DO, FACAM (DIPL)
3401 N. Kennicott Ave.
Arlington Heights, IL 60004
(800) 255-7030 FAX (708) 255-7700
CT, DIA, GP, NT, OSM, PM

Aurora

Thomas Hesselink, MD (D/C)
888 So. Edgelawn Dr., Suite 1735
Aurora, IL 60506
(708) 844-0011 FAX (708) 844-0500
A, CT, GP, NT, PM,
    Candida Belvedere

M. Paul Dommers, MD
554 S. Main St.
Belvedere, IL 61008
(815) 544-3112
AR, AU, CT, MM, PM

Chicago

Razvan Rentea, MD (P)
3525 W. Peterson, Ste. 611
Chicago, IL 60659
(312) 583-7793
GO, MM, PM

Geneva

Richard E. Hrdlicka, MD
302 Randall Rd., #206
Geneva, IL 60134
(708) 232-1900
A, BA, FP, NT, PM, YS

Glyn Ellyn

Robert S. Waters, MD (DIPL)
739 Roosevelt Road
Glen Ellyn, IL 60137
(708) 790-8100
CT, PM, OME

Hines

Ole Paly, MD
P.O. Box 1115
Hines, IL 60141
NO REFERRALS

Homewood

Frederick Weiss, MD
3207 W. 184th St.
Homewood, IL 60430
NO REFERRALS

Metamora

Stephen K. Elasser, DO, FACAM
205 S. Engelwood
Metamora, IL 61548
(309) 367-2321 FAX (309) 367-2324
CT, GP, HO, NT, OSM, PM

Moline

Terry W. Love, DO
2610 41st Street
Moline, IL 61252
(309) 764-2900
CT, NT, PM

Oak Park

Paul J. Dunn, MD (D/C)
715 Lake St.
Oak Park, IL 60301
(708) 383-3800
CT, HGL, NT, OSM, PM, YS

Ottawa

Terry W. Love, DO (DIPL)
645 W. Main
Ottawa, IL 61350
(815) 434-1977
AR, CT, GP, OSM, RHU, PM

St. Charles

Guillermo Justiniano, MD
77 Highgate Course
St. Charles, IL 60174
NO REFERRALS

Summit

Serafin C. Ilagan, MD
6252 S. Archer Rd.
Summit, IL 60501
(708) 458-0050
Gen. Surg.

Woodstock

John R. Tambone, MD
102 E. South St.
Woodstock, IL 60098
(815) 338-2345
A, CT, GP, NT, PM, HYP

Zion

Peter Senatore, DO
1911 27th St.
Zion, IL 60099
(708) 872-8722
CT, FP, GP

INDIANA

Clarksville

George Wolverton, MD (DIPL)
647 Eastern Blvd.
Clarksville, IN 47130
(812) 282-4309
CD, CT, FP, GYN, PM, PD

Delphi

Thomas R. Anderson, MD
651 Armony Road
Delphi, IN 46923
(317) 564-2777
FP, PM

Harold T. Sparks, DO (D/C)
3001 Washington Ave.
Evansville, IN 47714
(812) 479-8228
A, AC, BA, CT, FP, PM

Highland

Cal Streeter, DO (DIPL)
9635 Saric Court
Highland, IN 46322
(219) 924-2410 FAX (219) 924-9079
A, CD, CT, FP, OSM, PM

Indianapolis

David A. Darbro, MD (DIPL)
2124 E. Hanna Ave
Indianapolis, IN 46227
Indianapolis, IN 46227
(317) 787-7221
A, AR, CT, DD, FP, PM

Mooresville

Norman E. Whitney, DO (P)
P.O. Box 173
Mooresville, IN 46158
(317) 831-3352
AR, CD, DD, DIA, FP, NT

South Bend

David E. Turfler, DO (P)
336 W. Navarre St.
South Bend, IN 46616
(219) 233-3840
A, FP, GP, HGL, OBS, OSM

Valparaiso

Myrna D. Trowbridge, DO (D/C)
850-C Marsh St.
Valparaiso, IN 46383
(219) 462-3377
AC, AR, CT, GP, NT, OSM

IOWA

Des Moines

Beverly Rosenfeld, DO (P)
7177 Hickman Rd., #10
Des Moines, IA 50322
(515) 276-0061
GP, HGL, NT, OS, PM, YS

Sioux City

Horst G. Blume, MD (P)
700 Jennings St.
Sioux City, IA 51105
(712) 252-4386
CT, DD, Neuro., NT, OS, Pain
  Mgmt., S

KANSAS

Andover

Stevens B. Acker, MD (DIPL)
310 West Central, #D
P.O. Box 483
Andover, KS 67002
(316) 733-4494
CT, DD, FP, MM, PM

Garden City

Terry Hunsberger, DO (P)
602 N. 3rd. P.O. Box 679
Garden City, KS 67846
(316) 275-7128
BA, CT, FP, NT, OSM, PM

Hays

Roy N. Neil, MD (P)
105 West 13th
Hays, KS 67601
(913) 628-8341
BA, CD, CT, DD, NT, PM

Kansas City

John Gamble, Jr., DO (D/C)
1509 Quindaro
Kansas City, KS 66104
(913) 321-1140
GP, FP, DIA, DD, NT, OSM

KENTUCKY

Berea

Edward K. Atkinson, MD
P.O. Box 3148
Berea, KY 40403
NO REFERRALS

John C. Tapp
414 Old Morgantown Rd.
Bowling Green, KY 42101
(502) 781-1483
CT, GYN, MM, PD, P, RHU

Louisville

Kirk Morgan, MD
9105 U.S. Hwy. 42
Louisville, KY 40059
CD, CT, FP, MM, NT, YS

Nicholasville

Walt Stoll, MD (P)
6801 Danville Rd.
Nicholasville, KY 40356
CT, FP, NT, PM

Somerset

Stephen S. Kiteck, MD (P)
1301 Pumphouse Rd.
Somerset, KY 42501
FP, IM, PD, PM

LOUISIANA

Baton Rouge

Steve Kuplesky, MD
5618 Bayridge
Baton Rouge, LA 70817
NO REFERRALS

Chalmette

Saroj T. Tampira, MD (P)
812 E. Judge Perez
Chalmette, LA 70043
(504) 277-8991
CD, DD, DIA, IM

Manderville

Roy M. Montalbano, MD
4408 Highway 22
Mandeville, LA 70448
CT, FP, NT, PM

Natchitoches

Philip Mitchell, MD
407 Bienville St.
Natchitoches, LA 71457
(318) 357-1571 or (800) 562-6574

Newellton

Joseph R. Whitaker, MD (P)
P.O Box 458
Newellton, LA 71357
(318) 467-5131
CT, GP, IM

New Iberia

Adonis J. Domingue, MD (DIPL)
602 N. Lewis, #600
New Iberia, LA 70560
(318) 365-2196
GP

New Orleans

James P. Carter, MD (P)
1430 Tulane Avenue
New Orleans, LA 70112
(504) 588-5136
GP, NT, PM

Shreveport

R. Denman Crow, MD (P)
1545 Lone Ave., Ste. 222
Shreveport, LA 71101
NO REFERRALS

Slidell

Christy Graves, MD
1850 Gause Blvd., #205
Slidell, LA 70461
(504) 646-4415
IM

MAINE

Van Buren

Joseph Cyr, MD (P)
62 Main Street

Van Buren, ME 04785
(207) 868-5273
CT, GP, OBS

MARYLAND

Baltimore

Binyamin Rothstein, DO (D/C)
2835 Smith Ave., #209
Baltimore, MD 21209
(410) 484-2121
A, CT, GP, NT, OS, RHU

Laurel

Paul V. Beals, MD
9101 Cherry Lane Park, Suite 205
Laurel, MD 20708
(301) 490-9911
CT, FP, NT, PM

Pikesville

Alan R. Gaby, MD
31 Walker Ave.
Pikesville, MD 21208
(410) 486-5656

Rockville

Harry Lal, MD
21 Wall Street
Rockville, Md 20850
NO REFERRALS

Silver Spring

Harold Goodman, DO (P)
8609 Second Ave., Suite 405B
Silver Spring, MD 20910
(301) 881-5229
AC, CT, OS PMR, AU

MASSACHUSETTS

Barnstable

Michael Janson, MD, FACAM (DIPL)
275 Mill Way
P.O. Box 732

Barnstable, MA 02630
(508) 362-4343 FAX (617) 661-8651
A, CD, CT, NT, OME, YS

Cambridge

Michael Janson, MD, FACAM (DIPL)
2557 Massachusetts Ave.
Cambridge, MA 02140
(617) 661-6225 FAX (617) 661-8651
A, CD, CT, NT, OME, YS

Hanover

Richard Cohen, MD (DIPL)
51 Mill Street, #1
Hanover, MA 12339
(617) 829-9281
A, CD, CT, NT, PM, YS

Lowell

Svetiana Kaufman, MD (D/C)
24 Merrimack St., #323
Lowell, MA 01852
(508) 453-5181
A, AC, GP, GER, PM, RHI

Newton

Carol Englender, MD (P)
1340 Centre St.
Newton, MA 02159
(617) 965-7770
A, FP, NT, PM, Env. Medicine

West Boylston

N. Thomas La Cava, MD (D/C)
360 West Boylston St., Suite 107
West Boylston, MA 01583
(508) 854-1380
NT, PD, PM

Williamstown

Ross S. McConnell, MD
732 Main Street
Williamstown, MA 01267
(413) 663-3701
DD, NT, PM, HO

MICHIGAN

Atlanta

Leo Modzinski, DO, MD (DIPL)
100 W. State St.
Atlanta, MI 49709
(517) 785-4254 FAX (517) 785-2273
BA, CT, FP, GP, NT, OSM

Farmington Hills

Paul A. Parente, DO (DIPL)
30275 Thirteen Mile Rd.
Farmington Hills, MI 48018
(313) 626-7544
BA, CT, GP, PM

Albert J. Scarchill, DO (DIPL)
30275 Thirteen Mile Rd.
Farmington Hills, MI 48018
(313) 626-7544
BA, CT, FP, GP, MM, OSM, PM

Flint

William M. Bernard, DO (P)
1044 Gilbert Street
Flint, MI 48532
(313) 733-3140
A, CT, FP, GER, OSM, PM

Kenneth Ganapini, DO (P)
1044 Gilbert St.
Flint, MI 48532
(313) 733- 3140
FP, GP, OSM, PM, YS

Grand Haven

E. Duane Powers, DO (DIPL)
P.O. Box 170
Grand Haven, MI 49417
RETIRED

Grand Rapids

Grant Born, DO (DIPL)
2687 44th St. S.E.
Grand Rapids, MI 49512
(616) 455-3550 FAX (616) 455-3462
A, CT, FP, GYN, PM, PMR

Tammy Guerkini-Born, DO
2687 44th St. S.E.
Grand Raopids, MI 49512
(616) 455-3550
CT, GP, PM, YS, Laser

Linden

Marvin D. Penwell, DO (DIPL)
319 S. Bridge Street
Linden, MI 48451
(#313) 735-7809
A, CT, FP, GE, GYN, OSM

Novi

Thomas A. Padden, DO
39555 W. Ten Mile Rd., #303
Novi, MI 48375
(313) 473-2922
FP, PM

Pontiac

Vahagn Agbabian, DO (P)
28 No. Saginaw St., Suite 1105
Pontiac, MI 48058
(313) 334-2424
CT, DD, DIA, GER, IM, OME

St. Clair Shores

Richard E. Tapert, DO (DIPL)
23550 Harper
St. Clair Shores, MI 48080
(313) 779-5700
CT, GP, NT, PM

Williamston

Seldon Nelson, DO (P)
4386 N. Meridian Rd.
Williamston, MI 48895
(517) 349-2458
AR, CT, GP, NT, OSM

MINNESOTA

Minneapolis

Michael Dole, MD (D/C)
10700 Old Country Rd. 15, Suite 350
Minneapolis, MN 55441

(612) 593-9458
FP, PM, YS

Jean R. Eckerly, MD (DIPL)
10700 Old Country Rd. 15, Suite 350
Minneapolis, MN 55441
(612) 593-9458
CT, IM, NT, OME, PM

Tyler

Keith J. Carlson, MD
210 Highland Ct.
Tyler, MN 56178
(507) 247-5921
AC, GP, CT

Wayzata

F.J. Durand, MD
3119 Groveland School Rd.
Wayzata, MN 55391
NO REFERRALS

M. S. C. Durand, MD
3119 Groveland School Rd.
Wayzata, MN 55391
NO REFERRALS

MISSISSIPPI

Coldwater

Pravinchandra Patel, MD
P.O. Drawer DD
Coldwater, MS 38618
(601) 622-7011
CT, FP

Columbus

James H. Sams, MD (D/C)
1120 Lehmburg Rd.
Columbus, MS 39702
(601) 327-8701
AN, CT, GP

Ocean Springs

James H. Waddell, MD (P)
1520 Government Street
Ocean Springs, MS 39564
(601) 875-5505
AC, AN, Au, CT

Shelby

Robert Hollingsworth, MD (DIPL)
Drawer 87, 901 Forrest St.
Shelby, MS 38774
(601) 398-5106
CT, FP, GYN, OBS, PD, S

MISSOURI

Festus

John T. Schwent, DO (D/C)
1400 Truman Blvd.
Festus, MO 63028
A, CT, FP, NT, OBS, OSM

Florissant

Tipu Sultan, MD (P)
11585 W. Florissant
Florissant, MO 63033
(314) 921-7100
A, AR, CT, HGL, PM

Independence

Lawrence Dorman, DO
9120 E. 35 Street
Independence, MO 64052
(816) 358-2712
AC, CT, MM, OSM, PM

James E. Swann, DO
2116 Sterling
Independence, MO 64052
(816) 833-3366
CD, CT, DD, FP, IM, S

Joplin

Ralph D. Cooper, DO
1608 E. 20th Street
Joplin, MO 64804
(417) 624-4323
FP, GP, GYN, OS, S

Kansas City

Edward W. McDonagh, DO, FACAM
(DIPL)
2800-A Kendallwood Pkwy.

Kansas City, MO 64119
(816) 453-5940 FAX (816) 453-1140
CD, CT, DD, FP, HO, PM

James Rowland, DO
8133 Wornall Rd.
Kansas City, MO 64114
(816) 361-4077
AC, CT, DD, GP, HYP, OSM

Charles J. Rudolph, DO, PhD,
  FACAM (DIPL)
2800-A Kendallwood Pkwy.
Kansas City, MO 64119
(816) 453-5940 FAX (816) 453-1140
CD, CT, DD, FP, HO, PM

Moutain Grove

Doyle B. Hill, DO (P)
601 No. Bush
Moutain Grove, MO 65711
(417) 926-6643
A, CT, FP, GP, NT, OSM

Richmond

Emerson W. Ireland, DO
703 Willard Blvd.
Richmond, MO 64085
(816) 776-6933

Springfield

William C. Sunderwirth, DO (P)
2828 N. National
Springfield, MO 65803
(417) 869- 6260
CT, DIA, GP, OSM, PM, S

St. Louis

Harvey Walker Jr, MD, PhD,
  FACAM (DIPL)
138 N. Meramec Ave.
St. Louis, MO 63105
(314) 721-7227
CT, DIA, HGL, IM, NT, PM

William C. Sunderwirth, DO (P)
307 South Street

Stocton, MO 65785
(417) 278-3221
CT, DIA, GP, OSM, PM, S

Sullivan

Ronald H. Scott, DO (P)
131 Meridith
Sullivan, MO 63080
(314) 468-4932
GP, GER, GYN, NT, PM, OSM

Union

Clinton C. Hayes, DO (D/C)
100 W. Main
Union, MO 63084
(314) 583-8911
CT, GP

NEBRASKA

Omaha

Eugene C. Oliveta, MD (P)
8031 W. Center Rd., #208
Omaha, NE 68124
(402) 392-0233
CT, HYP, NT, PM, P, PO

Ord

Otis W. Miller, MD (D/C)
408 So. 14th Street
Ord, NE 68862
(308) 728-3251
CT, FP, NT, P, YS

NEVADA

Incline Village

W. Douglas Brodie, MD (D/C)
848 Tanager
Incline Village, NV 89450
(702) 832-7001
DD, FP, GP, IM, NT, PM

Las Vegas

Steven Holper, MD
3233 W. Charleston, #202

Las Vegas, NV 89102
(702) 878-3510

Ji-Zhou (Joseph) Kang, MD (P)
5613 S. Eastern
Las Vegas, NV 89119
(702) 798-2992
A, AC, GP, IM, NT

Paul McGuff, MD
3930 Swenson, #903
Las Vegas, NV 89106
RETIRED

Robert D. Milne, MD (P)
2110 Pinto Ln.
Las Vegas, NV 89106
(702) 385-1393
A, AC, CT, FP, NT, PM

Terry Pfau, DO (P)
2810 W. Chelston, #55
Las Vegas, NV 89102
(702) 258-7860
A, AC, CT, OSM

Robert Vance, DO (DIPL)
801 S. Rancho Drive, Suite F2
Las Vegas, NV 89106
(702) 385-7771
A, CT, HO, MM, OSM, PM

Reno

David A. Edwards, MD
4600 Kietzke Lane, Ste. M-242
Reno, NV 89509
(702) 829-2277
A, AC, CT, DD, PM, YS

Michael L. Gerber, MD (DIPL)
3670 Grant Drive
Reno, NV 89509
(702) 826-1900
CT, MM, OME

Corazon Ilerina, MD (P)
4600 Kietzke Ln., #M242
Reno, NV 89502
(702) 829-2277
CT, PM, Biol. Med.

Donald E. Soll, MD (D/C)
708 North Center St.
Reno, NV 89501
(702) 786-7101
A, AR, CT, HGL, HO, PUD

Yiwen Y. Tang, MD (P)
380 Brinkby
Reno, NV 89509
(702) 826-9500
A, CD, CT, HGL, HO, PM

NEW JERSEY

Bloomfield

Majid Ali, MD (D/C)
320 Belleville Ave.
Bloomfield, NJ 07003

Cherry Hill

Allan Magaziner, DO (DIPL)
1907 Greentree Rd.
Cherry Hill, NJ 08003
(609) 424-8222 FAX (609) 424-1832
CT, NT, OSM, PM

Denville

Majid Ali, MD (D/C)
95 E. Main Street
Denville, NJ 07834
(201) 586-4111 FAX (201) 586-8466
A, PM, Pathology

Edison

C. Y. Lee, MD (DIPL)
952 Amboy Avenue
Edison, NJ 08837
(908) 738-9220 FAX (908) 738-1187
A, AR, AU, CT, DD, OME

Ralph Lev, MD, MS FASM (DIPL)
952 Amboy Avenue
Edison, NJ 08837
(908) 738-9220 FAX (908) 738-1187

Richard B. Menashe, DO (D/C)
15 South Main St.

Edison, NJ 08837
(908) 906-8866
A, CD, CT, HGL, NT, YS

Rodolfo T. Sy, MD (D/C)
952 Amboy Avenue
Edison, NJ 08837
(908) 738-9220 FAX (908) 738-1187

Elizabeth

Gennaro Locurio, MD (P)
610 3rd. Ave.
Elizabeth, NJ 07202
(908) 351-1333
A, AC, CT, FP, AU, HYP

Ortley Beach

Charles Harris, MD (P)
1 Ortley Plaza
Oryley Beach, NJ 08751
(908) 793-6464
A, BA, CT, DD, FP, GER

Ridgewood

Constance Alfano, MD (P)
74 Oak Street
Ridgewood, NJ 07450
(201) 444-4622
A (food), Candida, CT

Skillman

Eric Braverman, MD (D/C)
100-102 Tamark Circle
Skillman, NJ 08558
(609) 921-1842
A, CT, DD, FP, IM, PM

Somerset

Marc Condren, MD
15 Cedar Grove Ln., #20
Somerset, NJ 08873
(908) 469-2133

West Orange

Faina Munits, MD (DIPL)
51 Pleasant Valley Way
West Orange, NJ 07052
(201) 736-3743
A, CD, DIA, DD, HGL, PM

NEW MEXICO

Albuquerque

Ralph J. Luciani, DO (DIPL)
2301 San Pedro N.E., Suite G
Albequerque, NM 87110
(505) 888-5995
AC, AU, CT, FP, OSM, PM

Gerald Parker, DO (P)
6208 Montgomery Blvd. N.E., Suite D
Albequerque, NM 87109
(505) 884-3506
A, CT, AC, AR, GP, HO

John T. Taylor, DO (P)
6208 Montgomery Blvd. N.E.,
Suite #D
Albequerque, NM 87109
(505) 884-3506
A, AC, AR, CT, GP, HO

Roswell

Annette Stoesser, MD (P)
112 S. Kentucky
Roswell, NM 88201
(505) 623-2444
A, CT, DIA, DD, FP, NT

Santa Fe

Shirley B. Scott, MD
P.O. Box 2670
Santa Fe, NM 87504
GE, MM, PM, YS

NEW YORK

Bronx

Richard Izquierdo, MD (P)
1070 Southern Blvd., Lower Level
Bronx, NY 10459
(212) 589-4541

Brooklyn

Gennaro Locurcio, MD (P)
2386 Ocean Parkway

Brooklyn, NY 11223
(718) 375-2600
GP, NT, PM

Tsilia Sorina, MD (P)
2026 Ocean Ave.
Brooklyn, NY 11230
GP, NT, PM

Michael Teplitsky, MD (P)
415 Oceanview Ave.
Brooklyn, NY 11235
(718) 769-0997 FAX (718) 646-2352
BA, CD, DIA, IM, PM

Pavel Yutsis, MD (D/C)
1309 W. 7th St.
Brooklyn, NY 11204
(718) 259-2122 FAX (718) 259-3933
A, CT, FP, NT, PD, PM, YS

East Meadow

Christopher Calapal, DO (D/C)
1900 Hempstead Tnpke
East Meadow, NY 11554
(516) 794-0404
A, CT, FP, NT, OSM, YS

Falconer

Reino Hill, MD (P)
230 West Main St.
Falconer, NY 14733
(716) 665-3505
CT, FP, PM

Great Neck

Mary F. Di Rico, MD (D/C)
1 Kingspoint Rd.
Great Neck, NY 11024
NO REFERRALS

Huntington

Serafina Corsello, MD, FACAM
  (DIPL)
175 E. Main Street
Huntington, NY 11743
(516) 271-0222 FAX (516) 271-5992
CT, DD, MM, NT, OME, PM

Lawrence

Mitchell Kurk, MD
310 Broadway
Lawrence, NY 11559
(516) 239-5540
CT, FP, GER, NT, OME, PM

Massena

Bob Snider, MD (D/C)
HC 61, Box 43D
Massena, NY 13662
(315) 764-7328
A, CT, FP

New York City

Robert C. Atkins, MD (DIPL)
152 E. 55th St.
New York, NY 10022
(212) 758-2110
CT, HGL, OME

Serafina Corsello, MD, FACAM
  (DIPL)
200 W. 57th St. #1202
New York, NY 10019
(212) 399-0222
CT, DD, MM, NT, OME, PM

Ronald Hoffman, MD, FACAM
  (DIPL)
40 E. 30th Street
New York, NY 10016
(212) 779-1744 FAX (212) 779-0891

Warren M. Levin, MD (DIPL)
444 Park Ave. So./ 30th St.
New York, NY 10016
(212) 696-1900 FAX (212) 213-5872
A, AC, CT, NT, OME, PM

Niagra Falls

Paul Cutler, MD, FACAM (DIPL)
652 Elmwood Ave.
Niagra Falls, NY 14301
(716) 284-5140 FAX (716) 284-5159

Oneonta

Richard J. Ncci, MD
521 Main Street
Oneonta, NY 13820
(607) 432-8752
FP

Orangeburg

Neil L. Block, MD (P)
14 Prel Plaza
Orangeburg, NY 10962
(914) 359-3300
A, CD, FP, IM, NT, PO

Plattsburgh

Driss Hassam, MD (P)
50 Court Street
Plattsburg, NY 12901
(518) 561-2023
GE, S

Rhinebeck

Kenneth A. Bock, MD, FACAM
  (DIPL)
108 Montgomery St.
Rhinebeck, NY 12572
(914) 876-7082 FAX (914) 876-4615

Suffern

Michael B. Schachter, MD, FACAM
  (DIPL)
Two Executive Blvd., #202
Suffern, NY 10901
(914) 386-4700 FAX (914) 386-4727
A, CT, NT, PO

Syosset

Steven Rachlin
MD8 Greenfield Road
Syosset, NY 11791
(516) 921-8181

Westbury

Savely Yurkovsky, MD (P)
309 Madison St.
Westbury, NY 11590
(516) 333-2929
A, CD, CS, CT, NT, PM

NORTH CAROLINA

Aberdeen

Keith E. Johnson, MD
188 Quewhiffle
Aberdeen, NC 28315
(919) 281-5122
DD, GP, GER, NT, PM, PMR

Leicester

John L. Laird, MD (DIPL)
Rt. 1 Box 7
Leicester, NC 28748
(704) 683-3101 FAX (704) 683-3103
A, CD, CT, FP, NT, PM

John L. Wilson, MD (D/C)
Rt. 1 Box 7
Leicester, NC 28748
(704) 683-3101
A, CT, Env. Med., NT, PM

Statesville

John L. Laird, MD (DIPL)
Plaza 21 North
Statesville, NC 28677
(704) 876-1617 or (800) 445-4762
A, CD, CT, FP, NT, PM

NORTH DAKOTA

Grand Forks

Richard H. Leigh, MD (DIPL)
2314 Library Circle
Grand Forks, ND 58201
(701) 775-5527
CT, GYN, MM, NT

Minot

Brian E. Briggs, MD (D/C)
718 6th Street S.W.
Minot, ND 58701
(701) 838-6011
CT, FP, NT

OHIO

Akron

Francis J. Waickman, MD (P)
544 "B" White Pond Drive
Akron, OH 44320
(216) 867-3767
A, Env Med, Cl Imm, YS

Bluffton

L. Terry Chappell, MD, FACAM
  (DIPL)
122 Thurman St.
Bluffton, OH 45917
(419)358-4627 FAX (419) 358-1855
AU, CT, FP, HYP, NT, PMR

Canton

Jack E. Singluff, DO (DIPL)
5850 Fulton Rd. N.W.
Canton, OH 44718
(216) 494-8641
CD, CT, FP, HGL, MM, NT

Cincinnati

Ted Cole, DO (P)
9678 Cincinnati-Columbus Road
Cincinnati, OH 45241
(513) 779-0300
A, CT, FP, NT, OSM, PD

Cleveland

John M. Baron, DO (DIPL)
4807 Rockside, Ste. 100
Cleveland, OH 44131
(216) 642-0082
CT, NT, PO

James P. Frackelton, MD, FACAM
  (DIPL)
24700 Center Ridge Rd.
Cleveland, OH 44145
(216) 835-0104 FAX (216) 871-1404
CT, HO, NT, PM

Derrick Lonsdale, MD, FACAM
(DIPL)
24700 Center Ridge Rd.
Cleveland, OH 44145
(216) 835-0104 FAX (216) 871-1404
NT, PM, PD

Douglas Weeks, MD (D/C)
24700 Center Ridge Rd.
Cleveland, OH 44145
(216) 835-0104 FAX (216) 871-1404
CT, HO, NT, PM, AC, PMR

Columbus

Robert R. Hershner, D0
1571 E. Livingston Ave.
Columbus, OH 43255
(614) 253-8733
FP, GP, GYN, IM, P, PD

William D. Mitchell, DO (DIPL)
3520 Snoufer Rd.
Columbus, OH 43235
(614) 761-0555
CD, CT, GP, IM, PM, OSM

Dayton

David D. Goldberg, DO (DIPL)
100 Forest Park Dr.
Dayton, OH 45405
(513) 277-1722
CT, GP, OSM, PM

Lancaster

Richard Sielski, MD (P)
3484 Cincinnati-Zainsville Road
Lancaster, OH 43130
(614) 653-0017
CT, FP, NT, PM

Paulding

Don K. Snyder, MD (P)
Route 2 Box 1271
Paulding, OH 45879
(419) 399-2045
CT, FP

Youngstown

James Ventresco, Jr., DO (P)
3848 Tippecanoe Rd.
Youngstown, OH 44511
(216) 792-2349
CT, FP, NT, OSM, RHU

OKLAHOMA

Jenks

Leon Anderson, DO (DIPL)
121 Second Street
Jenks, OK 74037
(918) 299-5039
CT, NT OSM

Norman

Howard Hagglund, MD
2227 W. Lindsey, #1401
Norman, OK 73069
(405) 329-4457
A, AC, AU, CT, GP, YS

Oklahoma City

Charles H. Farr, MD, PhD, FACAM
(DIPL)
10101 S. Western
Oklahoma City, OK 73139
(405) 691-1112 FAX (405) 691-1491
A, CT, NT, PM

Charles D. Taylor, MD (D/C)
3715 No. Classen Blvd.
Oklahoma City, OK 73118
(405) 525-7751
GP, GYN, OBS, PM, PMR

OREGON

Ashland

Ronald L. Peters, MD (P)
16507 Siskiyou Blvd.
Ashland, OR 97520
(503) 482-7007
A, CT, DD, FP, NT, PM, YS

Eugene

John Gambee, MD (D/C)
66 Club Road, Ste. 140
Eugene, OR 97401
(503) 666-2536
A, BA, CT, PM

Grants Pass

James Fitzsimmons Jr., MD (P)
591 Hidden Valley Rd.
Grants Pass, OR 97527
(503) 474-2166
A, CT

Salem

Terence Howe Young, MD (D/C)
1205 Wallace Rd. NW
Salem, OR 97304
(503) 371-1558
A, CT, GP, OSM, PM

PENNSYLVANIA

Allentown

Robert H. Schmidt, DO (P)
1227 Liberty PLaza Bldg., Suite 303
Allentown, PA 18102
(215) 437-1959
CT, FP, NT, PM

D. Erik Von Kiel, DO (D/C)
Liberty Square Med. Cntr., Suite 200
Allentown, PA 18104
(215) 776-7639
CT, FP, MM, NT, OSM

Bangor

Francis J. Cinelli, DO (P)
153 N. 11th Street
Bangor, PA 18013
(215) 588-4502
CT, GP, HYP

Bedford

Bill Illingworth, DO
120 West John St.
Bedford, PA 15522

(814) 623-8414
AN, CT, GP, NT, Pain Mgmt.

Bethlehem

Sally Ann Rex, DO (P)
1343 Easton Ave.
Bethlehem, PA 18018
(215) 868-0900
CT, GP, OS, PM, Occ. Med.

Coudersport

Howard J. Miller, MD
360 E. 2nd Street
Coudersport, PA 16915
(814) 274-7070
ASC, CT, GER, IM

Elizabethtown

Dennis L. Gilbert, DO (D/C)
50 North Market Street
Elizabethtown, PA 17022
(717) 367-1345
AC, CT, NT, OSM, PM

Fountainville

Harold H. Byer, MD, PhD (D/C)
5045 Swamp Rd., #A-101
Fountainville, PA 18923
(215) 348-0443
AR, CT, DIA, S

Greensburg

Ralph A. Miranda, MD, FACAM
  (DIPL)
RD. #12 Box 108
Greensburg, PA 15601
(412) 838-7632 FAX (412) 836-3655
CT, FP, NT, OME, PM

Greenville

Roy E. Kerry, MD
17 Sixth Avenue
Greenville, PA 16125
(412) 588-2600
A, DD, NT, YS, EM, OTO

Hazleton

Arther L. Koch, DO (DIPL)
57 West Juniper St.
Hazelton, PA 18201
(717) 455-4747
CT, GP, PM

Indiana

Chandrika Sinha, MD (P)
1177 So. Sixth Street
Indiana, PA 15701
(412) 349-1414
AC, CT, NT, PM, S

Lewisburg

George C. Miller II, MD
3 Hospital Drive
Lewisburg, PA 17837
(717) 524-4405
GYN, OBS, YS

Macungle

D. Erik Von Kiel, DO (D/C)
7386 Alburtis Rd., Suite 101
Macungle, PA 18062
(215) 967-5503
CT, FP, MM, NT, OSM

Mertztown

Conrad G. Maulfair Jr, DO, FACAM
  (DIPL)
Box 71 Main Street
Mertztown, PA 19539
(215) 682-2104 FAX (215) 682-6693
A, CT, HGL

Mt. Pleasant

Mamduh El-Attrache, MD (P)
20 E. Main St.
Mt. PLeasant, PA 15666
(412) 547-3576
BA, CT, DIA, GER, OBS, PO

Newtown

Robert J. Peterson, DO
64 Magnolia Drive
Newtown, PA 18940
(215) 579-0330
AR, CD, CT, DD, FP, GP, NT

Philadelphia

Frederick Burton, MD
69 W. Schoolhouse Lane
Philadelphia, PA 19144
(215) 844-4660
IM, CT, NT, PM

Jose Castillo, MD
228 South 22nd St.
Philadelphia, PA 19103
(215) 567-5845, 46, & 47

Mura Galperin, MD (P)
824 Hendrix St.
Philadelphia, PA 19118
(215) 667-2337
CT, FP

P. Jayalakshmi, MD (DIPL)
6366 Sherwood Road
Philadelphia, PA 19151
(215) 473-4226
A, AC, AR, BA, CT, DIA, DD

K. R. Sampathachar, MD (DIPL)
6366 Sherwood Road
Philadelphia, PA 19151
(215) 473-4226
AC, AN, CT, DD, HYP, NT

Lance Wright, MD (D/C)
3901 Market Street
Philadelphia, PA 19104
(215) 387-1200
DD, END, HYP, NT, PM, PO

Quakertown

Harold Buttram, MD (DIPL)
5724 Clymer Road
Quakertown, PA 18951
(215) 536-1890
A, CT, FP, NT

Somerset

Paul Peirsel, MD (P)
RD 4 Box 267 1A
Somerset, PA 15501
(814) 443-2521
CT, NT, Emerg. Med, Crit. Care

SOUTH CAROLINA

Charleston

David Younger, MD
383 Grove Street
Charleston, SC 29403
(803) 769-4649
GP, N, PM

Columbia

Theodore C. Rozema, MD (DIPL)
2228 Airport Road
Columbia, Sc 29205
(803) 796-1702 or (800) 992-8350
(NAT)
CT, FP, NT, PM

Landrum

Theodore C. Rozema, MD (DIPL)
1000 E. Rutherford Rd.
Landrum, SC 29356
(803) 457-4141 of (800) 992-8350
(NAT)
FAX (803) 457-4144
CT, FP, NT, PM

Rock Hill

Theodore C. Rozema, MD (DIPL)
2915 No. Cherry Rd.
(800) 992-8350
CT, FP, NT, PM

TENNESSEE

Jackson

S. Marshall Fram, MD
135 Weatheridge Dr.
Jackson, TN 38305
RETIRED

Morristown

Donald Thompson, MD (P)
P.O. Box 2088
Morristown, TN 37816
(615) 581-6367
CT, FP, GER, GP, NT, PM

Nashville

Stephen L. Reisman, MD (D/C)
417 East Iris Dr.
Nashville, TN 37204
(615) 383-9030
CT, GP, HGL, NT, PM, YS

TEXAS

Alamo

Herbert Carr, DO
P.O. Box 1179
Alamo, TX 78516
(512) 787-6668
CT, OSM, PM

Abilene

William Irby Fox, MD (P)
1227 N. Mockingbird Ln.
(915) 672-7863
CT, DIA, GP, GER, PMS, S

Amarillo

Gerald Parker, DO (P)
4714 S. Western
Amarillo,TX 79109
(806) 355-8263
A, AC, AR, CT, GP, HO

John T. Taylor, DO (P)
4714 S. Western
Amarillo, TX 79109
(806) 355-8263
A, AC, AR, CT, GP, HO

Austin

Vladimir Rizov, MD (P)
8311 Shoal Creek Blvd.
Austin, TX 78758
(512) 451-8149
AR, CT, DD, DIA, GP, IM

Dallas

Brij Myer, MD (D/C)
4222 Trinity Mills Rd., Suite 222
Dallas, TX 7587
(214) 248-2488
CD, DD, MM, PM, Pulm.

Michael G Samuels, DO (D/C)
7616 LBJ Freeway, #230
Dallas, TX 75251
(214) 991-3977
CT, NT, PM, OSM

J. Robert Winslow, DO (P)
2815 Valley View Lane, Suite 111
Dallas, TX 75234
A, CD, CT, END, PM, R

El Paso

Francisco Soto, MD (DIPL)
1420 Geronimo, D-2
El Paso, TX 79925
(915) 534-0272
CD, CT, DD, HO, PM, S

Houston

Robert Battle, MD (DIPL)
9910 Long Point
Houston, TX 77055
(713) 932-0552 FAX (713) 932-0551
A, BA, CD, CT, FP, HGL

Jerome L. Borochoff, MD (P)
8830 Long Point, Suite 504
Houston, TX 77055
CD, CT, FP, HO, PM

Andrew Campbell, MD
1441 Memorial Dr., #6
Houston, TX 77079
(713) 497-7904
FP, Immuno. Toxicology

Luis E. Guerrero, MD (P)
2055 S. Gessner, Suite 150
Houston, TX 77063

(713) 789-0133
AC, CT, FP, NT, PM, PO

Carlos E. Nossa, MD (P)
3800 Tanglewilde, # 1007
Houston, TX 77063
NO REFERRALS

Humble

John P. Trowbridge, MD, FACAM
 (DIPL)
9816 Memorial Blvd., Suite 205
Humble, TX 77338
(713) 540-2329 FAX (713) 540-4329
CT, NT, PM, YS, A, MM

John L. Sessions, DO (DIPL)
1609 South Margerat
Kirbyville, TX 75958
CT, IM, OSM

La Porte

Ronald M. Davis, MD (P)
10414 W. Main St.
LaPorte, TX 77571
(713) 470-2930
CT, GP, PM

Laredo

Ruben Berianga, MD
649-B Dogwood
Laredo, TX 78041
NO REFERRALS

Pecos

Ricardo Tan, MD (P)
423 S. Palm
Pecos, TX 79772
(915) 445-9090
AC, AU, CT, FP, NT, PM

Plano

Linda Martin, DO (P)
1524 Independence, #C
Plano, TX 75075
(214) 985-1377 FAX (214) 612-0747
CT, GP, NT, PM

San Antonio

Jim P. Archer, DO
8434 Fredericksburg Rd.
San Antonio, TX 78229
(210) 615-8445
A, CT, HO, NT, PM

Ron Stogryn, MD (P)
7334 Blanco Rd., #100
San Antonio, TX 78216
(210) 366-3637 FAX (512) 366-3638
A, CT, MM, NT, PD, YS

Sweeny

Elizabeth-Anne Cole, MD
303 N. McKinney
Sweeny, TX 77480
(409) 548-8610
BA, FP, NT, PM, OBS

Wichita Falls

Thomas R. Humphrey, MD (P)
2400 Rushing
Wichita Falls, TX 76308
(817) 766-4329
BA, FP, GP, HYP

UTAH

Murray

Dennis Harper, DO (D/C)
5263 S. 300 W., #203
Murray, UT 84107
(801) 288-8881
A, CT, OSM, TS

Provo

D. Remington, MD (D/C)
1675 N. Freedom Blvd., Suite 11E
Provo, UT 84604
(801) 373-8500
A, CT, FP, Env. Med.

VIRGINIA

Annandale

Scott V. Anderson, MD (P)
7023 Little River Tnpk., Suite 207

Annandale, VA 22003
(703) 941-3606
CT, DD, GP, MM, NT, PM

Sohini Patel, MD
7023 Little River Tnpk., Suite 207
Annandale, VA 22003
(703) 941-3606
A, CT, NT, PM

Mahmoud Salamatian, MD
7023 Little River Tnpk., 207
Annadale, VA 22003
(703) 941-3606
CD, IM

Hinton

Harold Huffman, MD (D/C)
P.O. Box 197
Hinton, VA 22831
(703) 867-5242
CT, FP, PM

Midlothian

Peter C. Gent, DO (DIPL)
11900 Hull Street
Midlothian, VA 23112
(804) 774-3551
CT, GP, OSM

Norfolk

Vincent Speckhart, MD (DIPL)
902 Graydon Ave.
Norfolk, VA 23507
(804) 622-0014
IM, Medical Oncology

Elmer M. Cranton, MD, FACAM
  (DIPL)
Ripshin Road-Box 44
Trout Dale, VA 24378
(703) 677-3631 FAX (703) 677-3843

VERMONT

Essex Junction

Charles E. Anderson, MD
175 Pearl Street
Essex Junction, VT 05452

(802) 879-6544
A, FP, NT, YS

St. Albans

Alan T. Lee, MD (P)
P.O. Box 306
St. Albans, VT 05478
(802) 524-1062
CT, GYN, OBS, YS

WASHINGTON

Bellevue

David Buscher, MD (P)
1603 116th N.E., Ste. 112
Bellevue, WA 98004-3825
(206) 453-0288
Env. Med/ Cin Ecol, GP, NT

Bellingham

Robert Kimmel, MD (D/C)
4204 Meridian, Ste. 104
Bellingham, WA 98226
(206) 734-3250
AC, CT, DD, FP, NT, PM

Fairchild

James P. De Santis, DO
8116 Palm Street
Fairchild AFB, WA 99011
NO REFERRALS

Kent

Jonathan Wright, MD (P)
24030 132nd S.E.
Kent, WA 98042
(206) 631-8920
A, CT, FP, MM, NT, END

Kirkland

Jonathan Collin, MD (DIPL)
12911 120th Ave. N.E., #A-50,
POB 8099
Kirkland, WA 98034
(206) 820-0547 FAX (206) 385-7703
CT, NT, PM

Port Townsend

Jonathan Collin, MD (DIPL)
911 Tyler Street
Port Townsend, WA 98368
(206) 385-4555 FAX (206) 385-7703
CT, NT, PM

Redmond

Maurice Stephens
13820 N.E. 65th St., #550
Redmond, WA 98052
NO REFERRALS

Seattle

Michael G. Vesselago, MD (D/C)
217 North 125th
Seattle, WA 98133
(208) 367-0760
CT, NT, FP, IM, MM, PM

Spokane

Burton B. Hart, DO (P)
E. 12104 Main
Spokane, WA 99206
(509) 927-9922 FAX (509) 927- 9922
CT, HGL, MM, NT, PM

Yakima

Murray L. Black, DO (P)
609 S. 48th Ave.
Yakima, WA 98908
(509) 966-1780
A, CT, FP, GP, OSM

Yelm

Elmer M. Cranton, MD, FACAM
 (DIPL)
15246 Leona Dr. S.E.
Yelm, WA 98597
(206) 894-3548 FAX (206) 894-2176
A, CD, CT, FP, HO, NT

WEST VIRGINIA

Beckley

Prudencio Corro, MD (P)
251 Stanaford Rd.
Beckley, WV 25801

(304) 252-0775
A, CT, RHI

Michael Kostenko, DO (D/C)
114 E. Main St.
Beckley, WV 25801
(304) 253-0591
A, AC, CT, FP, OSM, PM

Charleston

Steve M. Zekan, MD (P)
1208 Kanawha Blvd. E.
Charleston, WV 25301
(304) 343-7559
CT, NT, PM, S

WISCONSIN

Green Bay

Eleazar M. Kadile, MD (DIPL)
1538 Bellevue St.
Green Bay, WI 54311
(414) 468-9442
A, CT, P

Lake Geneva

Rathna Alwa, MD (DIPL)
717 Geneva Street

Lake Geneva, WI 53147
(413) 248-1430
AC, AR, BA, CT, HYP, IM

Milwaukee

William J. Faber, DO
6529 W. Fond du Lac Ave.
Milwaukee, WI 53218
(414) 464-7680
Neuro-Musculo-Skeletal

Robert R. Stocker, DO (DIPL)
2505 Mayfair Rd.
Milwaukee, WI 53226
RETIRED

Jerry N. Yee, DO (D/C)
2505 N. Mayfair Rd.
Milwaukee, WI 53226
BA, CT, GP, OSM

Wisconsin Dells

Robert S. Waters, MD (DIPL)
Race & Vine Streets
Box 357
Wisconsin Dells, WI 53965
CT, PM, OME

American College of Advancement in Medicine (ACAM) Physicians—Canada

ALBERTA

Calgary

Louis Grondin, MD, D/C
3rd Floor, 1504—15th Ave. S.W.
Calgary, Alberta
Canada T3C OX9
(403) 245-8008   FAX (403) 245-5212
Phlebology

J. Soriano-Grondin, MD, D/C
3rd Floor, 1504—15th Ave. S.W.
Calgary, Alberta
Canada T3C OX9
(403) 245-8008   FAX (403) 245-5212
AN,CT,Phlebology

Edmonton

Godwin O. Okolo, MD, D/C
132 Northwood Mall
9402 135 Ave.
Edmonton, Alberta
Canada T5E 5R8
(403) 476-3344
CD,CS,DIA,DD,GP,GER

Andrew W. Sereda, MD, D/C
#204 - 11 Fairway Dr.
Edmonton, Alberta
Canada T6J 2W4
(403) 430-9479
NT,Neuro.,PM

Tris Trethart, MD, D/C
10324 - 82nd Ave., #B102
Edmonton, Alberta
Canada T6E 1Z8
(403) 433-7401
NT,PM

K.B. Wiancko, MD, D/C
#205-9509 156 Street
Edmonton, Alberta
Canada T58 4J5
(403) 483-2703
FP,GE,GP,S

Grand Centre

Richard Johnson, MD, D/C
Box 96
Grand Centre, Alberta
Canada T0A 1T0
(403) 639-2760
GP,NT,OME,PM

BRITISH COLUMBIA

Kelowna

Alex A. Neil, MD, DIPL
170 Rutland Road, #12
Kelowna, B.C.
Canada V1X 3B2
(604) 765-2145
CT,GP,HYP,NT

Qualicum Beach

George Barber, MD,D/C
Box 39
#2 - 225 West 2nd Ave.
Qualicum Beach, B.C.
Canada V0R 2S0
(604) 752-5330
DD,FP,GER,HYP,IM,PM,P

Vancouver

Saul Pilar, MD,D/C
2786 West 16th Ave. #205
Vancouver, B.C. V6K 3C4

(604) 739-8858
A,DD,HYP,NT

Donald W. Stewart, MD, D/C
2184 W. Broadway, #435
Vancouver, B.C. V6K 2E1
(604) 732-1348   FAX (604) 732-1372
CT,GP

Zigurts Strauts, MD, D/C
3077 Granville St., #201
Vancouver, B.C. V6H 3J9
(604) 736-1105   FAX (604) 736-8857
AC,CT,FP,Thermography
Manipulative Therapy

MANITOBA

Winnipeg

Howard N. Reed, MD
302 Lamont Blvd.
Winnipeg, Manitoba
Canada R3P 0G1
RETIRED

ONTARIO

Blythe

Richard W. Street, MD, D/C
Box 100 - Gypsy Lane
Blythe, Ontario
Canada N0M 1H0

(519) 523-4433
GP,NT,PM

Smiths Falls

Clare Minielly, MD, D/C
33 Williams Street E.
Smiths Falls, Ontario
Canada K7A 1C3
(613) 283-7703
AN,CT,GP,NT

NOVA SCOTIA

Chester

J.W. LaValley, MD
227 Central Street
Chester, N.S.
Canada B0J 1J0
(902) 275-4555
GP

QUEBEC

St. Foy

Jean Yves Perreault, MD, D/C
2935 Long Champs
St. Foy, Quebec
Canada G1W 2G2
(418) 651-6408
CT,NT,Phlebology,Aesthetics

Notes

Chapter 2
Signs and Symptoms of Alzheimer's Disease

1. "There Were Times, Dear." Sandoz Pharmaceuticals Corporation, Lilac Productions, and SCETV, PBS, June 3, 1987.
2. *Stedman's Medical Dictionary*, 25th Edition. (Baltimore, MD: Williams & Wilkins, 1990), p. 444.
3. "The aging of America brings to light Alzheimer's, drug firms already researching therapy." *Medical Advertising News*, Vol. 6, No. 8, May 15, 1987, p. 2.
4. Kolata, Gina. "FDA panel approves test distribution of Alzheimer's drug." *The New York Times*, July 16, 1991.
5. Mace, Nancy L. and Rabins, Peter V. *The 36-Hour Day*. (Baltimore, MD: The Johns Hopkins University Press, 1991), pp. 9 & 10.
6. Katzman, Robert. "Early Detection of senile dementia." *Hospital Practice*, June 1981, p. 62.
7. Safford, Florence. *Caring for the Mentally Impaired Elderly*. (New York: Henry Holt & Co., 1986), pp. 18–27.
8. Ibid., pp. 27–35.
9. Ibid., pp. 35–43.

Chapter 3
Diagnostic Procedures for Dementia

1. Butler, Robert N. and Emr, Marian. "Alzheimer's disease: An examination." *TWA Ambassador*, November 1982, p. 69.
2. Katzman, Robert. "Early detection of senile dementia." *Hospital Practice*, June 1981, p. 61.
3. Hochman, Gloria. "Living with Alzheimer's." *The Philadelphia Inquirer Magazine*, December 1, 1985, p. 20.
4. Kra Siegried. *Aging Myths: Reversible Causes of Mind and Memory Loss*. (New York: McGraw-Hill, 1986), pp. 240–242.
5. Op. cit., Hochman, p. 50.
6. Op. cit., Katzman, p. 64.

Chapter 4
Pathological Brain Changes in a Patient With DAT

1. Jorm, A.F.; Korten, A.E.; and Henderson, A.S. "The prevalence of dementia: a quantitative integration of the literature." *Acta Psychiatr Scand* 76(5):465–479, Nov. 1987.
2. Evans, D.A. "Estimated prevalence of Alzheimer's disease in the United

States." *Milbank Quarterly* 68(2):267–289, 1990.

3. Roach, Marion. "Another name for madness." *The New York Times Magazine,* January 16, 1983, pp. 22–31.

4. Shibayama, H.; Kasahara, Y.; and Kobayashi, H. "Prevalence of dementia in a Japanese elderly population." *Acta Psychiatr Scand* 74(2):144–151, Aug. 1986.

5. Heston, L.L.; and White, J.A. *The Vanishing Mind.* (New York: W.H. Freeman and Co., 1991), pp. 15 & 16.

6. Selkoe, D.J. "Amyloid protein and Alzheimer's disease." *Scientific American* 265(5):68–78, November 1991.

7. Davies, P. "Alzheimer's disease and related disorders: an overview." In: Anderson, M.K., ed., *Understanding Alzheimer's Disease.* (New York: Charles Scribner's Sons, 1988), p. 4.

8. Needleman, H.L. "The behavioral consequences of low-level exposure to lead." In: Sakar, B., ed., *Biological Aspects of Metals and Metal-Related Diseases.* (New York: Raven Press, 1983), pp. 219–224.

9. Mahaffey, K.R.; Annest, J.L.; Roberts, J.; Murphy, R.S. "National estimates on blood lead levels: United States, 1976–1980. Association with selected demographic and socioeconomic factors." *New England Journal of Medicine* 307:573–579, 1982.

10. Singerman, A. "Clinical signs versus biochemical effects for toxic metals." In: Nordberg, G.F., ed. *Effects and Dose-Response Relationships of Toxic Metals.* (Amsterdam: Elsevier, 1976), pp. 207–225.

11. Thatcher, R.W.; Lester, M.L.; McAlaster, R.; Horst, R. "Effects of low levels of cadmium and lead on cognitive functioning in children." *Arch Environmental Health* 37:159–166, 1982.

12. Hunter, D.; Bomford, R.R.; Russell,

D.S. "Poisoning by methyl mercury compounds." *Quarterly Journal of Medicine* 9:193–213, 1940.

13. Clarkson, T.W. "Methylmercury toxicity to the mature and developing nervous system: possible mechanisms." In: Sakar B., ed., *Biological Aspects of Metals and Metal-Related Diseases* (New York: Raven Press, 1983), pp. 183–197.

14. Sandstead, H.H. "A brief history of the influence of trace elements on brain function." *The American Journal of Clinical Nutrition* 43:293–298, February 1986.

15. Frank, J. *Alzheimer's Disease, The Silent Epidemic.* (Minneapolis, MN: Lerner Publications Co., 1985), pp. 48–50.

16. Heston, L.L. and White, J.A. *Dementia, A Practical Guide to Alzheimer's Disease and Related Illnesses.* (New York: W.H. Freeman and Co., 1983), p. 52.

17. Office of Technology Assessment. *Losing a Million Minds: Confronting the Tragedy of Alzheimer's Disease and Other Dementias.* (Washington, D.C.: U.S. Government Printing Office, 1987).

18. Goldfarb, L.G.; Haltia, M.; Brown, P.; Nieto, A.; Kovanen, J.; McCombi, W.R.; Trap, S.; and Gajdusek, D.C. "New mutation in scrapie amyloid precursor gen (at codon 178) in Finnish Creutzfeldt-Jakob kindred." *The Lancet* 337:425, February 16, 1991.

19. Kovanen, J.; Haltia, M. "Descriptive epidemiology of Creutzfeldt-Jakob disease in Finland." *Acta Neurol Scand* 77:474–480, 1988.

20. Brown, P.; Rogers-Johnson, P.; Cathala, F., et al. "Creutzfeldt-Jakob disease of long duration: clinico-pathological characteristics, transmissibility, and differential diagnosis." *Ann Neurol* 16:295304, 1984.

Chapter 5
The Differential Diagnosis of Alzheimer's Disease

1. Safford, Florence. *Caring for the Mentally Impaired Elderly, A Family Guide.* (New York: Henry Holt and Company, 1989), pp. 10 and 11.
2. Nielsen, J. "Geronto-psychiatric period prevalence investigation in a geographically delimited population." *Acta Psychiat Scand* 38:307–330, 1962.
3. Kay, D.W.K.; Beamish, P.; and Roth, M. "Old age mental disorders in Newcastle-upon-Tyne, I. A study of prevalence." *British J Psychiatry* 110:146–158, 1964.
4. Essen-Moller, E. "Individual traits and morbidity in a Swedish rural population." *Acta Psychiatr Scand* [Suppl.] 100:1–160, 1956.
5. Small, G.W. and Jarvik, L.F. "The dementia syndrome." *The Lancet* 2(8313):1443, 1982.
6. *Diagnostic and Statistical Manual of Mental Disorders*, 3rd ed. (American Psychiatric Association, 1980).
7. Cummings, J.L.; and Benson, D.F. *Dementia: A Clinical Approach.* (Boston: Butterworths Publishing, 1983).
8. Folstein, M.J.; Folstein, S.E.; McHugh, P.R. "'Mini-Mental State,' a practical method for grading the cognitive state of patients for the clinician." *J Psychiatr Res* 12:189, 1975.
9. Folstein, M.; Anthony, J.C.; Parhad, I., et al. "The meaning of cognitive impairment in the elderly." *J Am Geriatr Soc* 33:228, 1985.
10. Gado, M.; Hughes, C.P.; Danziger, W., et al. "Volumetric measurements of the cerebrospinal fluid spaces in demented subjects and controls." *Radiology* 144:535, 1982.
11. Blass, J.P. and Barclay, L.L. "New developments in the diagnosis of the dementias." *Drug Devel Res* 5:39, 1985.
12. LaRue, A. "Neuropsychological testing." *Psych Annals* 14:201, 1984.
13. Reisberg, B.; Ferris, S.H.; De Leon, M.J., et al. "The global deterioration scale for assessment of primary degenerative dementia." *Am J Psychiatry* 139:1136, 1982.
14. Rosen, W.G.; Mohs, R.C.; Davis, K.L. "A new rating scale for Alzheimer's disease." *Am J Psychiatry* 141:1356, 1984.
15. Hughes, C.P.; Berg, L.; Danziger, W.L., et al. "A new clinical scale for the staging of dementia." *Br J Psychiatry* 140:566, 1982.
16. Benson, D.F.; Kuhl, D.E.; Hawkins, R.A., et al. "The fluorodeoxyglucose 18F scan in Alzheimer's disease and multi-infarct dementia." *Arch Neurol* 40:711, 1983.
17. Friedland, R.P.; Budinger, T.F., Koss, E., et al. "Alzheimer's disease: Anterior-posterior and lateral hemispheric alterations in cortical glucose utilization." *Neurosci Lett* 53:235, 1985.
18. Friedland, R.P.; Budinger, T.F.; Brant-Zawadzki, M., et al. "The diagnosis of Alzheimer-type dementia, a preliminary comparison of positron emission tomography and proton magnetic resonance." *JAMA* 252:2750, 1984.
19. Reynolds, C.F., 3rd; Kupfer, D.J.; Taska, L.S., et al. "Sleep apnea in Alzheimer's dementia: Correlation with mental deterioration." *J Clin Psychiatry* 46:257, 1985.
20. Small, G.W., and Matsuyama, S.S. "HLA-A2 as a possible marker for onset Alzheimer's disease in men" (in press).
21. Jarvik, L.F.; Matsuyama, S.S.; Kessler, J.O., et al. "Philothermal response of polymorphonuclear leuko-

cytes in dementia of the Alzheimer type." *Neurobiology of Aging* 3:93–99, 1982.

22. Peterson, C.; Gibson, G.E.; Blass, J.P. "Altered calcium uptake in cultured skin fibroblasts from patients with Alzheimer's disease." *N Engl J Med* 312: 1063, 1985.

23. Blass, J.P.; Zemcov, A. "Alzheimer's disease: a metabolic systems degeneration?" *Neurochem Pathol* 2:103, 1984.

Chapter 6
Aluminum Products All Around Us

1. *Physicians' Desk Reference*, 46th ed. (Montvale, New Jersey: Medical Economics Data, 1992).

2. Wigder, H.N. *Dr. Wigder's Guide to Over-the-Counter Drugs.* (New York: Dell Publishing Co., 1979).

3. Penna, R.P. *Handbook of Non-Prescription Drugs*, 6th ed. (Washington, D.C.: American Pharmaceutical Assoc., 1979).

4. *U.S. Code of Federal Regulations* 21, 182.1125-31, 182.1781, 133.173 (e)(1), 182.2727.

5. *Canadian Food and Drug Regulations*, Division 16, 1981.

6. Karacan, I., et al. "Dose-related sleep disturbances induced by coffee and caffeine." *Clin Pharmacol Ther* 20:682–689, 1976.

7. Brody, J.E. "Bodily interaction found to explain caffeine withdrawal headache." *The New York Times*, Apr. 24, 1982.

8. Weiner, M.A. *Reducing the Risk of Alzheimer's.* (Briarcliff Manor, New York: Stein and Day, 1987), p. 119.

Chapter 7
Aluminum Dust and Other Metallic Air Pollutants

1. Walsh, M.W. "Is aluminum related to

Alzheimer's disease?" *The Advocate*, December 11, 1990, p. B2.

2. Noble, H.B. "The air: Unsafe at any site." *The New York Times Magazine*, pp. 122–131, November 4, 1979.

3. Gordon, G. "New dimensions in calcium metabolism." *Osteopathic Annals* 11:38–59, 1983.

4. Weiner, M.A. *The Way of the Skeptical Nutritionist.* (New York: MacMillan, 1981).

5. Beisel, W.R. "Single nutrients and immunity." *American J Clinical Nutrition* 35:417–468.

6. Schneider, K. "Industries gaining broad flexibility on air pollution." *The New York Times*, p. A1, June 26, 1992.

7. "Research in Progress, Annual Report on Research Grants" (Chicago: Alzheimer's Association, 1990), p. 3.

Chapter 8
Aluminum-Contaminated Drinking Water, Milk, Tea, and Cookware

1. Martyn, C.N.; Osmond, C.; Barker, D.J.P.; Harris, E.C.; Edwardson, J.A.; and Lacey, R.F. "Geographical relation between Alzheimer's disease and aluminum in drinking water." *The Lancet*, January 14, 1989, pp. 59–62.

2. Flaten, T.P. "An investigation of the chemical composition of Norwegian drinking water and its possible relationships with the epidemiology of some diseases." Thesis no. 51, Institutt for Norganisk Kjemi, Norges Tekniske Hogskole, Trondheim, 1986.

3. Vogt, T. "Water quality and health—a study of possible relationship between aluminium in drinking water and dementia." *Sosiale og okonomiske studier* 61:1–99, Oslo: Central Bureau of Statistics of Norway, 1986.

4. Jorm, A.; Henderson, A.; and Jacomb,

P. differences in mortality from dementia in Australia: an analysis of death certificate data." *Acta Psychiatr Scand* (in press).

5. Yase, Y. "The pathogenesis of amyotrophic lateral sclerosis." *The Lancet* ii:292–296, 1972.

6. Yase, Y. "Environmental contribution to the amyotrophic lateral scelerosis process." In: Serratrice, G.; Cros, D.; Desnuelle, C., et al., ed. *Neuromuscular Diseases* (New York: Raven Press, 1984), pp. 335–339.

7. Gardner, N.J.; Winter, P.D.; and Barker, D.J.P. *Atlas of Mortality From Selected Diseases in England and Wales 1968–1978.* (Chichester, UK: John Wiley & Sons, 1984).

8. Lindegard, B. "Aluminium and Alzheimer's disease." *The Lancet,* February 4, 1989, pp. 267 and 268.

9. "Aluminum in the brain: new data." *Chemistry and Industry,* June 6, 1988, p. 346.

10. Coriat, A.M. and Gillard, R.D. "Beware the cups that cheer." *Nature* 321:570, 1986.

11. McGraw, M.D.; Bishop, N.; and Jameson, R., et al. "Aluminium content of milk formulae and intravenous fluids used in infants." *Lancet* I:157, 1986.

12. Bishop, N.; McGraw, M.; and Ward, N. "Aluminium in infant formulas." *Lancet,* Mar. 4, 1989.

13. Weaver, L.T.; Laker, M.F.; and Nelson, R. "Intestinal permeability in the newborn." *Arch Dis Child,* 54:236–241, 1984.

14. Sedman, A.B.; Klein, G.L.; and Merritt, R.J., et al. "Evidence of aluminium loading in infants receiving intravenous therapy." *N Engl J Med* 312:1337–1343, 1985.

15. Freundlich, M.; Zillervelo, G.; Abitbol, C.; Strauss, J.; Faugere, M.C.; and Malluche, H.H. "Infant formula as a cause of aluminium toxicity in neonatal uraemia." *Lancet* ii:527–529, 1985.

16. Wenk, G.L. and Stemmer, K.L. "Suboptimal dietary zinc intake increases aluminium accumulation into the rat brain." *Brain Res* 288:393–395, 1983.

17. Kaehny, W.D.; Hegg, A.P.; and Alfrey, A.C. "Gastrointestinal absorption of aluminium from aluminium-containing antacids." *New Engl J Med* 296:1389–1390, 1977.

18. Ward, N.I.; Watson, R.; Bryce-Smith, D. "Placental element levels in relation to fetal development for obstetrically 'normal' births: a study at 37 elements." *J Biosoc Res* 9 (part 1):63–81, 1987.

19. Flynn, A.; Miller, S.I.; Martier, S.S.; Golden, N.L.; Sokol, R.J.; and Del Villano, B.C. "Zinc status of pregnant alcoholic women: a determinant of fetal outcome." *Lancet* i:572–575, 1982.

20. Lo, G.S.; Settle, S.L.; Steinke, F.H.; and Hopkins, D.T. "Effect of phytate: zinc molar ratio and isolated soy bean protein on zinc bioavailability." *J Nutr* 111:2223–2235, 1981.

21. American Committee on Nutrition. "Aluminum toxicity in infants and children." *Pediatrics* 78:1150–1154, 1986.

22. DHSS Committee on Medical Aspects of Food Policy. *Present Day Practice in Infant Feeding: Third Report.* (London: HM Stationery Office, 1988).

23. French, P.; Gardner, M.J.; and Gunn, A.M. "Dietary aluminium and Alzheimer's disease." *Fd Chem Toxic* 27(7):495–496, 1989.

24. Flaten, T.P. and Odegard, M. "Tea, aluminium and Alzheimer's disease." *Fd Chem Toxic* 26:959.

25. Slanina, P.; French, W.; Ekstrom,

L.G.; Loof, L.; Slorach, S.; and Ceder-gren, A. "Dietary citric acid enhances absorption of aluminum in antacids." *Cli Chem* 32:539.

26. Flaten, T.P. and Odegard, M. "Dietary aluminium and Alzheimer's disease—a reply." *Fd Chem Toxic* 27(7):496–497, 1989.

27. Pike, R.L. and Brown, M.L. *Nutrition: An Integrated Approach*, 3rd ed. (New York: John Wiley, 1984), pp. 190 and 191.

28. Tennakone, K. and Wickramanayake, S. "Aluminium leaching from cooking utensils." *Nature* 325(6105):202, January 15–21, 1987.

29. Alfrey, A.C.; Mishell, J.M.; Burks, J., et al. "Syndrome of dyspraxia and multifocal seizures associated with chronic hemodialysis." *Trans Am Soc Artif Intern Organs* 18:257–261, 1972.

30. Alfrey, A.C.; Le Gendre, G.R.; Kaehny, W.D. "The dialysis encephalopathy syndrome: possible aluminium intoxication." *New Engl J Med* 294:184–188, 1976.

31. Mahurkar, S.D.; Smith, E.C.; Mamdani, B.H.; and Dunea, G. "Dialysis dementia—the Chicago experience." *J Dialysis* 2:447–458, 1978.

32. Davison, A.M.; Walker, G.S.; Oli, H.; and Lewins, A.M. "Water supply aluminium concentration, dialysis dementia, and effect of reverse-osmosis water treatment." *Lancet* 9:785–787, October 1982.

33. Bjorksten, J. "Recent developments in protein chemistry." *Chemical Industries* 48:746–751, June 1941.

34. Bjorksten, J. "Chemistry of duplication." *Chemical Industries* 50:68–72, January 1942.

35. Alrey, A.C. "Cassette No. 4 from conference of the American Academy of Medical Preventics, Denver, Colorado, November 2–4, 1979."

36. Alrey, A.C.; Hegg, A.; Miller, N.;

Berl, T.; and Burns, A. "Interrelationship between calcium and aluminum metabolism in idalyzed uremic patients." *Mineral Electrolyte Metab* 2:81–87, 1979.

37. Alrey, A.C.; LeGendre, G.R.; and Kaehny, W.D. "The dialysis encephalopathy syndrome. Possible aluminum intoxication." *New Engl J Med* 294:184–188, 1976.

38. Bjorksten, J. "Aluminum in degenerative disease." *Rejuvenation* 8(1):11–19, March 1981.

Chapter 9
How Aluminum Acts on the Brain

1. Doellken, P. "Ueber die wirkung des aluminum mit besonder beruecksichtigung der durch das aluminum verursachten lasionen im zentralnervensystem." *Naunyn-Schmiedebergs Arch Exper Path Pharmakol* 40:58–120, 1897.

2. Spofforth, J. "Case of aluminum poisoning." *Lancet* 1:1301, 1921.

3. Munoz-Garcia, D.; Pendlebury, W.W.; Kessler, J.B.; Perl, D.P. "An immunocytochemical comparison of cytoskeletal proteins in aluminum-induced and Alzheimer-type neurofibrillary tangles." *Acta Neuropathol* 70:243–248, 1986.

4. Rifat, S.L.; Eastwood, M.R.; Crapper-McLaughlan, D.R.; Corey, P.N. "Effect of exposure of miners to aluminum powder." *The Lancet* 336:1162–65, Nov. 10, 1990.

5. Perl, D.P. and Good, P.F. "The association of aluminum, Alzheimer's disease, and neurofibrillary tangles." *J. Neural Transm* [Suppl] 24:205–211, 1987.

6. Crapper McLaughlan, D.R.; McLachlan, C.D.; Krishnan, B.; Krishnan, S.S.; Dalton, A.J.; Steele, J.C. "Aluminium and calcium in soil and food

from Guam, Palau and Jamaica: implications for amyotrophic lateral sclerosis and parkinsonism-dementia syndromes of Guam." *Brain* 112:45–53, 1989.

7. Bjorksten, Johan. "The crosslinkage theory of aging.& *J. Amer. Geriatrics Soc.* 16, No. 4:408–427, 1968.

8. Pryor, W.A. "Free radical reactions and their importance in biochemical systems." *Fed. Proc.* 32:1862–1869, 1973.

9. Demopoulos, H.B. "The basis of free radical pathology." *Fed. Proc.* 32:1859–1861, 1973.

10. Demopoulos, H.B. "Oxygen free radicals in central nervous system ischemia and trauma." *Bull. Europ. Physiopath. Resp.* Resp. [Suppl.] 17:127–155, 1982.

11. Levine, Stephen A. and Kidd, Parris M. *Antioxidant Adaptation: Its Role in Free Radical Pathology.* (San Leandro, California: Allergy Research Group, 1985), pp. 14 and 15.

12. Crapper-McLachlan, D.R. and Dalton, A.J. "Alterations in short-term retention, conditioned avoidance response acquisition and motivation following aluminum-induced neurofibrillary degeneration." *Physiology and Behaviour*, 10:925–933, 1973.

12a. D.R. McLachlan, M.D., F.R.C.P.(C), Professor of Physiology and Medicine, Director, Centre for Research in Neurodegenerative Diseases, University of Toronto. Tanz Neuroscience Building, 6 Queen's Park Circle West, Toronto, Ontario, Canada M5S 1A8; telephone (416) 978–7461, teleFAX (416) 978–1878.

13. Crapper-McLachlan, D.R. and Tomko, G.J. "Neuronal correlates of an encephalopathy associated with aluminum neurofibrillary degeneration." *Brain Research* 97:253–264, 1975.

14. Crapper-McLachlan, D.R. and De-

Boni, U. "Aluminum in human brain disease—an overview." *Neurotoxicology* 1:3–16, 1980.

15. Crapper-McLachlan, D.R. and Van Berkum, M.F.A. "Aluminum: a role in degenerative brain disease associated with neurofibrillary degeneration" in *Progress in Brain Research,* Vol. 70, D.F. Swaab, E. Fliers, M. Mirmiran, W.A. Van Gool, and F. Van Haaren (Eds.) (Amsterdam: Elsevier Science Publishers, 1986), pp. 399–409.

16. Crapper-McLachlan, D.R.; Quittkat, S.; DeBoni, U. "Altered chromatin conformation in Alzheimer's disease." *Brain* 102:483–495, 1979.

17. Crapper-McLachlan, D.R.; Lewis, P.N.; Lukiw, W.J.; Sima, A.; Bergeron, C.; DeBoni, U. "Chromatin structure in dementia." *Ann. Neurol.* 15:329–334, 1984.

18. Lewis, P.N.; Lukiw, W.J.; DeBoni, U.; Crapper-McLachlan, D.R. "Changes in chromatin structure associated with Alzheimer's disease." *J. Neurochem.* 37:1193–1202, 1981.

19. Commissaris, R.L.; Cordon, J.J.; Sprague, S.; Keiser, J.; Mayor, G.H.; Rech, R.H. "Behavioral changes in rats after chronic aluminum and parathyroid hormone administration." *Neurobehavioral Toxicology and Teratology* 4:403–410, 1982.

20. Farnell, B.J.; DeBoni, U.; Crapper-McLachlan, D.R. "Aluminum neurotoxicity in the absence of neurofibrillary degeneration in CAl hippocampal pyramidal neurons *in vitro*." *Experimental Neurology* 78:241–258, 1982.

21. King, S.W.; Savory, J.; Wills, M.R. "The clinical biochemistry of aluminum." *CRC Critical Reviews in Clinical Laboratory Sciences* 14:1–20, 1981.

22. Hamilton, E.I. "Aluminum and Alzheimer's disease–a comment."

The Science of the Total Environment 25:87–91, 1982.

23. Mayor, G.H.; Keiser, J.A.; Makdani, D.; Ku, P.K. "Aluminum absorption and distribution: effect of parathyroid hormone." *Science (Washington)* 197:1187–1192, 1977.

24. Banks, W.A. and Kastin, A.J. "Aluminum increases permeability of the blood-brain barrier to labelled DSIP and beta-endorphin: possible implications for senile and dialysis dementias." *Lancet* 26:1227–1229, November 1983.

25. Lai, J.C.K.; Guest, J.F.; Leung, T.K.C.; Lim, L.; Davison, A.N. "The effects of cadmium, manganese and aluminum on sodium-potassium-activated and magnesium-activated adenosine triphosphatase activity and choline uptake in rat brain synaptosomes." *Biochemical Pharmacology* 29:141–146, 1980.

26. Lai, J.C.K.; Lim, L.; Davison, A.N. "Differences in the inhibitory effect of Cd2+, Mn2+ and aluminum 3+ on the uptake of dopamine by synaptosomes from forebrain and from striatum of the rat." *Biochemical Pharmacology* 30:3123–3125, 1981.

27. Wong, P.C. and Lim, L. "The effects of aluminum, manganese and cadmium chloride on the methylation of phospholipids in the rat brain synaptosomal membrane." *Biochemical Pharmacology* 30:1704–1705, 1981.

28. Yates, C.M.; Simpson, J.; Russell, D.; Gordon, A. "Cholinergic enzymes in neurofibrillary degeneration produced by aluminum." *Brain Research* 197:269–274, 1980.

29. Hetnarski, B.; Wisniewski, H.M.; Iqbal, K.; Sziedzic, J.D.; Lajtha, A. "Central cholinergic activity in aluminum-induced neurofibrillary degeneration." *Annals of Neurology* 7:489–490, 1980.

30. Wenk, G.L. and Stemmer, K.L. "The influence of ingested aluminum upon norepinephrine and dopamine levels in the rat brain." *Neurotoxicology* 2:347–353, 1981.

31. Wenk, G.L. and Stemmer, K.L. "Activity of the enzymes dopamine-beta-hydroxylase and phenyl-ethanolamine-N-methyl-transferase in discrete brain regions of the copper-zinc deficient rat following aluminum ingestion." *Neurotoxicology* 3:93–99, 1982.

32. Exss, R.E. and Summer, G.K. "Basic proteins in neurons containing fibrillary deposits." *Brain Research* 49:151–164, 1973.

33. Terry, R.D. "The fine structure of neurofibrillary tangles in Alzheimer's disease." *J. Neuropathology and Experimental Neurology* 22:629–642, 1963.

34. Terry, R.D.; Gonatos, N.K.; Weiss, M. "Ultrastructural studies in Alzheimer's presenile dementia." *Amer. J. Pathology* 44:269–297, 1964.

35. Brion, J.P.; Couck, A.M.; Flament-Durand, J. "Ultrastructural study of enriched fractions of 'tangles' from human patients with senile dementia of the Alzheimer's type." *Acta Neuropathologica (Berlin)* 64:148–152, 1984.

36. Wisniewski, H.M. and Wen, G.Y. "Substructures of paired helical filaments from Alzheimer's disease neurofibrillary tangles." *Acta Neuropathologica* 66:173–176, 1985.

37. Crapper-McLachlan, D.R. and DeBoni, U. "Aluminum in human brain disease—a review." *Neurotoxicology* 1:3–16, 1980.

38. Wisniewski, H.; Iqbal, K.; McDermott, J.R. "Aluminum-induced neurofibrillary changes: its relationship to senile dementia of the Alzheimer's type." *Neurotoxicology* 1:121–124, 1980.

39. Kolata, G.B. "Clues to the cause of senile dementia." *Science (Washington)* 211:1032–1033, 1981.

40. Blessed, G.; Tomlinson, B.E.; Roth, M. "The association between quantitative measures of dementia and of senile changes in the cerebral grey matter of elderly subjects." *British J. Psychiatry* 114:797–811, 1968.

41. Wilcock, G.K. and Esiri, M.M. "Plaques, tangles and dementia, a quantitative study." *J. Neurological Science* 56:343–356, 1982.

42. Crapper-McLachlan, D.R. and DeBoni, U. "Brain aging and Alzheimer's disease." *Canadian Psychiatric Association J.* 23:229–233, 1978.

43. Crapper-McLachlan, D.R.; Krishnan, S.S.; Dalton, A.J. "Brain aluminum distribution in Alzheimer's disease and experimental neurofibrillary degeneration." *Science (Washington)* 180:511–513, 1973.

44. Crapper-McLachlan, D.R.; Krishnan, S.S.; Quitkat, S. "Aluminum neurofibrillary degeneration and Alzheimer's disease." *Brain* 99:67–80, 1976.

45. McDermott, J.R.; Smith, A.I.; Iqbal, K.; Wisniewski, H.M. "Brain aluminum in aging and Alzheimer's disease." *Neurology* 29:809–814, 1979.

46. Perl, D.P. and Brody, A.R. "Alzheimer's disease: X-ray spectrometric evidence of aluminum accumulation in neurofibrillary tangle-bearing neurons." *Science (Washington)* 208:297–299, 1980.

47. Perl, D.P. and Pendlebury, W.W. 6Aluminum accumulation in neurofibrillary tangle-bearing neurons of senile dementia Alzheimer's type (SDAT)-detection by intraneuronal X-ray spectrometry studies of unstained tissue sections." *J. Neuropathology & Applied Neurology* 43:349, 1984.

48. Klatzo, I.; Wisniewski, H.; Streicher, E. "Experimental production of neurofibrillary degeneration. I. Light microscopic observations." *J. Neuropathology & Experimental Neurology* 24:1877199, 1965.

49. Wisniewski, H.; Terry, R.D.; Hirano, A. "Neurofibrillary pathology." *J. Neuropathology & Experimental Neurology* 24:163–176, 1970.

50. Wisniewski, H.; Sturman, J.A.; Shek, J.W. "Chronic model of neurofibrillary changes induced in mature rabbits by aluminum." *Neurobiology of Aging* 3:11–22, 1982.

51. Bugiani, O. and Ghetti, B. "Progressing encephalomyelopathy with muscular atrophy induced by aluminum powder." *Neurobiology of Aging* 3:209–222, 1982.

52. Kosik, K.S.; Bradley, W.G.; Good, P.F.; Rasool, C.G.; Selkoe, D.J. "Cholinergic function in lumbar aluminum myelopathy." *J. Neuropathology & Experimental Neurology* 42:365–375, 1983.

53. Selkoe, D.J.; Liem, R.K.H.; Yen, S.H.; Shelanski, M.L. "Biochemical and immunological characterization of neurofilaments in experimental neurofibrillary degeneration induced by aluminum." *Brain Research* 163:235–252, 1979.

54. Dahl, D. and Bignami, A. "Immunochemical cross-reactivity of normal neurofibrils and aluminum-induced neurofibrillary tangles. Immunofluorescence study with anti-neurofilament serum." *Experimental Neurology* 58:74–80, 1978.

55. Yates, C.M.; Simpson, J.; Russell, D.; Gordon, A. "Cholinergic enzymes in neurofibrillary degeneration produced by aluminum." *Brain Research* 197:269–274, 1980.

56. Marquis, J.K. "Aluminum neurotoxicity—an experimental perspec-

tive." *Bull. Environmental Contamination and Toxicology* 29:43–49, 1982.

57. Yamane, Y. and Ohtawa, M. "Effect of aluminum chloride on binding of 4-hydroxyamino-quinoline l-oxide to nucleic acids." *Gann* 69:477–486, 1978.

58. Karlik, S.J.; Eichhorn, G.L.; Lewis, P.N.; Crapper-McLachlan, D.R. "Interaction of aluminum species with deoxyribonucleic acid." *Biochemistry* 19:5991–5998, 1980.

59. DeBoni, U.; Seger, M.; Crapper-McLachlan, D.R. "Functional consequences of chromiatin-bound aluminum in cultured human cells." *Neurotoxicology* 1:65–81, 1980.

60. Sanderson, C.L.; Crapper-McLachlan, D.R.; DeBoni, U. "Altered steroid-induced puffing by chromatin-bound aluminum in a polytene chromosome of the blackfly *Simulium vitatum*." *Canadian J. Genetics and Cytology* 24:27–36, 1982.

61. Sanderson, C.; Crapper-McLachlan, D.R.; DeBoni, U. "Inhibition of corticosterone binding *in vitro*, in rabbit hippocampus by chromatin-bound aluminum.< *Acta Neuropathologica (Berlin)* 57:249–254, 1982.

62. Sarkander, H.I.; Balss, G.; Schlosser, R.; Stoltenburg, G.; Lux, R.M. "Blockade of neuronal brain RNA initiation sites by aluminum: a primary molecular mechanism of aluminum-induced neurofibrillary changes?" In *Brain Aging: Neuropathology and Neuropharmacology* (Aging, Vol. 21). Cervos-Navarro, J. and Sarkander, H.I. (Eds.) (New York: Raven Press, 1983), pp. 259–274.

63. Markesberry, W.R.; Ehmann, W.D.; Hossain, T.I.M.; Alauddin, A.; Goodin, D.T. "Instrumental neutron activation analysis of brain aluminum in Alzheimer's disease and aging." *Annals of Neurology* 10:512–516, 1981.

64. Hamilton, E.I. "Aluminum and Alzheimer's disease—a comment." *The Science of the Total Environment* 25:87–91, 1982.

65. Bjorksten, J.A. "Dietary aluminum and Alzheimer's disease." *The Science of the Total Environment* 25:81–84, 1982.

66. Caster, W.O. and Wang, M. "Dietary aluminum and Alzheimer's disease—a reply." *The Science of the Total Environment* 25:85–86, 1992.

67. Banks, W.A. and Kastin, A.J. "Aluminum increases permeability of the blood-brain barrier to labelled DSIP and beta-endorphin: possible implications for senile and dialysis dementias." *The Lancet* 26:1227–1229, November 1983.

Chapter 10
Dental Amalgam Dementia and Other Mercury Poisons

1. Valentine, Tom. "Dental mercury." *Search for Health* 1(2):52–69, November/December 1992.

2. Alsleben, H. Rudolph and Shute, Wilfrid E. *How to Survive the New Health Catastrophes*. (Anaheim, California: Survival Publications, Inc., 1973), pp. 212 and 213.

3. Ibid., pp. 216–220.

4. McAlpine, D. and Araki, S. "Minamata disease: an unusual neurological disorder caused by contaminated fish." *The Lancet* 2:629–631, 1958.

5. McAlpine, D. and Araki, S. "Late effects of an unusual neurological disorder caused by contaminated fish." *A.M.A. Archs Neurol.* 1:522–530, 1959.

6. Takeuchi, T. "Pathology of Minamata disease." *Acta Pathol Jpn.* 32 (Suppl 1):73–99, 1982.

7. Gen, O. et al. "Urinary beta-2-microglobulin does not serve as diagnostic tool for Minamata disease." *Arch Environ Health* 37(6):336–341, November/December 1982.

8. Bakir, F. et al. "The employment of a thiol resin in mercury poisoning." *Science* 181:230–241, 1973.
9. Rustam, H. et al. "Evidence for a neuromuscular disorder in methylmercury poisoning." *Arch Environ Health* 30:190–195, April 1975.

Chapter 11
Body and Brain Pathology of Mercury Toxicity

1. Warren, Tom. *Beating Alzheimer's.* (Garden City Park, New York: Avery Publishing Group, Inc., 1991).
2. Eggleston, David. "Effect of dental amalgam and nickel alloys on T-lymphocytes: Preliminary report." *J. Prosthetic Dentistry* 51 (5):617–623, May 1984.
3. Eggleston, David and Nylander, Magnus. "Correlation of dental amalgam with mercury in brain tissue." *Research and Education* 56 (6):704–707, Dec. 1987.
4. Nylander, Magnus; Friberg, Lars; Lind, Birger. "Mercury concentrations in human brain and kidneys in relation to exposure from dental amalgam fillings." *Swed. Dent. J.* 11:179–187, 1987.
5. Queen, H.L. *Chronic Mercury Toxicity—New Hope Against an Endemic Disease. Doctor's Guide for Lifestyle Counseling.* (Colorado Springs, Colorado: Queen and Company, 1988).
6. Hemenway, Caroline. "Amalgam declared dangerous." *Dentistry Today*, February 10, 1989.
7. Denton, Sandra. "The mercury cover-up." *Health Consciousness Magazine*, June 1989, pp. 1–6.
8. Clarkson, T.W.; Friberg, L.; Hursh, J.; Nylander, M. In *Biological Monitoring of Toxic Metals.* (New York City: Plenum Press, Feb. 1988).
9. *Proceedings of the International Conference on Biocompatibility of Materials.* (Tacoma, WA: Life Sciences Press, Nov. 1988).
10. Ahlrot, U. and Westerlund, P. *Nutrition Research,* supplement of 1985, p. 403: Second Nordic Symposium on Trace Elements in Human Health & Disease, Odense, Denmark, Aug. 1987.

Chapter 12
Studies Prove Dental Amalgams Promote Alzheimer's Disease

1. Hahn, L.J.; Kloiber, R.; Vimy, M.J., et al.: "Dental 'silver' tooth fillings. A source of mercury exposure revealed by whole-body image scan and tissue analysis." *FASEB J* 3:2641–2644, 1989.
2. Bjorklund, G. "Mercury as a potential source for the etiology of Alzheimer's disease." *Trace Elements in Medicine* 8(4):208, 1991.
3. Wenstrup, D.; Ehmann, W.D.; and Markesbery, W.R. "Trace element imbalances in isolated subcellular fractions of Alzheimer's disease brains." *Brain Research* 553:125–131, 1990.
4. Report to the International Academy of Oral Medicine and Toxicology, Orlando, Florida, February 1, 1992.
5. Paulson, Tom. "Dangers in fillings indicated. Scientists parallel dental amalgams and lead poisoning." *Seattle Post-Intelligencer*, February 25, 1992, p. 1.
6. Huggins, H.A. "Mercury protective prototocol." T.E.R.F. P.O. Box 2589, Colorado Springs, Colorado 80901.
7. Godfrey, Michael E. "Chronic illness in association with dental amalgam: report of two cases." *Journal of Advancement in Medicine* 3(4):247–255, Winter 1990.
8. Kahn Van, N. "Heavy metal poisoning: mercury and lead." *Ann. Int. Med* 76:779–792, 1972.
9. Thompson, C.; Markesbury, W.R.; Eh-

mann, W.D., et al. "Regional brain trace element studies in Alzheimer's disease." *Neurotoxicology* 9:1–8, 1988.

Chapter 13
Lead Poisoning of the Brain

1. Neergarrd, Lauran. "Lead paint: youngest face risk to health." Associated Press, *The Advocate*, February 1, 1993, pp. A1 and A8.
2. Fine, P.R., et al. "Pediatric blood lead levels: a study of 14 Illinois cities of intermediate population." *JAMA* 221:1475, 1972.
3. Cohen, C.J., et al. "Epidemiology of lead poisoning: a comparison of urban and rural children." *JAMA* 226:1430, 1973.
4. Patterson, C.C. "Contaminated and natural lead environments of man." *Arch. Environ. Health* 11:344, 1965.
5. *Lead: Airborne Lead in Perspective.* National Research Council–National Academy of Sciences, Washington, D.C., 1972.
6. Goyer, R.A. and Rhyne, B.C. "Pathological effects of lead." *Internat. Rev. Pathol.* 12:1, 1973.
7. Goyer, R.A. and Chisolm, J.J. "Lead" Chp. 3 in *Metallic Contaminants and Human Health*. Douglas H.K. Lee, ed. (New York: Academic Press, 1972).
8. Tucker, A. *The Toxic Metals* (London: Earth Island Ltd., 1972), p. 88.
9. Gordon, Garry. *Lead Toxicity*. (Sacramento, California: Sacramento Medical Preventics Clinic, Inc., Dec. 1974), p. 2.
10. *Minerals Yearbook*, Vol. 1. U.S. Dept. of the Interior, prepared by the staff of the Bureau of Mines, U.S. Government Printing Office, Washington, D.C., 1970.
11. Murozumi, M., et al. "Chemical concentrations of pollutant lead aerosols, terrestrial dusts, and sea salts in Greenland and Antarctic snow strata." *Geochim. Cosmochim. Acta* 33:1247, 1969.
12. Lederer, L.G. and Bing, F.C. "Effect of calcium and phosphorus on retention of lead by growing organisms." *JAMA* 114:2457, 1940.
13. Shields, J.B. and Mitchell, H.H. "The effect of calcium and phosphorus on the metabolism of lead." *J. Nutr.* 21:541, 1941.
14. Kostial, K., et al. "Reduction of lead absorption from the intestine in newborn rats." *Environ Res.* 4:360, 1971.
15. Six, K.M. and Goyer, R.A. "Experimental enhancement of lead toxicity by low dietary calcium." *J. Lab. Clin. Med.* 76:933, 1970.
16. Quarterman, J., et al. "The influence of dietary calcium and phosphate on lead metabolism." *Trace Substances in Environmental Health-VII*. Delbert D. Hemphill, ed. (St. Louis: University of Missouri Press, 1973), p. 347.
17. "U.S. plans a system for tracking levels of lead in children's blood." *The New York Times*, August 29, 1992, p. 10.
18. Kopito, L., et al. "Chronic plumbism in children." *JAMA* Vol. 209, no. 2, July 14, 1969.
19. Balch, James F. and Balch, Phyllis A. *Prescription for Nutritional Healing*. (Garden City Park, New York: Avery Publishing Group, Inc., 1990), p. 29.
20. "Succimer approved to treat severe lead poisoning in children." *BioProve Newsletter*, May 1991.

Chapter 14
Cadmium Poisoning Around Us and In Us

1. Sugawara, N. and Sugawara, C. "Cadmium accumulation in organs and mortality during a continued oral uptake." *Arch. Toxicol.* 32(4):297–306, 1974.

2. Nomiyama, K.; Yasuo, S.; Akiko, Y.; and Nomiyama, H. "Effects of dietary cadmium on rabbits: I. Early signs of cadmium intoxication." *Toxicol. Appl. Pharmacol.* 31(1):4–12, 1975.

3. Powell, G.W.; Miller, W.J.; Morton, J.D.; and Clifton, C.M. "Influence of dietary cadmium level and supplemental zinc on cadmium toxicity in the bovine." *J. Nutr.* 84(3):205–214, 1964.

4. Petering, H.G.; Johnson, M.A.; and Stemmer, K.L. "Studies of zinc metabolism in the rat: I. Dose-response effects of cadmium." *Arch. Environ. Health* 28(2):93–101, 1971.

5. Palmer, K.C.; Snider, G.L.; and Hayes, J.A. "Cellular proliferation induced in the lung by cadmium aerosol." *Am. Rev. Resp. Dis.* 112(2):173–180, 1975.

6. Schroeder, H.A.; Vinton, W.H.; and Balassa, J.J. "Effects of chromium, cadmium, and lead on the growth and survival of rats." *J. Nutr.* 80(1):48–54, 1963.

7. Schroeder, H.A. "Renal cadmium and essential hypertension." *JAMA* 187(5):359, 1964.

8. Schroeder, H.A. "Cadmium hypertension in rats." *Amer. J. Physiol.* 207(1):62–66, 1964.

9. Doyle, J.J.; Bernhoft, R.A.; and Sandstead, H.H. "The effects of low level of dietary cadmium on blood pressure. Na, K, and water retention in growing rats." *J. Lab. Clin. Med.* 86(1):57–63, 1975.

10. Tarasenko, N. and Vorobeva, R.S. "Hygienic problems connected with cadmium use." *Vestn Akad Med. Nauk.* 28(10):37–43, 1973.

11. Fox, M.R.S. "Effect of essential minerals on cadmium toxicity: A review." *Food Sci.* 39(2):321–324, 1974.

12. Koller, L.D.; Exon, J.H.; and Roan, J.G. "Antibody suppression by cadmium." *Arch. Environ. Health* 30(12):598–601, 1975.

13. Nordberg, G.F. "Effects of long-term cadmium exposure on the seminal vesicles of mice." *J. Reprod. Fertil.* 45(1):165–168, 1975.

14. Miller, W.J.; Lampp, B.; Powell, G.W.; Salotti, C.A.; and Blackmon, D.M. "Influence of a high level of dietary cadmium on cadmium in milk, excretion, and cow performance." *J. Dairy Sci.* 50(9):1404–1408, 1967.

15. *Ind. Health* 12(3/4):175–177, 1974.

16. Washko, P.W. and Cousins, R.J. "Effect of low dietary calcium on chronic cadmium toxicity in rats." *Nutr. Rep. Int.* 11(2):113–127, 1975.

17. Pond, W.G. and Walker, E.F. "Effect of dietary Ca and Cd level of pregnant rats on reproduction and on dam and progeny tissue mineral concentrations." *Proc. Soc. Exp. Biol. Med.* 148(3):665–668, 1975.

18. Hill, C.H.; Matrone, G.; Payne, W.L.; and Barber, C.W. "In vivo interaction of cadmium with copper, zinc, and iron." *Jour. Nutr.* 80(3):227–235, 1963.

19. Banis, R.J.; Pong, W.G.; Walker, E.F.; and O'Connor, J.R. "Dietary cadmium, iron, and zinc interactions in the growing rat.T *Proc. Soc. Exp. Biol. Med.* 130(5):802–806, 1969.

20. Ohkata, Kazuyoshi. "Effects of low calcium diet and cadmium addition on concentrations of cadmium, zinc and copper of body tissues." *Nichidai Igaku Zasshi* 31(3):105–124, 1972.

21. Mason, K.E.; Young, J.O.; and Brown, J.E. "Effectiveness of selenium and zinc in protecting against cadmium induced injury of the rat testis." *Anat. Rec.* 148(2):309, 1964.

22. Lucis, O.J. and Lucis, R. "Distribution of cadmium 109 and zinc 65 in mice of inbred strains." *Arch Environ Health* 19(3):334–336, 1969.

23. Suzuki, S.; Taguchi, T.; and Yoko-hashi, G. "Dietary factors influencing upon the retention rate of orally administered CdCl3 in mice, with special reference to calcium and protein concentrations in diet." *Ind. Health* 7(3/4):155–162, 1969.

24. Maji, Taizo and Yoshida Akira. VTherapeutic effect of dietary iron and ascorbic acid on cadmium toxicity of rats." *Nutr. Rep. Int.* 10(3):139–149, 1974.

Chapter 15
Brain Iron Imbalance as a Source of Alzheimer's Disease

1. Herbert, V. "Introduction and medicolegal consideration." In *Diagnosis and Treatment of Iron Disorders* (New York: HP Publishing Co., Nov. 10, 1990), p. 4.

2. Goodman, L. "Alzheimer's disease: a clinico-pathologic analysis of twenty-three cases with a theory on pathogenesis." *J Nerv. Ment. Dis.* 118:97, 1953.

3. Connor, J.R. and Benkovic, S.A. "Iron regulation in the brain: histochemical, biochemical, and molecular considerations." *Ann Neurol* 32:34–44, 1992.

4. Cannata, J.B.; Fernandez-Soto, I.; Fernandez-Menendez, M.J.; Fernandez-Martin, J.L.; McGregor, S.J.; Brock, J.H.; Halls, D. "Role of iron metabolism in absorption and cellular uptake of aluminum." *Kidney Int.* 39:799, 1991.

5. Fraga, C.G.; Oteiza, P.I.; Golub, M.S.; Gershwin, M.E.; Keen, C.L. "Effects of aluminum on brain lipid peroxidation." *Toxicol. Lett.* 51:213, 1990.

6. Blass, J.P. and Gibson, G.E. "The role of oxidative abnormalities in the pathophysiology of Alzheimer's disease." *Rev. Neurol.* 147:513, 1991.

7. Gibson, G.E. and Peterson, C.P. "Aging decreases oxidative metabolism and the release and synthesis of acetylcholine." *J. Neurochem.* 37:978, 1981.

8. Crichton, R.R. and Charloteaux-Wauters, M. "Iron transport and storage." *Eur. J. Biochem.* 164:485, 1987.

9. Hill, J.M. "Iron concentration reduced in ventral-pallidum, globus pallidus, and substantia nigra by GABA-transaminase inhibitor, gamma-vinyl GABA." *Brain Res.* 342:19, 1985.

10. Bourre, J.M.; Pascal, G.; Durand, G.; Masson, M.; Dumont, O.; Picotti, M.J. "Alterations in the fatty acid composition of rat brain cells (neurons, astrocytes and oligodendrocytes) and subcellular fractions (myelin and synaptosomes) induced by a diet devoid of n-3 fatty acids." *J Neurochem.* 43:342, 1984.

11. Larkin, E.C. and Rao, A. "Importance of fetal and neonatal iron: adequacy for normal development of central nervous system." In *Brain, Behaviour, and Iron in the Infant Diet.* Dobbing, J., Ed. (New York: Springer-Verlag, 1990), chap. 3.

12. Kabara, J. "A critical review of brain cholesterol metabolism." *Prog. Brain Res.* 40:363, 1973.

13. Mason, R.P.; Shajenko, L.; Chambers, T.E.; Grazioso, H.J.; Shoemaker, W.J.; and Herbette, L.G. "Biochemical and structural analysis of lipid membranes from temporal gyrus and cerebellum of Alzheimer's diseased brains." *Biophys. J.* 59:592, 1991.

14. Arai, H.; Kogure, K.; Sugioka, K.; Nakano, M. "Importance of two iron-reducing systems in lipid peroxidation of rat brain: implications for oxygen toxicity in the central nervous system." *Biochem. Int.* 14:741, 1987.

15. Subarao, K.V. and Richardson, J.S. "Iron-dependent peroxidation of rat brain: a regional study." *J. Neurosci. Res.* 26:224, 1990.

16. Jesberger, J.A. and Richardson, J.S. "Oxygen free radicals and brain dysfunction." *Intern. J. Neurosci.* 57:1, 1991.

17. Zaleska, M.M. and Floyd, R. "Regional lipid peroxidation in rat brain *in vitro*: possible role of endogenous iron." *Neurochem. Res.* 10:397, 1985.

18. Bose, S.K.; Andrews, J.; Roberts, P.D. "Hematological probelms in a geriatric unit with special reference to anemia." *Gerontol Clin* 12:339–346, 1970.

19. Calvey, H.D. and Castleden, C.M. "Gastrointestinal investigations for anemia in the elderly in a prospective study." *Age and Ageing* 16:399–404, 1987.

20. Mowat, A.G. "Hematological abnormalities in rheumatoid arthritis." *Semin Arthritis Rheum* 4:195–219, 1971.

21. Short, C.L.; Bauer, W.; Reynolds, W.E. *Rheumatoid Arthritis.* (Cambridge, Massachusetts: Harvard University, 1957), p. 350.

22. Merry, P.; Kidd, D.; Blake, R. "How safe is it to give parenteral iron to a patient with rheumatoid arthritis (RA) and iron deficiency anemia?" *Brit J Rheumatol* 28:22, 1989.

23. Edwards, C.Q.; Griffen, L.M.; Kushner, J.P. "Disorders of excess iron." *Hospital Practice* 26(3):30–36, April 1991.

24. Bomford, A. and Williams, R. "Long term results of venesection therapy in idiopathic hemochromatosis." *Queensland J. Med.* 45:611, 1976.

25. Niederau, C. et al. "Survival and causes of death in cirrhotic and non-cirrhotic patients with primary hemochromatosis." *New England J. Med.* 313:1256, 1985.

Chapter 16
Excessive Tissue Manganese as a Cause of Antisocial Behavior

1. Otten, M. "Bill targets CYA wards for probes on violence." *Sacramento Union*, Oct. 1, 1989.

2. Schauss, A.G. "Comparative hair mineral analysis results of 21 elements in a random selected behaviorally 'normal' 19–59 year old population and violent adult criminal offenders." *Int. J. Biosocial Res.* 1:21–41, 1981.

3. Maugh, T.H. "Hair: a diagnostic tool to complement blood serum and urine." *Science* 202:1271–1273, 1978.

4. Schroeder, H.A. and Nason, A.P. "Trace metal in human hair." *J. Invest. Derm.* 53:71–78, 1969.

5. Klevay, L.M. "Hair as biopsy materials: Progress and prospects." *Archives of Intern. Med.* 138:1127–1128, 1978.

6. Katz, S.A. "The use of hair as biopsy material for trace elements in the body." *Am. Lab.* 11:44–52, 1979.

7. Myers, R.J. and Hamilton, J.B. "Regeneration and rate of growth of hair in man." *Ann New York Acad. Sci.* 53:562–568, 1951.

8. Rook, A. "The growth and replacement of hair in man." In: A.J. Rook and G.S. Walton eds., *Comparative Physiology and Pathology of the Skin.* (Philadelphia: F.A. Davis, 1965), p. 191.

9. Cromwell, P.F.; Abadie, B.R.; Stephens, J.T.; Kyler, M. "Hair mineral analysis: biochemical imbalances and violent criminal behavior." *Psychological Reports* 64:259–266, 1989.

10. Doisy, E.A. "Trace element metabolism in animals." In *Proceedings of the University of Missouri's Sixth Annual Conference on Trace Substances in Environment Health.* Hemphill, D.D. ed. (Columbia, Missouri: Univ. Missouri Press, 1980), p. 193.

11. Papavasilliou, P.S.; Kutt, H.; Miller, S.T.; Rosal, V.; Wang, Y.Y.; Aronson, R.D. "Seizure disorders and trace metals: Manganese tissue levels in treated epileptics." *Neurology* 29:1466–1473, 1979.

12. Donaldson, J. "Manganese in the Canadian environment." In P. Stokes, ed. *National Research Council of Canada* #26193. Associate Committee on Scientific Criteria for Environmental Quality. National Research Council of Canada. SSN 0316-0114, 1988, p. 122.

13. Cotzias, G.C. "Manganese in health and disease." *Physiological Review* 38:503–532, 1958.

14. Cawte, J. "Accounts of a mystery illness. The Groote Eylandt Syndrome." *Aust. New Zealand J. Psychiatry* 18:179–187, 1984.

15. Barbeau, A.; Inoue, N.; Cloutier, T. "Role of manganese in dystonia." In: *Advances in Neurology*. Eldridge, R. and Fahn, S. eds. Vol. 14. (New York: Raven Press, 1976), p. 339.

16. Penalver, R. "Manganese poisoning." *Ind. Med. Surge. 24:107, 1955*.

17. Banta, R.G. and Markesbery, W.R. "Elevated manganese levels associated with dementia and extrapyramidal signs." *Neurology* 27:213–216, 1977.

18. Cawte, J. and Florence, M.T. "A manganic milieu in North Australia: Ecological manganism: Ecology; diagnosis; individual susceptibility; synergism; therapy; prevention; advice for the community." *Int. J. Biosocial Med. Res.* 11:43–56, 1989.

19. Donaldson, J.; Labella, F.S.; Gesser, D. "Enhanced autoxidation of dopamine as a possible basis of manganese neurotoxicity." *Neurotoxicology* 2:53–64, 1981.

20. Donaldson, J.; McGregor, D.; LaBella, F.S. "Manganese neurotoxicity: a model for free radical mediated neurodegeneration." *Can. J. Physiology & Pharmacol.* 60:1398–1405, 1982.

21. Graham, D.G. "Oxidative pathways for catecholamines in the genesis of neuromelanin and cytotoxic quinones." *Mol. Pharmacol.* 14:633–643, 1978.

22. Graham, D.G. "Catecholamine toxicity: a proposal for the molecular pathogenesis of manganese neurotoxicity and Parkinson's disease." *Neurotoxicology* 5:83–96, 1984.

23. Das, K.C.; Abramson, M.B.; Katzman, R. "Neuronal pigments: Spectroscopic characteristics of human brain melanin." *J. Neurochem.* 30:601–605, 1978.

24. Smyth, L.T.; Ruhf, R.C.; Whitman, N.E.; Dugan, T. "Clinical manganism and exposure to manganese in the production and processing of ferromanganese alloy." *J. Occupational Med.* 15(2):101–109, Feb. 1973.

25. Barbeau, A. *Neurotoxicology* 5:13–36, 1984.

26. Donaldson, J. *Neurotoxicology* 8:451–462, 1987.

27. Donaldson, J. In: "Manganese in the Canadian environment." In Stoles, P. ed. *National Research Council Publication Number 26193*. (National Research Council of Canada, 1988), p. 122.

28. Florence, T.M.; Stauber, J.L.; Fardy, J.J. "Biological studies of manganese on Groote Eylandt." In: The proceedings of a conference held at Darwin N.T. entitled *Research on Manganese and Metabolism—Groote Eylandt, Northern Territory*. Cawte, J. ed., 1987, pp. 23–35.

Chapter 17
Chelation Therapy Restores Demented and Senile Minds

1. Walker, M. *The Chelation Way: The Complete Book of Chelation Therapy* (Garden City Park, NY: Avery Publishing Group, 1990).

2. *A Textbook on EDTA Chelation Therapy.* (ed.) E.M. Cranton. (New York: Human Sciences Press, 1989), pp. 9 and 10.

3. Demopoulos, H.B.; Pietronigro, D.D.; Flamm, E.S.; Seligman, M.L. "The possible role of free radical reactions in carcinogenesis." *J. Environmental Pathology and Toxicology* 3:273–303, 1980.

4. Demopoulos, H.B. "Control of free radicals in the biologic systems." *Fed. Proc.* 32:1903–1908, 1973.

5. Skoog, D.A. and West, D.M. "Volumetric methods based on complex-formation reactions." In *Fundamentals of Analytical Chemistry* (New York: Holt, Rinehart, & Winston, Inc., 1969), pp. 338–360.

6. Schauss, A.G. "Utilizing hair trace element analysis in the treatment of violent juvenile and adult offenders." *Int. J. Biosocial Res.* 1(3):42–49, 1981.

7. Brody, J.E. "Lead-poisoning harm held to be partly reversible." *The New York Times,* Apr. 8, 1993, p. A18.

8. Walker, M. *The Chelation Answer: How to Prevent Hardening of the Arteries and Rejuvenate Your Cardiovascular System* (New York City: M. Evan, 1982), p. 14.

9. Harmon, D. "The free radical theory of aging." Read before the Orthomolecular Medical Society, San Francisco, California, May 8, 1983. (Available on audio cassette from Audio-Stats, 3221 Carter Avenue, Marina Del Ray, CA 90291.)

10. McLaughlin, D.R. "Aluminum toxicity in senile dementia: Implications for treatment." Read before the Fall Conference, American Academy of Medical Preventics, Las Vegas, Nevada, Nov. 8, 1981.

11. Cranton, E.M. and Frackelton, J.P. "Free radical pathology in age-associated diseases: Treatment with EDTA chelation, nutrition, and antioxidants." *J. Advancement in Med.* 2(1/2):9, Spring/Summer, 1989.

12. Demopoulos, H.B. "Molecular oxygen in health and disease." Read before the American Academy of Medical Preventics Tenth Annual Spring Conference, Los Angeles, California, May 21, 1983. (Available on three audio cassettes from Instatape, P.O. Box 1729, Monrovia, CA 91016.)

13. Demopoulos, H.B.; Pietronigro, D.D.; Flamm, E.S.; Seligman, M.L. "The possible role of free radical reactions in carcinogenesis." *J. Environmental Pathology and Toxicology* 3:273–303, 1980.

14. Demopoulos, H.G.; Pietronigro, D.D.; Seligman, M.L. "The development of secondary pathology with free radical reactions as a threshold mechanism." *J Amer. Col. of Toxicology* 2(3):173–184, 1983.

15. Schaefer, A.; Komlos, M.; Seregi, A. "Lipid peroxidation as the cause of the ascorbic acid induced decrease of ATPase activities of rat brain microsomes and its inhibition by biogenic amines and psychotropic drugs." *Biochem Pharmacol* 24:1781–1786, 1975.

16. Ito, T.; Allen, N.; Yashon, D. "A mitochondrial lesion in experimental spinal cord trauma." *J. Neurosurg.* 48:434–442, 1978.

17. Halstead, B.W. *The Scientific Basis of EDTA Chelation Therapy* (Colton, CA: Golden Quill Publishers, 1979).

18. Sukoff, M.H.; Hollin, S.A.; Espinosa, O.E., et al. "The protective effect of hyperbaric oxygenation in experimental cerebral edema." *J. Neurosur.* 29:236–239, 1968.

19. Higgins, A.C.; Pearlstein, M.S.; Mullen, J.B., et al. "Effects of hyperbaric oxygen therapy on long-tract neuronal conduction in the acute phase of spinal cord injury." *J. Neurosurg.* 55(4):501–510, 1981.

20. De La Torre, J.C.; Kawanaga, H.M.;

Rowed, D.W., et al. "Dimethyl sulfoxide in central nervous system trauma." *Ann. NY Acad. Sci.* 243:362–389, 1975.

21. Walker, M. *DMSO: Nature's Healer* (Garden City Park, New York: Avery Publishing Group, 1993).

Chapter 18
Proof That EDTA Chelation Therapy Has Efficacy in Brain Disorders

1. Perl, D.P.; Brody, A.R. "Alzheimer's disease: X-ray spectometric evidence of aluminum accumulation in neurofibrillary tangle-bearing neurons." *Science* 208:297–299, 1980.

2. Crapper-McLachlan, D.R.; Krishnan, S.S.; Quittkat, S. "Aluminum, neurofibrillary degeneration, and Alzheimer's disease." *Brain* 99:68–80, 1976.

3. Lerick, S.E. "Dementia from aluminum pots?" *N. Engl. J. Med.* 303:164, 1980.

4. Crapper-McLachlan, D.R.; Krishnan, S.S.; Dalton, A.J. "Aluminum distribution in Alzheimer's disease and experimental neurofibrillary degeneration." *Science* 180:511–513, 1973.

5. McDermott, J.R.; Smith, A.E.; Iqbal, K.; Wisniewski, H.W. "Brain aluminum in aging and Alzheimer's disease." *Neurology* 29:809–814, 1979.

6. Grumbles, L.A. "Radionuclide studies of cerebral and cardiac arteriography before and after chelation therapy." *New Horizons in Holistic Health II* (a symposium), May 27, 1979, Chicago, IL (Verbal presentation available on audio cassette, InstaTape, Inc., P.O. Box 2926-D, Pasadena, CA 91165).

7. Casdorph, H.R. "EDTA Chelation Therapy II: Efficacy in Brain Disorders." *Journal of Holistic Medicine* 3(2):101–117, Fall/Winter 1981.

Chapter 19
The Administration and Effects of Chelation Therapy

1. Schroeder, H.A. *The Poisons Around Us.* (Bloomington, IN: Indiana University Press, 1974).

2. Kopito, L.; Brilet, A.M.; Schwachman, H. "Chronic plumbism in children: Diagnosis by hair analysis." *JAMA* 209:243–248, 1969.

3. Vitale, L.P., et al. "Blood lead—an inadequate measure of occupational exposure." *J. Occup. Med.* 17(3):155, 1975.

4. Bessman, S.T.; Doorembos, N.J. Editorial, "Chelation." *Ann. Intern. Med.* 47:1036–1041, 1957.

5. Halstead, B.S. *Scientific Basis of EDTA Chelation Therapy.* (Colton, California: Golden Quill Publishers, 1979).

6. Seppalainen, A.M. et al. "Subclinical neuropathy at 'safe' levels of exposure." *Ach Environ. Health,* 1975.

7. Graham, A. and Graham, F. "Lead poisoning and the suburban child." *Today's Health,* March, 1974.

8. Caprio, R.J.; Margulis, H.I.; Joselow, M. "Lead absorption in children and its relationship to urban traffic densities." *Arch. Environ. Health* 28:195–197, 1975.

9. Freeman, R. "Reversible myocarditis due to chronic lead poisoning in childhood." *Arch. Dis. Child* 40:389–393, 1965.

10. Perl, D.P. and Pendlebury, W.W. "Aluminum neurotoxicity—potential role in the pathogenesis of neurofibrillary tangle formation." *The Canadian J. Neurological Sciences* 13(4):441–445, Nov. 1986.

11. Crapper-McLachlan, D.R.; Lukiw, W.J.; Kruck, T.P.A. "New evidence for an active role of aluminum in Alzheimer's disease." *The Canadian J. Neurological Sciences* 16(4):490–497, Nov. 1989.

12. McDonagh, E.W.; Rudolph, C.J.; Cheraskin, E. "The effect of EDTA chelation therapy plus supportive multivitamin-trace mineral supplementation upon renal function: A study in serum creatinine." *J. Holistic Medicine* 4:146–151, 1982.

13. McDonagh, E.W.; Rudolph, C.J.; Cheraskin, E. "The effect of EDTA chelation therapy plus supportive multivitamin-trace mineral supplementation upon renal function: A study in blood urea nitrogen (BUN)." *J. Holistic Medicine* 5(2):163–171, 1983.

14. Sehnert, K.W.; Clague, A.F.; Cheraskin, E. "The improvement in renal function following EDTA chelation and multivitamin-trace mineral therapy: A study in creatinine clearance." *Medical Hypothesis* 15(3)307z310, 1984.

15. Riordan, H.D.; Cheraskin, E.; Dirks, M., et al. "Another look at renal function and the EDTA treatment process." *J. Orthomolecular Medicine* 2(3):185–187, 1987.

16. Oliver, L.D.; Mehta, R.; Sarle, H.E. "Acute renal failure following administration of ethylenediaminetetraacetic acid (EDTA)." *Texas Medicine* 80:40–41, Feb. 1984.

17. Rudolph, C.J.; McDonagh, E.W.; Barber, R.K. "Effect of EDTA chelation on serum iron." *J. Advancement in Medicine* 4(1):39{45, Spring 1991.

18. Cranton, E.M. and Frackelton, J.P. "Free radical pathology in age-associated diseases: Treatment with EDTA chelation, nutrition, and antioxidants." *J. Holistic Medicine* 6:6–37, 1984.

19. Blake, D.R.; Dieppe, P.A.; Halliwell, B.; Gutteridge, J.M. "Hypothesis, the importance of iron in rheumatoid disease." *Lancet* 2:1142–1144, 1981.

20. Demopoulos, H.B. "Control of free radicals in biologic systems." *Federal Proceedings* 32:1903–1908, 1973.

21. Crosby, W.H.; Likhite, V.V.; O'Brien, J.E.; Forman, D. "Serum iron levels in ostensibly normal people." *JAMA* 227:310–312, 1974.

22. Nitsu, Y.; Chikara, A.; Takahashi, F.; Goto, Y. "Concentration dependent sedimentation properties of ferritin: implications for estimation of iron contents of serum ferritins." *American J. Hematology* 18:363–371, 1985.

23. Rahko, P.S.; Salerni, R.; Uretsky, B.F. "Successful reversal by chelation therapy of congestive cardiomyopathy due to iron overload." *JACC* 8:436–440, 1986.

24. Zylke, J. "Studying oxygen's life-and-death roles if taken from or reintroduced into tissue." *JAMA* 259:960–965, 1988.

25. Gutterridge, J. "Ferrous-salt-promoted damage to deoxyribose and benzoate." *Biochem J. (Great Britain)* 243:709–714, 1987.

26. McDonagh, E.W.; Rudolph, C.J.; Cheraskin, E. "The effect of EDTA salts plus supportive multivitamin-trace mineral supplementation upon renal function: A study of serum creatine." *J. Holistic Medicine* 4:146–151, 1982.

27. McDonagh, E.W.; Rudolph, C.J.; Wussow, D.G. "The effect of intravenous disodium ethylene diamine tetraacetic acid (EDTA) upon bone density levels." *J. Advancement in Medicine* 1:79–85, 1988.

Chapter 20
Clinical Studies That Show the Worth of EDTA Chelation

1. Meltzer, L.E. and Kitchell, J.R. "The treatment of coronary artery disease with disodium EDTA." In *Metal Binding in Medicine*, ed. M.J. Seven. (Philadelphia: J.B. Lippincott Co., 1960), pp. 132–136.

2. Meltzer, L.E.; Kitchell, J.R.; Palmon, F.

"The long term use, side effects, and toxicity of disodium ethylenediamine tetraacetic acid (EDTA)." *American J. Medical Sciences* 242:51–57, 1961.

3. Kitchell, J.R.; Palmon, F.; Aytan, N.; Meltzer, L.E. "The treatment of coronary artery disease with disodium EDTA—a reappraisal." *American J. Cardiology* 11:501–506, 1963.

4. Cranton, E.M. and Frackelton, J.P. "The current status of EDTA chelation therapy in the treatment of occlusive arterial disease." *J. Holistic Medicine* 4:24–33, 1982.

5. Casdorph, H.R. "EDTA chelation therapy, efficacy in arteriosclerotic heart disease." *J. Holistic Medicine* 3:53–59, 1981.

6. Casdorph, H.R. "EDTA chelation therapy, efficacy in brain disorders." *J. Holistic Medicine* 3:101–117, 1981.

7. Crapper-McLaghlan, D.R. "Aluminum toxicity in senile dementia—implications for treatment." Presented to the Fall 1981 meeting of AAMP.

8. Crapper-McLaughlan, D.R., et al. "Altered chromatin conformation in Alzheimer's disease." *Brain* 102(3):483–495, Sept. 1979.

9. Crapper-McLaughlan, D.R. "Intranuclear aluminum content in Alzheimer's disease, dialysis encephalopathy, and experimental aluminum encephalopathy." *Acta Nueopathol* (Berlin) 50(1):19–24, 1980.

10. Karlik, S.J. and Crapper-McLaughlan, D.R. "Interaction of aluminum species with deoxyribonucleic acid." *Biochemistry* 19(26):5991–5998, Dec. 1980.

11. Crapper-McLaughlan, D.R. and DeBoni, U. "Brain aging and Alzheimer's disease." *Canadian Psychiatric Assoc. J.* 23(4):229–233, Jan. 1978.

12. DeBoni, U. and Crapper-McLaughlan, D.R. "Paired helical filaments of the Alzheimer type in cultured neurones." *Nature* 271(5645):566–568, Sept. 1978.

13. King, G.A.; DeBoni, U.; Crapper-McLaughlan, D.R. "Effect of aluminum upon conditioned avoidance reponse acquisition in the absence of neurofibrillary degeneration." *Pharmacol. Biochem. Behav.* 3(6):1003–1009, Nov.–Dec. 1975.

14. Crapper-McLaughlan, D.R., et al. "Alzheimer degeneration in Down syndrome. Electrophysiologic alterations and histopathologic findings." *Arch. Neurol.* 32(9):618–623, Sept. 1975.

15. Crapper-McLaughlan, D.R., et al. "Aluminum: a possible neurotoxic agent in Alzheimer's disease." *Trans Am. Neurol. Assoc.* 100:154–156, 1975.

16. Crapper-McLaughlan, D.R., et al. "Aluminum neurofibrillary degeneration and Alzheimer's disease." *Brain* 99(1):67–80, Mar. 1976.

17. Crapper-McLaughlan, D.R. and Tomko, G.J. "Neuronal correlates of an encephalopathy associated with aluminum neurofibrillary degeneration." *Brain Research* 97(2):253–264, Oct. 1975.

18. Dalton, A.J.; Crapper-McLaughlan, D.R., et al. "Alzheimer's disease in Down's syndrome: visual retention deficits." *Cortex* 10(4):366–377, Dec. 1974.

19. DeBoni, U. and Crapper-McLaughlan, D.R. "Illuminated microelectrode for tissue culture." *Tissue Cell* 6(3):383–384, 1974.

20. Crapper-McLaughlan, D.R. "Brain aluminum distribution in Alzheimer's disease and experimental neurofibrillary degeneration." *Trans Am. Neurol. Assoc.* 98:17–20, 1973.

21. DeBoni, U. and Crapper-McLaughlan, D.R. "Intracellular aluminum binding; a histochemical study." *Histochemistry* 40:31–37, June 26, 1974.

22. Tomko, G.J. and Crapper-McLaughlan, D.R. "Neuronal variability: nonstationary responses to identical vis-

ual stimuli." *Brain Research* 79(3):405–418, Oct. 25, 1974.

23. Crapper-McLaughlan, D.R. "Experimental neurofibrillary degeneration and altered electrical activity." *Electroencephalogr. Clin. Neurophysiol.* 35:575–588, Dec. 1973.

24. Crapper-McLaughlan, D.R. and Dalton, A.J. "Alterations in short-term retention, conditioned avoidance response acquisition and motivation following aluminum induced neurofibrillary degeneration." *Physiol. Behav.* 10:925–933, May 1973.

25. Crapper-McLaughlan, D.R. and Dalton, A.J. "Aluminum-induced neurofibrillary degeneration, brain electrical activity, and alterations in acquisition and retention." *Physiol. Behavior* 10:935–945, May 1973.

26. Crapper-McLaughlan, D.R. "Brain aluminum distribution in Alzheimer's disease and experimental neurofibrillary degeneration." *Science* 180:511–513, May 4, 1973.

27. Krishnan, S.S. and Crapper-McLaughlan, D.R. "Determination of aluminum in biological material by atomic absorption spectrophotometry." *Analytical Chemistry* 44:1469–1470, July 1972.

28. Tatton, W.G. and Crapper-McLaughlan, D.R. "Central tegmental alteration of cat lateral geniculate activity." *Brain Research* 47:371–387, Dec. 12, 1972.

29. McDonagh, E.W.; Rudolph, C.J.; Cheraskin, E. "An oculocerebrovasculometric analysis of the improvement in vascular stenosis following EDTA chelation therapy." *J. Holistic Medicine* 4(1):21–23, Spring/Summer 1982.

30. Casdorph, H.R. and Farr, C.H. "Treatment of peripheral arterial occlusion, an alternative to amputation." *J. Holistic Medicine* 5:3–15, 1983.

31. Gotto, A. "The status of EDTA chela-

tion therapy in Texas." *Texas Medicine* 84:36–37, 1984.

32. Sehnert, K.W.; Clague, A.F.; Cheraskin, E. *Medical Hypothesis* 15(3):307–310, 1984.

33. Carter, J.P. *Racketeering in Medicine: The Suppression of Alternatives.* (Norfolk, VA: Hampton Roads Publishing Co., 1992), pp. 89–91.

34. Olszewer, E. and Carter, J.P. "EDTA chelation therapy: a retrospective study of 2,870 patients." *Medical Hypothesis* 27:41–49, 1988.

35. Olszewer, E.; Sabbag, F.C.; Carter, J.P. "A pilot double-blind study of sodium-magnesium EDTA in peripheral vascular disease." *The J. National Medical Assoc.* 82(3):57–60, 1990.

36. McDonagh, E.W.; Rudolph, C.J.; Cheraskin, E. "The effect of EDTA chelation therapy plus multivitamin/trace mineral supplementation upon vascular dynamics: ankle/brachial doppler systolic blood pressure ratio." *A Textbook on EDTA Chelation Therapy: J. Advancement in Medicine* 2(1,2):159–166, 1989.

37. Rudolph, C.J.; McDonagh, E.W.; Barber, R.K. "Effect of EDTA chelation and supportive multivitamin/trace mineral supplementation on chronic lung disorders: a study of FVC and FEV1." *J. Advancement in Medicine* 2(4):553–561, 1989.

38. Blummer, W. and Cranton, E.M. "Ninety percent reduction in cancer mortality after chelation therapy with EDTA." *J. Advancement in Medicine* 2(1,2):183–188, 1989.

39. Rudolph, C.J.; McDonagh, E.W.; Barber, R.K. "An observation of the effect of EDTA chelation and supportive multivitamin/trace mineral supplementation on blood platelet volume: a brief communication." *J. Advancement in Medicine* 3(3):179–184, 1990.

40. Rudolph, C.J.; McDonagh, E.W.; Bar-

ber, R.K. "A nonsurgical approach to ostructive carotid stenosis using EDTA chelation." *J. Advancement in Medicine* 4(3):157–168, 1991.

41. Adams, W.J. and McGee, C.T. "Chelation therapy: a survey of treatment outcomes and selected sociomedical factors." *J. Advancement in Medicine* 5(3):189–197, Fall 1992.

Chapter 21
The Anti-Alzheimer's Disease Diet

1. Kahn, C. "Withstanding Alzheimer's fit brains do better." *Longevity*, March 1992, p. 22.

2. NHA Fax Update. "'Lorenzo' gets rave reviews." *Townsend Letter for Doctors* 117:373, April 1993.

3. Maeda, K., et al. "Improvement of clinical and MRI findings in a boy with adrenoleukodystrophy by dietary erucic acid therapy." *Brain Development*, 14:409–412, 1992.

4. Moss, R.W. *Cancer Therapy*, (New York: Equinox Press, 1992).

5. Yehuda, S., et al. *Intl. Journal of Neuroscience*, 32:919–925, 1987.

6. Connor, W.E., et al. "Dietary effects of brain fatty acid composition." *J Lipid Research* 31:237, 1990.

7. Balch, J.F. and Balch, P. *Prescription for Nutritional Healing* (Garden City Park, NY: Avery Publishing, 1990), p. 40.

8. Rudin, D.O.; Felix, C.; Schrader, C. *The Omega-3 Phenomenon* (New York: Avon Books, 1987).

9. Barton, R.G., et al. "Dietary omega-3 fatty acids decrease mortality and Kupffer cell prostaglandin E2 production in a rat model of chronic sepsis." *J. Trauma*, 31:768–773, June 1991.

10. Cerra, F.B., et al. "Improvement in immune function in ICU patients by enteral nutrition supplemented with arginine, RNA and menhaden oil is independent of nitrogen balance." *Nutrition*, 7:193–199, May/June 1991.

11. Connor, W.E. and Connor, S.L. *The New American Diet*. (New York: Simon & Schuster, 1986).

Chapter 22
Dietary Brain Boosters and Memory Pills

1. Evans, D.A.; Funkenstein, H.; Alber, M.S., et al. "Prevalence of Alzheimer's disease in a community population of older persons: higher than previously reported." *JAMA* 262:2552–2556, 1989.

2. Werbach, M.R. *Nutritional Influences on Mental Illness* (Tarzana, California: Third Line Press, Inc., 1991), p. 95.

3. Abalan, F. "Alzheimer's disease: The nutritional hypothesis." *J. Orthomolecular Med.* 3(1):13–17, 1988.

4. Evans, J.R. "Alzheimer's dementia: Some possible mechanisms related to vitamins, trace elements and minerals, suggesting a possible treatment." *J. Orthomolecular Med.* 1(4):249–254, 1987.

5. Thomas, D.E., et al. "Tryptophan and nutritional status of patients with senile dementia." *Psychol Med.* 16(2):297–305, 1986.

6. Shaw, D.M., et al. "Senile dementia and nutrition." *Letter. Br. Med. J.* 288:792–793, 1984.

7. Martin, D.C. "B12 and folate deficiency dementia." *Clin Geriatr Med.* 4(4):841–852, 1988.

8. Strachan, R.W. and Henderson, J.G. "Dementia and folate deficiency." *Quart. J. Med.* 36:189–204, 1967.

9. Hoffer, A. and Walker, M. *Smart Nutrients* (Garden City Park, NY: Avery Publishing Group, 1993).

10. Hoffer, A. *Orthomolecular Medicine for Physicians* (New Canaan, Connecticut: Keats Publishing, 1989), p. 152.

11. Keatinge, A.M.B., et al. "Vitamin B1,

B2, B6 and C status in the elderly." *Irish Med. J.* 76:488–490, 1983.

12. Wagner, H.N., Jr.—interviewed in *Psychology Today,* July 1985.

13. Gibson, G.E., et al. "Reduced activities of thiamine-dependent enzymes in the brains and peripheral tissues of patients with Alzheimer's disease." *Arch Neurol.* 45:836–840, 1988.

14. Blass, J.P., et al. "Thiamine and Alzheimer's disease. A pilot study." *Arch. Neurol.* 45:833–835, 1988.

15. Gottfries, C.G. *Clin. Psychiatry News,* September 1989.

16. Repasy, A., et al. "Utility of routine vitamin B12 levels in the workup of dementia." Abstract. *Psychogeriatrics,* Dec. 1987, pp. 32–33.

17. Abalan, F. and Delile, J.M. "B12 deficiency in presenile dementia." Letter. *Biol. Psychiatry* 20(11):1251, 1985.

18. Cole, M.G. and Prchal, J.F. "Low serum B12 in Alzheimer-type dementia." *Age Ageing* 13:101–105, 1984.

19. van Tiggelen, C.J.M. "Alzheimer's disease/alcohol dementia: Association with zinc deficiency and cerebral vitamin B12 deficiency." *J. Orthomol. Psychiatry* 13(2):97–104, 1984.

20. Inada, M., et al. "Cobalamin contents of the brains in some critical and pathologic states." *Int. J. Vitam. Nutr. Res.* 52(4):423–429, 1982.

21. Geland, B. "Presentation to the European College of Neuropsychopharmacology." *Clin. Psychiatry News,* Sept. 1989.

22. Schorah, C.J., et al. "Plasma vitamin C concentrations in patients in a psychiatric hospital." *Human Nutr. Clin. Nutr.* 37C:447–452, 1983.

23. Burns, A. and Holland, T. "Vitamin E deficiency." Letter. *Lancet,* April 5, 1986, pp. 805–806.

24. Jackson, C.V.E., et al. "Vitamin E and Alzheimer's disease in subjects with Down's syndrome." *J. Ment. Def. Res.* 32:479–484, 1988.

25. Wisniewski, K.E., et al. "Occurrence of neuropathological changes and dementia of Alzheimer's disease in Down's syndrome." *Ann. Neurol.* 17:270–282, 1985

26. Sylverster, P.E. "Ageing in the mentally retarded." In J. Dobbing, et al., eds. *Scientific Studies in Mental Retardation* (London: Macmillan, for the Royal Society of Medicine, 1984), pp. 259–277.

27. Ward, N.I. and Mason, J.A. "Neutron activation analysis techniques for identifying elemental status in Alzheimer's disease." *J. Radioanalyt. Nucl. Chem.* 113(2):515–526, 1987.

28. Fujita, T. "Aging and calcium as an environmental factor." *J. Nutr. Sci. Vitaminol. (Tokyo)* 31 Suppl S15–S19, 1985.

29. West, R.D. "Aluminosilicates and Alzheimer's disease." Letter. *Lancet* 2:682, 1985.

30. Glick, J.L. "Dementias: the role of magnesium deficiency and an hypothesis concerning the pathogenesis of Alzheimer's disease." *Medical Hypotheses* 31(3):211–225, 1990.

31. Candy, J.M., et al. "Aluminosilicates and senile plaque formation in Alzheimer's disease." *Lancet* 1:354–357, 1986.

32. Corrigan, F.M., et al. "Aluminium and Alzheimer's disease." Letter. *Lancet* 2:268–269, 1989.

33. Howard, J.M.H. "Clinical import of small increases in serum aluminum." *Clin. Chem.* 30(10):1722–1723, 1984.

34. Brewer, G.J., et al. "Oral zinc therapy for Wilson's disease." *Ann. Intern. Med.* 99:314–320, 1983.

35. Burnet, F.M. "A possible role of zinc in the pathology of dementia." *Lancet* 1:186–188, 1981.

36. Constantinidis, J. "Alzheimer's dis-

ease and the zinc theory." *Encephale* 16(4):231–239, 1990.

37. Michel, P.F. "Chronic cerebral insufficiency and ginkgo biloba extract." In A. Agnoli et al., eds. *Effects of Ginkgo Biloba Extracts on Organic Cerebral Impairment* (John Libbey Eurotext Ltd., 1985), pp. 71–76.

38. Wesnes, K., et al. "A double blind, placebo-controlled trial of Ginkgo biloba extract in the treatment of idiopathic cognitive impairment in the elderly." *Hum. Psychopharmacol* 2:159–169, 1987.

39. Weitbrecht, W.U. and Jansen, W. "Primary degenerative dementia: therapy with Ginkgo biloba extract." *Fortschr. Med.* 104:199–202, 1986.

40. Taillandier, J. "Ginkgo biloba extract in the treatment of cerebral disoders due to aging." In E.W. Funfgeld, ed. *Rokan.* (New York: Springer-Verlag, 1988), pp. 291–301.

41. Bartus, R.T.; Dean, R.L.; Beer, B.; Lyspa, A.S. "The cholinergic hypothesis of geriatric memory dysfunction." *Science* 217:408–417, 1982.

42. Ashford, J.W.; Sherman, K.A.; Kumar, V. "Advances in Alzheimer therapy: cholinesterase inhibitors." *Neurobiol. Aging* 10:99–105, 1989.

43. Small, G.W. "Tacrine for treating Alzheimer's disease." Editorial. *JAMA* 268(18):2564–2565, November 11, 1992.

44. Selkoe, D.J. "Deciphering Alzheimer's disease: the pace quickens." *Trends Neurosci* 10:181–184, 1987.

45. Tanzi, R.E.; St. George-Hyslop, P.H.; Gusella, J.F. "Molecular genetic approaches to Alzheimer's disease." *Trends Neurosci.* 12:152–158, 1989.

46. Gottfries, C.G. "Pharmacology of mental aging and dementia disorders." *Clin. Neuorpharmacol.* 10:313–329, 1987.

47. Collerton, D. "Cholinergic function

and intellectual decline in Alzheimer's disease." *Neuroscience* 19:1–28, 1986.

48. Piccinin, G.L.; Finali, Giancarlo; Piccirilli, M. "Neuropsychological effects of 1-deprenyl in Alzheimer's type dementia." *Clinical Neuropharmacology* 13(2):147–163, 1990.

49. McLachlan, D.R.C.; Dalton, A.J.; Kruck, T.P.A.; Bell, M.Y.; Smith, W.L.; Kalow, W.; Andrews, D.F. "Intramuscular desferrioxamine in patients with Alzheimer's disease." *Lancet* 337:1304–1307, June 1, 1991.

50. Dean, W. and Morgenthaler, J. *Smart Drugs & Nutrients* (Santa Cruz, California: B&J Publications, 1990).

Appendix 2
The Protocol for the Administration of Chelation Therapy

1. Bjorksten, J. *Longevity, A Quest.* (Madison, Wisconsin: Bjorksten Research Foundation, 1981), p. 162.

2. Rudolph, C.J. and McDonagh, E.W. "The chelation carrier solution: An analysis of osmolarity and sodium content." *J. International Academy of Preventive Medicine* 8(1):26–34, 1983.

3. McDonagh, E.W.; Rudolph, C.J.; Cheraskin, E. "The effect of EDTA chelation therapy plus supportive multivitamin-trace mineral supplementation upon renal function: A study in serum creatinine." *J. Holistic Medicine* 4:146–151, 1982.

4. McDonagh, E.W.; Rudolph, C.J.; Cheraskin, E. "The effect of EDTA chelation therapy plus supportive multivitamin-trace mineral supplementation upon renal function: A study in blood urea nitrogen (BUN)." *J. Holistic Medicine* 5(2):163–171, 1983.

5. Sehnert, K.W.; Clague, A.F.; Cheraskin, E. "The improvement in

renal function following EDTA chelation and multivitamin-trace mineral therapy: A study in creatinine clearance." *Medical Hypothesis* 15(3)307z310, 1984.

6. Riordan, H.D.; Cheraskin, E.; Dirks, M., et al. "Another look at renal function and the EDTA treatment process." *J. Orthomolecular Medicine* 2(3):185–187, 1987.

About the Authors

H. Richard Casdorph, M.D., Ph.D., is a skilled doctor of allopathic medicine. He currently practices internal medicine and specializes in cardiovascular disease at the Casdorph Clinic in Long Beach, California. He is a Diplomate of the American Board of Internal Medicine and a Fellow of the American College of Physicians. He has been chief of the department of internal medicine at Long Beach Community Hospital and is former assistant clinical professor of medicine at the University of California Medical School, Irvine.

Having graduated from the Indiana University Medical School on June 15, 1953, Dr. Casdorph completed a rotating internship at Indiana University Medical Center in 1953–1954, went on to receive his training in cardiovascular medicine at the Mayo Clinic (the Mayo Foundation) in 1954–1955 and 1957–1961, and was awarded his Ph.D. in medicine from the University of Minnesota on December 14, 1961. He has taught at the UCLA Medical School and has an extensive medical publications record.

Dr. Casdorph is a former president of the American College of Advancement in Medicine, a non-profit professional membership society dedicated to educating physicians on the latest findings and emerging procedures in the fields of preventive and therapeutic medicine. He received a research fellowship from the National Institutes of Health, completed a special course in radioisotopes for licensure, and attended the School of Aviation Medicine, Air University, United States Air Force. For two years, Dr. Casdorph was Flight Surgeon and Captain, United States Air Force Medical Corps, 1611th USAF Dispensory, McGuire Air Force Base, New Jersey.

Dr. Casdorph graduated as a Phi Beta Kappa in 1949 from West Virginia University, where he underwent his premedical education, and went on to become a member of Alpha Omega Alpha honor fraternity at Indiana

University Medical School. He is listed in *Who's Who in the West*, the *Dictionary of International Biography*, and *The Blue Book Leaders of the English-Speaking World*. In October 1980, the American Academy of Medical Preventics presented him with its Highest Achievement Award.

Among the professional societies to which Dr. Casdorph has belonged are the Long Beach District Medical Society, the Los Angeles County Medical Association, the American Medical Association, the Long Beach Heart Association (of which he has been a member of the board of directors), the American College of Physicians, and many more. He has had 105 clinical journal papers published on aspects of treatment and diagnoses for cardiovascular disease, dementia, brain syndromes, diabetes, and excess blood fats. His book, *The Miracles*, was published in 1976 by Logos International, Inc. Dr. Casdorph was editor of the medical textbook, *Treatment of the Hyperlipidemic States*, which was published in 1971 by the Charles C. Thomas Co. The text was written by seventeen of the world's foremost authorities in the field of lipid disorders. Moreover, Dr. Casdorph has made more than 150 media appearances on the subjects in which he specializes. He is expert on the topics encompassed here.

Morton Walker, D.P.M., having left almost seventeen years of practice as a doctor of podiatric medicine in 1969, has since worked fulltime as a professional freelance medical journalist. His special areas of interest are wholistic medicine, orthomolecular nutrition, and safe, natural, nontoxic, alternative/complementary methods of healing/curing illness and disease.

Dr. Walker is the author of 56 published books (including six bestsellers each with over 100,000 copies sold) and over 1500 magazine, newspaper, and clinical journal articles. He has presented his book concepts on more than 1200 media events, including national, international, and local radio and TV talk shows, press interviews, lectures, videos, audiotapes, and news conferences.

The winner of 22 medical journalism awards and medals, Dr. Walker was given the 1981 Orthomolecular Award by the Institute of Preventive Medicine, which states: "For outstanding achievement in orthomolecular education. In the face of adversity you have persevered giving new meaning to the right of each citizen to choose his own medical treatment." He was recognized with the 1979 Humanitarian Award from the American College of Advancement in Medicine "for informing the American public on alternative methods of healing." Moreover, this author/lecturer received two Jesse H. Neal Editorial Achievement Awards from the American Business Press, Inc. for the best series of magazine articles published in any audited American magazine in the years 1975 and 1976. In September 1992, he received "The Humanitarian Award" from the Cancer Control Society for being "The World's Leading Medical Journalist Specializing in Wholistic Medicine."

Dr. Walker also has to his credit ten William J. Stickel Annual Awards for Research and Writing and Annual Hall of Science Awards for Scientific Exhibits, bestowed by the American Podiatry Association in the years 1958, 1960, 1961, 1962, 1964, and 1968 (most of those years he won two podiatry awards, including 1964, when he received both the coveted Gold Medal and Silver Medal from the American Podiatry Association). Dr. Walker has also been awarded a half-dozen Maxwell N. Cupshan Memorial Awards for research and writing from *The Journal of Current Podiatric Medicine*.

He learned investigative journalism for informing the medical consumer after leaving podiatric practice by working fulltime on local newspapers. For five years thereafter, Dr. Walker instructed continuing education students at the University of Connecticut in two courses, "Writing Nonfiction for Publication" and "Writing Fiction for Publication." Now, from his home in Stamford, Connecticut, he combines medical knowledge and writing ability in his highly successful career as a professional medical journalist and author.

Index